HUNTED LIKE ANIMALS

Christopher S. Warner

None who have always been free can understand the terrible fascinating power of the hope of freedom to those who are not free.

PEARL S. BUCK

1

As he crouched in the brush, Sparrow watched the *ven* freeze in its tracks not ten paces away. They stared at each other for a few heartbeats, neither flinching. Sparrow made a quick assessment of her value—a mature doe, he concluded. He admired the subtle white markings around her eyes and marveled at her transitory bravery. Usually, he was the hunter while the *ven* was the prey. Today, the day of The Hunt, he was the prey and the doe merely an observer. For a moment Sparrow thought the *ven* somehow understood the situation, as if she shared a common bond with him.

The heavy crunching of underbrush awoke the instinct in both of them. The *ven* leapt away with a few elegant bounds; the man hunkered down, trying to estimate the distance to his pursuers. Sparrow knew that by listening carefully he could figure out which way the hunters plodded. He could sneak away in a different direction and find a new place to hide until the telltale sounds returned. Garnet had taught him this before his death, and it had kept Sparrow alive more than once.

The Overlords hunted with effective patience, slowly and surely until they reached their bag limit, but their size always gave away their approach. The noise was still some distance away. He had plenty of time to listen and decide where to go next.

For a moment he wondered if anyone had been caught yet. His close friends Sage and Thrush had eluded the draw this time, which pleased Sparrow, but others he knew weren't as fortunate. Since Sage had been named, he was entered in the draw only once per passing winter. Thrush could be chosen any time, as could Sparrow and many of his younger friends— the boys and girls who liked to listen to his stories. He smiled, remembering their faces last night by the fire. He thought of the eldest of his sisters, Faith, who was now safe from The Hunt but secluded with the other women and thus out of Sparrow's everyday reach.

Sparrow cleared his thoughts and listened intently for many heartbeats, until he was sure the Overlord party had turned away from him. They hadn't come close enough to detect his smell. They had probably picked up someone else's. While slow and clumsy, the hunters pursued relentlessly until they had reached their goal. Someone would make a mistake. The Hunt wouldn't end until enough of the Ruck did. When the Overlords sent more than one party it often ended quickly, lasting no more than a day. Garnet's listening tactics didn't work as well when the noises from two or three sets of lumbering monsters competed. When only one party invaded, The Hunt could go on for much longer. One of Sparrow's favorite stories for the children was about such a time, a few generations back. A group of chosen Ruck, led by the legendary Eagle, eluded the hunters for more than six sunsets. In the end, Eagle gave himself up to satisfy the bag limit and secure another season of life for the rest of the Ruck.

Today, Sparrow had heard only one party. He wished it were otherwise; he preferred a quick Hunt. When he hunted the *ven* he tried to take them with one arrow, cleanly. Per custom, he always apologized as he let loose the bowstring and sent his arrow to its mark. He wondered if the Overlords apologized to the Ruck when they threw down the lightning bolt and claimed a scalp.

Convinced that no other party was near, Sparrow settled into a small ditch. He rubbed fresh dirt on as much of his body as he could reach, smearing it onto his forehead and face, under his arms and even around his genitals. It wouldn't fool a hunter's nose close-up, but it would limit the range by which they could locate the path he had traveled. He patted his small *ven*-hide pouch, making sure he could get to it quickly if necessary. He then sunk back into the ditch, listening and resting.

The doe startled him this time. She had returned without Sparrow noticing—perhaps he had fallen asleep for a moment. If so, she might have just now saved his life. They stared at each other until Sparrow had to laugh out loud, despite himself. With that, the doe wandered off casually, as if it were merely a game, and she was now bored with it. Just before disappearing back into the woods, the *ven* stopped and stared at Sparrow again.

Sparrow knew it was odd, but it seemed like the doe wanted something from him. He also knew he needed to get up and move, because he didn't know how long he might have been asleep. Gently brushing off his cover, he emerged from the ditch and moved slowly toward the *ven*. She waited until he had moved a few steps, then she hopped off. Sparrow followed. The doe glided between the shrubs and trees, almost losing him once. After they had covered about the width of his village, she abruptly stopped. A heartbeat later Sparrow heard the crunching and the doe leapt away, safely hidden again by mid-stride.

Sparrow hunkered down and listened to every multi-legged footstep. They were coming directly from the south, the direction he was heading. No doubt. That always made escape a little more difficult under Garnet's tactics. Turning around wouldn't work; they would pick up his scent more easily if they continued on their path for even a short time. He would have to choose between east and west and hope they would miss his scent when they passed by.

He never got to make that decision.

"*Eeeeee-unhh!*" The squeaky boyish voice startled Sparrow, but he reacted quickly enough to see Dreamer tumble into the brush after leaping (falling?) from the branches of a large pine about 30 paces away. For a few heartbeats, Sparrow froze, waiting to see if the black-haired boy was hurt and what he might do next, until Dreamer jumped to his feet and thrust both fists into the air. He began a victory dance, of sorts, shifting his weight from foot to foot and waving his arms, fists still clenched. Then, after skipping happily in a circle through the brush, Dreamer took off running. Sparrow mentally measured his speed and direction and realized that the boy would intersect the Overlords' path in short order. Even if he passed them by, they would almost certainly pick up his scent—and while in his current fantasy, Dreamer would have no chance to elude them.

Sparrow chased the boy, staying just close enough to keep him in sight. How could he help the boy without further endangering them both? He knew that Dreamer wouldn't snap out of his fantasy in time to protect himself. The boy enjoyed Sparrow's stories more than anyone, losing himself in the telling and re-telling. Dreamer's mother, Lotus, had given him that name even before he left the women. Nothing in his behavior since then had warranted changing it. Many in the village wondered how he had survived numerous hunts. Some guessed that his mother's strange powers had been passed to him; others figured he was just plain lucky. Hoping the boy's good fortune would hold out, or that God would intervene and turn him in a better direction, Sparrow tried to listen for the hunters even as he chased the boy. Finally, Sparrow decided that Dreamer's only chance this time was his own intervention.

Breaking into a full run and disregarding the brambles that raked his sinewy arms and legs, Sparrow closed on the boy. He overtook Dreamer so fast that he almost stumbled on top of him but managed to dodge to the boy's right, wrapping his left arm around his shoulders and dragging him down. Dreamer screamed in surprise and struggled to get away, his instincts for The Hunt returning as soon as the reverie ended so suddenly. With Sparrow holding tight, the boy realized what was happening and went limp.

They had landed in a sparse clearing, small, but without any immediate cover. Sparrow re-focused on the hunters' approaching clamor—he thought they might emerge at any moment. He dragged himself and Dreamer to their feet and took two steps away, moving in the best direction he could guess under the circumstances. He heard the Overlords' shrieking voices and destructive footfall behind him. He could smell them now, the wet-wolf smell that reminded the Ruck of death —and which now meant they were on his trail.

A few more steps and he let go of Dreamer, who had finally got his legs under him. Sparrow forced out "Run, boy" as he accelerated. Another shape flashed by him, about ten paces away, moving back toward the hunters. Another boy, this time Chance, older and more experienced than Dreamer, but not yet a man.

"*Fug!*" Sparrow said, slowing down. Dreamer passed him. "Run, boy, don't stop!" Sparrow yelled after him, stopping, putting his back to the nearest tree and looking for the older boy.

Most of the Ruck recognized that Chance was the fastest of all the young boys and girls. And he liked to gamble. Justin named him more than a winter ago because of his escapades during The Hunt—more than once he had led the Overlords on a lengthy chase and lived to tell about it.

Sparrow picked up Chance's shape again—he had paused about twenty paces away, as if waiting for the hunters to see him. "Chance," Sparrow yelled, "run now!" The boy obeyed immediately, dashing in exactly the opposite direction that Sparrow and Dreamer were going. And the Overlords emerged.

Three of them, at top-speed, obliterating a swath of foliage with their thick, tree-trunk legs. They shot lightning bolts, more than one from the screeching sound of it, but Sparrow couldn't be sure because he had already broken into a sprint. He hoped they would follow him, so he made a best guess to run away from both Chance and Dreamer. He ran and waited for the bolts to follow, but the next screech he heard was farther off than he expected. They were chasing Chance. Sparrow stopped again. Another screeching, this time followed by the unmistakable soul-rending scream of a Ruck losing his final Hunt.

All Sparrow could do now was run. He paused for a heartbeat, trying to guess the best route to find Dreamer again. He couldn't be sure that the Overlords had reached their limit. He ran, he searched, but he couldn't find the boy. With resignation, he found another suitable hiding place in the underbrush and pulled out his pouch. He scooped some of the flowers from inside and crushed them carefully between his hands, rubbing the pieces around his body as he had before with the dirt. Sighing, he settled into the undergrowth and inspected his cuts and bruises. Nothing serious. Chance's scream echoed in his ears while the image of Dreamer escaping farther into the woods—only to be lost again in a fantasy that might invite further danger—ran through his head.

Before long, the piercing horn sounded thrice, signaling the end of The Hunt. Perhaps Chance's death had satisfied the limit. How many this time? Two or three? That had been the usual for three winters now, when only a few newborns had survived. At least, it seemed, Dreamer had survived today's hunt. Sparrow trudged back to the village, apprehensive about finding out who else had died, as well as telling his story about Dreamer and Chance.

Most of the children and men had assembled by the time Sparrow reached the Circle. All were waiting quietly, as the black-cloaked, masked Overseer had not yet departed. Justin faced the Black One, with old man Coot at his shoulder, listening in (it was said that Coot had counted 30 winters!). Sparrow, after receiving thankful hugs from his sisters and brothers—including Willow, Badger, Archer, and Clay—approached his friends Sage and Thrush. As he walked around the edge of the

Circle, Sparrow saw Dreamer whispering with some other boys and girls. Sparrow allowed a faint smile for the boy's survival, nodding to his friends just before he stopped by Sage's side.

"I heard Chance die. No others," Sparrow whispered.

"We had guessed. We wondered about you, and no one has seen Violet," Sage said.

Sage then whispered to his younger brother Thrush, who was pulling at the new but still sparse facial hair around his chin. Thrush stopped his fidgeting momentarily and sighed, then continued the nervous habit while waiting with the rest of the Ruck for the Overseer to leave. Sparrow hoped that two was the limit.

When the Black One backed off into the woods to resume its post on the Point, Justin and Coot turned to join the Circle and everyone closed in, some of the children holding hands, others beginning to weep as the death of those they were missing was about to be confirmed. Justin moved slowly to the center of the Circle, standing on the low, flat expanse of rock there—a space large enough for a few of the Ruck to stand together, which they called the Stone. Justin's ruddy brown face was grave.

"We have lost two of our children today," said Justin. "We must grieve. But first, we must sing their virtue. Then we must remember our names. We must renew our pledge never to let the Ruck disappear from the land."

Several children cried and wailed again, while the men stood stoic. Justin paused, allowing the children to settle down.

"Chance and Violet were taken from us today. We loved them and we will remember them. Chance made us better when he showed us that the spirit of the Ruck can be challenged, but not broken. He gave us hope when he eluded the Overlords many times in The Hunt. Finally, he gave his life for us. Violet gave her life, too, before she had lived enough of it. She always welcomed us with her smile and entertained us with her dance. Because of their sacrifice, the Ruck will go on."

Justin paused again, allowing for more crying and comforting of siblings and friends. Chance had several brothers and sisters who wept and fell to their knees. Their mother, Diamond, had passed away in childbirth after her eleventh child, but an astounding nine of them remained, even after Chance's death today. The oldest daughter, Ash, who was nearing womanhood, comforted the younger ones. Mountain, Chance's oldest brother and along with Sparrow one of the oldest men in the village, quietly left his usual position by Hawk's side and tried to help his sister calm the others. All of Violet's siblings were older and more subdued, but they and Violet's younger friends still sobbed—even Spider let herself cry for a few moments.

Justin continued. "It is now time to honor the heroes of The Hunt. Does anyone wish to step forward?"

Sparrow, Dreamer, and a brown-skinned, thin girl named Onyx took one step forward into the Circle. Justin bowed his head to them, slightly.

"Please come to the Stone and speak your truth for all to hear," he said. The three obeyed, while Justin moved to the edge of the Circle next to Coot. Sparrow stepped atop the ceremonial surface; he was the oldest of the three testifiers, which meant he would speak first.

"Chance sacrificed his life for all of the Ruck today. He also saved two of us during the Hunt. Dreamer and I were trying to elude the Overlord party when Chance charged out between us, diverted their attention, and allowed Dreamer to run off. I turned back to see if I could help Chance, but they were upon us both, shooting lightning. Dreamer and I ran. They pursued Chance. I heard his death-scream only heartbeats later."

Sparrow stepped down and rejoined his friends, replaced by Onyx. Her thin frame made her appear a bit frail and gawky, but she stood straight, if not tall, looking directly at Justin, and trying not to let her tears fall as she spoke.

"Hawk saved me today. I'm sad about Chance and Violet, but I'm grateful to Hawk for his bravery. I thought I was hiding, but I heard the Overlords coming and I didn't know where to go. He appeared from nowhere, like he was following the hunting party ... or following me. He used his own flowers to disguise my scent. He told me to run, while he stayed there. I don't know how he lived ... they were ... so close ...." she trailed off, choking back tears. Turning to face Hawk, she forced out a "Thank you," awkwardly stepped off the Stone and went to stand with him. Shadow moved a step back to let Onyx squeeze in as Hawk put one hand on her shoulder.

Dreamer climbed up next, slowly turning around to look at everyone as he spoke, gesturing frequently towards his friends, and wiping a tear from his eye now and again.

"Sparrow is the best. He helped save me. He was helping before Chance got there. I was, um, I was pretending to ... I jumped out of a tree and was running when he pushed me down. Then the monsters came ... they were smashing everything, and, um, Sparrow told me to run while he, um ... went back to help Chance. They would've shot me if he ... I just wish ... I mean ..." He started to cry now, too, overwhelmed, and ran over to Chance's brothers and sisters and began to hug them.

Justin stepped back to the rock. "It is the law. Some must die while others live. Our heroes have helped save as many as possible. We honor them."

Everyone, except for Hawk and Sparrow, knelt and cupped both hands over their chests, fingers overlapped. They were silent for ten heartbeats, and then they rose.

"The Ruck go on. We remember our names. Sparrow, step up. Berry, step up. Rabbit, step up.

Sparrow re-entered the Circle, after a brief hesitation, but before either of the others had stepped up. He was somewhat surprised—he had been Sparrow for four winters and had expected to keep the name until his death. The other two also entered the Circle cautiously. Berry, a boy a little older than Dreamer, with blushing red cheeks and a sly grin, came next, taking a place on the other side of the Stone. Rabbit emerged last. A healthy girl about Dreamer's age, she had wild pale hair that complemented her smooth features and brilliant blue eyes. She huddled close to Sparrow, her head almost resting on his bicep.

Justin turned slowly in a full circle as he spoke. "We have known the names of Berry, Rabbit, and Sparrow for a few winters. Each of them has drawn The Hunt and returned to the Ruck.

"Rabbit returned from another hunt today. Her speed and agility have carried her back to us each time. But she is growing and changing, as all Ruck children do. In the spring, her beauty began to unfold slowly, like a patient flower. She has continued to bloom, even now as we approach another winter. And so, we will now know her as Blossom, and we will remember her name."

She hesitated, but Sparrow pushed her forward. She glided to the Stone, took Justin's outstretched hand, and stepped up. He kissed her forehead, as would a father. She smiled. A low hum swept through the villagers, turning into the subtle chanting of "Blossom." She smiled again and resumed her place at the edge of Circle, among friends.

Justin resumed his slow turn. "Berry has been known to us since he left the women. His antics since last winter have made us laugh and made us angry. To him, it seems everything is a game. It is not. But he reminds us that we must laugh. We have been without Coyote for too long, but our wait is now over."

Unlike Blossom, the boy didn't hesitate at all. Cheeks flushing brighter, the color of fresh berries, he leaped onto the Stone. Justin held him by both arms and kissed him on the forehead. Quickly, Coyote returned the kiss, pecking Justin on the cheek and causing the man to falter for a heartbeat. The hum swept rapidly through the villagers, with laughter and "Coyote" intermingled.

The boy jumped from the Stone with arms outstretched, reminding Sparrow of his encounter with Dreamer during The Hunt.

Justin turned. "We have known the name Sparrow for four

winters. He has become a man in that time. He has saved our younger children before, and again today. He delights us with his stories, helps feed us with the *ven*, and brings us children with the women. He tells our children many stories, with at least one having great meaning for us. He helps us remember Eagle, and so we now remember his name."

For several heartbeats, Sparrow couldn't move. The story of Eagle had sustained his hope during the difficult winters and when friends died in The Hunt. To be given such a legendary name ... how does one act? Somehow, his legs moved him to the Stone, and he took Justin's hand. He barely noticed the kiss and then realized he was approaching Coyote, who had bowed very low to one knee, grinning. The humming turned softly to "Eagle" and faded.

Justin raised his hands, palms upward. "We are the Ruck; we remember. We must survive. We now eat and re-gain strength. We thank the *ven* for keeping us fit and ready for The Hunt."

Again, a low hum swept among the villagers, turning into a brief cacophony, as siblings and friends fell naturally into groups to talk about the new names or to lament their lost.

Eagle, Sage, and Thrush started laughing again, and so everyone gathered around the small fire smiled and giggled, too. A few of them were still nibbling on the roasted *ven*, or drinking water from ceramic mugs, but most had gotten their fill and were just enjoying each other's company on a pleasant fall evening. Before long it would be too cold to relax like this, after sundown, without protection against the cold. Eagle sat with his back against a tree, while the others sprawled around him in a haphazard semi-circle, some sitting cross-legged, others stretched out on their backs or leaning back on elbows or propped up against each other.

"The look on his face ... I don't think I can ever forget.

Never." Thrush's voice squeaked as he spoke; the change was happening. Soon, he would become a man. The squeaking didn't seem to concern him. "I mean, kissing Justin is *groans* anytime, but during the naming ... !"

Dreamer lay on his back with knees raised, staring up at the stars, while Willow rested against the incline of his shins. She had done little but stare in admiration at her older brother, Eagle, since they assembled for the feast. A couple of smaller children played nearby, chasing each other, jumping and falling and enjoying all of it. One of them seemed to be playing by himself—Badger, who could occupy an entire evening just digging holes in the dirt.

At the edge of the semi-circle, Raven and Fly lay side by side, locked in an eternal kiss. Raven's perfectly long black hair cascaded across Fly's face and over his back, as if to conceal their activity, but their infatuation was no secret. They had been at this for days, it seemed; stopping only to eat, sleep, or do their chores (not to mention, The Hunt). Not unusual for boys and girls their age, but still it could be embarrassing—or at least distracting—for those around them, especially when they began to caress each other's genitals and erogenous zones, moaning with adolescent desire. Eagle remembered his first forays into sexuality; it had been a few winters now since he had behaved that way. He thought of Ruby, the first girl he had ever kissed or fondled, who had been with the women for more than three winters now and was a mother of three small children. He wondered if any of them were his. Sometimes one could guess, at least by appearance, when the children had grown old enough for their features to be defined. Hers were still young, and they hadn't even left the women yet, so Eagle didn't get to see them enough to hazard a guess.

Now, he was too old for the young girls remaining in the village. At least *he* thought so. Eagle knew that some of the younger men took liberties with the older girls, but he wouldn't. Of course, no one dared go all the way with a younger girl—any child conceived by such a union would be killed by the Black One, who always found out, somehow. In any case, the villagers frowned upon intercourse with girls who hadn't begun the bleeding. Still, a variety of pleasures could be had without risking conception and many of the older girls sought out the men, having tired of foolish boys. Several had approached Eagle; he always declined, politely, which only seemed to give them hope that he would change his mind. His glance happened on Ash, who reclined on her right elbow next to Sage, with her legs elegantly tucked under her left hip. Eagle found himself following the smooth line of her leg, up past her slim waist, around her curved breast, until his eyes met hers. He should have known she would be watching him, especially after his ascension earlier at the Stone. She had made her intentions clear one moon ago, and she seemed to follow him everywhere, even tonight after her brother's death, along with her younger brother Nardo. She offered a sly smile, lips parted just so. He returned the smile, but forced himself to look away.

"So, Sage," Eagle said, looking just past the man to avoid Ash's gaze, "what wise words do you have for us tonight?"

Sage frowned, giving Eagle a look that could start a fight under different circumstances. "Why destroy such a tranquil moment with words? Let the children play, let the lovers embrace ... let the men rest and keep their heavy thoughts to themselves." He winked at Eagle and glanced askew at Ash. "The Hunt is over, until the next season. The Ruck go on."

Heather, who had been playing *stones* with Nardo, spoke. "Sage, what will my brother, Coyote, do now? Will I still see him?"

Nardo, a burly young boy a few winters younger than Heather, had tossed the central stone into the air and deftly scooped up a few surrounding it, but dropped them just as quickly when the girl spoke. "*Fug*, you made me miss," he said.

Sage turned to Heather, who usually wore a chain of small purple flowers, except in the winter. She was fair-haired with rosy cheeks like her brother. "Of course, you will still see him, girl. He will be here for all of us, to make us laugh exactly as Justin said. I suspect he will have more than a few more antics for us, involving Justin, Coot, and myself. Indeed! Our Coyote will remind the Ruck to celebrate life—he will grow and change, as he should, but he will still be your brother."

Heather smiled, snatching the central stone from Nardo and resuming the game. The boy lunged across the *stones* and pushed her, almost knocking her backward.

"Nardo, stop it!" Ash scolded, stressing the boy's name as if she had yelled at him a thousand times. "If you can't play right, just leave."

Everyone stopped for a moment, reacting to the older sister's admonition. Sage made a pained expression and rubbed his ear; Newt, Double, Happy, and Rachel stopped their running and chasing for a moment. They resumed quickly enough, after Newt started a little chant.

"Nardo's in trouble, Nardo's in trouble," she said quietly at first, until they had all picked it up, skipping in a ring and waving their arms.

Nardo sprang up and charged at the other children, banging into Happy, a boy a few winters older than Nardo and a little bit taller but also slighter of build. They tumbled down, with Happy laughing the entire time, apparently enjoying what was turning into an impromptu wrestling match. The other kids came to his rescue, trying to pull Nardo away as he fought them off, all of them screaming like they had seen an Overlord for the first time, until Thrush intervened, dragging the boy to his feet.

"That was fun!" Happy said, flat on his back.

"Let him go, Thrush," said a dulcet, authoritative voice from the growing darkness.

Thrush obeyed as Hawk entered the fire lit area. Hawk seemed larger than usual in the dimly lit edge of the fire, his cropped black hair framing his face. Nardo ran up to him, grabbing hold to his well-muscled leg.

"I've been looking for you, boy. I want you to go with Shadow, back to my yurt, and wait for me."

"What did I do?" Nardo asked, his bravado fading slightly.

"Nothing, boy. I just want to speak with you and a few others. Shadow, take him."

Shadow appeared from behind Hawk. He hesitated, as if unsure of the order. Hawk made it clear. "I have some private matters, Shadow. Please take Nardo back to my yurt and wait for me."

Shadow, a boy of Happy's age and a full head taller than Nardo, put both hands on the boy's shoulders and gently turned him around. They left silently, but Nardo looked over his shoulder several times before they disappeared.

Hawk's tone softened. "Go about your play, children. Nardo is fine." He stepped forward, past Thrush, and helped Happy to his feet while smiling thinly. "Perhaps we can arrange a real wrestling match for you, Happy. I think you would enjoy it."

"*Yeeeeee*! I sure would!"

Hawk turned to Eagle, who hadn't moved from his spot against the tree. Sage and Ash had stood up and parted in front of Hawk's presence.

"Eagle," he said, evidently forcing out the new name. "Please come with me. We must talk."

Standing up, his back still to the tree, Eagle allowed himself a slight grin. He could see that they were all staring at him, waiting to see what he would do. Even Raven and Fly had broken the seal between their lips. He saw Thrush edging forward, as if waiting for a high sign during one of their excursions for *ven*.

"My pleasure, Hawk." Taking a few steps forward, he clapped Sage on the back and raised an eyebrow to Ash. "It is getting late, these children should be getting back to their yurts, don't you think?

Sage started to reply, but Ash cut him off. "Yes, it's late. Let's go everyone."

The children began to groan and whine, but Ash was ready for that. "We'll race back to the Circle—first one there gets to stay up until Eagle returns."

A chorus of exclamations rang out like it was the first day of winter snow. Newt took off running, her skinny legs flailing wildly. The rest of the young children chased after her, except for Raven and Fly, who got up and started off hand in hand, preferring to enjoy a little extra time together by way of a slow journey. Finally, Ash, Thrush, and Sage left together, with the eldest and wisest of the three turning to speak to Eagle as they departed.

"Perhaps I was wrong about letting the men keep their heavy thoughts to themselves, Eagle. I shall await your return."

Hawk shifted his glance between Eagle and Sage as the group departed, a quizzical look now occupying his usual granite face.

"What is it, Hawk?" Eagle leaned back against the tree, folding his arms. His long hair almost blended in with the bark, but his green eyes stood out, the reflection of the firelight flickering in them. He and Hawk were nearly the same height, but Hawk's body the more muscular and mature.

Hawk paused, carefully composing his words. "I wanted to congratulate you on your naming. You have earned it. Over the last two winters you have grown as a man, survived several Hunts, and become a proficient hunter yourself. You have helped feed the Ruck by bringing in the *ven* and helped save our children in The Hunt. We need men like you and me for the Ruck to go on. I was glad to hear the name of Sparrow called today after The Hunt. I had spoken to Justin a few times in recent moons, telling him that I thought your leadership should be recognized. I believe he was waiting for the right moment. Your saving of Dreamer made it possible today."

"Thank you," Eagle said, a little surprised by Hawk's praise. "You honor me with your kind words."

"You are welcome. But now you have a greater responsibility than ever before. I must admit that I was surprised by the name you received. Of course, I offered no suggestions; it is up to Justin, Coot, and Sage to determine our names. Yet, I *was* surprised. There hasn't been an Eagle among us for many winters. We remember his name, of course, and at some time, there should be another. Still, I wonder, is this the right time? Will you be able to carry on bearing such a name?"

"Only the Ruck can answer that. I merely do my best, Hawk. Did you know whether you could carry on with such a name as Hawk, when the Justin-before named you?"

Hawk bristled, took a deep breath, and nodded. "I never doubted myself. For the Ruck to carry on, doubts will not do."

"It seems that you doubt me." Eagle almost regretted his words as soon as they escaped his lips, but he believed Hawk was testing him—and it was the first response that occurred to him. "What should I say ... that I don't deserve to be Eagle?"

"No. Please don't twist my meaning. Remembering our names and carrying on doesn't mean all things will be as they were. Mostly, I wanted to see what you would say. You are Eagle now, but you shouldn't expect to be the same as the Eagle-before. He was a great leader, and someday you may prove so, too. It seems you understand that."

"Yes."

"Then understand this as well. I am the oldest of the men —aside from Coot—and I am the leader of the Ruck. I am the best hunter. The name of Eagle won't change any of this. Still, I want you to work with me to make sure the Ruck go on. I want you to become a father to the children, as I have. I can't guide all of them; I need other men to join with me. Men like Mountain who has pledged to serve the Ruck under my guidance. And perhaps Falcon, who was also given an important name in the previous Hunt. I have spoken to him, too, told him the same things I am telling you. We must lead the children properly."

"I agree, we must lead the children. I am willing to work with you, Hawk. I will continue to be a father to the children. I ..."

Hawk interrupted. "Then the first thing you must do is to stop filling their heads with some of the nonsense you put into your stories."

Eagle recoiled, nearly bumping his head against the tree trunk. "Nonsense? No, Hawk, the stories are important. We need them for the Ruck to go on. I won't stop telling the stories."

"You are half-right. The stories are important. They help us remember. But some of them are harmful. They give the children the wrong ideas. And there are other young men who can carry on the telling. It isn't for you anymore. You are Eagle now. Leave it to Fly—or one of the others."

Eagle bristled now, leaning forward. Only a leaf's length separated the two men, for a heartbeat, until Eagle relaxed and rested his back against the trunk again.

"You have given me much to consider, Hawk. Your words are heavy, but it is getting late. You heard Ash's promise to the children. We should make our way back. I will think about what you have said." Eagle began to move around Hawk's left arm, but the older man seized Eagle's wrist.

"Think hard, then," Hawk said, holding on for a few more heartbeats.

Eagle continued on his way to the yurts, without answering. He heard Hawk following him, but he never looked back.

2

Eagle watched the sun rise over the Point, following the slowly receding shadow emanating from the Black One on the other side of the valley. The Overseer, at its post, ubiquitous. The eyes and ears of the Overlords. Eagle wondered, but doubted, whether the old story was true—the Black One was once one of the Ruck.

He also reflected on his discussion with Sage, three nights before, after Hawk's threats and commands. Not true, it wasn't a discussion. More like an angry man ranting and a patient man listening. If not for Sage's well-timed counsel, blood might have been shed that night—or the next day. Eagle hated to admit it because the Ruck rarely resorted to violence against their own.

At first, he told Sage he was going to tell the stories that very night, calling the children from their sleep and challenging Hawk's edict in front of the entire village. Next, he said he would go straight to the heart of the matter and challenge the man to a *gant* after the sun rose, publicly questioning his loyalty to the Ruck. In either case, he realized Hawk wouldn't have let the challenge go without answer. Even among the Ruck, when two men create such a dispute, violence awaits.

Sage had reminded him of the legendary Eagle, and how his boon to the Ruck had been one of patience and perseverance, not rash action. He asked Eagle to look within, for three days: fasting, watching the sunrise over their village, making a secret journey into the heart of the Ruck. He had told Eagle to go hunt the *ven*, to watch the children play, and to observe the painstaking labors of the crafters. Only then, would the proper path reveal itself.

Now as Eagle watched the third sun rise from his perch, the righteous path became clear. He would walk through the village again today to speak to the crafters and complete his secret journey. Sage had proved himself a good friend, yet again. His advice always benefited all of the Ruck, as well as the individual. He wondered if Hawk had also sought Sage's counsel. Maybe he would go to Coot or Justin first. It occurred to Eagle: he might encounter Hawk in the village. The first two days of fasting were spent mostly on his own, hunting, thinking, and meditating. Sage must have thought of that. If they did meet today, Eagle would be able to temper his emotions.

He shed his blanket, stretched his limbs, and welcomed the warmth of the sun on his face. The cold loomed. Already they slept with extra skins and coverings, but during the day a single layer of clothing still sufficed. It would change soon enough. Another winter to count and, he hoped, to survive.

Standing and stretching his torso, Eagle wondered if they had preserved enough *ven* and *veg* to nourish the Ruck. The men continued hunting for as long as possible, but a harsh winter could drain their supply of *pem* and exhaust all of the *veg*. Eagle decided to spend the next few days hunting, bringing in as many *ven* as he could. His stomach grumbled, and he realized all his thinking about food had made him hungry. Just one more day of fasting. For now, another gulp from his water skin would have to do. He picked up the blanket, threw it over one shoulder, and headed down to the village.

Looking first for Archer, his sister and the crafter he knew best among all the Ruck, Eagle happened upon Dreamer. The boy acted out his current fantasy near Archer's yurt, dancing around the small smoldering fire. Eagle froze; the boy hadn't noticed his arrival. He hoped to observe Dreamer's entire story, perhaps it would give him another clue on his journey. He had to stifle a chuckle. The boy appeared to be playing three different roles in whatever story his imagination had invented. One character was large and strong, another haughty, and the third appeared to be a child (himself?). They were arguing about something, although Eagle couldn't quite discern the meaning. He observed for some time, but before the story had ended Dreamer suddenly gasped and halted, finally seeing Eagle's bemused face.

"It's okay, son." Eagle said, quickly. "I was enjoying your story. Please, tell me what happens next."

Dreamer only shrugged. "Um ... I don't know."

"It was interesting. I could see the people, but not exactly what they were doing. I'd like to see more."

"It's just a ... I'm just pretending." Dreamer looked up into the sky. "Do I have to tell you, Eagle?"

"Of course not. But I would like it if you did."

Dreamer continued looking up, lolling his head from side. Eagle wondered if the boy had retreated to his dream-world again, or if was only acting like it to avoid the conversation. Just then, Eagle saw Archer and Tanner out the corner of his eye. They were coming back from the village's breakfast together.

"Okay Dreamer," Eagle said. "Maybe you can tell me about it later." He waved to the girls. Almost young women, really. They were two winters younger than Ash: born only a moon apart. Like her brother, Archer had a slender, sinewy body, but her hair and eyes were much darker than his. She kept it cropped close, almost like Hawk's (Eagle realized he had never noticed that before). Tanner, shorter than Archer by about one thumb, had more curves, with orange hair braided in one long strand down her back. They probably had two more winters before joining the women. Both of their departures would be felt in the village; they had developed exemplary skill in their crafts. Coot had said that Archer handled the bow better than anyone he had seen since he was a boy. Tanner was named three winters ago, prematurely, after the accidental death of her mentor, and she had honed her skill admirably. They stopped and Archer hugged Eagle.

"So, brother, you haven't left for good after all," Archer said as she held him for an extra few heartbeats. "Was your hunt successful?"

Eagle smiled as they parted. "Yes. I brought in six *ven*."

Dreamer squealed. "*Yeeeeee*! Six!"

All three of them turned to Dreamer. He was dancing again and didn't appear to be paying attention. No one seemed sure if he was listening to them or if his fantasy had somehow coincided with their conversation.

Eagle shook his head playfully, shrugging and chuckling. "He's been making me laugh since I got here. I was looking for you, Archer. And Tanner, if you don't mind, I would like to meet with you in a little bit."

Both girls paused, as if surprised. "Is something wrong, Eagle?" his sister asked.

"No, not at all." Eagle didn't understand her reaction at first, but then he realized his request might have sounded a little vague and mysterious the way he blurted it out. His fasting had made him a little dizzy at times. He had been thinking about his journey since before daybreak, but of course they didn't know that. And he rarely came to talk to Tanner unless it was about needing some article of *ven*-hide, which he would say right away.

"I'm sorry," he continued. "I didn't mean to alarm you. I'm just following Sage's advice. He told me that I should watch the Ruck for a day, especially the crafters. If it doesn't bother you, I would like to share part of the day with you … to watch you work and remember the importance of your tasks."

The girls now looked even more perplexed, especially Tanner. "There isn't much to see," she said. "You know what *ven*-hide looks like. You're wearing my leggings now. It sounds weird. I mean, I don't really care, but it sounds strange."

"Please, indulge me." Eagle looked into Tanner's eyes. She seemed a bit embarrassed and shifted her gaze over to Dreamer (still dancing). "I won't hinder you; it might even be fun," Eagle said.

Archer grabbed him by the arm, giggling. "I'll take him first, Tanner, and find out what this is all about. See you later." She dragged Eagle to her work area, still giggling, while Tanner harrumphed and turned toward her yurt, her orange braid flailing behind her.

Archer's work area was really just a pile of her tools and supplies that she kept covered with *ven*-hide scraps sewn together, resting just outside of her small yurt. She let go of her brother and knelt beside it, dragging the cover away to reveal the pile. It was a mess. Eagle always wanted to tidy it up when he came to see her. He occasionally bothered her about organizing everything. Today, he sat down cross-legged and faced her without mentioning it.

Archer collected up a few stones that she had begun working into points. She examined them while she talked, still kneeling.

"No comments about my mess? This *is* a strange morning. Maybe Tanner was right."

"In a way, I guess." Eagle breathed deep. "I suppose I should tell you what this is all about."

"That would be nice."

He lowered his voice. "After the naming, Hawk came looking for me. He lectured me about being a man. Told me to stop telling the stories, to let Fly take my place from now on."

Archer had just chosen one of the points and set down the others. Now, she concentrated on her brother. "That's silly."

"It's an insult. I was ready to throw the *gant*. Sage talked me out of it. He advised me to go off on my own for a few days—to hunt and fast. He also said to come back to the village on the third day and observe the Ruck. That's what I'm doing now. I started with you, because you're my sister. Now that I think of it, I guess I started with Dreamer."

"I see." Archer now weighed a few cutting stones in her palm, picked a small one and began to chip away with it. "You won't learn much by watching me do this. You know how to shape a point."

"I don't think that's what Sage meant. I think he meant that I should share the day with the Ruck to remember how the village feels. A *gant* would change things, wouldn't it? It has divided the Ruck before—I tell a story about it."

"I know you do. It still sounds silly. I don't understand Sage sometimes. I mean, you've seen me make points before."

"You are good at it. I've taken many *ven* with your points."

"I'm not as good as Fletcher. She's younger than me and already better at it.

"But she isn't teaching other children how to shoot, is she?"

Archer smiled widely as she worked. "I enjoy that. I guess I'm pretty good at that." She paused and looked up at Eagle, with excitement in her eyes. "Why don't you come back later and watch my lesson?"

"That's a good idea."

"Of course it is." She cocked her head to one side. "I guess Sage is pretty smart after all."

They laughed with each other and talked for a little while, until Eagle realized the sun was edging its way across the morning sky and that he had better move on. He had lost track of the day after Archer had asked him to talk about their mother. She hadn't seen Honey since she left the village, but Eagle visited the women once per moon with the other men. He told Archer that Honey was as beautiful and kind as ever, and that she always asked about her children when they could steal a moment together to talk. Honey had lived almost as long as Coot they reminded themselves, which was something to be grateful for. Most of the villagers were orphans, especially the older children. As Eagle got up to leave, he leaned over and hugged his sister's shoulders with one arm. She rested her head on his arm for a heartbeat and then went back to her work.

He found Tanner quickly. She had her hands inside a large round wooden bowl, mashing something watery. Eagle greeted her and sat down a few feet away. He smelled a wafting earthy odor, probably from whatever she was mashing. He said nothing more, observing, until she sighed and looked up.

"Are you just going to sit there and stare at me?" she asked.

"Not if it offends you. I don't know much about your work. I just wear your leggings and shirts." Eagle smiled. "I was going to watch you work for a little while, maybe ask a few questions."

"I guess that's okay."

"What are you doing now?"

"Making a dye. You didn't kill any *ven* that color, did you?" She thrust a finger at him, straight from the bowl, sending a trail of dye drops in an arc toward him. "Sorry."

"Missed me." Eagle looked at his leggings while she continued mashing. They had two shades of brown, which helped to hide him in the woods. He had never really thought about how they got that way, only how much concealment they offered. Function, more than form, had always been his concern. Looking at them more closely now, he noticed a few small designs around the calf, within the mixture of dyes. Although he had never really thought much about the designs before, Eagle now recognized some important images for the Ruck—images of the *ven* and the bow and the Circle.

"I never noticed the significance of these designs before. You are very talented."

Tanner lifted her head from the bowl again and stopped her mashing. She stood up, with the bowl tucked under one arm, and began to walk away. She looked over her shoulder, saying, "Thanks. Most people don't ever notice."

Eagle followed her swinging curvy hips and orange braid as she went around the back of her yurt to the small shelter where a number of *ven*-hides hung under a large piece-meal sewn hide. All shapes and sizes, scraps, strips and sides hung from nearly every available thin branch rafter. The dye and hide commingled to produce a strong odor within the shelter, making Eagle feel a little giddy for a few heartbeats. He realized that much of his efforts ended up here—they used every usable part of the *ven* and thanked them for it. She had lots of projects going on, it seemed. Eagle looked around while Tanner fussed with things. She finally seemed content to go about her activities and let him observe. He watched closely while she applied the new dye to what appeared to be several fresh skins. She used some kind of moss, or something that he might have used as tinder, as well as a balled-up piece of cloth. She seemed to lose herself in the process, completely ignoring him, and muttering to herself now and then. She didn't rush, but she had handled all the pieces before long.

She looked up at him like the conversation hadn't paused. "So, what's this all about? What do you want from me?"

Eagle stuttered, briefly, as her question startled him. "Nn ... nothing. I just wanted to visit with you and watch you work. It has proven valuable already."

"Why? You should be out hunting or something."

"I have been hunting for two days, you heard me say that before."

"So? This is just strange. Don't you think I'm a little too young for you, anyway?"

This time, Eagle stammered. "Wh ... no, I ... it's not that, really, I just came to watch you work. It was Sage's idea."

"Now I'm really scared. Hawk says Sage has his head in the clouds."

Eagle paused—that seemed to answer part of his question about with whom Hawk had sought counsel.

"Forgive me," Eagle said. "I should have started out by telling you that. My thoughts were heavy, and Sage advised me to clear my head by fasting and observing the Ruck. I guess it does sound strange, but it's been helpful."

Tanner shrugged, returning her attention to the work.

"Do you visit with Hawk often?" Eagle ventured.

"Sure. I hang around with a couple of Ruck who hang around with him. Hawk saved me in my first Hunt. I don't think he was much older than your friend Thrush at the time. That's when he was named."

"Hawk cares very much about the children. As do I. I want to make sure the Ruck go on."

Tanner looked over her shoulder at him. "I believe you," she said, softly. She turned back to her work. "We all do. But the Ruck should have one leader."

Eagle looked up at the sun and saw it edging overhead. "You obviously have a lot of work to do. I should go. Thank you, Tanner. I look forward to your new designs."

As he walked toward Fletcher's yurt, Eagle wondered how much Tanner knew. Her comment could have been a coincidence, but she obviously had her eyes open. He also realized the strength of Hawk and the influence he had on the villagers. Hawk had saved many children, earning their allegiance. Hawk deserved to be a leader, but Eagle knew he was wrong about the stories. Eagle began to think about finding a way to keep the stories alive without having to challenge Hawk.

He searched around Fletcher's area. Very similar to his sister's, he noticed. The three young crafters lived close together, sharing the same fire and each other's company. Fletcher was one winter younger than the other two, one of the sisters of Chance who were born to Diamond (all orphans now). She looked much like her older sister, Ash. After calling her name in case she was inside the yurt, Eagle turned around and thought about whom he should try next. When Archer appeared, it occurred to him that everyone would be taking the high-sun break before long.

"She's out gathering feathers, I think. She has stayed by herself since The Hunt. She and Chance grew up together."

Eagle nodded, understanding. He and Archer had lost siblings, too. Sometimes, the other children would mourn for a full moon; sometimes they bounced back more quickly. The Hunt affected everyone differently; they were used to it and it horrified them at the same time.

"Thanks for telling me. I'll go look for Potter or Weaver or Carver, before the break." Eagle set off toward the middle of the village—the male crafters lived on the other side, so he decided to see who was out and about while on his way.

As he approached the Circle, he saw a group of the smaller children playing. About a dozen of them, occupied with a variety of activities, apparently without any supervision at the moment. He saw Badger first, digging in the dirt as usual and dangerously close to disturbing the Circle. Nearby, Double and Fish were playing stones. Eagle marveled at how much Double looked like her older sister, Butterfly, with her golden-brown hair gently falling about her shoulders and complimenting her tanned features. He braced himself against Fish. For the last two moons the little girl had rushed him and grabbed both legs in an enduring hug every time she saw him. Eagle would have to break loose, forcibly, because she never seemed to want it to end. The other children were a little farther off, running around and playing some kind of free-form game. It looked like Opal and Newt and ... Red, he was unmistakable ... but before he could identify them all, Fish spotted him.

She got up and ran all in one motion, hooking her arm around his legs as she flew by him, swinging around him and latching on with both arms around both legs.

"Sparrow! I mean, Eagle! Give me a ride!" She quickly let slide her grip, taking only his left leg, sliding down and sitting on his foot with her arms and legs wrapped around.

"Okay, Fish." He dragged her along, stiffening the leg Fish had claimed, while hobbling four or five steps. Fortunately, she wasn't heavy—she had left the women only two winters before. Unfortunately, the others now wanted a turn, and they were charging and screaming, led by Badger. They overwhelmed Eagle, sending him and themselves into a pile of screaming, giggling worms.

"What's going on out here?" an older girl screeched. "Eagle, what are you doing?"

The boys and girls rolled around and some of them started to break off and straighten up. Eagle lifted his head, shook off Shorty—where had he come from?—and propped himself on one elbow. Shrew glared at Eagle, hands on hips.

"I ... I was just passing through," Eagle said. A couple of the children giggled but stopped once Shrew's glare had swept over them. "It all started when Fish rushed me ..."

"It's time for the break," Shrew interrupted. "And I don't want to hear any complaining." The children started to dust themselves off and head over to the yurts by the Circle. Shrew waited a few heartbeats then turned back to Eagle, who had gotten up. "You're always getting those children worked up, aren't you?" she said.

"Honest, I just walked up, on my way to find Potter."

"Well, you just keep on going then. It's hard enough keeping these children from breaking each other's necks as it is." Shrew turned away before Eagle could reply.

He watched her leave. Tall and skinny, she always held her head high. She tied her black hair in a single braid but kept it much shorter than Tanner's. She was only slightly older than Archer and Tanner, but she had matured much more quickly. Everyone knew she was on her way to join the women. And she made sure that everyone knew she wasn't happy about it. It was as if she were trying to shorten the children's childhood to make up for losing some of her own. Still, she kept them occupied, cared for, and safe. She would continue to do so until moving in with the women.

Eagle realized someone was chuckling behind him. He listened for a few heartbeats; it was definitely Sage.

"Ambushed by children, an angry woman, and a mediocre hunter, all in one break time," Sage said, approaching. Eagle turned around.

"Mediocre? Eagle replied. "You give yourself too much credit."

"I was just about to have some water. Please join me, Eagle."

They clasped each other on the back and went to Sage's yurt. They sat inside, with the flap open. Eagle told him about the morning, his hunting the days before and his plans for the rest of the day. Sage told him that Potter had left the village for the day, collecting materials along with some other boys. Sage had also seen Weaver and Bison leaving the area together earlier, for what he didn't know.

Eagle enjoyed the respite. When Sage began to chew on the *pem*, Eagle remembered how hungry he was. He thought he would be used to it by now. He would eat well tonight. The water refreshed him, though, so he thanked his friend for the break and went off to see if Weaver and Carver could be found.

He steered as far from the children as he could, passing between a few yurts. He realized that he was near Hawk's area, but it was the best way now. No sense in avoiding everyone—he wanted to stay away from Shrew in particular. He happened to come upon Weaver and Bison, who were sitting outside of someone's yurt, still enjoying the mid-day break. They gave a start when he appeared.

"Why are you sneaking up on us like that?" Bison demanded. He stood up and faced Eagle. He was a strong young man with an expansive chest, covered with a small sleeveless shirt, even as the weather became colder. He kept his brown hair cropped short, like Hawk's, but he always wore a string of *ven*-hide around his head, just across his forehead. He was a few winters younger than Eagle, but probably stronger physically.

"Relax, Bison. I was just trying to avoid Shrew." Eagle regretted the comment as soon as he said it. The other thing everybody knew about Shrew was how she felt about Bison and how much he tried to avoid her.

"You're asking for it!" Bison threatened, holding his fist in the air.

Weaver intervened. "Come on, Bison, you know you aren't the only one who tries to stay away from Shrew." He lowered his voice. "Break is about done; let's move before she hears us."

Bison heeded his friend, the younger brother of Sage. They went behind the yurt and kept moving outward from the Circle until they were definitely out of earshot. Eagle trailed them and finally, when they had stopped, Bison told Eagle to leave them alone.

"Actually, I was looking for Weaver," Eagle answered. "I was hoping to speak with you and ask some questions about your work." Before they could reply, Eagle continued. "I know it sounds weird, but your brother suggested it. What are you doing now?"

"We were gonna go practice archery." Weaver said.

"May I go with you? We can talk while we walk, and then I'll leave you alone."

Bison turned his back and started off. Weaver shrugged and followed him. Eagle caught up to him quickly and walked by his side. Weaver was only one winter younger than Bison, but he was smaller and wirier. His fair, shoulder length hair often swept into his eyes—he sometimes tied as much of it as he could into a small clump, but today it fell free. He had a small, furry, pubescent moustache. Eagle easily matched the boy's pace and began talking.

"What do you do each day, normally?"

"I don't know. Same as everyone else. I work, I eat, I practice … sometimes I hunt. I hang out with girls whenever I can."

"Who do you like?"

"Forget it. I'm not telling you. You can't make me."

Eagle reminded himself that he didn't have the same rapport with this brother of Sage. While Thrush had wanted to become friends with his brother's friends, Weaver did his own thing.

"Okay. I was just curious since you brought it up." Eagle waited a few steps before he continued. "I guess I thought I'd be able to catch you while you were working. You make lots of the things the Ruck need to go on. You are important to us. I was just thinking that without your skill, we might all freeze in the winter, so I wanted to learn more about it."

Weaver slowed down a bit, letting Bison pull away from them. "Thanks for saying so, but why all of the sudden?"

"Your brother said I should observe the Ruck and reflect on who we are. I went to him for counsel. He also suggested that I fast and hunt alone for a few days. It has all been helpful to me. I'm talking to all the crafters, because each of you has something important for the Ruck. I've begun to wonder: how do you choose an apprentice? Do you have one?"

"I have been showing a couple of children, like I was shown. They aren't real interested, but they could carry on if ..." he trailed off.

They walked a bit further in silence now. They saw Bison had already reached the range; he was covering the fixed target—made from thatch, mud and wood—with a new piece of felt. Eagle saw Weaver smiling; it was obviously one of his works, another combination of function and form. A mixture of swirling colors, the emerging pattern highlighted four distinctive targets of differing sizes, surrounding one small patch of black in the middle.

"That's nice," Eagle said. "Mind if I try it out?"

"Old men are always first, aren't they?" Weaver answered.

Bison tacked the target in place, and then joined them. Realizing that Eagle was going to take the first shot, he snorted, folded his arms and stood off to the side. Relaxing and taking measured breaths, Eagle took his short bow from his back, strung it quickly and knocked an arrow. He shot with only a heartbeat's aiming, and the arrow pierced the edge of the central black target. He took another shot and buried the arrow in the next smallest patch of color, which looked a lot like a fleeing *ven*.

"Excellent work, Weaver," he said, striding off to retrieve his arrows. Eagle waved to the two young men after he had replaced the arrows in his quiver. He headed back toward the yurts around Hawk's area, to look for Carver, leaving them to their practice.

As Eagle approached the small clearing at the end of the large group of yurts where Carver, Weaver, and Potter slept and worked, he saw that Carver was instructing a couple of other children. All three had their backs to him. Eagle thought quickly, deciding to observe without their knowledge, if possible. Unfortunately, he was out in the open. Seeing Potter's work area lean-to between him and Carver, he made a quick dash for its cover. He knelt at the back edge of the structure and looked out between the clutter, wondering if he had gone unnoticed.

Apparently, Eagle had moved quickly enough, because they continued their work without interruption. He watched Carver, a rotund young man one winter younger than Thrush, patiently showing the two children how to whittle a stick into some desired form. He couldn't tell exactly what they were attempting to make with their stone knives—much like the one Eagle used to skin *ven*—and it was hard to hear Carver's instructions and guidance, but after studying them for a while, Eagle recognized the children as Shrub and Fox.

All three of them worked diligently and both of the apprentices paid attention to their mentor. Carver had a pleasant voice and manner; he kept them at ease, encouraged their enthusiasm. He had a funny habit that became more and more apparent as Eagle watched. Any time he stressed something in his lesson, he would sweep the fingers on his right hand through his bowl-cut black hair and exhale deeply. This happened three or four times and after each sweep, Shrub and Fox went back to their own carving, as if it were a signal for them to carry on.

Eagle concentrated on Fox for a while. Her sharp, brown features and lithe body had caught his attention before. She was way too young for Eagle and he had never thought otherwise, but many of older boys sought her attention, including Thrush. Eagle remembered one of the storytellings, when Thrush had made subtle advances on her, and she had returned his foray with friendly smiles, bright blue eyes, and gentle touches on his arms and legs. They had walked off together after Eagle had finished the story, but Thrush later told him that she hadn't even let him kiss her that night; they just held hands and walked around. It just made Thrush want her even more. Now, she seemed quite content in working with the wood; in fact, she seemed different than the times he had seen her with Thrush or Ox or Rock. When she was around the boys, she played coy and carefree, letting them lavish attention on her without really doing anything to encourage or discourage them. Here, under Carver's tutelage, she seemed intense and focused on what she was doing. Eagle had never seen that side of her—it left him more impressed by her than ever before.

"*FUG*! It's all messed up!" Shrub's outburst demanded Eagle's attention. Although the bushy-haired boy was about the same age as Dreamer, he was noticeably small for his age. That didn't stop him from tangling with the other children— he had won several wrestling matches organized by Hawk and Mountain. He was quick to react to pressure, from his own making and from others. In this case, he was upset about his own mistake.

Carver said some soothing words, moving toward him, but Shrub recoiled and looked like he was going to lash out. Carver kept talking, sweeping his hair twice, until the boy allowed him near enough to offer suggestions on how to fix the mishap. Carver took the boy's stone knife, with his permission, and began to alter the wood's surface. He then returned it to Shrub, who continued working like nothing had happened at all.

Eagle quietly shifted until he was sitting more comfortably. He continued to watch for a while, as the sun began its slow descent and shadows started to fall across the village. Carver and his apprentices continued their routine, the elder boy showing them little tips and tricks along the way and complimenting them occasionally on their work. They seemed to appreciate his praise; it was sincere but sparing—and genuine, Eagle thought. Finally, he decided to move on. He could cut through the copse between here and the area where he kept his yurt and then go back to Archer's to observe her lesson.

When he approached the cluster of yurts that included his own, he saw a group of young children gathered around the central campfire area. Much like at Carver's, the children were preoccupied by their mentor, Fly. Raven sat nearby (Eagle realized he hadn't seen them separated in days). A couple of the children noticed Eagle's approach; when he stopped beside a tree, they said nothing, reverting their attention to Fly. Eagle sighed, lightly, hoping to God that Fish wasn't there. He loved her, but right now he hoped to watch Fly's storytelling without his knowledge. Fish could change that quickly. He couldn't see them all and some of them couldn't see him, so Eagle stood still, hoping to disappear from their thoughts long enough for him to observe his apprentice.

Fly had his back to Eagle, facing the children. He had every one of them captivated. Animated, he paced a bit back and forth as he told the story of the *washer*. His audience giggled, smiled at each other, and blurted out things they enjoyed about the story. Eagle himself had to hold in a chuckle or two. Fly told the funny stories well. The *washer* had meaning, but it also made the children laugh.

Near the end, Fly began to spin in a tight circle, pretending to be a pair of leggings in the *washer*—churned round and round until the *tek* had cleaned them. He spun into the ground and lay there stretched out like he was drowned. The children squealed, and a couple of them leapt up from the back of the group, laughing and jumping. Fish looked straight at Eagle. He braced himself.

"Sparr ... uhh ... Eagle!" She rushed him again.

He timed her advance precisely, reaching down and snatching her in the crook of his left arm, lifting her into the air over his shoulder, and wrapping both arms around her like a sack of *veg*. She screamed in pure delight. He spun her around and placed her back on the earth all in one motion.

"Do it again!" Fish yelled, but by then, Fly and Raven had approached, with children in tow.

Raven spoke first. "Sneaking up on us, Eagle? Why?" She winked at him.

"Just listening to a good story." Eagle picked up Fish, throwing her back over his shoulder again. This time he lowered her upside down behind his back, holding tightly to her ankles.

"That was a great story, Fly," he said. When he felt Fish pressing into the ground he bent down and gently released her.

"Thanks." Fly seemed a little embarrassed but accepted the praise humbly. "I like telling the stories."

Other children were lining up for rides, but Eagle held them off. "I have to go see my sister, Archer," he said.

"*Fug*," said Raven. "We're supposed to take some of these kids to Archer for their lesson." She looked up at the sun, continuing its descent. "I hope we're not late."

"That's where I'm going. Follow me," he yelled to everyone, taking off at a jog.

They all ran together, screaming and laughing, until they reached Archer's area. He called her name, but instead, Tanner appeared.

"She left for the range." Tanner said. She disappeared quickly, retreating to her work area.

They ran again, led by Eagle and trailed by Fly, who herded the slower ones to keep up. They ran across the Circle, hearing Shrew cursing them from behind. They ran around Sage's and Coot's yurts, up the ridge and into the open area alongside the range.

Archer had just two students. As they slowed, Raven yelled at the children who were still giggling and running around.

"Fish, Badger, Double, Snow! Come over to Archer with me. The rest of you go back with Fly." She now herded, pushing them all to archer.

"I'm staying here, too, Fly," Eagle said. "I'll talk to you later tonight."

The boy nodded and led the younger children away again. Eagle strolled up slowly, allowing his sister and Raven to organize the students before he reached them. Copperhead and Blossom were the two students who were already there. Archer got them all lined up in front of the three targets, two children to each. She barked instructions at them, about how many arrows to shoot, what to aim for and how to take turns. After she had explained the entire process, she walked up to Badger, who had been digging in the dirt with his bare toe while she talked. (Shouldn't he be wearing shoes in this weather, Eagle wondered). She asked him to tell her what she had just said. Badger apparently had no idea. He shrugged. So, Archer explained the whole thing again and asked Blossom to tell her what she had just said. The young girl had the general idea, and so, satisfied, Archer moved off to the side, barking at them to begin. Raven had stood off to the far side of the students, listening and watching Archer.

Each child took a shot before Eagle moved up beside his sister. He was about to speak but she beat him to it.

"We're burning sunlight. Why are you making my students late for class?" she accused, arms folded.

"No, honest, I stumbled upon them … Fly was telling a story, and … Raven can tell you."

Archer squinted at him sidelong out of one eye. "I guess I can give you that, then. It will just have to be a shorter lesson."

Eagle sighed. "Thanks. It's been a strange day. Tanner was right. I seem to have been at odds with almost everyone! This is much harder than hunting and fasting." He paused and chuckled. "I guess that's what Sage wanted me to realize," he said, under his breath.

The children had taken their second shots, waiting afterward as Archer had instructed. Archer had started off toward her students as Eagle muttered his thoughts, but when she heard him mumble those afterthoughts, she gave him a puzzled glance.

Eagle's sister resumed her instruction of the children, giving them a new target. She went over to Raven's side this time and spoke to her. Eagle watched the next rounds and saw that Snow, a boy two winters younger than Dreamer with almost white hair, was a decent marksman. As far as Eagle knew, neither Snow nor his fraternal twin Fern had ever been hunting, yet; even though the boy was young, Snow could probably help them bring in *ven*. The other children varied in proficiency, none standing out as superior or lacking in basic skills. Everyone finished their rounds, except for Badger, who was again scrawling with his toes. Archer ran up to him and gave him and everyone a brief lecture on the importance of paying attention during the hunt. Badger, shamefaced, took his last shot and missed horribly, and so added the embarrassment of having to retrieve it in the brush behind the targets. Archer returned to Eagle's side.

"What do you think?" she asked.

"I think they're learning. Snow is good. I was thinking that he should go hunting with the older boys sometime. Has he ever been?"

"No. But I agree with you. Tell me when you plan to take him, and I'll make sure he's ready."

They watched as the students took their next round of shots, four each this time. By then the sun had nearly disappeared beyond the far hills. It was getting harder and harder to see. Archer ordered the children to retrieve and store their arrows and then she led them all back to the Circle to prepare for the evening meal.

Their noses told them the roasting had already begun. They arrived to find that Hawk and Rock had brought in several ven from the day's hunt. Eagle ate well that night, hanging out near Sage's yurt, with Sage, Thrush, Ash, Coot, Star, and a variety of children who came and went freely. Throughout the evening, Eagle watched the various groups of Ruck, spread around the circle or near their yurts, enjoying the special meal and one another's company. He saw that Hawk spent most of the time with Mountain, Rock, Scar, Bison, Shadow and—most interestingly—Fox and Shrew. But the most unusual event of the night didn't involve any of them.

While everyone was still eating, Coot excused himself and disappeared into the woods, apparently to relieve himself privately. Eagle observed Coyote following discreetly. Looking around, Eagle wondered if anyone else had seen the young boy stealing into the trees after the old man, but no one seemed to take any notice. Trying not to be distracted by his friends,

Eagle kept his attention on the area where Coot and Coyote had entered.

Soon, the boy darted out and ran directly toward Eagle's group, waving something over his head. Coot pursued, just a few steps behind, naked below the waist! Eagle screeched with laughter, and when the others turned to look at him, he pointed to the developing spectacle. Coyote flew past, waving the old man's leggings, howling raucously and leading a chase around the village until everyone had a glimpse of Coot's predicament. The oldest of the Ruck nearly collared the boy twice, but Coyote twisted and spun away, howling again. Finally, the boy relented, tossing the leggings aside and scampering back into the trees near the group of yurts where Eagle slept. Coot grabbed his leggings, pulled them on swiftly and returned to the group, stoic and tall, as if this kind of thing happened every night. That made everyone laugh harder—Eagle noticed that even Hawk and his usually no-nonsense group had fallen about laughing, giggling, and pointing at the old Coot.

As the evening wore on and some of the boys and girls started to pair up, something occurred to Eagle. It would be interesting to spy Thrush from time to time, to see if he was watching Hawk's group. He was. Whenever Fox flirted with Bison or Rock or Peacock, Thrush focused on them, pulling constantly at his tuft of chin hair. Eagle found the whole thing interesting. Shrew was all over Bison and having some success tonight—he was actually talking to her and not trying to get away. Eagle wondered whether Bison stuck around because of Fox. She had both young men quite aroused with her playful touches and evocative poses. Meanwhile, Shrew followed Fox's lead, gradually getting some of Bison's attention, especially after it became evident that Rock was winning Fox's hand tonight. Several things happened almost all at once: Rock and Fox started to kiss; Thrush jumped to his feet and then realized how he looked, sitting down again, turning his back on Hawk's group, and staring into the brush; Bison got up and stretched, saying he was taking a walk; Shrew got up and followed him

(Bison didn't protest and pretended not to notice). Star said something to Eagle, something he didn't quite catch.

He turned to her. "I'm sorry, Star, my mind was wandering."

She laughed at him and turned to look at Ash and Sage, who also chuckled. "I asked if you were still with us. I guess not."

Eagle blushed faintly, realizing that while he was watching the interplay, others were too. Some were watching him as well. "Guilty," he said. Star looked beautiful tonight, as did Ash. Eagle wished he were Bison and Thrush's age again, just for one night. Star's interest in him was even stronger than Ash's, he thought, and he had dreamt about her more than once. She would go to the women soon, he knew. She stared at him with her perfect green eyes, until he turned away, meeting Ash's suspicious stare. He looked down into his hands.

"I think I'm worn out from the last three days and this large meal is making me sleepy," Eagle said, still looking at his hands. "I think I'll go back to my yurt." He looked up, quickly passing his attention to each of his friends, who smiled, or in Coot's case, winked back at him.

As Eagle stood up, Star leaned over and took Thrush's hand. "Come on, Thrush, I want to talk to you," she said. She stood up, pulling his arm and dragging him to his feet. He looked sullen at first, but grinned when she put her arm around his waist and rubbed against him. "Good night, everyone." She waved to everyone, including Eagle, who had paused for a second.

"Good night," he replied. "Good night," he said again, this time to everyone.

Back inside his yurt, he thought about the day, and all three days. Sage had given him good advice. It didn't solve anything, of course. Still, now he had a better idea of what he had to do about Hawk's directive.

◆ ◆ ◆

Several days of hard rain had disrupted the Ruck's routine,

but they were all getting back to normal a couple of days after the clouds broke. Most of the Ruck wore extra layers of clothing now—the rain had brought a chill that remained even after the skies cleared. Winter threatened, but they still had time to hunt and carry on most of their regular activities, at least for a while longer.

Two days ago, Eagle had taken Snow along with some of the other boys on a hunt—the boy had nearly taken a *ven* with his first shot. Yesterday, Eagle had organized some foot races with many of the children, teaching them the proper form for all out speed, setting up several rounds and giving the children a good workout, one they enjoyed thoroughly. He had seen Hawk take notice. The man watched some of the races and cheered on the children while sitting with Mountain and Star and some of the older boys and girls. Falcon and Joy had helped Eagle organize everything, while Justin served as the starter and official judge. Most of the villagers watched or participated at some point during the afternoon. Even Wolf was seen there, watching for a little while and talking to Ash. The winners —Nardo, Nettle, and Peacock—received small figurines fashioned by Potter and Carver (Eagle had visited them during the rainy days and arranged it all). Everyone got hugs and applause. Peacock, after his victory, strutted around the field; the young girls just couldn't get enough of him.

Today, Eagle had other plans. He had talked to Fly a few times about doing more of the storytelling. Fly couldn't wait, he was already gathering small groups of kids together and telling some of the easier stories, but he really wanted to do more, and so he listened to everything Eagle told him on those rainy days. During those tutorings, Eagle learned that it was Hawk who had worked out arrangements with Shrew to let Raven and Fly play with some of the kids that third day of Eagle's secret journey (and since). It worked out just fine, Eagle remembered thinking, and he planned to use the information tonight.

All day, Eagle walked around the village and the woods,

talking to the children about the races and asking if they wanted to do that again before the weather got too cold—and inviting them to join Fly for a special storytelling after the evening meal. Archer quizzed him a little, because she knew he didn't usually do that sort of thing—he told the stories to whomever wanted to hear them, and often it was spontaneous rather than planned. Nonetheless she agreed to encourage some of the less interested children to attend.

So did Joy, who always found the fun in any activity—and had a way of coaxing people to get involved and enjoy themselves. During the foot races, Joy had volunteered to help without Eagle ever asking. He appreciated it. He made sure to get her help for tonight. On the other hand, Buck was somewhat indifferent. Eagle had sought him, because he knew many of the young girls liked the boy, especially those younger than him, and he hoped Buck's presence would help fill out the audience. Buck hinted that he would be there if Tanner came. Until then, Eagle didn't know that Buck had an interest in Tanner. Eagle knew he couldn't go to Tanner himself without risking Hawk learning about the storytelling too soon. Of course, Hawk would get wind of things, but approaching Tanner might jeopardize Eagle's plan. He contemplated asking Archer to help him but decided against it. He believed Buck would show up just in case Tanner was there.

After the evening meal, Fly got things started, as Eagle had instructed. He and Raven herded some of the children together for some free play in the clearing near Eagle's yurt. Eagle stoked the fire and waited for other children to arrive, while Fly and Archer tried to round up as many as they could. Soon enough, two dozen girls and boys had crowded into the clearing, their combined squeals, laughter, and yelling creating a cacophony that made Eagle smile broadly. Some of the older boys and girls joined, as well as some of the men. He saw Fish in the very front of the group, along with Badger and Snow and Fern and others. It pleased Eagle to see that Fish had restrained herself at this time—she seemed to understand the gravity of the situation. Fish did smile and wave, and Eagle waved back, but she stayed put, holding hands with Fern.

Before long, Eagle saw Hawk arrive. He remained at the edge of the brush, with Shadow at his heels and Bison and Shrew at his flank. Eagle gave the signal to Fly, who called them to order in the traditional fashion, patting his hands together and against his chest and thighs, slowly getting the other children to join in. The cacophony of voices subsided as the patting grew in strength, until they were all in rhythm. Then Fly stopped abruptly.

"Once upon a time," Fly bellowed, "the Ruck were different. We tell the stories to remember the time and to remember our names." The children slowly stopped their patting and quieted down, but the youngest ones squirmed in anticipation.

"Many winters ago," Fly continued, "the Ruck-before lived in villages all across the land. There were many, many, many of us, more than we could ever count. The villages were bigger than our entire valley, and the Ruck sometimes called them *sitties*, because you had to sit and wait for a *cart* to take you from one end to the other."

Fish and the others giggled and made faces at each other. Somebody said, "That's silly."

"It's true," Fly answered. "The Ruck-before had the *tek* and they did dozens of amazing things every morning. The *sitties* were so big, you could fit a hundred of our village inside just one part of them. And the *carts* were part of the *tek*; they rolled by themselves on wheels the size of an archery target. The Ruck-before could control them with the power of their thoughts, make them go wherever they wanted to go in the *sitties*, but sometimes they had to sit and wait in the *cart*, while other *carts* went first."

Fly began to shuffle around in a circle, pretending to be inside a cart, and stopping once in a while, lowering his behind as if to sit, waiting a few heartbeats and starting up again.

"Every Ruck-before had a *cart*," he said, still puttering around in a circle. "The leaders sometimes had two or three each. Some of the *carts* could hold a dozen Ruck and some of the *carts* could carry the Ruck AND their *ven* from the day's hunt AND sacks of *veg* and bowls and stones and anything they could dream of taking from one clearing in the *sittie* to another. These kinds of *carts* were called *pickemups*, because the Ruck had a special *tek* that made it easy to pick up huge stones and bags of *veg* as big as Eagle's yurt and put it right into the *cart* without a Ruck even lifting a finger.

"Even with the *carts*, the Ruck couldn't move everywhere because the land was so big. And there were lots of *sitties*, all over the place. If you wanted travel far in one day, you used another kind of *tek*—so amazing that you might not even believe it."

"Tell us!" screamed a girl named Leaf, and everyone giggled at her outburst. She looked embarrassed, but Eagle was pleased to see her there—she used to come to many of the storytellings when she was Fish's age, but he hadn't seen her at one for a while. He saw that she was sitting near Buck, along with several other girls including Blossom, Spider, and Willow. Eagle guessed they had all come because of Buck. He started to look for Tanner, but the Ruck children settled down again as Fly continued the story, his circling *cart* now at a stop.

"You see," he said, pausing for effect, "if you wanted to get from one *sittie* to another, you had to fly on a big bird." Fly stretched out his arms and leaned forward, leaving his place in front of the group and circling them all, zooming faster and faster. Everyone laughed and made faces now, even some of the men, Eagle noticed, including Oak and Falcon, who must have shown up sometime after Fly started the telling. Even though some of the children had heard this story before, Fly's performance always produced laughter. Justin had given him the name because of this very story, and the boy lived up to it every time.

"They called them birds, but they were really the highest of *tek* and they could carry everyone in our village at one time!" He slowed down in front of the group and reached down to pick up Finch, one of the smallest boys in the village. With the boy squealing, Fly slung him onto his back and started zooming around again. By now, many of the children were standing and cheering and talking to each other about the story and whether they believed such a thing even possible. Eagle took the opportunity to spy Hawk's reaction. As usual, the man was intent on the activity at hand and showed little sign of emotion, but the Ruck around him seemed to be enjoying themselves. Even Shrew laughed a little while she tried to squeeze Bison's arms from behind in a quick embrace, which he shrugged off, gently.

Fish and Snow lead a group of the smaller children in shouts of "Me, too!" and "My turn!" and "I want to fly!" as Fly began to slow down and swoop in for a landing. He got down on all fours and Finch reluctantly slid off, while the other children immediately swarmed around the young storyteller, lobbying for their flight.

Eagle thanked God for the flow of events—he couldn't have asked for better circumstances to continue his plan. He casually moved over to the children, sweeping up Fish as he had done during Fly's telling of the *washer* and helping Fly to his feet.

"Okay, settle down, the story isn't over yet," he said. "And even the big birds needed time between flights, to regain their strength for the next journey." He ushered the children back to their places, dropping Fish right in front and patting her on the head.

"The Ruck-before had many wonders of *tek*, like the *cart*, the bird and the *washer*." But that was not what made them strong." Eagle took the telling position, while Fly rested on one knee a few paces behind him. Eagle took a deep breath and spoke.

"Their strength came from their beliefs, their hard work and their knowledge. They built the big *sitties* slowly, passing down their crafts and ideas from mother to child. They started like us, in small villages, but some of the men and women traveled together to start a new village. And then some of them started another, and another, until villages sprouted up like Tiller's *veg* across the land. There were no Overlords then, no Overseer. The Ruck-before traveled and explored, finding many incredible things and learning more and more until they could use the *tek* to make even more unbelievable things."

Eagle paused. He swept his glance across the gathered Ruck, but the only one he cared about right now was Hawk. Bison and the others (there seemed to be even more now) stood silently, some of them with arms folded. Hawk's demeanor hadn't changed. Eagle pressed on.

"As the villages grew, they became *sitties*. Sometimes, the *sitties* of the Ruck-before fought against each other, sometimes they helped each other. Different leaders gained strength at different times. Each leader spread his ideas among the villages and *sitties*, gaining followers and building more and more places for the Ruck-before to thrive and survive. The competition among the *sitties* continued, sometimes with actual fighting, and sometimes in new forms. They fought with words or in contests, like our wrestling matches and foot races. But they did fight, and they did kill each other, and it threatened to wipe out the Ruck-before.

"Then a strong leader asked them all to work together, to build even better *tek* and share it with everyone throughout the land. He traveled from place to place, telling everyone about his ideas, making friends and spreading his belief that the Ruck could someday do impossible things, like touching the stars. His name was Flag, and he led the entire Ruck-before. Every Ruck in every in village pledged allegiance to Flag and his beliefs."

Eagle paused again, this time because something he couldn't explain told him to stop. Usually, he breezed through this part of the story of Flag, but he suddenly realized that the next thing would have been Flag's symbol, the Eagle. In the last couple of days, he had tried to collect his thoughts on how he would handle the telling today. He had decided not to make the jump from Flag to the Eagle of the Ruck-now. Nevertheless, he had almost moved into that tangled thicket. He took another deep breath, then continued.

"Flag taught the Ruck-before many things and they all loved him. He wanted justice for all of the Ruck, and he fought for the well-being of those who weren't as strong as the others. He stood up for the meek and risked his life so that others could go on. In time, Flag and his followers had built agreements between many villages and *sitties*, until they all joined together into what they called the *glowful village*. Great *tek* fires burned from the highest point of each village, creating a warm glow that covered all the land after the sun had set. When the fires were first started, all the leaders gathered in one place and declared themselves united, naming the land the *Yewessay*."

Slowly and softly the time-honored chant rose from the children, "*Yewessay, Yewessay, Yewessay*." Eagle waited for a few heartbeats, then began to speak over the chant, as it faded out just as smoothly as it had started.

"Yes, the *Yewessay* was a wonderful land, and it went on after Flag died. He asked the children to remember his words, and so his beliefs passed on from mother to child, even after the Overlords came and stole the *Yewessay*. We know many of his teachings, still. Some we must not forget, or else the Ruck won't go on."

Eagle took his last pause. "Flag told his followers never to forget the most important thing the Ruck have. *Freedom*. No matter what happens to us, our *freedom* is a part of us. It is like our blood—it flows within us. If we lose our blood, we die. If we lose our *freedom*, we die. It is something we must believe in—it can't be given to us or taken away, except by ourselves.

"The Ruck-before picked their own mates, they traveled wherever they wanted, they lived wherever they wanted—by the mountains, by the oceans, by the prairies. The Overlords changed that. They took our land, stole all of the *tek* and killed many, many of the Ruck-before. But they didn't take away our *freedom*. We can still believe in our God, we can still remember our names and the time-before, we can still teach our children about *love, liberty, and perfect happiness*. We can still hunt and feed the children, we can still craft and play and dance. We can still choose who we want to love, even if we can't choose our mates. We can still travel as we choose every day, even if restrained by the Black One at the *tekline*. We can still choose to fight for our *freedom*, every day, by choosing to believe in it.

"Flag told us to let *freedom* bring us glory! He told us to hold up the *Hand of the Free* and to forever honor the *Stone of the Brave*! We must not forget!"

Eagle raised his right fist as she spoke the last words, looking into the sky. The children started to chant *Yewessay* again. Fly stood up, resuming the patting to match their vocal rhythm. The chants faded again as the children and the men started to talk to each other and break into smaller groups. Eagle slowly lowered his eyes to scan the Ruck. He met Hawk's eyes and they held each other's gaze for three heartbeats, until Hawk turned his back and strode off. His followers slowly turned and followed.

Eagle took another deep breath and scanned the rest of the Ruck. He wondered how long it would take for Hawk to act. More importantly, he wondered what the man would do, and who might side with him.

That same evening, with the winter chill demanding extra blankets despite the roaring fire, Eagle gathered some of his friends to the same clearing where Hawk had delivered his message the night of The Hunt. It seemed a fitting place. Ash, Sage, and the others enjoyed the get-together, which they figured would be the last time before winter prohibited such nocturnal gatherings, while Eagle shifted uneasily and said little as the evening wore on. Coot was absent, as it was his duty that evening to accompany the Black One with the delivery of the winter's supply of *pem* and *veg* to the women at the compound —he would also return with supplies of soap and candles made by the women. Fly joined the group briefly, hand-in-hand with Raven, to thank Eagle for the chance to lead the telling. He didn't stay long, leaving with Raven for the private warmth of his yurt. Star and Thrush hung around a little longer before they left together. Some of the younger children came and went freely, but soon they had all departed for their familiar fires and cozy yurts, leaving Sage and Eagle alone.

"Bold moves, my friend." Sage said.

"What other advice would you have given?"

"Sometimes it's not 'what', but 'how'. You obviously came here tonight expecting Hawk to confront you after the telling."

Eagle eyed his friend, slowly nodding his reply. "Yes ... I did." A shiver prompted him to pull the blanket tighter around himself. "He is more patient than I thought. I shouldn't underestimate him."

"What you did was right, but perhaps you moved too quickly."

"I don't know."

The two men sat together in silence, staring into the cold night air. Finally, Sage stood.

"It's cold, it's late. I'm going back," he said.

During the walk home, Eagle's thoughts swirled around the events of the past few weeks. A fitful sleep caused him to wake several times during the night.

Eagle eased back into his routine after a few days. Many of the men hunted during those last days before the onset of winter. They had seen the first snow flurry. It didn't stick, but the warning was all they needed. Eagle had begun to take Snow, Chase, and Ram with him on a regular basis. The boys, Ram and Snow, seemed to enjoy the cold weather hunts. Chase, normally one of the best hunters, still excelled (including taking almost as many *ven* as the two boys combined), but she seemed to enjoy it less than during the warmer moons. The foursome, along with other children joining them occasionally, brought in more than two-dozen *ven* in a three-day span.

On the last day of the three, as the hunting party was securing the catch for the trip back to the village, Hawk and Shadow surprised them all.

"Need some help?" Hawk said, appearing in their midst, with Shadow nearly attached to his left shoulder blade. The boy carried a slain *ven* slung across his back.

Eagle's party gasped in unison, started. When they had caught their breath, Eagle stepped forward. "We ... we're okay," he said.

"I see." Hawk turned to the children, who were staring at the two men. "Carry on," he ordered, and they snapped back to their work. Hawk turned away, walking off. "Stay here, Shadow. Come with me, Eagle."

Eagle paused. He didn't like being ordered. It reminded him of why he had decided to challenge Hawk in the first place. He waited a few seconds, before following. They went out of earshot of the children before Hawk stopped, turning to face Eagle, who closed to an arm's length before stopping.

"We must put an end to this foolishness," Hawk said.

"What do you mean?"

"You know too well. You are as transparent as an insect's wings."

"Say what you came to say, Hawk."

The older man cocked his head slightly, glaring at Eagle. His dark eyes threatened to burn a hole right through his rival's. "I told you to stop telling the stories. You chose to ignore my advice, and your choice could ruin what the Ruck have achieved."

"No. My choice helps the Ruck go on. The stories are important."

"The stories are necessary to keep the children on the right path. They should be told by children, like Fly, not by the men.

Not by the leaders. And certainly, the men shouldn't tell the children stories that give them a false hope."

"I agree."

"Then why would you tell the *freedom* story? Fly was doing fine. You shouldn't have stepped in," he said, sternly, like Eagle had heard him do with Nardo. "I thought we had agreed that the boy would take over the tellings."

Eagle bristled and started moving to his left, trying to circle Hawk, who countered easily. They circled, slowly, as they continued speaking.

"Hawk, I said that I would think about it. I did. I now think you were right. Fly should take over the tellings ... but he's not ready yet. He could carry on if I died in the next hunt, out of necessity, as we all do. But he's still young; he is just about to see his tenth winter."

"Go on," Hawk said, after Eagle's long pause.

"Fly needs to learn." Eagle said. "I was teaching him more about the telling. I thought it would be fun to give the children a good time while doing it."

"You are teaching him the wrong things," Hawk snapped.

"What? I am teaching him the legends."

"Yes, your favorite legends."

"They are the legends that our ancestors told us, Hawk. You know that. What other legends should I tell them? How else can the Ruck go on?"

Hawk had slowed down, and Eagle matched his movement. "I have given this much thought, Eagle. I believe we have already forgotten what our stories mean. The *tek* and the marvels and even *freedom*. It's all nonsense. Filling our children's heads with impossible dreams, of traveling anywhere they like, will only destroy our village sooner."

"You don't believe the stories at all?" Eagle stopped, overwhelmed.

Hawk slowed and closed the gap between them, stopping a bent arm's length away. "I do believe they have value, but I think they are remnants of a past we can never reclaim. We should use them to entertain the children and to teach them more about how to survive our real circumstance."

"You don't believe we can be *free*?"

"The Overlords rule us completely, Eagle. They impose the bag limit, not us. Just as we are the masters of the *ven*, they are our masters. They grant and take away life."

"Only God can do that," Eagle said.

"Another story for which our understanding has been lost for generations."

Eagle frowned and sighed deeply. "I must not believe that, Hawk. God must exist and his mysterious ways we simply cannot explain. It is possible that the Overlords do rule us as completely as we rule the *ven*. But you aren't suggesting that they are gods, are you?"

"Call them whatever you like. I am saying that they might as well be gods. The only way for the Ruck to survive is by playing the Overlords' game. The stories you are telling threaten our chances to survive the game. To stay alive."

"Without the hope of *freedom*, why bother?" Eagle threw up his hands and stomped back toward the children.

"You know that we will be ordered to join with the women soon. If you resume the tellings after we return, I will publicly confront you. There should be one leader. That is me."

Eagle fought the urge to turn around. The challenge was made. Nothing more had to be said.

3

Even after giving birth to thirteen children and raising them all until they left to join the main village, Honey still enjoyed running the nursery. She watched the toddlers as they ran, stumbled, and fell within the confines of the play area; she smiled and laughed as they helped each other up and resumed their games. She held her infant of three moons to her breast and glanced over to Rose, who was nursing her own baby, now about seven moons from the womb. Honey saw the radiant serenity on her younger friend's face and wondered if she herself still looked that way when nursing her own babies. She still felt that way, but the many winters and the many births had taken a toll on her appearance, she knew. While Honey half-envied Rose's elegant beauty, the feeling had always been tempered by the bond they had forged shortly after Rose had joined the women four or five winters ago.

Rose had been Blossom when she left the village, Honey remembered. In fact, Honey had given her the name of Rose, partly because of the softly glowing hue of her cheeks and her long, shapely limbs, but also because her beauty came with a sometimes-thorny attitude and wit that caught aggressors unaware. While the infant at Rose's breast was her third living child, she had become more beautiful than ever.

Just then, as if she knew Honey was staring at her, Rose lifted her bright blue eyes, smiled at Honey, and tossed her long black hair over her shoulder. She wore it loosely, unlike many of the other women who either cropped their hair or wore braids.

"What are you thinking, Honey?" Rose asked, gently shifting her infant without breaking its suckling.

Involuntarily, Honey shifted her child, too. "To be honest, I was wishing I were still as beautiful as you are. Perhaps then, the men would still welcome the chance to lie with me."

"Don't be silly. After a moon in the village with boys and girls, the men lust for the chance to make love with any of us. They might as well wear a blindfold, at least for the first night. I doubt that they even recognize which one of us they draw until after they have spent themselves and their blood leaves the one head and returns to the other."

Honey chuckled as she caressed her child's skull. "In that case, perhaps we should be wearing the blindfolds," she said, which made them both laugh out loud, demanding the attention of the toddlers and crawlers secured in the play area. Honey made her cooing noise, which signaled the children to go back to their play. One by one they returned to their activities, some of the older toddlers talking and giggling and running, while the ones who could crawl were dragging themselves in the dirt or fiddling with their toys in an apparent effort to unravel the mysteries of creation itself.

"I wish they would calm down like that for me," Rose said. "How do you do it?"

"I don't know; it's just something I discovered a long time ago. There's no trick, I don't think. I don't even know why it works. Have you tried it?"

Rose shrugged. "A few times, especially with my own. At first, I thought it had worked, but Marvel proved that wrong. She does as she likes, unless you or Lotus are around."

Now Honey shrugged. "Do you think so? I haven't had much success with controlling her. She is extraordinary."

"That's a nice way to put it." Both of the women looked out over the children, which included their own and those of other women who were busy with the daily chores. Marvel, by far the tiniest of the toddlers, was bossing around the others as she seemingly organized a new game or activity. She tossed her own frazzled black hair, just like her mother had done, and gave simple and quick orders to her subjects.

"Do you ever wonder who the father is?" Rose asked. "I mean, with Marvel, her features don't tell me the truth. Is it strange to wonder?"

"Of course not. We all do, sometimes. And sometimes we can tell … you know that. But I never dwell on it. It doesn't matter, as long as the Ruck go on."

"Yes, I guess so. But Marvel has made me think about it more than usual. She began to speak earlier than most of the others and even though she is small, she seems to be a natural leader. I can't help but wonder."

Honey nodded. "I understand. Sometimes, one like Marvel is born. Lotus gave her that name very early, because of her special qualities. Still, it doesn't matter who the father is. Most of the time, I think it's better that none of us ever really knows. We can guess, but we're never really sure. All that matters is the children are cared for when they reach the village."

Rose shrugged again and they sat in silence a little while longer until their infants had had their fill. Honey stood up and stretched her short legs, now holding her small daughter up against her shoulder and gently patting its back. Even standing, Honey was only about a head taller than Rose sitting. She kept her honey-brown hair in multiple braids, which revealed a round, comely face with a few freckles around her nose. She gently rocked back and forth, while Rose also got up and stretched, mimicking her elder's example.

They turned when they heard a young woman calling Honey's name. Butterfly glided over to them, her golden hair flowing. She stopped on the other side of the low wooden barricade that surrounded the play area, shifting from foot to foot and gently biting her lip. She had arrived at the compound just before the last hunt, after emerging as perhaps the most beautiful of all the women—and following an awkward stage in the village where she had struggled with the older boys teasing her about her rapidly developing attributes.

"Coot is here, with the Black One," she said, nervously. "They want to speak with you." She paused, then added, "Does that mean something is wrong?"

"No, Butterfly, it is the way of things. Please tell Coot I will arrive as soon as the children are cared for." Honey smiled to Rose. Butterfly would understand soon enough.

The young woman fluttered out of sight, to deliver the reply, before Honey could continue.

"Here, let me hold your child," Honey said to Rose. "Please go and find Lilly or Jade. *Fug*! I should have told Butterfly to come right back. *Ehhhhhh*, it makes no difference. Please find someone else to help you here so I can attend to Coot and the Black One."

Rose chuckled as she handed over her boy infant. "Maybe you ought to sit down first, *gramma*. You'll need your strength tonight. And your blindfold."

Honey almost snatched the child from Rose's arms, in retort. They eyed each other for a heartbeat, all in fun, until Rose laughed from her belly and ran off to find one of the younger women.

It didn't take long. Rose returned, with Butterfly as it turned out, who fluttered around and played with the children while Rose picked up another crawling infant who needed feeding. Honey waved goodbye and covered her eyes dramatically, sending the women into one last round of laughter that carried Honey to the compound entrance on wings of mirth.

Coot wore his ceremonial face, as expected. He stood just inside the compound gate, with the Black One filling the gateway itself. Coot said the required words and then told her of the draw. Three nights, ten men, starting with Coot. Both of the Ruck smiled for a few heartbeats, Coot reaching out his hand —despite the Overseer's looming—and squeezing Honey's. She felt a wave of warmth and energy. His lips moved, but he said nothing audible; it was merely the silent signal they had developed over the years, a secret code that the Overseer would never understand. They, Coot and Honey, the oldest of the

Ruck, who had seen almost sixty winters between them. They who had suffered through the life and death of more than a hundred Ruck; they who had long ago decided they were half-siblings; they who had fallen in love despite all their efforts to the contrary.

"I understand," she said, releasing herself from Coot's grip. "The women will be ready."

The Black One retreated, allowing Coot to exit. Honey dutifully closed the gate and sighed.

Honey surveyed the women and children gathered around the compound's central meeting area. They huddled close together for warmth and comfort. The small fire lit their faces; children laughed or slept or pleaded with their mothers for attention. Lotus sat by Honey's side, a huge grin on her angular amber face, her narrow dark eyes sparkling in amusement. Honey tried to follow her gaze to the source, which turned out to be Ruby struggling to keep hold of her tiny infant while also trying to stop one of her rambunctious little boys from crawling all over the young woman sitting next to her, named Faith.

Honey and Lotus continued to watch, while their own toddlers quietly played together between them and their infants slept in *ven*-hide pouches strapped against their breasts. Faith cradled her own sleeping infant and turned her back to Ruby's boy. Faith wore her shoulder length brown hair in three braids, much like her mother's style. Ruby, whose flushed cheeks looked as if they would burst, dragged her over-stimulated toddler off Faith's back by grabbing his overalls. The boy squealed, protesting without quite uttering any understandable words.

It was still hard for Honey to adjust to being a *gramma*. Rose's earlier jibe repeated in her thoughts as she watched Faith and Ruby do their best to comfort their infants while keeping the rambunctious boy in check. Including Faith, Honey would see two of her grown children this night, as Sparrow would return with the men very soon. That made her smile, but she still felt odd about Faith being a mother now. Really, it made her feel old.

Lotus interrupted her thoughts. "Shouldn't we begin, *gramma*?

"Yes," Honey replied. "Thank you."

Honey stood and stretched out her arms, palms up. The women began to hush their children and gradually the only sounds were pops and crackles from the fire pit.

"Coot came with the Black One today," Honey said. "Our men will be visiting us soon." The other women, all except Butterfly, were unsurprised. While they didn't always know the exact day, the men always came about the time of the new moon. But they waited patiently for Honey to explain the draw.

"Ten men will visit us for the next three nights. As always, the first man drawn by Justin will pair with the oldest among us, and the rest of the men shall follow in order by most winters-seen still less than the first drawn. When the youngest man is paired, the order continues with the oldest man not drawn until all the men are paired." Honey paused, searching out Butterfly among the gathering. She wasn't actually the youngest, Honey knew, but she was the newest and would thus need the most explanation. Butterfly looked more bewildered than scared or worried.

"The draw of ten means that at least one young boy will become a man tonight on his first visit to the compound, because only nine joined us for the last moon. It may also mean all nine of the men have survived The Hunt. As we know, we can never be sure until the men arrive and tell us of the events of the last moon in the village. This is a time of great happiness and terrible sadness for us. We will remember those who do not return, and we will embrace those who do. We will mourn for any lost children and we will pray to the Goddess to give us more to replace them. The Ruck must go on."

The women nodded, somberly. They waited, some of them seemingly leaning forward and waiting for more from Honey.

"Oh yes, I almost forgot, the draw begins with old Coot." Honey couldn't help but smile when she said it. She realized Lotus and the others would take notice, but she didn't care.

"They will join us later tonight. We have plenty of time to prepare."

On cue, Nightingale stood up and began to sing softly. Her tiny infant rested between her breasts, safely held in the pouch, while the little girl who was cuddling with her stood up and clutched Nightingale's leg during the song. The tall woman sang one full verse, her voice gradually increasing from almost a whisper to nearly speaking level as she reached the chorus. Her voice steady now, she gracefully raised her arms and started to direct the other women to join in on rounds, until all of them were singing the chorus and swaying to the harmonies they were creating. A few of the older toddlers tried to join in, not getting the words right but doing their best to mimic their mothers' tune. As she swayed to the rhythm, Nightingale picked up her toddler, holding the girl on her left hip, turning in a slow circle and smiling at everyone. The singer's leaf-brown face, framed by short cropped, curly, reddish-black hair, shown for a heartbeat in the fire's glow when she turned to Honey and Lotus. After a wink from Honey, Nightingale set down her daughter and directed the waning of the rounds until once again she was the only one singing, faintly now for one final chorus. A couple of the toddlers clapped their hands and Marvel shattered the mood, shouting "Again!"

Rose shushed her precocious child while some of the younger women giggled along with the children. Nightingale sat again, pulling her daughter into her lap and pulling a blanket around herself and both her children. Lotus stood next. She stood a few thumbs shorter than Nightingale, but that didn't diminish her presence.

"Thank you, Nightingale," she said. "We have much to give

thanks for this evening. And we have much to ask for in the next few nights. When our men return to us, we will enjoy their warm embrace on a cold night—and the Goddess willing, we will bear their children so the Ruck can go on. We sing our praises to thank the Goddess for another new moon and the continuation of our sisterhood. We dance to invigorate our bodies, to cleanse our cares of everyday life, and to ready ourselves for the men. As we prepare the earth for the acceptance of seed, we prepare ourselves for the seed of the Ruck."

Lotus reached into a pocket on her heavy cloth poncho, throwing a handful of powder into the fire. It blazed fiercely for a few heartbeats, releasing a plentiful plume of smoke that carried a pungent flowery odor. Lotus breathed deeply for a few heartbeats, inhaling the fragrance, as did the other women. Honey noticed that a few of the children made faces or held their noses. The cloud slowly dispersed in the cold air, but the smell remained, blanketing the gathering.

Next, Lotus reached inside of her poncho and removed something wrapped in thin, smooth fabric. The other women all produced a similar package. None appeared quite the same —sometimes the fabric was rough and heavy, sometimes bright and flimsy, sometimes it was wrapped in plain twine, other times in dyed fabric strips. Lotus sat down again, and some of the women shifted themselves or moved their children in order to have a bare space of earth in front of them. Even the children watched quietly. The women then untied the packages without removing the fabric, laying the covered item directly in front of them. Only Ruby abstained—it was still too soon after giving birth to her infant. Butterfly lagged behind the others, uncertain of the next move, mimicking the fair-haired Jade who had joined the women only a few moons earlier and sat next to her now.

Lotus recited a short verse and threw another handful of the powdered herb into the fire. The flash illuminated her face for several heartbeats. The intensity revealed in the face of Lotus gave Honey a start. As the fragrance wafted once more over the gathering, Lotus dug into the cold earth with both hands. Honey and the other women followed her example, until all of them had dug a small hole about the width and depth of their hands. They waited again for Lotus, who threw a third and final handful of herb into the fire. The smell was now overwhelming, and a couple of children coughed and complained.

Lotus ignored them, carefully unrolling the fabric to reveal a small clay fetish, a woman large with child, which she cupped between both hands and raised over her head. Others did the same, including Butterfly, whose mouth fell agape when she lofted the fetish.

Lotus spoke again, uttering another verse that the others echoed softly. They set their fetishes down into the earth and gently filled in the dirt over top, leaving a small mound where the hole had been. Lotus pinched a bit of dirt, rubbing a smudge onto her forehead first, her breasts second, and between her legs third. She then leaned over to Honey, pinching a bit of dirt from hers and marking her in the same way. She proceeded to each woman, kneeling before her and repeating the ritual until they had all been touched. She reclaimed her place in front of the others, next to Honey.

The *gramma* rose again, a stern face set in the fire's glow as she spoke. "We are the land. We must sow the seed of the Ruck. We ... the women ... we ensure that the Ruck go on."

Honey let out a soft chuckle and began to smile. "But let's not forget to have fun, too. We'll hear stories of our children, good and bad, and we'll enjoy the company of men again. It is a serious time; it is a carefree time."

She gracefully unhooked her child, handing the pouch and child over to Rose. Honey then moved over to pick up two drums against the room's wall while Jade and Mantis stood up. Neither of them had children with them, but that was about all they had in common. Mantis towered over Jade—they were the tallest and shortest women in the compound and several winters apart. Honey handed one of the drums to Nightingale, who somehow managed to hold it and both her children at the same time. Honey sat down next to her and they started to play, slapping out a rhythm that started the two dancers moving.

Despite their differences, Mantis and Jade made a pleasing pair. They looked like they had practiced their dances well during the last moon, preparing for this cold night. Mantis stamped her feet and swung her long black single hair braid in a tight circle. Her well-proportioned long body seemed perfectly tuned to the beat. Jade's wide hips swung back and forth in rhythm, stamping her feet with a slower but well-timed co-ordination with her partner. As she neared the fire, Jade's eyes lit up and everyone was reminded of why Lotus had given her that name when she arrived.

Soon, Honey put her drum aside. Nightingale continued playing, managing this time to release her toddler—who began dancing (sort of)—without missing a beat. Honey started dancing after dodging the toddler, trying to follow Jade's moves. Lilly stood now, joining in and trying to match the frenetic pace of Mantis.

The eleven women laughed and celebrated for a while longer that evening, taking turns dancing, drumming and holding each other's infants. They sweated and cheered, chased the children, and sang again in rounds. Finally, the women hugged each other, gathered up their children and went back to their individual yurts—the ones they slept in only when the men came to share them. Ruby rounded up the young orphans, Curly and Peck—who were about to dig up some of the fetishes—and herded them along with her little boy, Lamb, and her un-named toddler who had accosted Faith earlier in the evening. Now, only Lotus and Honey remained.

"Poor Ruby. But somebody has to watch those girls these three nights." Honey spoke as she secured her infant's pouch, with help from Lotus, still breathing heavily after all of the dancing. "It felt so good to dance. I really had no choice, though. I had to offset the anticipation! Being with Coot is all I can think about."

Lotus shrugged. "You know how I feel about it. It's necessary for the Ruck to go on. But I still say we're better off without the men around."

"Your sons will turn into men someday, too, you know."

"Goddess willing, yes. But they won't be my concern, then." Lotus leaned closer to Honey and stroked her hair. "Men are so preoccupied with themselves. You know I prefer a woman's company."

Honey smiled and gently spun away. "But this isn't the night for that. Let's go—they'll be here soon. And you don't want to keep Justin waiting."

"Don't I?"

"No." Honey laughed and glanced over her shoulder as she left the gathering area with her toddler on her hip and a bounce in her step.

Her children slept soundly on the other side of the yurt's partition, tired from the earlier activities. Honey had slipped away for just a dozen heartbeats, long enough to remove the barricade from the compound entrance and run back to her yurt. She waited for an eternity until she heard them entering and dispersing amid not-so-hushed voices. The yurt flap parted, letting in a rush of cold air and the pervasive smell of the main campfire—and revealing the silhouette of her lover.

Honey lifted herself to her knees from her cross-legged position and at the same time felt Coot drop to his knees, the flap closing behind him. They embraced, deeply, feeling their energy passing back and forth between them. Honey had chosen not to light any candles, so they couldn't see each other very well in the darkness of the closed yurt, but it didn't matter. Their fingers traced every inch of each other's face, neck, ribs, hips, and back, taking in more than their eyes could ever perceive, while they tantalized each other with small kisses and subtle bites.

Coot pressed against Honey, his heavily bearded mouth finding her delicate lips and devouring them. He tasted like the memory of a childhood treat. When he pressed harder, she succumbed, leaning back onto the bed of thin pillows and *ven*-hide as he fell on top of her, now devouring her neck and earlobes. She moaned—thankful that Coot could still find the exact spot that made her head spin. Most of the other men hadn't caressed her earlobes the way Coot had; those who experimented didn't succeed. She felt herself melting, but she couldn't let go just yet.

"Coot," she whispered, "oh my ... Coot, my children ... are they ...?"

"Alive, yes," he muttered, in between kisses. "And so are we." He began to untie Honey's poncho and stopped kissing her just long enough to pull it over her head. He slowly circled her left breast with his tongue, and she laughed. He played exclusively with the left one and he would never say why.

"There is much to tell, Honey," he said, lifting himself above her, like doing a push-up. "It can wait. Tonight is for us." He began to gently lower himself enough to reach her ears again.

She reached out and found his hard member straining against his leggings. She untied them while he nipped at her earlobes. Finally, she freed him, and she turned her head, forcing his mouth to hers and slipping her tongue through his lips. She stroked him gently with both hands as they kissed for some time, Coot holding himself above Honey until the combination of her fondling and his own weight caused him to pull back. He dropped again to his knees, this time between her legs. Now he untied her leggings, pulling them off and leaving her naked and shivering slightly even within the yurt's shelter. Leaning across her, Coot fumbled in the dark for a heartbeat, grabbing the poncho and giving it back to Honey. He paused to pull off his own leggings, which Honey had left barely halfway down.

Honey smiled as she pulled the poncho back over her head and shoulders. Coot never rushed; it didn't surprise her that he would take the time to make sure they were warm and comfortable. She felt him reach between her legs just as her head popped out. She leaned back onto the bedding, moaning softly again.

For quite some time, Coot teased and tantalized Honey. She gently rolled her head from side to side and moaned faintly as he warmed her insides with his sensual massaging of her legs, hips, and genitals. She wanted to moan louder when he lay between her legs on his belly and lowered his head, but she didn't want to wake her children. He carried her on wave after wave of sensation as he licked and sucked her endlessly. She felt on the verge of explosion several times, but he wouldn't let her reach climax.

Finally, he climbed on top again, raising himself above her as before. She guided his erect member inside her. He began moving in slow measured strokes and lowered himself to reach her ears again with his teeth. He started to pick up his pace and it seemed to Honey that he was matching the beat from the dancing celebration earlier in the evening. Coot's ear-nibbling became too much, she wanted to scream and laugh out loud at the same time, and so, instead, she pushed him off (he relented easily) and rolled onto her knees. She pushed him onto his back and straddled him.

When Honey began to ride Coot, he reached one hand up to massage her genitals. She raised and lowered herself over his erection and leaned forward so they could kiss again. In rhythm, they accelerated their pace until both of them shook and shuddered, unable to stifle their groaning but at least managing not to cry out as they brought each other to a powerful crescendo.

◆ ◆ ◆

Rose's infant fell asleep quickly, but Marvel had different ideas. She pestered her mother, asking precocious questions about the night's pending events. She wanted to know which man was coming to visit, why he had to stay with them anyway, and why all the women had buried those clay toys before the singing and dancing. These and other new questions flustered Rose, but she managed to maintain her composure as she readied the beddings, matter-of-factly replying she was fairly certain it would be Sparrow unless something had changed greatly in the village during the last moon. Of course, Marvel had been around when the men had visited before, but she had never shown any particular interest in the purpose of the visits, much less the details. Lately, she had taken greater interest in everything around her. Even though she was young, it wouldn't be too long before she left for the village.

Rose scooped up her tiny, insightful daughter and gave her a hug like it might be the last time she would ever have the chance. Sitting on the bedding, they cuddled, cooed, and whispered to each other. This comforted Marvel, sapping some but not all of her present inquisitiveness. It took some more convincing, and the promise of something special the following day, before Rose eventually persuaded Marvel to lie down with her brother behind the hanging cloth partition. After waiting long enough to be convinced of her daughter's slumber, Rose took two of the candles Lotus had made for her, left the yurt to light them from the campfire and returned to place them in wooden holders near the bedding. Just moments later she heard the men enter the compound and split up to their respective destinations. The yurt flap opened, letting in a gust of cold air that made the candles flicker.

Eagle stooped to enter and lowered himself to one knee while making sure the yurt flap was closed tightly against the cold. He paused to allow his sight to adjust to the dim candlelight. Rose smiled and waited for him, sitting cross-legged on the bedding. They had been together before, but not in a number of moons, as the draw had determined. They spent a few heartbeats taking each other in; both had grown and matured since their last meeting. Eagle broke the silence.

"Rose, I am Eagle now." He paused. "That sounded strange, didn't it? I just ... I figured you should know ... before we ..."

Rose patted a spot on the bedding just in front of her. "Please, join me ... Eagle."

He complied. They faced each other now, staring into each other's eyes. Rose's bright blue eyes held Eagle's gaze. He reached up with his right hand and stroked her loose black hair, running his fingers through it like a thick comb. She put one hand on his knee while reaching for his cheek with the other. She guided him closer, and they began to kiss, gently, exploring each other's lips and tongues while their hands wandered over each other's curves and muscles.

Rose broke off, leaning back onto one elbow and stretching out her legs. Eagle reclined beside her and started stroking her hips and thighs.

"You are a different man, Eagle." Rose blurted out. "Has a new name changed you so much?"

Eagle had to laugh. He had asked himself that same question during the last few days. "I like to think the name is a reflection of the change, not the cause. It has been a while since we were paired together, and much has happened in that time."

"I understand." She leaned over to kiss him again and they continued their foreplay. Neither seemed inclined to rush; both took great interest in exploring with their hands and mouth. Eventually, Eagle untied Rose's leggings and tugged at them playfully. She rolled onto her back and lifted herself enough for him to pull them off completely and then rolled back onto her side. They played with each other a little longer —with Eagle rubbing her genitals and penetrating her with his fingers until she became wet—and then Rose returned the favor, taking down his leggings while she licked and rubbed his erection.

They laughed and enticed each other a little longer, kissing more earnestly while their intensity was building beyond playfulness. Breathing more heavily now, Rose looped her arm around Eagle's neck as she rolled onto her back again, dragging him on top of her. He entered her in one smooth stroke, her wetness allowing him to do so without any resistance.

Eagle thrust and withdrew again and again at a steady but unhurried pace. Both of them began to grunt and groan as their pleasure increased and Eagle's thrusts grew stronger and more forceful. Finally, Rose's groans turned to gasps and Eagle drove himself even harder and deeper within her until they both let out throaty exclamations and reached near simultaneous climax.

As their breathing returned to normal and Eagle lay heavily now on top of her, Rose thought she heard movement behind the cloth partition. She was too spent to think much of it, and she didn't really care just then. Eagle lifted his weight from her, sliding over slightly and resting himself on one forearm. He offered soft kisses to Rose's forehead and lips, which she returned. They cuddled like this for a while, without speaking, until both of them fell asleep.

Honey watched Coot as he napped, knowing he would wake up soon and be ready to go again. She had lit two small candles so she could now see him clearly. She sat cross-legged next to him, with a heavy blanket wrapped around her—she had covered his naked lower half with *ven*-hide. She hoped he would want to talk a little bit; she couldn't wait any longer to hear about her children and the rest of the village. Luckily, he began to stir, so she helped wake him by rubbing his genitals through the hide.

"Lover?" she said, almost whispering. "It's time to tell me all the news."

Coot groaned and muttered something, then abruptly sat up, covering her hand with his, over his crotch. "That's how I always want to be woken up." Lifting his head and torso, he now rested on both elbows.

"There's a lot to tell," he said. "Maybe we should wait until morning." He shifted his weight to one elbow and eased his fingers lightly up Honey's thigh.

She playfully swatted away his hand. "Start with my children, you old tease."

"Okay. All of your children are alive and well." He reached for her thigh again and she swatted it away again.

"Details, lover, details. The night is still young, even if we aren't. We have plenty of time."

"Okay, okay. Let's see ... Badger is growing fast. He still loves to play in the dirt and so he still bears that name. I've heard that he has had some trouble in some of his lessons. I have been thinking that maybe his preoccupation with the soil can be turned to our advantage. I've asked Tiller to take him into the fields after the winter.

"Willow is still wonderful. She hasn't lost any of her grace or mild temperament. She helps out with the smaller children, assisting Shrew just for fun. You'd be proud of her. Lately, I've noticed she has been hanging around some of the older boys in the evenings—not the men, mind you, but boys like Buck. In fact, I think she has taken a specific fancy to him, much like many of the young girls. She is looking much more like you, but I suspect she'll be a little taller. No surprise there!"

Honey laughed and squeezed his thigh. "Watch it, lover. I've done my duty tonight. If you want more, you'll have to behave."

"An empty threat if I ever heard one." Coot smiled. "Anyway, this brings me to Archer. She has done very well since the last winter, taking over ... well, you know. She teaches the children well—I watched her conduct a couple of lessons this moon. I hope we can find someone to take her place after she comes here to the compound. That shouldn't be for at least two more winters." Coot paused, pulling at his beard.

"Hmmmm ... Clay and Ox. They haven't changed much. They're boys being boys. Oh, here's a juicy bit—I saw Ox go off with Fox once or twice."

Coot paused again for a few heartbeats, apparently composing his thoughts. "Now that brings me to Sparrow." He pulled at his beard, thoughtfully.

"Yes, what?" Honey demanded.

Coot chuckled. "Oh, I really wanted to keep you in suspense, but I don't know how to do it right. I'll just tell you."

Honey waited for a few heartbeats, but Coot still hadn't continued. She reached for his groin and this time her threat seemed real enough.

"Okay, okay," he said. "He is Eagle, now."

Honey looked confused, then proud. "Eagle? Really?"

"Yes, Justin named him after The Hunt. It was due, after being Sparrow for so long and surviving Hunts and becoming a father figure to a number of the children. Justin was waiting for the right time. Even Hawk had gone to Justin and recommended that your son be re-named ... but I don't think it turned out exactly the way Hawk wanted. Justin surprised us all, and so far, he hasn't felt it necessary to explain why he gave such a legendary name to your son ... well, at least he hasn't explained it to me. I accept it—it is our way and Justin has every right to give the names as he sees fit. I think the naming was wise."

"What happened in The Hunt to give Justin the opportunity?" Honey asked, her voice lowering, respectfully, in deference to those who must have died.

Coot told her everything—about Eagle and Hawk saving Dreamer and Onyx and about the rivalry brewing between the two men since Eagle's naming. They talked about this for some time—until Honey had heard more than she really wanted to know. It was always frustrating to hear of such goings on in the village when she couldn't do much to influence them. So, Coot moved on to other things—he told her about the loss of Chance and Violet. About the fortune of recent good hunting, about Fly and Eagle's stories, and the races and other games. About the re-naming of the other two children, now Blossom and Coyote. They laughed out loud—having to cover their mouths and hold their aching stomachs as they made a great effort not to wake the children—when Coot told Honey about Coyote stealing his leggings that night.

After they had calmed themselves, Honey curled up beside Coot and they began to kiss again. Soon, she had turned around and shed the blanket, climbing on top of him and facing his feet. She straddled his face, and then lowered her head to take his newly recovered erection into her mouth. She licked and sucked him while he did the same for her, until he teased her gently to another climax. Coot slid from underneath her as she remained on her knees and he entered her from behind. It didn't take long for him to fill her, and this time she rolled onto her back and held her legs up in the air as he collapsed beside her. She prayed to the Goddess for his seed to take purchase— she wanted to bear his child rather than another man's. It was selfish of her, but all that mattered was for the Ruck to go on, and he was the best of the men as far as she was concerned.

She started to speak to Coot again, her legs still in the air, but he had passed out already. She held her position until her hips and legs ached, finally relaxing and falling asleep herself.

Honey peered over Coot's shoulder and through the open yurt flap, watching the children playing out in the commons. He sat cross-legged in front of her, just outside the entrance to the yurt; she knelt behind him. His reddish-brown hair and beard were a mess of tangles—he obviously didn't comb either often, if ever, although he did somehow manage to keep them from getting filthy. She didn't mind taking care of it for him; in fact, she hoped the grooming would keep him around a little longer that morning. They had been making small talk and enjoying the slightly warmer than usual morning while the children played. She wanted him to stay longer. She hated the tradition whereby the men would depart soon after sunrise to hunt, or fish, or just plain go away during daylight, returning the next evening to visit the next woman's yurt. It made no sense, really, and she doubted whether the Black One or the Overlords cared what the men did during the day, as long as they all did their duty during their conjugal visits. She had argued this point with Coot and Justin a few times—they wouldn't listen. Just two days and three nights every moon—why couldn't they stay with their women and youngest children for that time? It seemed like they really wanted to escape the morning after, and she just couldn't let that go.

"Coot, why don't you stay for a little while longer? You could play with the children, or help me with a few chores, or just relax."

"Honey, you know the answer. I'd love to stay here today. I wish we could be together every day. We can't ignore our ways merely for our own pleasure. If I stayed here too long it would set a bad example for the younger men, like Wolf and Earnest."

"*Fug*. Don't hide behind tradition. If you don't want to stay, just say so."

Coot leaned back to look into her eyes. "Lover, it's not about what I want. It's about what's best for the Ruck." He leaned forward again and pointed to the children. "What I want ... is to know which of those children are mine. What I want is to live with you in our own yurt, raising our own children and sharing each other's love. But I also want to make sure the Ruck go on and so I make my choices accordingly. We both know what can happen if we try to defy the Overlords. We steal our moments together, like right now, but we must recognize the constraints and choose our time wisely."

Honey shook her head. Coot's uncanny ability to combine common sense with sincere feelings was maddening. "Fine. Just stay as long as you can, lover. Don't rush out."

"Combing my matted shrub of a head can't be rushed. It's a good excuse as long as we don't stretch the truth. Besides, it feels really good … and I doubt you're done yet, so …."

Coot's thought trailed off as both he and Honey watched Eagle emerge suddenly from Rose's yurt. He was holding Marvel under one arm at first, before hoisting her high into the air with both arms and spinning around several times. The little girl screamed in sheer delight and begged him to do it again when he set her down. She wobbled around in mock dizziness. Rose appeared at the yurt entrance, smiling wryly as she dropped Eagle's bow and quiver. Soon, other toddlers ran up to join Marvel in the begging. They all swarmed around Eagle; he pretended to be overwhelmed by their numbers as they tugged at his leggings, allowing himself to be pulled down to the ground and falling in a heap with five or six of them landing on top of him. Rose came forward and told them to go back and play where they were before, so she could say goodbye to Eagle. Marvel took the hint—she marshaled the toddlers in the cutest retreat Honey had ever seen.

Honey continued to comb Coot's hair while both of them observed the younger couple in silence. Eagle and Rose clasped each other's hands and leaned together for a quick peck on the lips. They said a few words to each other, it appeared, and then Eagle picked up his items and strode off. He disappeared from the commons, heading toward the main gate.

Honey was about to comment on the scene when Justin stepped into their view from around the side of the yurt. He blocked their view of the commons and his scent wafted up to Honey's nostrils. She recognized the lingering odor of Lotus' sex on Justin. A bit startled by that, she wondered if he noticed any traces of their nocturnal activity.

Justin ran his brown fingers through his curly cropped dark hair. "Mine could use a bit of combing, too, Honey. Of course, you know, Lotus wouldn't oblige."

Honey stifled a laugh, but Coot didn't bother to conceal his amusement. "You'd be a fool to even ask," he said.

"Come on, friend," Justin replied, extending a hand to help lift Coot from his seat. "It's time to go."

Coot sighed, ignoring his friend's gesture. "Just a few more minutes, Justin. Let Honey finish." He leaned back a little, pressing against her. She squeezed his shoulder with the comb-less hand. Justin shrugged and turned to watch the children.

As Honey reluctantly finished up her combing, a few of the younger men gathered and headed toward the main gate. Honey took stock of them: Sage was there, along with the fair-haired and boyish-looking Earnest, the tall and powerful dark-skinned Oak and the new young man, Wolf, who seemed to be tagging along more aimlessly than with intent to join the others. He turned for a moment, as if to look directly at Honey as she watched. His steely eyes caught her gaze for a heartbeat —he would be visiting her tonight, she realized—and then he turned away abruptly. The four men departed toward the gate all at once.

As if on cue, Falcon emerged from Storm's yurt and quickly scanned the area. Honey smiled when she saw him; he was the next best lover to Coot, in her opinion, but he was mostly business and she noticed that Storm hadn't come out to see him off. Falcon waited for a short time until Mountain appeared from the entrance to Nightingale's yurt. Falcon hurriedly called out to Mountain, by far the tallest and most powerful man in the village, as he was saying goodbye to Nightingale by giving her a big kiss and a few gratuitous squeezes of her rump. They also took off toward the gate.

"We must go now," Justin said, with his authoritative voice. "The others have all left."

"So they have." Coot said, sighing again. He leaned back again, searching out Honey's lips and they kissed deeply for what they knew might be the last time in at least a moon. They said nothing more as they finally separated. Honey watched the two men leaving the commons. When they were out of sight, she threw the comb carelessly off to the side, slumped down from her knees to her buttocks, and choked back a few tears.

Eagle exited the compound gate without knowing exactly what he was going to do this day. He had considered waiting around for Sage or one of the other men, but the only one he had seen upon leaving Rose's yurt was Coot, still basking in the presence of Honey. He had decided against approaching the old man and his mother during the brief time they had together—and he thought it would be strange to linger in the commons until someone else showed up. It had also occurred to him that the next man to emerge might be Hawk, which wasn't the most pleasant prospect. So, he left the compound and figured he could wait outside or maybe go off on his own for some more reflection.

He wouldn't fast this time—he would need his strength for the next two nights—but Eagle knew he had some thinking to do. Hawk's warning echoed in his head. In just two more days he would have to deal with whatever action Hawk decided to take, or he would have to force the action himself. Still hearing Hawk's voice in his head, he started off into the woods.

A heartbeat later, Eagle nearly jumped out of his skin. Someone had grabbed him by the elbow, from behind. He spun around, finding Hawk, staring wide-eyed.

"I thought you were trying to ignore me, Eagle," Hawk said, relaxing and almost smiling. "It seems you weren't even listening. I called out to you several times."

Eagle took a couple of short breaths and regained his composure. He didn't know what to say in the moment.

"Was she so good that you left the compound in a daze?"

"That's none of your business," Eagle answered, starting to turn away again.

"Maybe not. Tonight, it will be."

Eagle stopped, turning slowly. A weird feeling came over him. It surprised him. The thought of Hawk pairing with Rose bothered him. He wasn't sure why. He hadn't even thought about her much before last night.

"What do you want, Hawk?"

"I thought we might spend the day together."

Eagle realized he was making a face, despite himself. Taking a few deep breaths, he tried to relax. "What did you have in mind?"

"Nothing in particular. But it's a warm day, at least for this season, and I thought we might hunt together—and talk." Hawk breathed deeply now, apparently considering his next words, so Eagle waited. "When we go back to the village, we should have this whole thing settled."

Many thoughts flew through Eagle's head in the next few heartbeats. Retort after retort surfaced; he rejected them all. Hawk spoke the truth. They should settle this as men, on their own, if possible. He had his doubts about the likelihood of it, but he wanted to try.

"I agree," he said. "Let's go hunt for a little while. I'm sure the women and children could use some more *pem* for the winter."

The hunting was mostly pretense. Even though this morning continued to prove warmer than any day in several, winter had arrived and the *ven* were scarce. The creatures could cross the *tekline*, it was known, and they tended to disappear during the colder months. Eagle and Hawk traveled largely in silence, wandering this side of the valley, looking for tracks they didn't expect to find. It made a good buffer between their previous encounters and the ensuing discussion, Eagle thought. As the sun moved directly overhead, Hawk picked up fresh sign. Neither of the men could expect it to prove fruitful. Eagle just shrugged, and so Hawk lead them on the trail, until they surprised two young *ven* grazing on a remaining patch of grass in the sunlight. Each man deftly knocked and loosed an arrow. Their training took over, each felled one of the pair.

Hawk broke the silence as they prepared the corpses for travel, using their sharp stone knives. They sat and chewed a piece of *pem*, speaking of the nice weather, telling an anecdote about one of children, or musing over a cloud. All banalities, Eagle knew, but he welcomed them. During a pause, his mind went to the place where he watched the Black One the morning after he became Eagle. He thought he would like to go there again now. He knew the conversation would turn sooner or later, and the Point seemed like a good place for it. He told Hawk he was ready to start moving again. He added that he would like to lead for a while, before they took the *ven* back to the compound. Hawk grimaced while nodding his assent.

Eagle led them to the spot. Hawk laughed now, a throaty, malevolent laugh. It sounded strange, since he hadn't done so in Eagle's presence for some time.

"It seems we both have claimed the same spot, again," he said. He looked directly toward the Overseer, above on the ridge. "Do you come here to watch him?"

Eagle nodded, although he didn't find it as funny as Hawk apparently did. He had considered this a refuge, but no longer.

Hawk began to unburden himself of the *ven*. Eagle hesitated, and then eventually followed. Finally, they sat together, staring out and up to the Black One.

"Now that we are here," Hawk began, "we can talk as men. Perhaps we may even understand each other. This place is important—as it seems both of us have discovered. The Black One stands there, watching us for the Overlords, who rule us. What does that tell us?"

"That depends," Eagle said. "Each man sees a thing in his own way. It is no different than the race where some of the children thought Willow had won while others thought Moon had beaten her."

"This is different, Eagle. This is about survival. Children's games like your races or my wrestling matches have no part in determining whether the Ruck go on. As men, we play the game of the Overlords. As fathers to the children, we must choose wisely in this game. We must make decisions that will keep us alive, in The Hunt and beyond. I believe we can live longer than old Coot, and better, if we understand the rules of their game. So again, I ask you, what does the Black One's perpetual vigil tell us?"

"It is a reminder that we are prisoners," Eagle said, flatly. "But it is also a reminder that we can regain *freedom*."

"You are half-right. We are prisoners. We won't have *freedom*. We can have life, in one form or other. But teaching the children that the Ruck can overcome the Overlords' and somehow reclaim your legendary *Yewessay* ... it is foolish and harmful."

"God gave us the will to choose. Even the Overlords can't take that away from us. They can corral us with the *tekline*, they can force us to live and breed according to their plan. They can kill us in The Hunt or destroy us all at any time. Still, they can't rule every piece of our lives." Eagle pointed to the Overseer. "Although it watches over us constantly, it doesn't know everything we do. It can't hear our thoughts; it can't stop our feelings, and it can't stop us from believing in *freedom*. Ultimately, it can't force us to live, which means we are still in control of our lives."

Hawk had frowned throughout Eagle's argument, still facing the Black One. Now he turned to look at Eagle, who met his stare.

"Again, you are half-right. We can choose to die. It happens sometimes, I'm sad to say, but that doesn't mean *freedom*. That is a coward's escape. The *freedom* you tell the children about is very different. You claim we can escape our imprisonment and roam the land as we please. That will never happen. It is just a story to help our young from succumbing to the despair that otherwise makes them choose to die. If your God exists, which seems unlikely, then that is the only thing he gave us, the right to end our lives. He certainly didn't give us the strength to defeat the Overlords."

Eagle turned away, clenching the right side of his jaw. He

breathed deeply, feeling Hawk's gaze and breath at his shoulder. He steadied himself, fighting off the urge to get up and leave, or worse, to grab Hawk and shake some sense into him. Questioning his ideas was one thing; questioning his faith was another. Clenching his jaw even tighter, Eagle stared out at the Overseer for several heartbeats. Hawk fell silent as well. Finally, after Eagle had regained himself, he spoke again.

"Just because you don't believe we have the strength to overcome doesn't mean there is no God."

"God hasn't come to our aid. Why should I believe in him?"

"If there is no God, how did we get here? Who created us? Who gave us the power to think, to be able to question our lot?"

"It doesn't matter. Who gave the Overlords the power to imprison us?"

Eagle shook his head and briefly threw up his hands, still avoiding Hawk's gaze.

"Did your God create the Overlords, too?" Hawk continued. "If not, who created them? The women believe in a Goddess. Who is right?"

Eagle let out a long sigh. "I told you: everyone sees things in a different way. I believe there is God. My mother believes in the Goddess. We can both be right. Maybe they are one and the same. Maybe both exist. I'll admit it's not easy to accept. It is a matter of faith. But I'll also say this: your beliefs don't give us any hope of escaping our prison."

"No, you're wrong there," Hawk answered, no turning his attention back to the Overseer. "I believe we can escape the village and enjoy the same privilege as the Overseers. It has nothing to do with gods and Goddesses. It has everything to do with understanding the game of the Overlords."

"I thought you said we couldn't escape." Eagle looked askance at Hawk.

"I said we couldn't have *freedom*. I believe we can escape the village. Some of us have." Hawk pointed again to the Black One. "Him," he said.

For a few heartbeats, Eagle sat confused, then he turned to

face Hawk again. "You don't mean you think the old story is true? Of all the stories to believe in ..."

"I'm sure of it." Hawk interrupted, and then paused, as if considering something before he continued. "The Overseer was once one of the Ruck. And I know there is more than one of them. They were men who proved their worth in The Hunt, learned the secret, or otherwise figured out the game. They have been rewarded for their strength, given the elevated position of Overseer. After that, who knows what a man could achieve. That is our way out."

Eagle had turned to study the Black One again. "Those are strange ideas, Hawk. What proof do you have?"

"No more or less proof than you have for your God." Hawk allowed another throaty chuckle. "But I do know this: There is more than one of them; I have seen the changing of the guard. I have sat here and watched them many times. Another changing will occur near sundown."

Hawk stood and stretched. Involuntarily, Eagle stood as well.

"Meet me back here before sundown." Hawk continued. "You will see." Hoisting the *ven* onto his back, Hawk left Eagle standing there, staring at the Black One, and wondering.

◆ ◆ ◆

Eagle returned to the spot first, not wanting to be late. The setting sun cast his own shadow in front of him as he stood for a while before deciding to sit and wait for Hawk. This unusually pleasant winter day had already begun to pass. He shivered and wrapped his arms around himself to hold in as much warmth as possible. In case Hawk was late, Eagle watched the Black One carefully, resuming his musings about his rival's ideas about its nature. Hawk had called it a man—this was unthinkable to Eagle. He had always called the Black One "it" and always thought of it as something other than himself. Certainly not one of the Ruck. That aside, it had never really occurred to Eagle that there might be several Overseers. It made him feel like a foolish child who knew nothing of the world. Eagle grew anxious to see if Hawk was correct, and fortunately, his rival arrived before long.

"It will be soon," Hawk said, taking a seat next to Eagle as before. Neither man spoke after that; they focused their complete attention on the Black One across the valley. Eagle was almost afraid to blink, not knowing what to expect and not wanting to miss whatever was about to happen. Hawk seemed more relaxed, until he thrust his extended finger and said "There!"

Eagle had seen it; a sudden, bright blue flash of light and the appearance of another Black One, who immediately changed places with its counterpart. The Overseer they had been watching took one step away and disappeared. It was all done in just a few heartbeats.

Hawk stood, abruptly, triumphant. "Now you have seen it."

"What was that the flash? It looked sort of like the *tekline*." Counter to Hawk, Eagle drew himself up slowly. Eagle remembered the one time he had seen the *tekline* ignite, encompassing one of his playmates, Sprout, back when he was a boy—an accident that happened when they had strayed too far from the village. He shuddered, unable to keep the horrifying image of his friend burning alive from filling his mind.

"That would make sense," Hawk replied. "But it doesn't happen every time. Or, at least, we can't see it every time. If it's not the *tekline*, it's something like it. Convinced?"

Eagle swallowed and shrugged, regaining only a bit of his composure. His throat was dry. He struggled to speak. "It … it proves there is more than one Overseer. And it brings up many questions. It doesn't prove they are from the Ruck."

"I suppose not. But I'm sure of it. I can feel it in my bones, Eagle."

Eagle didn't know how to respond. They stood there a little longer, awkwardly, as they both fell silent again. As much as

Hawk grated on his soul, Eagle had to acknowledge that he had taught him something important today.

"Thank you for showing this to me, Hawk. It grows cold, and I think it's about time for us to re-join the women."

Hawk nodded, and they traveled in silence back to the compound, moving quickly to ward off the mounting chill.

◆ ◆ ◆

Eagle left Nightingale's yurt early the next morning, before daybreak. She was mildly offended, even though he had assured her it had nothing to do with her. He had kissed her deeply to help ease the offense. It was the truth—he wanted to avoid Hawk and the other men, preferring to be on his own for the day. Leaving early enabled him to get out of the compound before anyone else saw him.

Now, as he sat by the edge of the river, not many paces from the lagoon that butted up against the compound—and wrapped in a blanket he had taken from Nightingale's yurt —his thoughts returned to the Black One. His mind whirled, trying to discount the possibility that Hawk could be correct about its (actually their, he now knew) origins. Images of the *tekline* flash from last night commingled with those of Sprout from many winters ago. These thoughts threatened to hurl Eagle into a bout of depression. He had been staring at the icy flow of the river for some time—exactly how long he had no idea. The sun had risen and had begun to warm him a little, but not enough to shed the blanket just yet. Weaver's cloth gave him both warmth and security against the reality of the harsh winter and lessened his increasing feelings of captivity, but ultimately, he knew he was fooling himself.

He got up and moved, throwing the blanket over his shoulders. He shook his legs and rubbed his arms vigorously. While pacing back and forth, his thoughts kept returning to the changing of the Overseers. He desperately wanted to make sense of it all. Finally, he sat again, putting his back against the edge of a rock that protruded from the riverbank. He tried to calm his mind, asking God for help. There had to be a reason for Hawk's revelation—a reason for which even Hawk had no inkling. Nothing came to Eagle, not for a while longer, but he continued to ask for help, even murmuring aloud, almost beseeching his God to reveal the meaning of the Overseers.

Instead, when he opened his eyes, he saw Rose. He blinked for several heartbeats until he was sure it really was Rose. She had come down to the lagoon to bathe, it seemed, without noticing him. He watched her as she removed her clothes, shivering against the cold but apparently refusing to let it dissuade her purpose there. Her naked form made him draw in his breath, sharply. He realized he hadn't seen her like this before; it was always under the cover of darkness, or perhaps in the dim glow of candlelight. Rose stretched her arms to the sky, and he couldn't help but fix his gaze on her hardened nipples standing out against her firm breasts, at once complaining against the cold air and rejoicing in the *freedom* of nakedness.

She knelt down, grabbed two handfuls of sand from the edge of the water, an let the sand sift between her fingers. Then she quickly plunged herself into the water, wading in to a deeper spot but staying safely away from the river's more rapid current. She let out a high-pitched yelp, expelling some of the fierce chill she had endured from the icy water. The sound made Eagle gasp again, his jaw dropping in surprise. She plunged again, submerging her entire body under the water for a few seconds, exploding to the surface just as quickly and exclaiming at the top of her lungs as she shook the water from her loose-hanging hair. She started to swim toward Eagle; he ducked away, instinctively, hiding behind the rock.

As he watched her swim and listened to her sporadic exclamations, his thoughts returned to two nights ago, when he spent the night in Rose's yurt. It occurred to him that it was much more interesting with her than with Nightingale. Not because of the sex itself—both women were accomplished lovers. With Nightingale, it felt like the usual visit with one of the women—a matter of course—and now, in contrast, his night with Rose felt like more. They hadn't talked much that night, and still he felt that they had understood each other well. They had connected on a level beyond the necessity of ensuring that the Ruck would go on.

Then, as Rose lifted herself out of the water for a moment, her body glistening in the sunlight, Eagle remembered that Hawk had been with Rose last night, while he was with Nightingale. He watched Rose turn; she started to swim back to the point where she had entered. He couldn't help but visualize Hawk and Rose together, in her yurt, doing what must be done. It burned him like no fire he had ever approached. He tried to put the thought out of his mind, but it was replaced by the brief exchange with Hawk from the previous morning.

"Was she so good that you left the compound in a daze?"

"That's none of your business."

"Maybe not. Tonight, it will be."

Eagle's face and chest burned again. He stood up, throwing the blanket off his shoulders and welcoming the cold air. He had never felt this way before. It was understood; all the women shared all the men, as the draw determined. He had never questioned it, not once. It was necessary for the Ruck to go on. Now, his head throbbed, and his heartbeat quickened. He tried to remember who would be with Rose tonight.

When Rose had reached the edge of the river where she entered, he regained himself, realizing he was now standing in open view. She would probably see him, and so he felt a flush of embarrassment. Still, he wanted her to see him. He wanted to speak with her; he wanted to hold her and help her ward off the chill. It was forbidden. They all knew the rules—spend the nights together and the days apart. Eagle considered the risk for a few heartbeats. When Rose emerged from the water, squealing and shaking the water from her hair again, he decided. He picked up the blanket and strode toward her.

She looked up and almost exclaimed aloud, but somehow

squelched the instinct. Eagle advanced quickly, without a word, and wrapped the blanket around her. Her bright blue eyes, already wide and sparkling from her icy swim, grew even wider as she huddled within the blanket. She spun her head from side to side, not to shake the water from it this time, but to see if anyone else could witness their interaction. Understanding, Eagle tried to usher her to a more secluded spot between some trees at the lagoon's edge and the compound fence. She allowed him to guide her, pointing to her clothes and a blanket she had left where she undressed. Eagle let her go, stepping back to sweep up the items as she continued to move toward the spot he had indicated. He rejoined her in a few leaps and bounds, handing her the second blanket and gently placing her clothes at the trunk of a tree.

Eagle couldn't speak, despite his urge to do so. He watched as she dried herself, unashamedly, wrapping one blanket around her head and drying up the water with the other. Finally, she spoke.

"You were watching me," she whispered.

"Ah, yes. Yes. I'm sorry. I ..."

"That's okay. I don't mind," Rose said, her eyes still gleaming. Her surprised expression softened into a faint smile. "Still, it is forbidden. If anyone saw us, it could be trouble. We're making it worse by talking now. And if the Black One saw us ..."

"I know. I'm sorry. I was just sitting there, thinking, and suddenly there you were." Eagle paused and Rose waited. Hundreds of thoughts flooded his mind, only one came to his lips. "You were so beautiful, so alive ... it made me think about our night together, and how I wish we could be together every night."

"That can't happen, Eagle. It's a wonderful compliment." Now, she paused, and Eagle waited, shifting his gaze uncomfortably as she dropped the blanket, reached for her clothes, and dressed. "It was quite nice to be with you, though. I enjoyed our time together."

"More than with Hawk?" It came out of his mouth, unbidden, and he felt like a foolish boy as soon as he said it.

She laughed, discreetly. "We are already on dangerous ground, Eagle. Let's not make it worse. You know we all do what must be done. It's no shame to enjoy it. Your mother taught me that. We put aside our desires to make sure the Ruck go on. Every man who comes to my yurt receives my warmth."

Eagle felt his face redden more intensely, which made him feel even more foolish. "Yes, of course ... I didn't ... I mean, I just ..." he stammered unable to finish.

Rose reached out and put her finger to his lips. "Enough," she said. "You are a sweet man. I meant it when I said I enjoyed being with you. I hope we are drawn again, soon. You must not let your rivalry with Hawk interfere with our duty. The Ruck must go on. And now you must go away, and I must return to the women."

They both hesitated for a few heartbeats. Finally, Eagle nodded, and began to leave, but she surprised him, grabbing his arm and pulling him close enough to land a kiss on his lips, and then letting go just as quickly. Startled, he fell off balance as she ran away. He watched as she fled, her loose black hair flowing behind her. Scooping up the wet blanket, Eagle trudged away in the opposite direction, his mind and emotions whirling yet again.

That night, several of the men converged on the compound gate at once, huddling close together for extra warmth on what became a wind-chilled evening. Eagle saw Hawk among them, and so he tried to avoid the man, falling to the back of the group. Hawk fell back as well, until they were nearly shoulder-to-shoulder as they filed through the gate.

"I hope tonight with Nightingale is as good as last night," he muttered. "Rose was incredible."

Eagle bit back his words and held back his fist. All the

thoughts from the lagoon rushed back to him. Luckily, Sage arrived behind them, and he changed the moment.

"Eagle. How are you?" he asked, clapping his friend on the shoulder. He glanced at Hawk and nodded curtly. Hawk simply moved forward with the other men.

"Relax," Sage said. "One more night to enjoy."

As much as he tried, Eagle couldn't muster any words. He walked in behind Hawk and made his way directly to Storm's yurt.

His agitation lingered when he opened the flap and stooped through. Storm had two candles lit; they flickered from the breeze brought in with Eagle, and he saw her sitting cross-legged in front of the cloth that separated the yurt in two. Eagle stared at her, but he wanted to see Rose. It pained him to see Storm's short-cropped red hair instead of Rose's long flowing strands. Storm was comely, and friendly, but in that heartbeat, anyone but Rose would have been a disappointment for Eagle. Suddenly it flashed in his mind that Justin would be with Rose tonight.

Finally, Storm spoke. "Eagle, come sit with me. Please stay quiet, Trey and the baby have just fallen asleep."

Still in his funk, Eagle stood there until she had to speak again. "Eagle?" she ventured.

He grunted and sat down beside her. He began to pull off his things, oblivious to the growing cold and insensitive to Storm's presence. She leaned back, frowning.

"Aren't you even going to say hello?" she asked.

A blast of wind shook the yurt. It startled both of them, and sounds of the baby stirring behind the partition demanded Storm's attention. She crawled past him, peering around the edge of the hanging blanket. Eagle stared at her silhouette and snapped back to the present. He thought about Storm and her children. She had lost her first two in childbirth and both deaths had occurred during fierce thunderstorms. Trey was the third child and first survivor. Eagle remembered his mother telling him all about it on the night when they were first paired—they had talked in whispers all night, defying the Overlord's intentions. Another blast of wind was followed about ten heartbeats later by a distant clap of thunder. Storm fully reappeared after checking her children.

"They are restless tonight," she said, lifting her eyes as if looking through the yurt roof out into the cloudy sky. Her face, while pretty, appeared haggard, older than her actual winters. She sighed, turning back to Eagle. "And what's wrong with you?"

"I have a lot on my mind." Eagle said, still ruminating.

"I'm so sorry for you," Storm said, icily. "Look, I don't deserve this treatment, Eagle. I don't know exactly what your problems are, but if it's about this rivalry with Hawk, you can just leave it at the door. We both know why we're here. Deal with it like a man or get out."

Eagle was taken aback. He hadn't realized how transparent his feelings and actions were. He wondered how much she knew—did she know about the lagoon, had the women circulated the stories about the village? Or what? He felt like a child, once again. She was right; she deserved better.

"Hello." Eagle said, reaching out to stroke her cheek.

She allowed a thin smile.

"I'm sorry I have been so rude," he continued, still stroking her cheek. He leaned over to kiss her. Their hands began to roam over each other's bodies, and before long Eagle had begun to undress her. They did their duty, satisfying each other in a pleasant, but somewhat perfunctory, manner. Their relative brevity turned out to be advantageous, because the thunder rolled closer and closer until shortly after they had finished, when a bolt of lightning lit the compound, and the immediate thunder rattled Storm's yurt with another tremendous clap. Storm's startled baby began to cry, which woke Trey, too, and she went to comfort them. She stayed behind the partition for a while. Eagle fell asleep before she could return.

When he left her yurt in the morning, they said a civil goodbye and Storm kissed Eagle on the cheek. The rain and wind had left a bit of debris around the compound and a few of the women and children were out collecting it. Eagle saw Wolf and Mountain leaving together. He moved quickly to catch up with them. He also noticed that some of the women had gathered already, making new fetishes for the next visit by the men. His mother had explained the ritual to him. Although he never quite understood, right now it comforted him a little. It was a familiar sight, and as he followed the other two men out of the compound it gave him a feeling of getting back to the routine after three unusual nights and two days of strange events. He hadn't seen Rose as he departed, which caused him both a relief and a regret, even though he did look for her among the women.

He let Wolf and Mountain continue on their own while he took his own path back to the village. The image of Rose stretching her naked limbs to the sky before plunging into the cold lagoon occupied his thoughts all the way back to his own yurt.

4

He didn't completely recover until after the next visit to the women. Now, two moons later, Eagle stood at the edge of the Stone and watched the men and the children preparing for their last night before The Hunt. He reflected on the events of the last two winter moons, which had seemed to pass slower than all the combined winters he could remember.

Eagle had slept with Butterfly and Lilly the first two nights of the next visit to the women. Because Lilly was the youngest, he ended up visiting with his mother on the final night. It helped him more than he could have imagined. They talked until sunrise. He shared his feelings for Rose; Honey told him that she understood because of her feelings for Coot. While Eagle knew his mother loved the old man, she had never spoken of it in such a way before that night. They dared to share their deepest feelings and desires in life, disregarding the reason the Overlords had put them together in the draw. They defied their masters again, together—mother and grown son. Eagle cried in his mother's arms and it felt good.

Partly, he cried because he was the only man who could visit with his mother. He was overwhelmed by the thought while they were talking about the simplest things. The other men's mothers had all died—rarely did the Ruck have a grown man and his mother alive at the same time. The boys weren't allowed to see their mothers after leaving the compound, so it happened only by accident or with intent to deceive the Overlords. It made Eagle feel like the luckiest man in the village.

He hoped that his brother, Ox, would survive enough hunts to take his place among the men, eventually sharing the same experience with Honey.

Partly, he cried because the weight of the last two moons had fallen heavy on his heart. Eagle couldn't stop thinking about Rose. He also couldn't bring himself to share his thoughts with anyone, not even Sage. Coot set the example they all followed: although the old man's love for Honey was evinced by his actions, he never talked about her with any of the other men. That night, secretly sharing his deepest thoughts with his mother in her new-moon yurt, Eagle breathed relief.

He had kept his feelings wrapped tightly inside, much like the villagers had wrapped extra layers of clothing to insulate their bodies against a harsh winter. Eagle and the other men had organized the children into groups to stay together in the larger yurts during the several days when the ground froze, thin layers of snow covered the ground, and the wind bit into the flesh like a bird's talons. Some of the older children—predominantly Shrew, Archer, Star, Bison, and Potter—helped to watch and entertain the other children, keeping them warm and in good spirits as they all struggled against the challenge of winter.

The decrease in village activity helped to quell the rivalry with Hawk, and for that, Eagle had welcomed the winter's harshest days. It also gave him little to do, other than ruminating on the events of his visit to Rose, Nightingale, and Storm. The image of Rose by the lagoon haunted him. He awoke abruptly one night, sweating, in a yurt full of the Ruck huddled together for warmth against the freezing night. He had been dreaming about the night in Rose's yurt—he could feel her under him, could smell her hair and taste her tongue as they explored each other's bodies—but suddenly, over his shoulder, Hawk sat watching, observing them as he had the Black One from their spot. Eagle's rage and embarrassment shook him from this dream, and he found himself staring at the back of

Star's head, his left leg half-draped over her hips as she cuddled with a couple of the younger children.

Eagle told his mother about that night, and others like it, when he couldn't sleep because of the recurring dreams about Rose, Hawk, and some of the villagers. Mother and son traded stories and tidbits throughout the night about those winter months. They talked about Star for some time, as she would soon be ready to join the women. They often returned to the subject of Hawk and Rose. Honey observed that Eagle's dreams revolved around the two of them nearly every time. Her prompting made him reflect on his feelings during the course of the second winter moon.

He learned that Jade had become pregnant—probably two moons ago. Honey said this came as good news for all the women, because Jade hadn't conceived since joining them a winter before. The women considered it bad luck not to bear a child soon after leaving the village. When a woman failed to conceive over two consecutive winters, she usually became ill and often died. Eagle noticed that his mother shivered when she reminded him.

Eagle remembered playing with Jade as children in the village. She had seen only a few winters less than he had. They had grown up together, playing games and learning skills from the elder children, even surviving The Hunt together. The one and only night when they went together, after flirting, echoed in Eagle's mind. He hadn't thought of it in some time, but it must have been four summers ago. He remembered the warm night and the feast, almost smelling the roasting *ven* in his memory. The smallest children were racing around the fire, while the older children were breaking off into groups and often into pairs.

He and Jade were among a group of children with Sage and Faith and—well, those weren't any of their names then, he was starting to say, when his mother waved him on, nodding her understanding—and led by Garnet. As Eagle talked about the night with Jade, it somehow reminded him of the recent time when Coyote stole Coot's leggings. Eagle started to tell the story, too, until Honey said she had heard it from Coot. The two of them couldn't stifle a brief burst of laughter at old man Coot's expense.

It occurred to Eagle, with a start, that night was the only time he and Jade had ever been together. As boys and girls, they had kissed and touched each other in still private places. They never got together again, and Jade seemed to avoid him after that, mostly hanging around with the children who followed Hawk. Finally, foolishly, Eagle recalled Sage's words at that time: "She is keen for you this summer, Sparrow." He hadn't comprehended it, then. With the aloofness of only eleven or twelve winters, he had quickly moved on to flirting with other girls after that one summer night with Jade. No wonder she had avoided him, after his rudeness! Eagle's mood deepened when he realized this, but his mother calmed him, saying, "We all do things we regret. Jade is fine, her life has taken its own path."

Eagle also learned that Butterfly turned out to have a beautiful singing voice, which no one had ever perceived. Shy and quiet when she lived in the village, although not withdrawn, she usually spoke softly and only when spoken to. Rose beamed when she told Eagle about the ritual two nights ago, describing the enthusiasm and power Butterfly displayed when the women were singing. She drowned out the other women in her round, and eventually they all fell silent, both surprised and delighted by the unexpected performance. Only Butterfly and Nightingale remained in voice at the end of the song, as the younger woman matched the skill of her elder, harmonizing perfectly until they pierced the hearts of all the women there, drawing tears of joy from their sisterhood.

Butterfly had emerged as beautiful to the eye as to the ear. Watching the men prepare for The Hunt, now, Eagle remembered the night he had recently spent with her. Butterfly had welcomed him to her yurt with confidence. Moreover, she exuded the aura of experience, even though she lacked it. He could smell her now, strangely, remembering how the musk of her aroused body penetrated the cold yurt as they pleased each other. It was different with Lilly; she was still timid. Eager, yes, but uncertain. As his mind wandered, Eagle had felt his mother's quizzical stare. He must have been making a strange face as he remembered the two nights before he visited Honey.

Fortunately, the thought prompted him to ask about Lilly, and so they moved on. Honey told him she believed Lilly had already conceived, even though it wasn't yet showing. Honey also believed that Lilly was even farther along than Jade. Still, the stress of not knowing for sure had made Lilly's adjustment even more difficult. Although she was younger than Butterfly, she had gone to the women a season earlier because her body had matured faster. Even so, she hadn't quite outgrown her gawkiness and she struggled to adapt to life in the compound. Clumsy and awkward, strong and determined—that's how Eagle remembered her. And her wild, curly hair ... he remembered, too. He recalled seeing her during her first archery lesson, and nearly his last. Her hair had framed a resolute face, focused on the target. A steady aim, too, landing the arrow close enough for the kill. Yet, when she turned to her friends, jubilant, she tripped over her own feet, ground her face into the earth, and nearly lost a tooth. Eagle said he hoped that Lilly began to show soon, because he knew she would bear skillful hunters. Honey promised to pass on the compliment, predicting evidence before the next moon.

She gave news about Faith and her infant boy, who had survived the critical first several moons of life. Faith had settled in well among the other women; Honey reminded Eagle this was now his sister's second winter away from the village. Having her mother as one of the leaders of the compound must have been difficult and helpful in equal measure. Faith had the advantage of a ready confidant, an older woman who had every reason to make sure she understood the way of life within the compound walls. At the same time, as the daughter of Honey—the oldest and most fruitful of the Ruck women—she must have felt a weight of obligation. Just as rare for a grown man to visit his mother, no one could remember a time when mother and daughter lived among the women together, both still bearing children and ensuring the Ruck would go on. Eagle thanked God for giving Faith a child so soon after leaving the village. His mother's rejoinder, as she echoed Eagle's sentiment but instead offered her thanksgiving to the Goddess, made him chuckle and think of the debate with Hawk at the spot where they watched the Black One. Again, with a start, it occurred to Eagle that he had yet to draw his sister. Her quick pregnancy excused her from several moons' visits, and in the draws since she gave birth they had simply not been paired. It comforted Eagle because he didn't want to pair with his sister. Still, he hoped that they, too, could share a night talking, in defiance of the Overlords' commands.

With all of the talk about the women, Eagle's thoughts often wandered to Rose. Once more he found himself contorting his face while his mother eyed him. She seemed to be calling him back from the reverie, even though no words were said as she huddled under a blanket against the cold. That's when he confided much to his mother. He admitted that he couldn't stop thinking about Rose lying with other men. And trying to remember with whom she had ever lain. Especially, how many times with Hawk over the winters? Embarrassing, but he had to say it ... tonight she was with Coot! He imagined Coot running around naked below the waist as he had during Coyote's prank, but this time the old man was chasing Rose until they tumbled together and made love.

How could Honey accept it, he asked, knowing what must be happening and yet also knowing it must happen? How could she quell her feelings—knowing the one who loves her is with another, even if it must be so for the Ruck to go on? Honey didn't answer; she only nodded and reached out to take her son's hand. Eagle's lament subsided, but he couldn't stop thinking about Rose. He revealed the deepest of his fears—Rose didn't feel the same for him. That she behaved the same with

Hawk, or Coot, or the younger man, Earnest (who had shared Rose's yurt the first night this moon).

Honey drew Eagle closer. They hugged as he wept. They embraced for a while, sharing their warmth and connection. Gently, Honey whispered to him a story about Rose, one from her early time at the compound. It was high summer, and Rose had just missed her first circle. The men were about to return for the three nights. Rose panicked; she sought out Honey and begged for advice on how to please a man when she might already have a child within her! Rose had blushed and mumbled and finally forced out the words. At first, Eagle smiled when his mother talked about Rose's natural sensuality and how odd it was to see her in such a state that day. She had Coot, Justin, and Garnet in the draw. (Eagle choked a thankful sigh when Hawk wasn't on the list.) Honey tried to recite Rose's words—words so precious, Honey thought: 'They are the eldest, and I can't disappoint them' ... or something like that.

Honey giggled a bit as she related the rest of the story, about how she helped Rose re-discover her confidence while they undressed, compared their bodies and talked about which men could give them the greatest pleasure. That day, Honey said, Rose accepted an important truth: the duty of the Ruck women could bring pleasure without shame. It didn't make complete sense to Eagle, which pleased him because the whole thing had become strangely exhilarating and awkward at the same time. Mother and son finally fell silent and released each other, re-settling under separate blankets. While the story made Eagle uncomfortable, at least it had broken the spell of his obsession with Rose's lovers for a few moments.

Honey asked for more news about the village. Eagle's first thoughts went to what was to come—the last days of winter and the upcoming Hunt—before he snapped his fingers and some of his usual spark reappeared in his eyes. He couldn't believe he hadn't told his mother about Coyote's latest trick. He guffawed, stifled it, and chuckled despite himself before telling her the entire tale.

They had all huddled together on one of the freezing nights, a collection of Ruck men and children fighting off the chill by pressing warm bodies under heavy blankets, telling stories by candlelight, playing *stones,* and sleeping in shifts. Eagle and Coot had organized this group of children, using the yurt where Raven and Fly often gathered the children on rainy days. There were about a dozen of them, including Raven and Fly, Fish, Fern and Snow, Huff, Coyote, Leaf, Star, and ... well, others who came and went.

Eagle held the last watch while Coot napped along with some of the children. Those who couldn't sleep—or hadn't yet fallen under Eagle's slumber spell—listened intently as he told them the stories about the *tek.* Outside, Eagle knew from his quick inspection during Coot's watch, snow fell in the valley and seemed determined to stick. He hadn't told the children —the last thing he needed was for Fish to rouse all the others with talk of snowballs, races, and *boggans.* Later in the morning, if the wind calmed and the sun returned to warm them, they could have their fun. During the cold night, staying inside the yurt meant survival. Eagle did his best to bore them to sleep or at least soothe them with uninspired versions of the familiar stories they knew so well. It worked, mostly, and only a few of the children were awake in the dead of night. Eagle found himself distracted during one story, by an intermittent rustling and shifting from a group of sleepers. He had thought nothing of it because it ended without incident.

The next morning, when sunrays began to penetrate the village through gaps in the hills, Eagle shook Coot to wake him. The sight he found nearly made him trip backwards over the other sleepers. The old man's face had been altered (decorated?) into a ridiculous mask! Coot stood up at the ready, alarmed by Eagle's reaction. The children shrieked in laughter and fear. Coot's full brown beard had been streaked with wide swaths of yellow; his eyebrows had been made green and thick with something sticky and matted. His nose was a blood red ball—Eagle recognized it as one of Tanner's favorite dyes

—and much of his usual swarthy skin had been coated with a grey-white ash. The mask itself elicited plenty of shrieks and howls, but Coot's counter-reaction made his visage even more outlandish, as he screwed up his nose and mouth in a puzzled grimace until the children were either screaming in terror or screeching in delight.

Eagle's gaze swept over the children to assess the level of panic. He settled on Coyote, who stood still, beaming. The boy wore a smudged line of color from his hairline down to the tip of his nose—the same hues as Coot's face. While he wore the smudge like a prize, he also waggled his fingers in front of his face, flaunting the evidence. By then, Coot had realized that he himself was the source of the disturbance. Coot scanned the yurt just as Eagle had done. Touching his beard, the old man felt the yellow paint and looked even more puzzled. Just then, the three of them exchanged glances, and the story unveiled itself all at once, as Coyote dashed to the yurt's entrance flap and burst through.

The boy tripped over the still fastened flap ties, but he was way ahead of the pursuing Coot, who had to push his way past the wild-eyed children. Eagle tried to keep them inside—a mistake, as he couldn't possibly corral them all. It only put him farther behind the chase as the children poured out of the warm yurt and squealed at the thin blanket of snow. When Eagle emerged, the frosty smell of the wind struck him first, followed by the hint of smoke from a small fire nearby. Children ran pell-mell chasing after Coyote and Coot. The boy took the path out of the village and toward the gentle surrounding hills. Evidently, Coyote had planned his escape, because as he dodged between a few yurts he emerged carrying a small *boggan*.

Coyote continued to elude Coot and kept distance between them, holding the flat piece of treated wood over his head as he moved farther away from the village, still trailed by Eagle and the gaggle of children. Hawk joined the madness, sprinting up from behind and keeping pace now. Smoky wisps reached

Eagle's nostrils, and he understood that Hawk had been tending the fire. More children, who were already out and about with Hawk or Mountain, joined the chase. As Coyote finally crested the hill, with Coot now only an arm's-length behind him, Hawk stopped and began to laugh. On cue, many of the children stopped, too. Eagle slowed a few steps later. They all watched as Coyote launched himself, belly-first, onto the *boggan* and hurtled down the hill. An exasperated Coot shook his fist at the downhill-fleeing boy, who soaked in the glory of the other children's cheers.

Of course, the children rode the *boggans* all morning until the sun melted patches of grass back into the snow. All the men helped, organizing the lines of those waiting their turn, quickly slicking the bottoms of the *boggans* with shards of soap, and accompanying the youngest children down the hill. Rarely had the whole village come together during these winter months, but the Ruck enjoyed this day in unity. Eagle fell silent after his telling of the tale, acknowledging with a nod at his mother's insistence to relay her compliments to the trickster. Ruminating, he noted how few his interactions with Hawk had been during the winter.

And thus, most importantly in the long night with his mother, Eagle had begun to understand more about his rivalry with Hawk. While it had seemed to diminish during the harsh winter, the effects of the season had merely forced their disagreements into hibernation—just like the snowstorms that had completely covered the village, the valley, and the hills, sending the *ven* into hiding for the winter.

He understood this more and more as Honey prodded him to talk about what had happened with Hawk. He told her about the mundane events, such as a footrace Eagle organized for the children and Hawk's nighttime wrestling matches. Even such simple things exposed the rivalry. During one of the races, Hawk had raised a dispute on behalf of a young girl, Grouch. She was one of the fastest children and a skilled hunter. Her disposition impeded her interactions with many of the children, but she had found a place with Beetle, Axe, and Fox, as well as some of the others who gathered with Hawk's group. As usual, Grouch ran with the leaders throughout the race, maneuvering for position during the final sprint. The surprise was Spider, who had also kept pace through the last turn. The two young girls separated from the foremost pack, nudging, elbowing, and finally tripping each other. Spider stumbled least and regained her footing; Grouch collapsed in a tumble and ended up on her back. Willow overtook them both, crossing the finish line a few strides ahead of the recovering Spider.

Eagle had ruled the trip was accidental, unintended, with neither girl bearing fault. He awarded the winner's necklace of polished pebbles to Willow. Spider and Grouch both complained; Eagle waved them off. Grouch skulked away and slumped to the ground in a heap. Spider imitated her opponent, which made some of children giggle. Hawk put an end to that, standing and taking up Grouch's cause. Everyone fell silent as Hawk accused Spider of purposefully taking down Grouch. Only Coyote was more mischievous than Spider, he reminded all of them. Hadn't she just the other night placed a bowl of cold water under Mountain's sleeping blankets in the communal yurt? A few of the children tittered again, remembering how the effects of the spilling cold water had launched the giant man like an arrow shot straight into the sky. Hawk silenced them with his glare. "Some tricks are funny, some are not," he boomed, slowly turning so all the children could see the seriousness of his argument. He continued, campaigning for Grouch as the true winner who deserved the victor's necklace—he said Spider's trick had stolen it from Grouch. Finally, he raised his hands above his head and called to Justin for an appeal to Eagle's ruling.

Justin rose and walked slowly toward Hawk, surveying the crowd, the race ring, and the two girls. While Justin walked, the children took sides, yelled out their individual verdicts, and tried to shout each other down. It seemed to take forever for Justin to reach the spot of the dispute, not to mention his decision. In hindsight, the overt divisions of children —those who favored Hawk and those who favored him— became obvious even then. During the actual moment, Eagle hadn't grasped the full significance. While Justin's deliberation crawled at a snail's pace, his announcement was brief. He upheld Eagle's ruling—there was no evidence that Spider had intentionally tripped her opponent. Hawk retreated, returning to his impassive stance, and the races continued, though subdued.

As the darkness now settled over the village the night before The Hunt, Eagle wondered how he had been so thick. Even after his visit with Honey one moon ago, a number of other little things were adding up, even though the winter's obligatory seclusion had cloaked them at the time. Walking around the perimeter of the Circle, now, and watching a few of the boys and men pair off before The Hunt, he remembered another incident, one which showed the trouble with Hawk had only just begun. It would surely continue when the weather warmed and the Ruck resumed their regular activities.

They had gathered for another frosty night in one of the communal yurts, arranged this time by Eagle and Falcon. With the help of Potter and Joy, the two men managed to get all the younger children settled under a pile of thick blankets. The routine on these nights varied little—excepting the antics of Spider and Coyote—and eventually Eagle pulled out some of his most trusted sleep-inducing stories. Falcon had drifted off, along with some of older children, and yet a few of the younger ones hung on and on, struggling to stay awake lest they miss one of their favorite stories. Relating the events of this night to Honey, Eagle tried to remember the group of children who he knew were awake. Among them, he was certain, were Moon and Sky, Herb, Nettle, and Fish. He remembered because Moon and Sky weren't really listening; they had cuddled together to kiss and play, which was part of the reason that Eagle had started a story about *freedom* —he wanted to focus on something other than their flirting. Who was listening mattered, he had told his mother, because one of them must have relayed the story to Hawk.

Eagle understood, now: whoever had passed it along had probably done so with complete innocence. His initial reaction the following night, when Hawk confronted him, was that Potter or perhaps even the young boy Red had been spying for Hawk. Surely, the simpler explanation made more sense. One of the little ones—Nettle or Herb or even Badger or Fish—had repeated part of the story of *freedom* for no other reason than to pass the time or to show off to friends. Before long, it had reached Hawk's ears.

Eagle sensed something amiss during the few daylight hours they had allowed the children to play unfettered. As the sun dipped beneath the hills, Hawk circled the village with Shadow and Grouch close behind. Shrew, Ash, and Star rounded up the children and were moving them into yurts supervised by Falcon, Oak, and Eagle. An unusual and perplexing happening, Eagle thought, but it came clear when Mountain approached him to say he would take over the organization of the children's yurt. Eagle stared at the giant man. No one ever seemed interested in arguing with Mountain. He had enormous patience as well as an intimidating physique. Standing there like a wall between Eagle and the yurt, Mountain raised his chin and gave a nod toward the spiraling Hawk.

Being called out didn't bother Eagle. Neither did he much consider his own safety as he strode over to his rival. It did bother him that the other Ruck had taken notice of everything. Eagle saw Thrush and Archer moving together, sort of trailing Hawk and his two followers in a tighter, inner circle. The smaller children had momentarily eluded their evening shepherds, straying off to play again or watching the events unfold. A couple of them spoke—Eagle recognized Fish's bold squeal above the others, asking "where is Eagle going?" Eagle could only wonder why he was going.

When Eagle approached Hawk, the older man had signaled to his bodyguards. Shadow and Grouch slowed down. Eagle turned shoulder to shoulder with Hawk and the two men walked off together. Archer and Thrush turned aside as well, helping to round up some of the remaining children. Soon, Eagle and Hawk disappeared into the nearby copse.

The earlier confrontations with Hawk had taught Eagle not to assume what would happen next. He waited for the older man to speak, studying Hawks movements as he slowed and took a stance amongst the sturdy pines. Hawk seemed as purposeful as ever, in no hurry to say whatever it was he meant to say. They faced each other at breath's range. Finally Hawk spoke. Eagle would remember the brief exchange like one of the stories he had told a hundred times to the children.

"It has been a long winter, Eagle, and difficult for all of us. Huddled together in a few yurts, having to bear the odor of days without bathing, eating scraps of *pem* and dried *veg* and trying to keep the children from beating each other senseless for lack of more interesting games. I know it isn't easy to keep them occupied. These are the times when your stories are most helpful. These are the times when the jaunts of Spider and Coyote keep us going. Still, it can also be a time of trouble, especially if the wrong stories are told or the wrong lessons are taught."

Hawk paused, drawing in a long breath. Eagle waited, motionless, thinking of himself tucked away in the underbrush as Garnet had taught him—listening for the next hint of the Overlords approach. Never move too soon, never move too late. Wait for the moment. He had made both mistakes in previous encounters with Hawk.

Hawk smiled, thinly. "It's okay. I understand. It's never easy to admit a mistake." He paused again. Eagle saw that Hawk expected a reply. No, he expected something more. Capitulation. Subservience. Yes, it had come to the point. Eagle remained still. He blinked, once, involuntarily.

Hawk lifted his chin and stared into the sky, turning back and leaning closer. Face to face now, Hawk's warm breath cut through the cold air and made Eagle blink again. "I won't give you another chance ... Sparrow." He exaggerated the insult with a pair of pointed fingers, twice raking Eagle's sternum. "I have offered you every chance to accept your role, without causing strife in the village. The children have taken notice. This is your last refusal. You leave me no choice."

"You gave me no choice. It just took me two moons to realize it." Eagle turned to leave, but Hawk seized him by the shoulders and spun him around. Jerking away, Eagle started to move around his elder until once again they circled each other.

"Realize this, boy. I am the leader of the Ruck. I will speak out against any further stories of *freedom* or God. I won't allow you to delude the children."

This time, Eagle broke the circle and widened the gap between them with two measured steps backward. Hawk stopped, watching, seemingly ready to strike, but never flinching. With a few more steps, Eagle felt a pine's trunk against his back. He turned and departed suddenly, without acknowledging Hawk's words. He found Thrush and Archer keeping a self-imposed watch nearby. They guided him to the yurt they had chosen, that of Falcon's gathering. Nothing was said, but the silence itself seemed to inform everyone in the yurt of what was to come. Eagle promised himself his next story of *freedom* would be told with more care, at the right time. Patience would serve him best, just as Garnet had taught him.

That was the last bitter cold night of the winter. Soon after, the weather improved. The Ruck began to return to their daily outdoor activities. Winter hadn't passed completely into spring, but the Ruck men and children could sense the imminent changes in the flora and fauna. It helped to renew their energies and enthusiasm. By the time the *ven* had begun to return—and hunting had resumed—almost everyone in the village had forgotten the effects of the harsh winter and set themselves to their appointed tasks, games, and lessons. Eagle welcomed the changes and busied himself with timely responsibilities—from organizing hunting parties to helping Tiller prepare the fields for a new season's planting of *veg*. All of the men had done similarly. The confrontation between Hawk and Eagle had paused again, albeit briefly.

Truly, for a number of days, a state of bliss seemed to blanket the village much like the snows had covered it only a short time ago. Children chased each other all day long; the artisans cleaned and organized their materials and tools; men took stock of the villagers and made plans for the moons to come.

The abrupt reappearance of the Black One reminded everyone of the bittersweet reality of the end of winter. When the Overseer came to speak with Justin during the mid-day break, it could mean only one thing: another visit by the men to the compound, followed by the seasonal transfer of the women and children to and from the compound, and ending with The Hunt.

Now, continuing to pace around the Circle, Eagle remembered the village gathering prompted by the Black One's unwelcome return a few days ago. Justin called the Ruck to the Circle and told them what the next several days would hold, even though all but the youngest children knew exactly what must happen. Eagle could still see Justin standing on the Stone, as he relayed the edict of the Overlords in a tone that suggested more an acceptance of fate than an active role in the proceedings. Justin gave a brief litany of the impending events and told everyone to prepare for them.

Earlier that day, Justin had gathered the eldest of the men to the Stone (Hawk, Eagle, and Coot) to determine which of older girls should go to join the women. That too, seemed a formality to Eagle. Only two were physically mature enough to consider seriously. The debate began with the usual question of whether to send both of the girls or only one. Hawk expressed his opinions first, most strenuously, preferring only one transfer. No one could imagine an argument against that, unless the women had suffered the rarity of recent multiple deaths, so Hawk made it clear whom he favored. Eagle had to repress an exasperated shaking of his head because Hawk's assertiveness seemed as obvious as *ven* tracks. In the end, they all agreed on the right choice. Shrew would leave the village and take her place among the women; Star would remain for one more season. Hawk didn't need to argue his case, but he had done so, anyway, as if to make a point.

Eagle's memory of the choosing was interrupted when he saw Hawk and Bison weaving through the yurts and entering Hawk's yurt together. It always troubled him, this pairing of men and older boys the night before The Hunt. Eagle accepted it, but he still couldn't condone the pairings. Garnet had said "if it helps the Ruck to go on then it must be," although Eagle's mentor had also advised him just to take care of himself. Eagle had turned a blind eye to it for some time, despite his feelings. Between two men ... well, it was their choice. A boy, even as old as Bison ... it did not sit well with Eagle.

He had considered speaking up before, and yet he had never done so. Pursuing it now would only divert him from all the decisions he had made since Hawk's ultimatum. And it was too well accepted, too rooted in the long story of how the Ruck would go on, to question lightly. Everyone knew the men were faster, stronger, and more agile after a night's sex, but any such activity with the young girls brought harsh retribution from the Overseer if a child was conceived—the death of the girl and the unborn child. Long ago, some of the men had chosen to pair with each other. It had carried on because the Ruck were convinced that it helped them to go on. Eagle paced around the Circle one last time before darkness completely enveloped the village. All the children had retired to their yurts. Eagle returned to his own and closed the flap.

He felt relieved that none of the younger children had come to him for comfort or advice. He had little to give after the recent visitation with the women, the transfer of Curly and Peck to the village—and Shrew to the compound—and spending much of his time pondering what to do about Hawk. As one of the elder men not chosen in the draw, Eagle had a responsibility to the whole village that evening. All of it had drained him but, for some reason, not being chosen for The Hunt had drained him most. Still, Eagle welcomed the quiet respite and hoped it would last. He needed it to plan, to reflect on what would happen after the Hunt. What if Hawk doesn't return? Of course, Eagle told himself, Hawk would return. So, what then?

He couldn't fix his mind to that because the thought of his recent visit with Rose pushed everything aside, again. In the up and down events of the end of winter, this draw had made his heart sing, even if momentarily, for Rose would be the last pairing of his visit. He had never felt such a surge of joy before any of the previous visits. He found himself hopelessly distracted the two nights before Rose, which he spent with Lotus and Mantis. Lotus didn't seem to mind his distraction at all. They ended up making love as if it were the drying of *pem*. Mantis gave him an earful, one which made Storm's admonition seem like foreplay. He didn't care. He performed his duty, even if dully, and all that mattered was another night with Rose.

She had received him with all the warmth he had come to expect from her. She matched even his most wonderfully imagined greeting when she embraced him the moment he stooped through the flap. She took his head in her hands and kissed him for what seemed like the entire winter. He inhaled deeply as they kissed, savoring the flowery scent in her hair and devouring her soft lips. With her breasts and belly pressed firmly against him, she finally, gently pulled her head away, and they smiled at each other in the candlelight. Their wordless embrace lifted Eagle's spirit higher than he thought possible. He took it as a sign: with so much love between them, words had no meaning.

She peeled away from him without turning from his gaze and drew him further into the yurt. He began to sit down when she knelt next to him, but she shook her head and began to fumble with the ties of his leggings. Eagle sighed and re-laxed as she tugged them down, lifting his hips and pulling the leggings past his *mocs*. Staying on her knees, she easily coaxed him with her hands and mouth. Eagle stroked her hair and cupped her cheek; she looked up into his eyes without stopping. Although he expected her to slow down and invite him onto the hides and blankets, she continued until his knees weakened and his head began to swoon. He shook the dizziness off for a few heartbeats and stared again into her eyes as she looked up at him, her blushing cheeks glowing in the shadowy candlelight. He motioned to the bedding; she simply shook her head again and took him deep into her mouth. Waves of pleas-ure rippled through his body, threatening to weaken his legs to the point of collapse. His breath quickened and he couldn't stifle a groan as he watched Rose continue. He made a final, feeble gesture to the bedding; again, she shook her head and seemed to take this as a sign to increase her voracity until she brought him to an incredible, shuddering climax that had him gripping her shoulders to avoid falling in a heap next to her.

Beaming, Rose guided him down to the bedding, and they both fell on their backs. Euphoric and embarrassed, Eagle struggled to catch his breath and clear his head, while she hummed to herself. Recovering proved difficult—his mind kept spinning in confusion as he tried to fathom why she had wasted his seed. Not only did it constitute rebellion against the Overlord instructions, but more importantly it could also deprive them of a chance to conceive a child, a duty which the Ruck men and women took most seriously. To go on, they must bear children whenever possible. Finally, the seriousness of it all took hold in his mind and he returned to his senses. Leaning up on one elbow, he turned to her and uttered the first word since his arrival.

"Why ...?"

"I'm pregnant."

Eagle recoiled as if Rose had slapped him in the face. She turned and propped herself on one elbow, facing him. Her face shone in the candlelight, cheeks on fire and smile as wide as the whole valley. Even the splendor of her naked body that day at the river paled by comparison.

"How can you be sure?" he asked. "Isn't it risky to … ?" Eagle faltered as some of the fog swept back through his mind and his member stirred with the memory of Rose's unusual act replaying in his memory.

"Lover, we can always have another go. The night is young, after all. It won't matter. I'm sure of it now. I wasn't sure before the ceremony, and even though I had missed my circle Honey and Lotus agreed that I must take part in the visit. Even last night, I still wasn't certain. This morning all the signs became clear. And right now, I can even feel it inside me."

Rose took Eagle's free hand and placed it against her belly. Of course, he felt nothing, it had to be much too soon for that. Nonetheless, the conviction in her eyes made him believe. He couldn't doubt her.

"It must be two moons now," she said. "That means you could be the father."

She could have slapped him again. A hundred thoughts raced through his head, but the pride of fathering another Ruck child—with the only woman he had ever loved in this way—overwhelmed all of them in those first precious few heartbeats. He scrambled to his knees and leaned over to hug Rose, taking in the wonderful aroma of her hair. She pulled herself to her knees now, and they clung to each other, making time stop.

All at once, logic commanded his thoughts, and Eagle realized it was just as possible that Hawk was the father. Or Justin.

As foolish as it made him feel even now, two days later, he still couldn't get past the possibility. Neither he nor Rose had spoken of it that night. She was far too understanding to speak openly, but it hung there in the air, like the fog that often settled in the valley, clouding his mind. They had cuddled together and talked the remainder of the night, enjoying each other's company, but Eagle's emotions ebbed and flowed.

He rejoiced in the notion that he and Rose would be having a baby. He floundered in the possibility the child was fathered by someone else—perhaps by Hawk.

Now, alone in his yurt, the thought plagued him. He tried to reassure himself. He and Rose had shared so much that night. He began to believe she felt the same way about him as he did about her. This thought offered comfort, but it couldn't dispel the other nagging feelings. For the last two days he had begun to convince himself that he and Rose had found what his mother and Coot treasured. This hope was the only salve for his pain.

He didn't sleep much this night before The Hunt. Each time he awoke, among many times before sunrise, he thanked God for keeping him safe from the draw.

5

Eagle and the rest of the villagers watched twelve of their kin trod off into the dense woods at the edge of the Hunting grounds.

They had assembled early; the sun peeked over the hills and spilled slim rays into the valley. Hawk led the single file procession while the ten children followed him in a line from oldest to youngest. Justin took up the rear. The older, unchosen ones said nothing, solemnly observing their companions' departure. Some of the younger children shed tears as they huddled together for support; others latched onto their elders. A few, like Dreamer, needed additional comfort. He stood in front of Eagle, sobbing and pressing his back against the man as if the bodily contact would somehow snap him out of an awful reverie. Eagle wrapped his arms around the boy's torso, swaying slowly. He also prayed to God, asking for quick and painless deaths to those taken during The Hunt. The only voices heard were those of Curly and Peck, the dark-haired twins who had joined the village just two days ago, having seen the passing of their fourth winters.

"Where are they going?" they asked in unison. "Why can't we go?" Peck asked.

Strangely, Eagle observed, their inappropriate outburst seemed to help. It broke the tension of the departure, and the unchosen Ruck disassembled as the procession disappeared into the pines. Star whispered to the twins and ushered them along with her, beginning their education in the ways of village life. Eagle walked with Dreamer until the boy suddenly skipped off, apparently immersing himself in a new, more pleasant fantasy. Eagle sought out Archer at her yurt.

They sat, making idle talk and sometimes retreating into their individual thoughts while Archer fiddled with her arrows and fletching. It reminded Eagle: Fletcher was one of the children drawn for The Hunt, which in turn reminded him of how difficult the time was for those not chosen. They could do nothing but wait for the return of the survivors. Sometimes that could mean more than a full day—or even six full sunsets, according to the legend of the Eagle-before.

This time, as it turned out, the survivors began to reappear well after nightfall. Most of the younger children had gone to their yurts. The men and some of the older children had gathered in their usual groups, enjoying the warmth of a small fire and trying to pass the time. When a Hunt went beyond the time of the evening meal, it would continue the following day, usually. In Eagle's group, gathered around Thrush's yurt, Sage had said as much. They had begun to prepare themselves for a night's rest and continuation of their vigil the following sunrise. Ash's sudden gasp and the appearance of Ox and Nardo, from south of the Circle, changed everyone's mood.

Eagle jumped to his feet and rushed to meet his brother and the younger boy. He grasped them both by the shoulders and welcomed them back with firm hugs and greetings. A lingering odor of dirt and wildflower filled Eagle's nostrils when he embraced his younger brother. He held Ox at arm's-length and saw the well-placed smudges on the boy's face, arms, and legs. He had learned the lessons well. In fact, Eagle realized, Ox was becoming a man and somehow in the last few moons Eagle had missed it. His shoulders had broadened, hairs grew under his nose and even after the grueling day in the woods, he stood tall and confident. Obviously, both of the boys were spent, but they still managed hearty smiles and hugs when the other Ruck came to greet them. The news had spread like dry leaves in a heavy wind. Even though no one had heard the usual three horn blasts, soon everyone in the village had been roused by the likes of Ash and Thrush, Joy and Scar, or Tanner and Bison, who had run from yurt to yurt to let everyone know The Hunt had ended. Others lit candles around the circle in preparation for the ceremonies.

The return of Ox and Nardo began the next, and most uncomfortable, stage of The Hunt. Welcoming the returning men and children became bittersweet when the reality began to take hold—some wouldn't return. Brothers, sisters, friends, and companions would all breathe a sigh of relief at one moment and feel their hearts ache the next, as the arrival of each surviving Ruck increased the likelihood that another would never return. A few initial survivors didn't dispel the hope of soon seeing a sibling or best friend, but when the count reached more than a handful, it was like a stab in the heart each time another child reappeared. It was one of the reasons that Eagle preferred to be among the chosen. And now, even though he had thanked God for keeping him safe the night before, he still had the feeling it would have been easier the other way around. Fortunately, it rarely took long for all of the survivors to return. The uncertainty lay in just how many would be reunited.

Ox said he had been on his own most of the time and he didn't know about anyone but Nardo—he had spied the younger boy after the horns sounded. Ox caught up to Nardo, and they returned together to the village. Nardo said he knew that Hawk had survived because they had stayed together throughout much of The Hunt. When the horns sounded, Hawk had told him to go on ahead while he tried to help the other survivors make their way back to the village. Nardo didn't know about anyone else. The news put Eagle oddly at ease. It surprised him—his first feeling about the news of Hawk's survival was relief. Before he could examine this feeling, shouts from the edge of the village alerted them to the arrival of Maize.

Spider ran out to meet the lanky, olive-skinned, and tawny-haired girl, who was already accompanied by Fox. Maize surprised Eagle even more than Ox—she had matured and had the look of a woman. The men had already identified her as one who might join the women before the next winter, but she must have changed much in the two winter moons. As she approached, a number of the other girls gathered around her with hugs and kisses. Compared to most of them, she was a woman—her curves and features rivaled those of Star. Eagle realized he had failed to notice many things during the winter. He vowed to be more attentive to all of the children. The girls seemed to give Maize extra attention, probably because her sister Violet had been lost in the previous hunt. Their comments sparked Eagle's memory. Spider was also her sister, and Scorpion, who had yet to return, was their brother.

As if the story of this Hunt had been arranged in advance, more voices from the perimeter signaled the return of Scorpion and Henna. By now, gathering groups of children ebbed and flowed. Their tears mixed with elated shrieks, and the emotions of the Ruck soared up and came down like a volley of arrows shot into the sky. Even fatigued, Scorpion helped ease the communal tension with a sarcastic re-enactment of a close encounter with the Overlord party—his brief ridicule of their hunting prowess made everyone chuckle and sigh. Eagle was glad that the boy didn't overdo it because other children still hadn't returned. Scorpion, known for his quick, stinging wit and agile physique, clearly understood the situation at hand, even with only ten winters marked. Meanwhile, Henna found herself surrounded by Fly, Raven, Fish, and others, as she had recently been hanging around with the group of boys and girls who seemed to favor Eagle. Her dark red hair against her light brown skin made her stand out in the group.

With the arrival of nearly half the chosen ones, the initial good cheer subsided. The Ruck gathering became much more subdued, almost solemn. They had all taken their places around the circle, not by anyone's order but simply by the comfort of routine. Certainly, Eagle knew, the return of more of the chosen would be welcomed but without the enthusiasm of the first few. And no one would feel slighted because most of them had lived through this before. While they never got used to it, they had adapted ways of coping with it. When the solid boy named Mace returned holding the hand of the smaller Iris, they were received with hugs, kisses, and tears, but without shouts, exclamations, or delight. Iris, who usually talked non-stop, barely uttered a word as she took her place among friends such as Leaf, Nettle, and Onyx. Mace joined up with Fly and the others, surveying the gathering as he and his friends whispered to each other, pointing out the others who had returned.

The boys and girls began milling about the circle. Voices fell to whispers and mutterings. Only three children remained unaccounted for, along with the two men, although Nardo reassured everyone that Hawk was still alive. Soon the Black One would arrive to confirm the deaths, but it didn't always arrive after all the survivors had returned. Eagle remembered: he himself had arrived after the Black One during the last Hunt. A wave of whispers swept around the circle with the names of Hawk, Justin, Fletcher, Opal, and Rachel permeating the chatter. If Nardo was correct about Hawk, then at least two of the other four had perished. The men cast knowing glances at each other from around the circle—the loss of Justin could create trouble and uncertainty in the village. Eagle noticed that Falcon had begun to edge his way toward Coot, slowly, to avoid alarming the children. Eagle left his siblings and followed Falcon's lead, stopping to squeeze Mace's shoulder and pat the nearby Ram (Mace's brother) on the back. In part, Eagle did so to make his movements seem more natural, but also because he was truly glad that Mace had returned. Eagle and Falcon had closed within whispering distance of old Coot. They didn't have a chance to consult with him before the rolling sound of low voices preceded the arrival of the young boy Opal, who always seemed to get along with everyone, and the beautiful darker-skinned girl named Rachel, who turned the heads of boys like Ox, Beetle, and Scorpion even though she never seemed to care whether anyone noticed her. Those two quickly mixed in with their friends amid more tears and embraces as the only remaining sounds become sobs and moans. The number of survivors added up to misery for the brothers and sisters of the last two children.

Eagle saw Falcon turning his head to Coot's ear. He leaned in closer, hoping to catch the gist, which seemed to be the simple question of what would happen if indeed Justin didn't return. There was no time for an answer. Hawk appeared at the edge of circle, making his way over to Mountain, Shadow, Grouch, Bison, and his other followers—and causing a momentary stir throughout the gathered Ruck. The Black One appeared, as if following Hawk, and moved into the center of the circle. It paused briefly beside the Stone and then walked deliberately over to Coot.

The old man hesitated for merely a heartbeat, taking a deep breath and stepping up to meet the Overseer just inside the circle. Listening intently, Eagle studied the black-cloaked creature as it confirmed to Coot what they had all guessed by now. Eagle heard the old man say "*Fug*" when the news of Justin had been confirmed. Eagle couldn't resist a glance toward Hawk as he measured the Overseer's size and stature. Although roughly the same height as the tallest of the Ruck men, it (he?) seemed much broader and thicker. Its oversized and thick-soled footwear bore no resemblance to those of the Ruck and gave it the appearance of something very different; its masked-face and large head gave no indication of kinship to the Ruck men. But these external features didn't preclude the possibility. Quite conceivably, a man could be disguised underneath all of that heavy black garb. Another glance toward Hawk confirmed that both men were thinking the same thing just then, as Hawk tilted his head ever so slightly and gave one calculated nod towards Eagle.

The Black One turned and strode off to its post after its message was relayed. Murmurs swept round the circle—Eagle heard the name Justin resonating among the gathered Ruck, almost floating to the surface of the whispers in rounds. He heard Thrush clearly; the boy was asking Sage whether another Justin would be named immediately. Curly (or Peck?) called out asking "Who was that?" which caused a ripple of nervous laughter, followed by Star again attempting to quiet them and help them understand about the Black One. When Coot moved to the center of the circle and stepped onto the Stone, the Ruck quieted.

"We have lost two of our family today," Coot said. "We must grieve. But first, we must sing their virtue. Then we must remember our names. We must renew our pledge never to let the Ruck disappear from the land."

A number of the children began to sob again, while Eagle and the other men stood motionless, impassive. Coot looked uncomfortable. The children crying seemed to upset him even more. He pressed on.

"Justin and Fletcher were taken from us today. We loved them and we will remember them. Justin lived to see twenty winters, providing a worthy example for all of the Ruck men and children. He was kind to us all, fair in all his judgments. He never put his own ideas before the good of the village. He will be missed, but I know his last judgment would be for all the Ruck to go on, never giving up hope. He gave his life so we could go on. Fletcher saw only half as many winters as Justin, but her contribution is no less meaningful. She fashioned her arrows with the utmost care, making sure that each of them flew straight and true. Her hard work has enabled us to bring in many *ven* for food and clothing—perhaps the most important thing in the village. And she taught others her craft, with enormous patience, so it would never be forgotten. Because of their sacrifice today, the Ruck will go on."

Coot drew a deep breath and waited. Fletcher's brothers and sisters let loose their grief, lamenting and hugging each other for support. Many of the children of Diamond had survived, with some reaching adulthood. Eagle knew Diamond had gone to the compound within a few moons of Honey and died giving birth to the little girl Weed four winters ago—or was it five? Eagle watched as her children comforted each other and accepted the best wishes of their friends. In each of the last two Hunts a child of Diamond was lost—first Chance, now Fletcher. And three of them had been chosen for this hunt. Still, a number of Diamond's children remained to grieve for their lost sister, including Mountain, Wolf, Ash, Happy, Opal, Nardo, and Weed. It seemed a strange time to think of it, but Eagle had been enjoying the task of memorizing recent Ruck lineage. At least those children had each other to console. Justin had no surviving siblings. Eagle closed his eyes for a few heartbeats and grieved for the loss of Justin.

When Diamond's children had collected themselves, Coot continued. "It is now time to honor the heroes of The Hunt. Does anyone wish to step forward?"

Nardo rushed forward. He stopped short, already several steps inside the circle, realizing he hadn't been given permission to approach the Stone. Meanwhile, Opal had taken the proscribed single step inside the circle and waited. Nardo seemed at a loss, unsure whether to go back or stand still. Coot seemed equally non-plussed. After a few heartbeats, the old man shrugged his shoulders and swiveled his head, motioning for the two boys to continue forward. He turned sullenly and stepped down from the Stone as he spoke.

"Please come to the Stone and speak your truth," he said. He moved back to the space near Falcon and Eagle.

Regaining his awareness of the situation, Nardo slowed down and let his older brother go first. Opal was two winters older, but Nardo had almost caught up to him in height. Opal stepped up onto the Stone and smiled gently, taking a long breath. It sounded to Eagle as if the whole gathering had relaxed. Somehow, Opal had a way of calming everyone around him. Eagle had seen it once before, during the summer wrestling matches. The boy had interjected himself into a scuffle between two of the older boys—Boar and Ram—and managed to settle them down without any of the men intervening. Eagle leaned over to Coot during the pause, nudging him and whispering, "Take heart, old man, with boys like Opal, the Ruck will go on." Eagle stepped sideways away from Coot just as the boy began. He thought to make his way back to Archer and the others, but he realized Willow had already edged over towards him. They leaned against each other.

"I think that Justin should be remembered as a hero today," Opal said. "Not just for his protection during The Hunt, but for everything he did for us. I know he loved everyone here. He helped us learn, he played with us and he was always fair when he judged our arguments. He always had time for talking, or hunting ... or just sitting around carving figures. Today, he took care of us again. He found me when the sun was going down ... and ... he told me that the Overlords were getting close. He told me which way to go. He didn't come with me. When I met Rachel on the way back, after the horn, she told me that Justin had also helped her before it got dark. I don't know what happened to him after that, but I think he helped to save both of us. I think he sent us one way so he could lead the Overlords away from the rest of us."

Opal stood there a little longer, twisting his trunk slowly and looking around the circle, with a few tears swelling in his eyes and rolling down his cheeks. Again, he breathed deeply, and the whole gathering seemed to inhale and exhale with him. He stepped from the Stone and moved toward his younger brother, briefly gripping his right arm as they passed each other.

Nardo stepped up. He shifted his weight back and forth. His enthusiasm had waned, but his nervous energy hadn't, and now it seemed he didn't know where to start. He scanned the gathering. This only made him hesitate further. The Ruck waited patiently until Nardo locked Hawk's eyes across the circle, and the boy's confidence rekindled.

"Hawk found me really quick. In the morning. He kind of snuck up on me, then he told me to stay with him and, um ...

then we moved around and, um ... looked for the others. Once, we found, um ... Ox ... and Hawk said he should go away from the Hunters. Just like always, Hawk made sure we were safe." Almost hopping from foot-to-foot, the boy turned to look at Coot, wide-eyed. A little late for remembering the ways of the circle, Eagle thought, but at least Nardo was thinking about it. Coot nodded to him, smiling as he approached. Nardo leapt off the Stone and ran back to stand with his brothers and sisters. Eagle pressed closer to Willow and smiled to Archer, Ox, Badger and Clay, who had assembled a little farther around the circle.

Coot stepped back to the speaking position. Given a little time to think and listen to the children, he seemed reassured. The old man stood straighter than before. "It is the law. Some must die while others live. Our heroes have helped save as many as possible. We honor them."

Everyone, including Hawk, knelt and cupped both hands over their chests, fingers overlapped. They were silent for ten heartbeats, and then they rose.

"The Ruck go on," Coot announced, boosting and deepening his voice. "We remember our names. Earnest, step up. Beetle, step up. Leaf, step up. Nettle, step up. Opal, step up. Finch, step up.

One by one, each of the Ruck came to the edge of the circle and took one stride within it. It took more than a dozen heartbeats for all of them to get there. Eagle counted six and wondered why Coot had chosen so many. It was unusual, but losing Justin had everyone reeling. Eagle had no desire to question Coot's intentions beyond this passing thought. Looking them over, Eagle realized the old man had called them out of order. Beetle, whose size had burgeoned since the last winter, was not far from becoming a man, while the slim and shorter Leaf hadn't even seen her tenth winter.

Coot turned slowly in a full circle as he spoke. "We have known this man," he started, gesturing to Earnest, "and these children for several winters. Most of them have drawn The

Hunt and each has always returned to the Ruck.

"Finch has been with us for one full winter now. He has readily learned about life in the village. He speeds from lesson to lesson with an eagerness of spirit we should all embrace. His name will be entered into the draw this coming season, but it will be Sparrow when it is, and we will remember it."

The boy began to move, and then stopped, unsure. Coot waved him, inviting him closer. The boy was emboldened when a low hum swept through the villagers, turning into the subtle chanting of "Sparrow." He flitted up to the Stone, taking Coot's extended hand. The old man kissed the young boy on the top of his head and ruffled his hair. Sparrow turned and paused, smiling all the way to his ears. He ran back to the edge of the circle to re-join his friends, getting hugs from Snow and Fern. Eagle smiled, glad for another child to have that name. He might have taken the naming as an insult, given to a boy so young, but Finch-now-Sparrow seemed destined for a succession of bird names. For a few heartbeats, Eagle felt like he was looking at himself in the past.

"One of our speakers this night, Opal, has also made huge strides in recent moons. He survived The Hunt today and inspired us all with this tribute to Justin. His words remind us of his thoughtful and caring ways. Who has ever been offended by Opal?" Coot paused; his right hand raised into the air before continuing. "Not one of us, I should think. He has shown us his love in many small ways, every day, without any expectations from any of us. His words give us strength tonight, and every night. We will now call him Dove, because he keeps us at peace with ourselves and with each other.

Modest as ever, Dove approached the Stone with carefully measured steps. His gentle smile remained as he accepted Coot's hand and pulled himself up. The old man kissed the boy on the head, spun him around to face the gathering, grasping him by both shoulders before releasing him to his friends and siblings. The rolling song of "Dove, Dove, Dove" swept through the Ruck three times before subsiding.

Coot turned to face the spry little girl named Nettle who often won the races and the wrestling matches in her age group. She stood one step in front of her sister, Raven. Eagle noticed that Fly stood another step behind, next to Nettle's brother, Boar. Their older sister Shrew had gone to the compound a few days ago; Raven and Boar had stayed close together and Fly had given Raven a little more space than usual. Eagle thought one of the siblings was missing but, before he could ascertain whom, Coot was speaking.

"Since her first day in the village, Nettle has shown her quickness in our games, in hunting *ven,* and in The Hunt. She makes us wonder if anyone can jump higher, run faster, shoot better. She understands what it means for the Ruck to go on. In less than ten winters she has proven her value to the village. I look forward to watching her grow. For now—maybe even a brief time—we will call her Rabbit."

Eagle grimaced. This time, he didn't understand why Coot had given this name, when it had previously belonged to a much younger Blossom. He wondered if Hawk would take offense. Searching the Ruck, Eagle found Blossom with her brothers, Potter and Parrot, who showed no signs of objection to the naming. Eagle turned back to see the girl leaping onto the Stone, getting a rushed kiss on the forehead from Coot and leaping back off. She ran around the Stone in several swift bounds and then sped over into the arms of her big black-haired brother, Boar. The gathered Ruck chanted "Rabbit, Rabbit" at a hurried, choppy pace until she waved to them from within her brother's embrace. Coot's choice had worked.

"I must apologize to Beetle, for I realize that he has seen more winters than Leaf, but I promise to explain why I call him next, you will see. It is no insult to Beetle. This boy is becoming a man, in stature—as we can all see—and in spirit, which is felt by all who know him. I remember when Justin named him Beetle, and why. Justin said he possessed a toughness like the shell of a beetle and a matching will to persevere. Since then, he has demonstrated bravery in The Hunt a number of times.

He is a loyal friend, a fierce competitor. He is sure to be one of the largest men in the village—someday. A name to match his eventual physique seems right, so we will call him Bear and we will remember his name.

The deep, drawn-out chant of "Bear" started at once and it sounded beautiful to Eagle's ears. It echoed in the night, filling the valley with a rumbling growl. The boy approached, reached out to grab Coot's forearm and hoisted himself up to the Stone. Coot was nearly yanked off as a result, but the thick-chested boy hung on and held the old man up there with him. They steadied themselves and Coot planted a kiss on Bear's forehead. Eagle noticed that Bear lumbered over to celebrate with Bison first, before re-joining his brothers and sisters, Hoop, Hemp, Henna, and Rachel. Eagle remembered that their oldest brother was Falcon. Eagle leaned forward in order to look past Willow and saw that Falcon was beaming as he watched his younger brother honored with such a strong name.

"Leaf and Earnest remain," Coot continued, taking a long pause. The girl and boy had stepped into the circle quite near each other, as it happened. "As I promised, I will explain why I had to name Bear first. It is the same reason that I must also speak of Earnest now. This young man has proven that he can be trusted by everyone in the village. He sets a fine example for our children, teaching them the value of virtue. He gives us hope as we strive for the Ruck to go on. A solid hunter, a good friend, and a trustworthy man. The kind of person the Ruck need in hard times. The kind of man who can settle our differences without choosing sides, who can see the truth in the smallest specks of evidence, who we know will be honest with us. A man we call Justin. A name we must remember."

It seemed to Eagle that the whole gathering had held its breath as Coot finished. Certainly, Earnest-now-Justin had. For several heartbeats no one even seemed to move until competing whispers rose among the Ruck, some of it a conglomeration of musings and wonder and some of it the subtle, measured mantra of the two-syllable name, "Jus-tin, Jus-tin."

Finally, the mantra won out, not because the chorus increased in volume but because the other whisperers had joined in or, at least, quieted. Finally, the young man approached the Stone and accepted Coot's arm-up. Once he was atop, he knelt on one knee, allowing the old man to kiss the top of his head. He stood tall and walked back to the edge of the circle, where his siblings had re-gathered. Star, Onyx, Sky, and Iris enveloped him. Even Buck made his way over to clap the back of his older brother.

Eagle scanned the Ruck and saw that most of the reactions to the naming seemed favorable. Finally, his gaze fell onto Leaf, the poor young girl who had often been teased by the others because of her ability to end up in embarrassing situations. Her name had come from one of her misfortunes, as she had fallen into a pile of leaves and dead undergrowth just a few days before The Hunt, emerging with a sticky head of leaves and twigs and other rotting *veg*. Now, she was standing there alone, as everyone digested the idea of a new Justin. Eagle wanted to step forward or shout to Coot. While it seemed like forever as he watched the young girl standing patiently, if not pathetically, Eagle realized it was probably no more than a few more heartbeats before Coot resumed speaking.

The old man had to hush the Ruck this time before turning to face the girl. "Leaf has shown us many times: even when challenged, the Ruck can go on. She has faced misfortunes that would dampen anyone's spirit, yet she has never given up in anything she tries to do. I have heard she is becoming skilled at carving, studying her lessons with vigor and enthusiasm. It is true, she is growing up—and while she will probably fall again, we can trust her to get up. And I believe we can trust her in all things, because many of us know she has never told a lie. The Ruck must be true to each other; we must trust each other. It is important to remember. And so ... you see ... I had to save this naming for last, because it won't do to have two Earnests, but it is vital we have one."

The young girl raced to the Stone, as if she had been re-leased from restraining bonds at the edge of the circle. She latched on to the old man's mid-section, squeezing with all her might. Coot managed to lean over and give her half a kiss on the head before she darted off to meet her siblings, Fisher and Fox, who stood near their older brother Bison. A soft, sober chant began, with "Earnest" lingering in the cold night air for a dozen heartbeats.

Coot raised his hands, palms upward. "We are the Ruck, we remember. We must survive. In the morning, we will eat and re-gain strength. We will thank the *ven* for keeping us fit and ready for The Hunt."

A final hum swept through the village, soft but enduring. The various groups of the Ruck dispersed, grateful to settle in for the night, to grieve, and to reflect.

◆ ◆ ◆

Eagle knew it was happening, but he hadn't anticipated the abruptness with which the villagers now divided themselves into distinct camps. Naturally, groups formed and changed over time, with the children and the men congregating with those who share the same interests. Yet, the groups had never been exclusive. Truly, they still weren't, but they had changed. The children didn't associate as freely with each other as they had several moons ago. It had been some time, for instance, since Nardo had joined Eagle's group for an evening around the fire, playing stones or chasing around the likes of Newt, Double, and Dreamer.

None of this pleased Eagle. Still, he had begun to see it as necessary. The day after The Hunt, with the feast of *ven* and even a little of the remaining dried *veg*, marked the most obvious divisions. It seemed to be the quietest, most sullen feast in Eagle's memory. Three overt groups emerged: Hawk's, Eagle's, the rest. And even though each large group had settled within easy earshot and vision around the circle, they seemed to have set unseen boundaries few cared to cross. Eagle's mind recited a litany, silently, as he watched Hawk's group throughout the day.

Mountain, Axe, Bison, Rock, Potter, Bear, Tanner, Shrub, Weaver, Boar, Copperhead, Fisher, Fox, Iris, Maize, Nardo, Grouch, Rabbit, Brute, Onyx, Ox, Peacock, Red, Shadow, Scar, Scorpion, and Hoop. They kept to themselves for most of the day and retired together for the night.

Eagle's group behaved much the same. While he didn't intend to collect them, they seemed to gravitate to him over the winter moons. Their names turned over and over in his mind throughout the feast, so much that the others had to snap him out of his musings on three occasions.

Archer, Sage, Raven, Fly, Badger, Ash, Willow, Thrush, Dreamer, Buck, Sparrow, Chase, Henna, Hemp, Earnest, Fish, Blossom, Joy, Rachel, Ram, Parrot, Mace, Newt, and Star.

If a certain few among the rest hadn't stopped to visit with the Ruck who had chosen Eagle or Hawk, there might have been no contact among the groups at all. The first to brave the invisible boundaries was Coot, who calmly visited both camps. He first sought out Joy and convinced her to play a game of *stones*, which attracted the attention of Badger, Fish, and Newt. When Badger and Fish started a game of their own, Coot asked Joy to accompany him on a little stroll. Joy agreed and Newt begged to go with them, so Coot swept the dark-haired little girl up into his arms and led them directly over to Hawk's group. Joy glided right into their midst and struck up a conversation with Fletcher and Fox. Eagle admired Joy's ability to connect with everyone. Her presence there with Coot gave hope to Eagle. Maybe the village hadn't suffered a complete rent.

Later, Star left Eagle's group and went to play with Curly and Peck, spending a little time talking to Falcon as she and the children drew figures in the dirt with sticks. She left the twins with Moon and Sky—when she returned, sitting close to Eagle, she had tears running down her cheeks. Squeezing back another flood of tears, she told Eagle she had instructed the children to stay with Falcon and the others—that while she would visit them every day, Moon and Sky would be teaching them from now on. She leaned against Eagle; he slid his arm around her shoulders. They huddled together for a while, watching Dreamer, Henna, and Earnest chasing each other around at the edge of the pines in some unfathomable game invented by Dreamer.

As the sun dipped closer to the hilltops, Eagle watched Mountain and Shadow building a campfire for the evening. Bison stood next to them, apparently asking them for permission to leave. Hawk called to Weaver, who joined them all by the fire. Words were exchanged, about what Eagle wasn't sure, but soon the older boys—led by Bison—gathered up their quivers and arrows and left Hawk's group. They immediately sought out Clay, who had stuck close to Falcon since the chosen had departed for the Hunt. Shrugging, Clay collected his gear, and the boys went off towards the archery range. Eagle noticed that Buck went to fetch his quiver and ran to catch up with them. When they returned a short time later, with the sun casting long shadows into the valley, they split up and rejoined their respective groups. Clay headed back toward Coot's blazing fire. Buck returned to sit next to Eagle (who was now starting a fire himself). Weaver and Bison plopped themselves down among the assembled group of Tanner, Fox, Grouch, Rock, and Scar.

Eagle observed Buck, who was watching Tanner's group as if missing even the tiniest movement would cause him great sorrow. Buck must be watching Tanner, Eagle thought. It made sense when Blossom and Rachel slinked over to sit with Buck, touching his leg, whispering in his ear, and pressing against him. Buck seemed to enjoy the attention, although the girls couldn't pry his focus from the other camp. With the sun setting and some of the boys and girls beginning to pair off, Buck now seemed oblivious to anything other than the small group of girls now being chatted up by Bison and the other boys in Hawk's camp.

This thought led Eagle to another while he tended his small fire. Once night had fallen, the groups had re-settled within their boundaries and none were crossing over. Usually, boys and girls would be mixing and matching and flirting and sneaking away together, often separating from their regular group of friends and exploring new relationships, even if only for this one night of festivities (like himself and Jade, those winters ago). Tonight, all the pairings came from within the groups. Eagle continued to coddle his fire while he made every effort to observe who went with whom.

In his group, Raven and Fly stayed close together, even though they hadn't left the open area of the feast. Ash and Thrush slinked off with arms around each other's waists. Ram and Joy were kissing nearby, apparently in no need of privacy. Blossom and Rachel, having failed to lure Buck, had turned now to Parrot and Mace. Star lingered close to Eagle. He enjoyed that. She seemed content to stay near, chatting now and then while allowing him to drift into his thoughts whenever he needed to. He smiled and said "thank you" to her. She made a face and Eagle realized his comment had come out of nowhere. "For being a friend," he clarified. She leaned over to hook his arm, pressing her head against his shoulder.

Falcon had several children gathered around him, mostly the younger ones, along with Oak, Wolf, and Clay. Spider and Coyote had left together at the same time as Ash and Thrush. Eagle wondered if they were going off to kiss and play or to plan their mischief. Moon and Sky had cuddled together at the edge of Falcon's group, having put the twins down for the night with the other smaller children. Eagle realized that only a few of the older girls hadn't aligned themselves with Hawk or himself—so the neutral older boys in Falcon's camp had no one to pair off with. No, that wasn't true, there was Heather. But she usually stayed by herself when others paired off. Her shyness appeared to make her invisible to Clay, Tiller, and Carver. Those boys didn't seem able to stop themselves from staring at the girls in Hawk's and Eagle's groups as they selected boys for the evening. Heather was now hanging around Bison—not saying much, just staying near him. It looked like she was watching him right then.

The girls near Hawk made their choices with the least possible subtlety. Fox had rounded them up in a semi-circle. They stood pointing, giggling, and whispering to each to other while the boys near the fire pretended not to care. The whispering turned to loud declarations of who was stronger, more handsome, or the best kisser. Joining Fox in the fun were Maize, Tanner, Onyx, Heather, and surprisingly, Grouch. The names of Bison, Boar, Rock, Potter, Bear, Peacock, and Ox were clearly spoken. The boys began grumbling. They stood up, mumbled and fidgeted—they even turned their backs to the girls and talked amongst themselves. When Fox came over and snatched Bear's arm, the pretense ended. No boy had the will to refuse. By the time the giggling had ended, Eagle saw that Bison and Maize, Potter and Tanner, Peacock and Heather, and Rock and Onyx had paired off and disappeared into the night. Only Grouch remained, standing there alone for a few heartbeats. Eagle thought she was ready to turn away, but after a dozen more heartbeats she sidled up to Ox and whispered something to him. He laughed and took her hand, escorting her through the nearby yurts and out of sight. Boar took a seat near Mountain and Hawk.

And then the hurtling objects slammed against Eagle, knocking him off his haunches and pounding the back of his head into the ground. A thudding beat echoed in his head, like the sounds of the mallets they sometimes used to tenderize the *ven*. Heavy weights pinned him to the ground, and everything went white and sparkly in front of his eyes. A screeching wave passed through his ears, turning to a giggling wail and finally mutating into a succession of threatening growls. Swallowing hard, Eagle blinked and blinked until flashes of orange and yellow pierced the whiteness and he felt sticky drips forming on his forehead. As the orange-yellow glow grew, the white faded to a black background and Eagle realized his face was no more than an arm length from the fire. A droplet fell to his lips and he tasted salt. Familiar voices seemed to murmur from far away—whose he didn't know—and the heavy weights slid off him. Someone—no, some two—linked his arms and lifted him to one knee. His vision remained blurry, and yet he recognized Star's soft but sinewy touch and thought he heard Buck asking Eagle to say his name aloud. Buck's question puzzled him for a few heartbeats, but he managed to steady himself as he kneeled. He saw Fish and Badger being held by two older girls, who were staring at him as if they had seen the Overlords taking a scalp during The Hunt. Eagle forced out "My name or your name, Buck?" and he heard a collective sigh trickle around him.

It took more than two dozen heartbeats before he could make sense of it all. Badger and Fish kept asking if he was okay, sobbing, saying they were sorry, that they didn't mean it. Eagle's tongue retreated into his throat; he coughed and sputtered.

Star jumped in. "It's all right, children. Eagle will be okay." She sounded so certain. It soothed Eagle as much as it did the children.

Fish's sobs lengthened into weeping and whining. "We ... only ... wanted ... to hear ... a story."

The words struck Eagle as hard as the assault. Fish had the right of it. This time, he recovered more quickly. With open arms, he called Fish to come to him and when she did, he wrapped his arms around her waist, hoisted her to his chest and spun her flailing legs around in a circle. She squealed and he laughed out loud before slowing down.

"A story, you say? Fish, you are brilliant." Putting the little girl down, Eagle staggered, woozy and nearly tripping himself. "Star, Blossom, everyone ... go round up our friends and tell them I will be telling a story tonight. Star, make sure that Curly and Peck know about it ... Mace, see if you can find Raven and Fly ... find whoever you can. Come back soon."

Eagle lowered himself to one knee, watching his young

friends doing as he asked. He steadied himself, kneeling by the fire and coaxing it to a larger blaze.

◆ ◆ ◆

Eagle remained by the fire until enough friends had gathered for Fly to begin the patting. A few at a time, the children joined in, sitting down and thumping their chests or legs in a syncopated rhythm. From Fish to Ram and Star, the children swayed and tapped in unison. The rhythm sped up; tapping turned to slapping. Barely over the noise, Eagle thought he heard the clamoring of Curly and Peck begging Falcon to join Eagle's children. When Ash and Thrush re-joined the group, Fly led the patting back down to soft fingertips. Eagle stood and faced them all. He kept his back to Hawk's camp.

"You know the many wonders of the *Yewessay*. Our fathers told us; I tell you. Our stories help the Ruck go on. They teach us and help us remember. They help us remember things like the *tek* ... strange but real."

Eagle pointed to Fly, who leapt to his feet and pranced around the edge of the fire. Eagle continued.

"They had the *carts* to help them cover the distance between the *sitties* and to zoom around faster than any of the Ruck can run." Eagle glared at Fly, pausing longer than he intended. A few heartbeats too late the boy took his cue and raced around the fire. Eagle saw that Curly and Peck had fled from Falcon's grasp—Falcon, Moon, and Sky pursued the rumbling twins right up to the gathering.

"They had the *sells* so they could talk to each other in different *sitties*." Fly perked up his ear and stopped his fruitless race. Staggering, he pretended to hold something small between his thumb and forefinger, just in front of his lips. He bobbled his head and moved his lips like he was telling a funny story. The children roared.

Curly or Peck shouted, "What's he doing?" Falcon shushed

them and sat them down, motioning for the others who had followed him over to do the same. He remained standing.

"They had the *birds* that carried them from one *sittie* to another." Eagle looked for Fish; she didn't disappoint. She rushed Fly with Badger in tow, and her wake stirred up the other young ones. Fly backed away without thinking, waving his arms. Eagle cut in front of the boy and scooped Fish into his arms. The others skidded to a stop.

Fly backed off all the way to Falcon's group. Eagle set the girl down and started to usher them back to their places. A burst of laughter erupted from the crowd, fingers pointing past Eagle. He turned and saw Fly sprawled on his back, just behind Spider, who knelt on all-fours. She rolled over, closer again to Falcon, who laughed with the others.

Eagle motioned for Fly to have a seat. The boy slouched back, embarrassed, to Raven, who smiled and hugged him when he sat down.

"It wasn't just the *tek*, they had other things, too," Eagle said. "They had animal friends, like the *dawg*. Cousins of the wolves we sometimes hear from over the hills, *dawgs* lived in peace with the Ruck-before. They lived in the yurts as part of the *famlee*. They loved the Ruck and would risk their own lives to save anyone in the *famlee*."

Eagle paused, spying the little girl Copperhead dragging Hawk to the edge of the audience. A few others tagged along: Ox, Bison, Hoop, Grouch, and Shadow.

"The *famlee* had a mother and father, brothers and sisters, *dawgs* and other animal friends. Sometimes ... the mother and father still lived with THEIR mother and father." Eagle paused for two heartbeats, this time for effect. "Even sometimes again," he whispered, leaning in toward the children around Fish, "their mother and father still lived with theirs!"

The youngest children all sucked in air at the same time, creating a collective gasp. Eagle continued before they could blurt out questions.

"Some things were more important than the *tek*. Knowing your father, living with a *famlee*, traveling wherever you wanted to go. The *birds* and the *carts* gave them the ability to travel faster. But without something even more important, they could never have traveled at all." Eagle withdrew to the fire as he spoke, kneeling in his previous spot, letting this thought hang in the air.

"No, it was never the *tek*. The Ruck of the *Yewessay* had something better. They had *freedom*."

The children breathed more deeply now, hanging on Eagle's next word. Hawk swooped to the end of the semi-circle.

"*Freedom*." Eagle stood as he repeated the word. "What does it mean? I believe it means we always control our lives. We choose—no matter what our situation. It's not something we earn; we just have it. We choose to eat, we choose to play, we choose to die. I believe we still have *freedom*. I choose to believe the Overlords can't rule us."

Hawk advanced as Eagle hurried out the last words. "That is a *fugging* lie," he said, halting within reach of Eagle and turning to the gathered.

"I have told Eagle that these stories will hurt the Ruck. They teach us lies that make our situation worse. The Overlords rule us absolutely. We can't fight them or disobey them. How many of you have seen them in The Hunt? How many of you have lost a brother or a sister to one of their lightning bolts?" Now Hawk let the words linger, turning to Eagle. "How many of us have seen ... one of our friends burned by the *tekline*?"

Eagle turned from Hawk, visually sweeping the assembled Ruck, whose numbers swelled now that Hawk had stepped up. Sweeping back, Eagle glanced at his rival before redirecting his attention to the gathering.

"I have seen a friend burned," Eagle said. "I don't want to see another. It doesn't mean we can't be *free*. All I say is that we choose ... we choose to be ruled by the Overlords or we choose not to be."

"Nonsense." Hawk said. "The evidence is obvious. The Overlords decide what happens to us. Their *tekline* holds us in this valley. That alone should be enough. But there's more. The Black One watches us at all times. Probably listening right now." The children gasped again. Hawk threw up his arms and asked Eagle "What choice do we really have?"

Eagle shook his head, advancing toward Fish again. "I have told Hawk what I think. His view gives us no hope. I think we have to start believing we can be *free* and find a way to live *free*."

"More nonsense." Hawk addressed the older children as well as the men standing around the edges of the gathering. "Talking about *freedom* can only destroy the Ruck more quickly. Believing in such ideas puts us in danger. Some will try to disobey the Overlords' rules and we will all be punished. It's better to recognize the truth of our situation and make sure the Ruck go on."

"Why should the Ruck go on if we are only slaves to the Overlords?"

Eagle suspected this question would change the course of the debate. He didn't expect the uproar the comment raised, as many of the Ruck gasped, shouted, stuttered, or yelled. He caught Sage's bewildered eye. No turning back.

"Really." Eagle let out an exaggerated sigh. "If Hawk speaks the truth, if he is right, why should we bother?" He plopped down near Fish and Badger, shrugging.

Small arguments broke out here and there accompanied by more startled looks and exasperated grumbles. Hawk hovered.

"I think ..." Eagle poked Fish in her ticklish spots. "I think the reason we are supposed to go on is so we can one day be *free* again. And I think we must take back our *freedom*, not wait for someone to give it to us."

"That's where you have it wrong, Eagle. Trying to leave or disobey will only get us killed faster. Don't forget the other stories, Eagle, the horrible ones. The stories about the Ruck who made love while still in the village, the ones who bore a child. The stories about the men who stole away to the compound. The ones who tried to teach the children to *reed* and *rite*. All of them mutilated, more of us punished, severely..."—

he pointed to Fish, Badger, and Copperhead—"... children like those taken from us without even the chance to survive The Hunt. You are suggesting we disobey and try to leave. I'm saying that is madness."

"It's madness to go on for no reason, which is what you suggest, Hawk."

"No. I say that we can achieve our *freedom* by proving ourselves to the Overlords. I think they are testing us." Hawk turned to the children. "I think our fathers and their fathers knew this truth: if the Ruck could go on long enough, we would prove ourselves worthy of a place among the Overlords."

Eagle stood, stretching. "We have been waiting a long time, it seems. I don't know what more we have to prove. I look around and see brave men, strong children. Fast runners, good hunters, talented crafters. And I see more on the way. The Overlords will never *free* us, we must make ourselves *free*."

"Eagle, you know some have tried." Hawk softened, taking a long, measured breath. "Why did none of our mothers and fathers try to leave? Because they knew what would happen. We have learned from experience. Rebellion means death."

"I'm not saying we should go grab our quivers and charge the *tekline*." A few chuckles rolled through the crowd. "I'm saying we can choose how to live. And for me, believing we can escape the Overlords is the reason to go on. I believe God gave us *freedom* and the Overlords can't take it away without our agreement. If we strive for *freedom*, we can have it. We can take small steps, here in the village while we plan how to get away. The Black One can't hear us all the time. Where is he now? Why hasn't he come to silence me?"

"The Overlords have no need to silence you. Your words mean nothing to them. But your actions will bring retribution. Are you saying we can escape the *tekline*?"

"Eventually. Yes. There must be a way."

"If it's so easy to leave, why haven't you? I will help you pack." Hawk's comment and flourish drew laughter from the Ruck. Eagle smiled and nodded.

"Okay, Hawk. I never said it was easy. I'm saying we have to believe we can. That's where we were when you so rudely interrupted my story."

"Clearly, we disagree. I can't support your ideas. I can't let them go unquestioned. I waited too long to interrupt. I think you are hurting the children." Hawk turned again to the men and older children. "Each of you will need to decide which of us to follow. Falcon and others, I understand it isn't easy to choose sides. And yet, hasn't it become clear for all of us to see? Eagle's ideas will be the death of the Ruck. If follow him, we won't go on. To those who would follow me, I say to you: our obedience to the Overlords will allow us to go on and someday earn our due place. To those who would follow Eagle, I say you will end up dead, and you will bring punishment upon the rest of us."

Hawk backed away. Bison, Shadow, and others surrounded him. Eagle let Hawk's words be the last. When Eagle declined to respond, Falcon and the rest separated, returning to their campfire. Eagle observed a few of the Ruck had hesitated: Copperhead, Buck, Clay, Curly, and Peck.

When Thrush and Ash came up to him, Eagle slapped Thrush on the back pre-emptively and said, "No, the time for talk has ended tonight. We should all rest and consider these events. Get the children to sleep, please."

6

Eagle slept well for the first night in some time. He woke with the sun and watched its inexorable rise above the hills, chasing away the dew and harkening the coming moons of warmth and growth. A pleasant dream from the night lingered in his memory as Eagle soaked in the shine, a simple dream about hunting with Garnet and his friends shortly after he was named Sparrow. His impulse was to fetch his bow and quiver, round up Sage and Thrush, and spend the full of daylight bringing in *ven* for the village.

Eagle's reason told him this impulse was foolish. While the spectacular sunrise gave him hope of a new season, the *ven* wouldn't be plentiful yet, if they had returned at all. And it would do no good to traipse off with the two brothers he hoped would remain his best allies, drawing attention to themselves the first morning after the argument with Hawk.

No, something with the children would serve his goals much better.

Why not combine the two ideas? Eagle smiled, mentally patting himself on the back. Gathering up some of the younger children on a crisp morning and getting them back to the idea of hunting, now that would do. It wasn't too soon to go out looking for *ven* spoor. It would give him a buffer from Hawk, a chance for some degree of normal village life to resume after the argument. And it would serve a useful purpose.

Eagle roused all the yurts in his camp, shaking loose the remaining sleepers like ants kicked from the mound. He then corralled the others who were already up and making their own fun. He grabbed the first five youngsters he could find, defining "young" as he went. He snapped up Chase, setting the limit at her count of winters, while judging Badger and Fish were now ready, at six winters, to learn more about hunting. That made three. He spun around to find Blossom staring at him from the edge of her yurt, wiping sleep from her eyes and squinting. Eagle raced to her, dragging Fish on his pant-leg and Badger by the scruff of the neck—and feeling another giggling child in close pursuit. Eagle's wild rush had some of the children screeching and laughing. Dropping Badger just in front of Blossom, he spun around again and caught Hemp in his now free arm. Eagle laughed out loud, and the children squealed for more.

"Come," he said. "We are going hunting." Pointing to each of the five he had selected, he continued. "If you have a bow, go get it. If you don't, follow me. We meet at the archery range."

Blossom, Hemp, and Chase all ran back to their yurts. Eagle pried Fish from his leg, promising to carry her. He lined her up next to Badger and scooped up both, one per shoulder. When he straightened up, getting ready to start off to Archer's yurt, he saw Dove watching from the imaginary edge of Falcon's camp.

Eagle stopped. He lifted his chin toward Dove and tilted his head toward his destination. He wanted to wave, but his arms were full. He made the motion again. Dove smiled, first waving and then nodding his understanding. Finally, the boy sighed and shook his head.

"No, thank you, Eagle," he called out. "Not today. Please, ask me again sometime."

Eagle nodded and started to run. Before long he realized, painfully, that carrying both of the young ones would wear him out. He slowed to a pace he could manage.

"Are you ready to learn how to hunt?" he asked.

"*Yeeee!*" Fish would have cheered the eating of dirt at that moment. Eagle chuckled. So would Badger—anytime. Right now, the boy didn't seem too keen on hunting.

"What about you, Badger?"

"I don't know."

They reached Archer's and Eagle let the matter drop. He saw his sister in her work area, looking up from her task as he approached. She had started early, like her brother. She shook her head, smirking, as he set down the children.

"You can't resist putting on a show, can you Eagle? After last night, I thought maybe you would understand. Sometimes, it helps to give something a rest, too."

"I'm just having fun. Right?" Eagle made a face at Fish.

"*Yeeee!*"

"These children need bow and arrow for our hunt today, Archer. Would you help us?"

Archer stood and gave her brother a hug. She whispered, "We'll talk later." They parted, and she grinned. "Yes, of course I will help. It's an honor to help the future hunters of the Ruck."

"Oh, and they need a lesson, as well, Archer. Can you help with that, too? My party is meeting at the range."

"Then I will meet you there with everything these young hunters need."

This time, Eagle asked the children to walk with him. They crossed the village to the south. Eagle saw Tiller out in the fields. He had never quite understood how the boy did the work, digging in the soil all day, planting seeds and cultivating the sprouts. Hunting was much more interesting. Of course, Badger insisted they stop and help the older boy with his digging. Eagle countered with an offer to stop and watch for a bit.

When Tiller realized they were watching him, he stood up and dawdled, uncomfortable. Eagle waved and Tiller sort of waved back. The boy turned away, revealing his curly, tangled mass of dark hair tied in a bunch at his neck, then turned around again, scratching his temple. He left a large dirt patch on his smooth, light brown skin. He seemed to be waiting for them to leave, so Eagle dragged the reluctant Badger by the neck again, and they pushed on toward the range.

The other three were waiting for them, half-practicing shots at the target, half-looking-over-their-shoulders and carrying on about how long it was taking for Eagle to arrive.

"We've been waiting forever," Chase whined. "We thought maybe you left without us."

"I wouldn't do that. We're waiting for Archer. She will give a quick lesson and then we'll go. Plenty of sunlight left."

Archer arrived after the older children had shot a round of arrows under Eagle's supervision.

"Children, fetch your arrows," Eagle said. "Your real teacher has arrived."

Archer called to Badger and Fish. She gave them their tiny new weapons while the other three retrieved arrows. Neither of them could hold the bow and pull the drawstring properly, but she would get them there in time. Today's outing didn't require them to shoot; it was only a first step. Eagle watched his sister's gentle persuasion. She guided them with her nimble hands, while the looks on their faces told Eagle they believed they were doing it themselves. She let them do it on their own, too, allowing them to imagine themselves as legendary hunters and marksmen. She asked Eagle to make sure they didn't hurt each other—even with the blunted points—while she tutored Chase, Hemp, and Blossom. She returned to Eagle's side once she had all the children occupied with their activities.

"You said some questionable things last night," she said.

"I didn't want it to happen this way."

"What do you mean?"

"All of this," Eagle said, "I didn't want this to become a fight. Neither of us is willing to budge a finger's length. Each of us believes so much in our way. And each of us cares about the children. I had to get it out in the open—the differences in our beliefs and our vision for the future. The Ruck must know their leaders and choose for themselves how to live."

Archer had turned her head to watch him speak. "I agree, brother. And I think there are others, too. You spoke for them. I think they will help you—we will help you."

"I'm counting on it."

Eagle wished he hadn't said that to his sister. He wanted to keep her out of his secret plans as much as possible. He wanted her help in simple ways, like the archery lesson, but not for the dangerous ideas that churned in his mind throughout the *ven* hunt.

The excursion proved uneventful. They found no spoor at all. It didn't surprise Eagle, although it disappointed all of them. Even though Eagle's purpose wasn't to bring in *ven*, the children's enthusiasm had him hoping they might find some after all. Still, Badger and Fish learned a lot from the older children, especially Chase. The young girl hit everything she shot at—no moving targets, but impressive practice, nevertheless. She glided through the brush, with elegant, effortless steps, leaps, and bounds. Chase set a valuable example for the younger ones.

Also, the birds were returning to roost. The mating calls, wood pecking, and fluttering of escape from the treetops hit the Ruck like unexpected thunder on a cloudless evening, especially after two moons of hibernation in the yurts. They spent a good part of the day spotting different kinds of birds and speculating on how many had returned. The birdsong filled their hearts with the promise of a new season.

Eagle even spotted a few wildflowers peeking up through the detritus in some of the clearings where they rested. He picked just one, tucking it safely inside his small pouch. He studied the spot carefully, planning to return later, harvest some of the flowers and teach the children how the delicate petals could save their lives.

When they returned at sunset, the children were spent. Ash and Thrush helped to fill their bellies and get them organized for the night. It gave Eagle an opportunity to pass a word to Thrush, discreetly.

"I'm going on another three-day journey, Thrush. Please tell your brother—and thank him again for his advice a few moons ago. When I return, I want to meet with both of you. I will need your help for what I have in mind. Say nothing to any other Ruck. When you see me the fourth morning, ask me to go hunting with you—and make sure Sage knows to join us."

Thrush started to respond, but Eagle turned away and admonished one of the children for not eating all her *ven* and *veg*. Eagle glimpsed the initial confusion in Thrush's face. He believed the boy would grasp the importance of caution in these matters. Indeed after a few moments, Thrush turned back to the younger children. He followed Eagle's example, making sure they all ate everything given to them.

Three campfires came alit as the groups of the Ruck settled in for the night. Eagle sighed as he watched Mountain and Hawk mentoring Bison and Fox on the subtleties of an enduring fire. It had proved easy to avoid confrontation for a day—perhaps too easy. Eagle wondered if the divisions were so deep that the village could fracture into separate pieces. The thought ran a chill up to his neck. He wondered if his plans were too drastic—if they would only hasten or cause a complete rift. By the time Eagle drifted off, sleeping by the fire instead of retiring to his yurt, his resolve for putting his plan in motion defeated his doubts.

When he stirred a while later, the whole village still slept. The sliver of a moon dipped toward the mountains. Eagle forced himself awake, chewed one last piece of *pem,* and left silently.

The orange-red sunrise heralded another magnificent day. Eagle walked the expanse of the valley while the sunlight lasted. He took inventory of the new wildflowers, collecting a sample of each one he found, deeply inhaling its fresh scent and memorizing every location. He counted the different birds, rodents, and bugs he observed, stopping to listen to the chatter of sparrows or watch the determination of a horde of black ants. He scoured the most used *ven* trails for any sign of their return, still finding none but gaining confidence they would reappear soon. A few times he simply stood and breathed, lifting his face to the sky and thanking God for the bounty of the valley.

His stomach grumbled most of the afternoon and without replenishment he grew fatigued before the sun had set. It didn't matter; Eagle pushed past his body's pleading for sustenance, drinking water from his skin at regular intervals and focusing his mind on his plans for escape. He wound his way to the spot where he and Hawk watched the Overseer, creeping in as he came closer, spying to see whether his rival had chosen this evening to visit the place himself. With no one around, Eagle perched at the edge of the spot and hoped he hadn't missed the changing of the Black One. He nearly had —the sudden flash surprised him because it happened merely heartbeats after he settled his back against a tree and wondered if he had arrived too late. For his plan to work, he would need precise timing. He already knew that, but this reminder served him well. He decided to return earlier the next day, and as many times as possible this moon, until he could feel in his bones the timing of the change.

On the second evening of his journey, Eagle realized that returning to the spot, daily, would be impossible. He thanked God for the insight and the forewarning. On his initial approach, he heard a throaty cough, the kind one makes when swallowing water down the air pipe. He froze. The coughing paused, sputtered, and was interrupted by Hawk's cursing his own misfortune. Eagle gambled—hoping he was far enough away to retreat without alerting the still coughing Hawk—taking quick strides, almost leaps, down the ridge. The light rain, which had been falling intermittently all day, helped cover his descent. As far as Eagle knew, Hawk never noticed him.

Eagle made haste to a spot he had visited yesterday, a place that might also afford a view of the Black One. It was less ideal, he thought, but close enough to get there in time. The approach proved more difficult in the steadily drumming rain but, when he alighted on a stone outcropping just beneath the main bluff and paused for a breath, he judged the vantage point here equal to the other spot. Although the scraggy rocks made it cramped and a little uncomfortable, he knew he could pull himself up to the bluff after the changing and re-settle for the night.

He guessed his position was no more than a village length from Hawk's spot. Normally, he could measure distance easily, but the mad dash to this spot made him more uncertain. He surveyed the hills, his eyes often returning to the Overseer, while he tried to confirm his guess. Suddenly, he saw the flash at the edge of his periphery, turning his head too late to see anything else. So, he learned, this spot required a more direct observation to witness the changing.

The rain sputtered shortly after Eagle had pulled himself up to the main bluff. He stretched on his back and drifted off. Heavy drops pounding on his eyelids snapped him alert. Hearing rolling thunder and blinking against the imminent downpour, he dragged himself back down the hill a little ways until he found the shelter of a thick pine. He pressed his back against a trunk and wedged himself between low limbs, hoping to avoid the brunt of the storm.

The rain had resumed during the morning of hunting—at least, Eagle's attempt at it. He traveled with an arrow knocked for some of the time, just for the feeling of it, but he detected no evidence of *ven* in the valley. He stayed as close to the *tek-line* as he dared. About the time his stomach complained to the point where even water had no effect, Eagle stumbled across a small party led by Falcon and Oak. They didn't speak, but the men saw each other through the brush. Eagle paused long enough to discern two of the children in the party—Clay and Happy. The latter saw Eagle, too. He waved, prompting Eagle to guffaw and wave, despite himself.

A faint drizzle persisted all afternoon. Eagle decided to try observing the village unnoticed. He snuck to the edge of copse where the Chosen entered for The Hunt. From there, he could see one of Tiller's fields (the one without the small pear trees), but he needed to get closer to examine even a portion of the village. As usual, Tiller labored with gusto, but he wasn't alone this time. Badger and the little girl Fern were helping him. A welcome sight—at least the younger children still associated with others from different camps. Tiller's acceptance of Badger also gave hope. Tiller worked on the far side; the children were digging near him and chattering. Eagle surmised that he could make a run to the oaks near the crafter's yurts without drawing their attention. With no alarm from Badger, Eagle guessed he had managed it.

Methodically climbing high and working to find a perch with a good view of the crafter's clearing, as well as part of Hawk's main area, Eagle finally propped himself above two sturdy limbs. The painstaking climb, added to his lack of nourishment, left him woozy. All he wanted for many heartbeats was to hold on tightly, catch raindrops on his tongue, and stare straight ahead. Only Potter could be heard, at first. Apparently, the boy hadn't noticed Eagle's ascent. Eagle almost fell asleep in his treetop nook, but he shook the haze from his mind and focused on Potter's activity—he was re-conditioning old scraps of clay. Later, Carver and Weaver returned to their work areas, with the shy little girl Tortoise and the bushy-haired Red, respectively, in tow for their lessons. Eagle noted that Potter and Weaver greeted each other, while neither of them ever spoke to Carver or his student. Eagle remembered that Carver had placed himself in Falcon's group. The trio seemed to tolerate, or rather ignore, each other's presence. Tiller's yurt rounded out the four surrounding the clearing and it still appeared to be in use. Eagle was glad they had all maintained their yurts and workplaces. He took it as a positive sign, even if they avoided interaction. Things hadn't fallen apart altogether.

Several times, Eagle fought off waves of drowsiness brought on by the tedium of the crafters' work combined with the gentle patter of precipitation. When Tiller finally returned from the fields, pushing a load of tools in his creaky cart, Eagle crept down the tree and headed back to the hills.

A flash of lightning and clap of thunder startled him after he had returned to the pine tree where he took refuge from last night's storm. Tucked under the pine, again, he slept uneasily the remainder of that night. The thunderstorm passed, although a steady rain continued into the morning.

Despite the lingering rain, Eagle found Tiller out in the field as the sun tried to penetrate the third morning's clouds. While he still couldn't understand the boy's enthusiasm for the task, Eagle admitted to himself an interest in the value of the *veg* Tiller cultivated. During his scouting the previous two days, he had seen some wild plants that looked like the ones Tiller grew and he wondered if he could have eaten them. Absorbed with his hoeing, the boy was oblivious to Eagle's approach. Tiller nearly swung the tool in instinctual defense when Eagle spoke to him. Once Tiller had recognized him, Eagle said he needed to ask a few questions.

The boy couldn't hide his skepticism, but he agreed to Eagle's request. They sat at the edge of the field by the trees that gave entrance to the grounds of the The Hunt. Tiller pulled a small digging tool from his belt, poking nervously at the muddy earth while they talked. Eagle glanced around to make sure no other early risers happened upon them.

"Badger seems very interested in your work," Eagle began. "I hope he is helping you and not hindering you."

Tiller lifted his head from the digging and shook it with eyes wide, as if that were an answer.

"I'm interested, too. I saw what looked like some wild *veg* out there." Eagle gestured to the surrounding hills. "I was wondering if they are safe to eat."

"I ... I ... don't know. I would have to see them ... I guess."

"Maybe you could join me for a little while, to take a look?"

Tiller made a face, digging with more vigor. "I ... I don't think that's a good idea, Eagle. I mean, uh, I uh, have a lot to do … you know, after the winter and everything."

"Of course." A few heartbeats of uncomfortable silence passed. "I wouldn't want to take you away from your fields. It looks like it takes a lot of work to grow the *veg*."

Tiller perked up; he seemed surprised by Eagle's comment. "Uh-huh. You have to be patient. First, the soil has to be …" he stopped abruptly, scratching his temple. "Well, you don't … you don't care about … all of that. It just takes time."

"Just like anything worth doing, Tiller. And I think I've used enough of your time this morning. Thank you." Eagle rose and stretched. His stomach complained again, loud enough for Tiller to hear. Eagle scanned the hills, wondering which way he should go and then picking the way that would take him across the archery range.

Tiller spoke after Eagle had taken a few steps. "Um, Eagle? There probably is some *veg* out there that you could eat. They grow … they grow fast after it rains. We call them *shrooms*."

Eagle returned. "Tell me more, please."

Tiller stood, glancing around. "Over here." He led Eagle into the nearby trees. His voice exuded excitement as he searched the ground. "They grow in the damp shade. Maybe … with the rain … we might … here!" He plucked the small cap and held it up for inspection. His tone changed. It reminded Eagle of the way Archer spoke during her lessons. "This one's okay. Look for ones like this. Don't eat them … yet. Some aren't good. Bring them back to me first."

Tiller's excitement ebbed quickly when he looked up into Eagle's eyes. He dropped his head, ashamed, still clutching the *shroom*. "I mean … if you …"

"That sounds like fun." Eagle said, extending his hand, palm-up, into Tiller's view. "I better take one, or I won't even have a chance."

Lifting his brown eyes but not his head, Tiller placed the *shroom* in Eagle's hand.

"Thank you, Tiller. I will return later."

Eagle kept his word, returning at the end of the day with a

pouch full of the *shrooms*. They were small and he wasn't sure they were the right ones. He found a large group of them beneath a thickly wooded area near the foothills. It took a while. The sun had finally pushed aside the clouds, and it was already on its way down. After picking his pouch full, Eagle continued his search for *ven* spoor, heading up into the hills from the *shroom* patch. The urging from his insides tempted him to eat a few, but he forgot all about the idea when he finally spotted signs of the *ven*. He was near the *tekline* when he found the early sign—probably just one or two of the creatures. It looked like they had crossed and then left just as quickly. It was enough to lift Eagle's sprit. He thanked God for their return and hoped the Ruck would see a few does before long.

He ran down some of the slopes and bounded across the crags and ditches in the foothills. When he returned to the *shroom* patch, he remembered his pouch and he slowed down. Although the spoor find had distracted him, and he needed to stay away one more night before connecting with Thrush and Sage in the morning, Eagle didn't want to renege on his word to Tiller. He stole back toward the fields, staying out of the sight of any wandering villager eyes. He had to wait a little while, peeking from the brush, until Tiller was alone, because the other crafters, their friends, and students stayed busy around the clearing for some time. Finally, the boy was pushing his tool cart back to his yurt after the others had departed, so Eagle made a dash.

He hurriedly passed the pouch to Tiller. "I found some. I'm sorry I can't stay right now. I'll talk to you later ... you can tell me later if I picked the right ones." Eagle saw Bison rounding the back of Hawk's nearby yurts and so he fled without waiting for an answer from the boy.

Eagle watched the changing from the new place, then enjoyed another wonderful evening atop the bluff. Over the three days, he had thought much about his plans for escape. Partly, he needed the time to convince himself, one way or the other. Partly, he needed a little extra time to make sure his plans made good sense. The fasting made his head light, but also made his thoughts clear. Focused on the Black One, Eagle had watched the flash and the changing quite clearly from the outcropping. Now, as he lay on his back on the bluff, staring at the darkening sky, he drifted off until a half-awake dream played in his mind. He saw himself darting across the *tekline* at the moment of the flash, racing past the Overseer and running—no, flying—forever over long open fields, bodies of water, and other unrecognizable hills and valleys.

When sun rose over the hills surrounding the Ruck's valley, he went directly to his yurt and grabbed a few pieces of *pem*. Chewing them outside, he was spotted by Ram and Parrot, who raised the alarm of his return. Children swarmed around him. Eagle almost choked on a piece of the dried *ven* as they grabbed and pulled and pressed. He laughed it off and played innocent to their inquiries of "where have you been." Instead, he dropped to the ground with them, tickling the youngest ones until they squirmed away. Thrush arrived, pulling off the diehards with Ram's help.

"Eagle, it is good to see you." Thrush said. "My brother and I are about to go hunting for spoor. Will you join us?"

Eagle dusted himself and stood up. Raven approached to give him a hug, and then she and Fly rounded up the children. Ram and Parrot lingered close-by, as did Star.

"I would be honored, Thrush. And it might not be only for spoor. I found tracks yesterday—the *ven* are returning!" Eagle raised his voice as he finished, making sure everyone could hear him. The Ruck rejoiced. His ploy thinned the crowd further, with the villagers dispersing to spread the news to other friends. Ram, Parrot, and Star remained, apparently waiting for an invitation to join the hunting party.

"Ram, would you please find Coot and Justin and make sure they know? It's important." Eagle said.

"Sure!" Ram said.

"Sure!" Parrot said. "Find Coot and Justin and make sure they know."

The boys ran off, leaving only Star. She leaned closer to Eagle, squeezing his arm. She whispered. "You won't get rid of me so easily."

"I know," he replied. "Thrush, would it be okay if Star joined us?"

Thrush paused, uncertain. "I ... if ... well, sure, Eagle, if that's what you ..."

Sage's appearance interrupted Thrush's stammering, for which he seemed grateful. "So, the *ven* have returned," he said. "Come on, Eagle my friend, show us what you have found." Sage didn't wait, starting off toward the woods. Eagle extended his arm to Star. She hooked hers through his, and she grabbed Thrush's hand with her free one as they all caught up to Sage.

When they reached the place where Eagle had found traces of the *ven's* return, they sat and talked in hushed tones, each of them except Eagle a taking turn on watch for any approaching Ruck. Eagle laid out his plans, telling them what he wanted each of them to do. They debated at first, questioning the boldness of his ideas, especially the part about him leaving the valley. Eagle assured them. He knew what must be done. In the end, they all agreed to do as Eagle asked, despite any reluctance.

They talked about whom else to involve—and those within their group Eagle didn't want involved. Eagle asked Thrush, Sage, and Star to work quietly within the village, avoiding attention and coordinating efforts while taking no action themselves. Meanwhile, he said, others would help him in the hills or perform specific tasks. Sage suggested that Ram would be the best candidate for helping prepare the escape. Star added Mace's name to the idea, keeping those brothers together. Eagle accepted both suggestions. He asked them if they thought Fly could carry on the story-telling—including the reinforcement of the *freedom* stories—with only occasional involvement himself. They decided that Fly would need guidance, but with Star as a messenger and Raven's ongoing work with the younger children, it could be done.

When they broached the subject of Falcon's group, Thrush grumbled and forced out Ash's name. She had told him she was thinking about going off with Clay, Tanner, or Carver (or all three!) to convince them to join us. His scowl told them all what he really thought about the idea. Eagle thanked him for being honest—and apologized when he said that Ash was precisely on target. Continuing friendships and courting rituals gave them their best chance to persuade those in Falcon's camp —especially Clay, who was Eagle's brother—and perhaps even Falcon himself. Star volunteered to coordinate the effort; the men chuckled when she cited her several winters' experience in that area. Eagle winked and encouraged Thrush to do his best to make connections with the girls in Hawk's camp. They all laughed when Thrush, smirking and blushing through his growing reddish-blond whiskers, said "I guess it couldn't hurt."

Eagle made it clear: he didn't want his brothers and sisters involved directly, if possible. Too many ways to slip there, he thought. He said he would rely on Archer to help with lessons for the children and other normal activities. At the same time, he didn't want Archer or Willow or Badger to know any details of the escape plans—not yet. Eagle asked his friends to let him include his siblings in his own time. No one argued, although Thrush asked about Ox, who had chosen Hawk's camp. Eagle's reaction surprised them. He raised his voice to normal levels, which sounded like a shout after their lengthy whispering, insisting that the boy was *free* to choose his way, just like Clay. They couldn't put any pressure on him just because he was Eagle's brother. He softened, aware of his relative outburst. Of course, Eagle said, he welcomed Ox as an ally if he could be convinced, like any other Ruck, to continue normal relations whenever possible.

Finally, they discussed whether to include Coot. They all counted him on their side. They agreed the old man had chosen Falcon's camp to delay an immediate rift in the village. Sage supported Coot's choice. It was important for the village, he said, and he stressed that it was just as important for Coot to know about Eagle's escape. Eagle ended the discussion; yes, of course he wanted to tell Coot, just not yet. He wanted to tell his brothers and sisters in time, too. Nodding to Sage, he promised to tell Coot before he attempted to escape the *tekline*.

They stared at each other for several heartbeats. Eagle broke the silence, saying they should actually do some hunting before they returned to the village.

To everyone's dismay, none of the Ruck hunting parties brought in *ven* for several more days. Others had found spoor, all near the *tekline*, but no actual sightings of their prey. Rain soaked the valley almost every day, making the hunting a little more difficult.

Eagle thanked God for the rain—and even for the delay in the return of the *ven*. The combination gave the Ruck a focus fitting with his plans. Working with Ram and Mace became easy; they made excursions every day, sometimes with others, sometimes just the three of them. Eagle made sure to take the younger ones with him sometimes; they needed to learn, and the search for spoor taught them patience and persistence. He knew the *ven* would return, and—although their supplies of *pem* and dried *veg* waned—he never questioned whether they would make it through, somehow.

Everyone welcomed the rain, although it began to dampen spirits as much as it saturated the valley floor. Everyone, except for Tiller. Eagle met him twice at sunrise before Falcon and Clay brought in the first *ven*. The first time Eagle went to fulfill his promise about the *shrooms*; later he went because he was beginning to enjoy Tiller's company. Eagle saw him as an important ally.

The boy described the mottled markings on the *shrooms* that Eagle had picked, showing him how to tell whether they could be eaten. Eagle had to admit: he still didn't get it, but Tiller's enthusiasm made the time interesting. Eagle asked what would happen if someone ate the wrong ones. Tiller hesitated; he wasn't sure. The Tiller-before had told him some *shrooms* could kill a Ruck; others might only make one fitful and feverish.

Eagle also visited Hawk's spot twice before the first *ven* was taken, hoping to see the man there. He had stopped trying to avoid Hawk all the time. Their paths had crossed in the village and out in the hills. They rarely spoke, aside from the perfunctory utterance of each other's names. Eagle realized Hawk would be undertaking his own plans. He began to see all things as constant maneuverings, each man trying to achieve the superior position. Each cultivating his own supporters and preparing for the next contest. Each trying to keep the other from discovering intentions. Eagle had found Hawk at his coveted spot, with Shadow, on his second visit. Ram had accompanied Eagle that evening.

"Hawk," Eagle said, "I haven't seen you here, much."

"I've been here."

"Me, too."

They said nothing else. Eagle and Ram remained, off to the side, for a while. Hawk sat silently, suspending whatever lesson he might have been teaching. Shadow couldn't resist frequent glares over his shoulder. Eagle took the mallet-like hint. On his way back to the village, he decided he would visit Hawk's spot every several days.

After Falcon and Clay brought in the first *ven*, the three groups of the Ruck tried to settle into a promising spring routine. More birds returned, Tiller's work began to show results, and children resumed their games and lessons. Successful hunting parties grew until it became a regular activity once again. The Ruck ate heartily, adding vigor and strength after the winter's toll. Many things were the same as any one of them could remember, although the differences made it impossible to feel normal.

Eagle tried to organize a large race. None of Hawk's children participated. Hawk held wrestling matches—he made formal invitations to the children from Falcon's group while he ignored those in Eagle's group. Eagle had encouraged Mace or Parrot or Chase to go, but they wouldn't. Eagle went himself, once, hoping they would tag along. They still declined. He saw Clay there, hanging near his brother, Ox. Clay had come to the races with Spider, Dove, and some of the youngest ones. Hawk ignored Eagle, but Shadow's and Hawk's older boys glared at him until he left after only one match.

The competition to recruit Falcon's group turned into a game itself, consuming much of Eagle's time day after day. He continued to visit Tiller, spent time talking to Ram and Mace about a personal relationship with God, and made special efforts to hunt with Clay, Happy, or Dove—and any of the children from Falcon's group. Copperhead joined them once, sticking close to Dove. Eagle saw them go off together later in the evening; in fact, this pairing escaped no one's attention. Rarely did the boys and girls crossover for fooling around, despite the plans Eagle and Star had laid for Thrush and Ash. Luckily, Copperhead's foray broke things open. Shortly before the visit to the women, Ash had paired off with Carver and Weaver on successive nights. Somehow, Star had managed to arrange a pairing of Clay and Rachel (it lasted three nights). Eagle noticed that Clay had also taken off with Fox at least once. Meanwhile, Buck continued pining, staring at the older gaggle of girls in Hawk's group almost every night and sulking as the pairings unfolded. Star had encouraged Buck to talk with Tanner, but he shrugged off the suggestion, preferring to brood.

Eagle observed several of Carver's lessons with Tortoise or Moon or Spider—openly now. He asked the children questions about their projects and whittled a bit himself while he sat with them. He took opportunities to observe the other crafters' lessons, including Tanner (who smoldered the entire time) and Potter or Weaver. Even while the crafters tried to ignore his presence, Eagle made a point to speak to the children they tutored, showing his interest in their activities regardless of what camp they had joined. Whenever possible, Eagle included Fern and Snow and Happy and others in his races and he organized a tournament of stones for the youngest children (Snow won, beating his twin sister in the final game).

More than once, Eagle and Hawk or their emissaries collided in their efforts to win over the children in Falcon's group. The maneuvering crept into daily life. Eagle and his friends tried to get to the children before their rivals did, rousing them early in the morning or pouncing on them after a meal and herding them off to a pre-arranged activity. Eagle learned of a morning where Star and Maize nearly dragged each other to the ground in a wrestling match worthy of Hawk's instruction, as they each tried to entice children from Falcon's group to join them for the day's activities. After cajoling the children with promises of great fun and trying to outdo the other's bribes, the girls (almost women, Eagle reminded himself) began to physically corral the children. The two of them simultaneously got their grips on poor Double. They nearly pulled the little girl's arms from the sockets until they realized they were hurting her, causing them to tear into each other with curses and threats. The verbal jabs became violent shoves; Falcon and Oak had to pry them apart when they started pulling hair.

Fly continued telling the stories. That, at least, was working. Hawk couldn't take those stories away from the children without some kind of replacement. Fly was much funnier than Eagle; he kept the sessions light and silly. Fish seemed to take a shine to him, as with Eagle. She had helped the boy act out the stories of the *washer* and the *carts*, Eagle learned one evening around the campfire with Star and Sage. Eagle still attended some of the tellings ... and he told a story himself once in a while. Nothing to rouse Hawk's ire. Oddly, the major difference in the storytelling was that Hawk attended many of them, accompanying his children. Hawk attended even more than Eagle during this moon.

On a warm morning just a few days before the men went to the women, Raven and Fly were collecting children for a story. Like others, Eagle had relaxed a little in the welcome sunrays and planned to visit his sister later in the morning. He saw Raven rounding up his children and Fly calling out to everyone else to attend his story of *dawgs,* and maybe something extra, so Eagle stuck around. Bison had already entered Falcon's camp, asking some of his peers to go hunting. Bison was talking to Clay about bringing some of the smaller children, when Fly's heralding captured their attention. Curly and Peck raced off without as much as a nod to Moon and Sky. Fern, Snow, and Happy wanted to go as well. Suddenly, Bison's party had dwindled to two: Clay and Spider. The burly youth strode over to Fly, clearing a path through the children who clamored around the boy and then poking him in the chest.

"Perhaps you should check to see if the children already have plans."

Fly stepped back, taken aback. "I'm sorry, Bison. I didn't mean ... I wasn't ..."

"Next time," Bison interrupted, "I won't be so *fugging* nice."

"Look, I'll tell the children we'll do it tomorrow," Fly said. The children groaned.

"Making me look like the bad guy," Bison said. "No. We'll all go to your storytelling. Let's go children."

They squealed and cheered. Bison picked up Peck and threw the girl over his shoulder and called out to his friends to meet for a story.

Eagle watched as the crowd swelled. He considered speeding up part of his plan. Hawk joined just when the patting began. Eagle joined in, too—when Fly started the telling—mulling over the situation at the rear of the assembled Ruck. The boy wasn't at his best, perhaps the larger group affected him or perhaps the encounter with Bison had left him anxious.

The children giggled when he imitated a *dawg's* life in the village, but even Fish didn't laugh out loud or call for more like usual. Eagle had decided not to push too hard at this telling, but towards the end of the story, Fly pushed a little too hard himself. He said, someday, the Ruck might be able to find a *dawg* that could become part of the *famlee.*

Hawk interjected. "That will never happen," he said, getting up to join Fly in front of the group. "The *dawgs* are all gone. Forever."

A low groan rose from the children. Eagle circled around the group to flank Hawk. "They might not be," he said. "We don't know what lies beyond the valley."

Hawk turned slightly, half-facing the children and half-facing Eagle. "And we never will. There's no escaping. We die if we try. How many times must I say it?"

"We can't give up hope, Hawk. Fly's story is about hope."

"False hope."

"There's no such thing." Eagle scanned the children, making eye contact with several of them. "Children, if you want to, you can believe we might find another *dawg,* some day."

"Or" Hawk said, "you can believe what your eyes tell you and not be fooled by false hope."

Eagle let Hawk have the last word, again. This already went farther than he cared for, at least right now. The children just sat there, not knowing what to do, until some of the older ones ushered the younger ones back to their respective camps.

It still occupied Eagle's thoughts when they stood in line outside the compound. Two more evenings at the bluff had helped a little, but not enough. Standing and waiting for his visit with Ruby, he focused his mind on how he would handle the next few days. No more distractions when he was with the women. He made a promise to himself to treat all three of the women just as he would if it were Rose. He could muse and plan during the days between each visit.

What still bothered him were Hawk's exact words. Eagle tortured himself trying to figure out whether they had hidden meaning. Did Hawk know about Eagle's plans to escape? Had he learned about Ram and Mace? Or was it all just a coincidence?

That first night with Ruby helped him. He came to understand more and more. These visits went beyond duty or pleasure. They healed, if he let them. He would miss them after he escaped.

When Ruby greeted him, she still held her infant to her breast. Eagle's heart melted. Numerous candles lit the entire yurt. He glimpsed Ruby's two toddlers—Lamb and a boy whose name he didn't know—drawing in the dirt near the yurt's divider. He knelt down by them and asked them to show him their designs. They hesitated, but Ruby smiled and told them it was okay. She finished her feeding, and Eagle saw a content glow in her cheeks. She ushered the children behind the screen, settled them in for the night, and snuffed several of the candles.

Eagle and Ruby relaxed in each other's arms for a while, without talking, waiting for the children to drift into slumber. Ruby hummed, almost inaudibly. Eagle could feel the vibrations as she leaned her head on his chest. Now and then he could hear her clearly, and he felt his eyes getting heavier as he relaxed. Ruby shook him and stared into his eyes with a sly smile while he recovered. She began by kissing him on all his fringes—his earlobe, his brow, his nose, his fingertips. At first, she wouldn't let him return the kisses. In time, she relented, and he rolled on top of her, exploring her lips with the tip of his tongue. They quickened, tugging at each other's clothing as their heat grew, sweating passionately for the first time since the winter visits. They didn't wait; Eagle entered her soon after they shed the last of their skins. He performed for as long as he could hold out, releasing deep inside Ruby as she pointed her toes toward the sky.

They dozed for a while and talked for a while. Things had changed in the compound. Shrew had been named Gazelle. Eagle looked surprised. Ruby laughed, then explained. "Lotus has predicted Gazelle's long legs will mature like the limbs of the fastest of the legendary creatures. In time, she will move as swift as the autumn wind."

Rose, Jade, and Lilly were all bearing children. Eagle sucked in air when Ruby confirmed what Rose had guessed a moon ago. The swirling thoughts of fatherhood threatened to distract Eagle's attention, but he fought them off. Also, with the addition of Gazelle and the loss of the Justin-before, nine men and women's names entered the draw. Unless another man died, it would be several moons before one of the older boys joined the visits for his first time, Eagle realized.

Several of the children were approaching the age of moving to the village or of being named. Ruby's own son was named recently, as Twig, because he had taken to always clutching one and using it to scratch designs in the dirt, just as Eagle had seen. Honey told Ruby a few children would probably be ready to move in a few moons. Lamb was still too young.

"*Ehhhhhh*! I almost forgot!" Ruby said. "Your mother asked me to give you a special hug for her." She wrapped her arms tightly around Eagle's back and pressed against his chest. She almost squeezed the air out of him. Eagle seemed surprised, although he smiled as she released him. She laughed again, so loud he thought she would wake the baby. "She told me that's the face you would make. Honey is the best."

When Eagle awoke to the sounds of the compound coming alive the next morning, he felt groggy. He and Ruby hadn't slept much. They had made love again before they faded—a slow, soothing intercourse. Now, Ruby was already nursing the infant; Lamb and Twig were gone.

"You better get out of here, lover," was all Ruby said. Eagle obeyed.

He had hoped to see Rose as he crossed the compound, but her yurt was closed up. He did see Marvel ordering around some of the other children. Lotus watched over all the children while reclining topless against a stout pine. She stared at Eagle while he paused to scan the area. Her whole face seemed to transform from a calm observer to a mischievous imp when they first made eye contact. He found himself offering an awkward wave in return, in spite of himself, and just as he remembered his last awkward visit with her. She just laughed out loud. He felt utterly foolish. He headed straight for the gate, avoiding the other men and heading off into the woods alone. Being reminded of his recent mishap with Lotus increased his resolve—he would always give his best with all the women in the future.

He wanted to be alone on the first day. He hoped he could spend the second day with at least one of the other men—anyone but Hawk. He remembered the day they had spent together during the visit before the winter. Back then, Hawk could infuriate Eagle with one breath and still manage to teach him something with the next. Now, neither of them could stand each other's presence at all, and Eagle felt he had nothing more to learn or gain from a day's hunting and talking with Hawk.

This mutual avoidance helped the development of his plans. At least Eagle had thought so before Hawk's comments at Fly's telling. Avoiding Hawk's attention during their reconnaissance work had proved far easier than he expected over the course of the moon. The struggle to gain the confidence of Falcon's children made it easy to slip off with Mace or Ram regularly. They had scouted and marked the *tekline* with great precision. He had taught them about God; he passed on what Garnet had given to him those winters ago. Most importantly, he and the boys had watched the changing of the Black One from Eagle's new perch on several occasions. Only once did they need to purposefully distract Hawk and the others to accomplish an evening's work. Ram had done just as Eagle instructed, challenging Shadow and Bison to wrestling matches after insulting them and drawing their ire. Hawk made a show of it all and others joined in, including Thrush, also as Eagle had instructed. The whole thing consumed the attention of Hawk and his followers for most of the evening—helping to remove Ram from suspicion and allowing Mace to get very close to the Black One.

It all seemed to be working out nicely. Maybe it was too easy; maybe Hawk was simply allowing him to think their planning had gone unnoticed. Perhaps one of the older boys had been spying on them the entire time while Hawk remained aloof and disinterested or pretended to be distracted by wrestling matches or hunting excursions.

All of these thoughts bounced around in Eagle's head the day after Ruby. He walked, he hunted a little, he sat at the far edge of the lagoon with his feet in the water. From time to time his mind drifted to other things, including the possibility he might see Rose while he sat there on the water, like the day they had kissed. None of the women ever came out—they followed the traditions of the visit, not daring to leave the walls of the compound and possibly encountering one of the men, as Rose had done that day. She was pregnant now, anyway, and even though he would have traded all his plans to hold her again, he knew it wouldn't happen that way.

He also thought about what might happen during the visit with his sister, Faith. This would be the first time they were paired since she went to the compound. They would be expected to couple, both by the need for the Ruck to go on and by the decree of the Overlords. He had no intention of letting it happen if he could avoid it. He didn't know what she would think, though, and he also had no desire to offend her if she expected him to do his duty like any of the men. After all, they were only half-siblings. Some of the women didn't seem to think it mattered, Eagle believed, just like some of the men and older boys found it acceptable to lie with each other before The Hunt. He was sure Faith and Honey had talked about it, but he couldn't be sure what would happen when the time came. And then he also wondered how she would act when Hawk visited her the next night.

As the sun fell behind the mountains, Eagle found himself wandering far from the compound, still fretting whether Hawk knew about his plans. Nevertheless, he kept his promise to himself, shaking the doubts from his head and running back to the compound. He joined the other men waiting outside the gate. None of them were talking when he arrived, and Honey appeared at the gate to usher them in just a few heartbeats later. Eagle stayed back, breathless, and entered last. He watched his mother go off with Sage while he made his way to his sister's yurt.

Faith met him at the flap, standing. She took his hand, squeezing gently and leading him into the yurt. More than a dozen candles on ceramic plates lit and warmed the chamber. She peeked around the *ven*-hide divider and came back. Eagle decided to sit; Faith paused, paced a few steps and looked down at him.

"Honey said this would be hard," she said. She crossed and uncrossed her arms.

"Please sit, Faith. It's good to see you."

Faith crossed her arms again, peeked around the divider at her only child and finally sat near her brother, facing him.

"What else did our mother tell you?" Eagle ventured.

"She said to give you a big hug. She said I would know what to do. But I don't. I begged her to tell me what to do."

Eagle smiled. "Our mother is wise. We're lucky. It seems you feel the same way I do. *Fug* the Overlords."

Faith's eyes opened like blossoms and Eagle saw her smiling teeth for the first time in a long time. Her crossed arms flew open like arrows from a bow. She threw herself at her brother, wrapping herself around his shoulders and knocking him to the side. They toppled one of the plates of candles, and they laughed while they snuffed the flames before any of the blankets could alight.

They talked until all the other candles melted half into nubs.

Faith told him how hard it was to be always a mother. Her

girl had so much energy and needed so much attention. Of course, all the women helped each other, but it still seemed more than she could handle. She finally adjusted during the recent winter, with special help from Honey and Lotus. Strangely, she admitted, it helped to know Ruby also had struggles with her children. Seeing a young woman who already had three children showed it could be done, even if it was never easy. The children needed constant supervision and love. Faith couldn't resist peeking behind the curtain one more time. She said one of the best things about the men's visits was sharing the yurt with her own baby for three nights. It was a refreshing diversion from living in the main chambers with all of the women, where they all cared for the children together.

They talked a little bit about the news that Ruby had given Eagle, and they talked a lot about Faith's little girl. Eagle admired Faith's devotion to the child. It occurred to him how excruciating it must be to watch the children depart for the village when the time came.

Eagle learned that Faith and Honey had talked about many things, including Eagle's rivalry with Hawk and the current situation in the village. Faith told him all of the women knew about the dispute between the two men. More to his surprise, Eagle also learned that the women were choosing sides just like the Ruck in the village.

Faith provided details of the split, which Eagle memorized:

Honey's women included Faith, Ruby, and Rose.

Lotus led a group that remained neutral, including Lilly, Nightingale, and Butterfly.

Jade, Storm, and Mantis closed ranks in support of Hawk.

Eagle woke early the next morning, hearing the baby crying. He and Faith gave themselves a good night's rest, and so he woke refreshed. He peered through a crack in the yurt flap, watching some of the other women's yurts. Faith's spot wasn't secluded; Eagle could see several others. Wolf was the first to emerge, almost as soon as Eagle started watching. Winking at Faith, Eagle pushed through the flap and followed the young man.

Wolf heard him approaching. He stopped at the gate.

Eagle spoke. "Wolf, would you care to hunt with me today?"

Wolf said nothing, wearing his faraway look until Eagle moved ahead, opening and holding the gate. Finally, Wolf said "Okay" and stepped out of the compound. They had started into the woods when Sage burst out of the gate and caught up to them. Eagle whispered to his friend: "You must have been awfully rude, or terribly inadequate, for Honey to turn you out so early in the morning!" Sage laughed in reply.

The hunting filled the day. Wolf rarely spoke, although he did listen to Eagle, who tried to explain his reasons for believing the Ruck must someday escape. Eagle did his best to surmise the solitary man's perspective. The only thing Wolf said besides "okay" and "go on" was that he favored the open telling of the stories. This alone emboldened Eagle. They stayed together right up until they passed through the gate in the evening: Wolf going to Storm's yurt, Sage finding Lotus waiting for him in the commons, and Eagle joining Butterfly.

Her musk filled his senses as soon as he entered the yurt. The arousing smell reminded him of their last visit. Butterfly seemed pleased to see him and welcomed him with all her usual enthusiasm. She took him down to the blankets and began to explore his body immediately, wasting no time in getting him fully aroused. During the long night of lovemaking, he thrust deeply inside her three times, releasing his seed and hoping the Ruck would go on.

He woke much later the next morning. Butterfly was gone. He shook the sleep from his eyes and left the yurt. He saw Falcon sitting next to Honey in front of her yurt, as they watched the toddlers playing chase and laughing. The man arose and approached. Eagle stopped in the middle of the compound to meet him.

"Let's go, Eagle. We are the last."

Eagle followed him toward the gate. Just at the edge of his vision, he saw Rose crossing the compound. She had just turned, but he saw her backside as she knelt in front of the soap vats. She showed no notice of Eagle. Still, even the brief sight of her was enough to lift him through the gates and on ahead of Falcon before he realized the other man was asking him a question.

"I said," Falcon repeated, "when will you have another race?"

"Uh, soon." Eagle said. He lied. He hadn't thought much about it. "Have the children been asking about it?"

Falcon shrugged. "Not exactly. I enjoy the races, just like I enjoy the wrestling. I think our children should be doing both."

"I agree, Falcon. I'll arrange one."

"Good. And make sure some of your children attend the wrestling matches."

The activities arranged by Falcon helped Eagle to get his mind off the lingering memory of Rose at the compound. He left elated, but when he reached the village, he was already glum. He allowed himself most of the first day to ponder how he might manage to see her again. By nightfall, he determined not to dwell on it. The next day Eagle closed the gate in his mind to Rose's image. He started talking to everyone about the biggest race of the season, to be held in a dozen mornings. Meanwhile, Hawk was drumming up support for his wrestling tournament, which would happen three days before the race. Although Ram and some of the others didn't want anything to do with Hawk's event, Eagle impressed upon them how important it was if they were to have any chance of swaying Falcon's children. Once he had Ram's agreement, the children's excitement grew for both events.

Justin and Falcon helped Hawk to supervise the various wrestling matches. Hawk seemed to welcome their assistance while the children came together in one large group to listen to the rules. The day started off with great promise. The three men helped the youngest children prepare for their matches, showing no favoritism—and they accepted Sage's offer to help as well. Eagle guessed his rival coveted the opportunity to work closely with the neutral men and cultivate their potential allegiance. Still, Hawk's actions showed nothing but respect for all of them, including Sage.

At the start, the children cared only for the thrill of the matches. About two dozen of them competed. Ram, Thrush, Buck, Willow, Henna, Earnest, Sparrow, and Newt represented Eagle's group. Henna bested everyone in her age group, while Nardo and Bison won the necklace of pebbles in their groups. Henna's performance surprised just about everyone except for Raven and Fly. Eagle learned later the same night that Henna had been practicing with them every day ... and wearing them out by all accounts. She basked in the congratulatory hugs and kisses from her friends, as did Hawk's winning duo. That night Henna went off with Mace. Eagle overheard Raven whispering to Fly, saying Henna had finally paired up with the solid, dark-haired boy who made her heart throb.

Early in the day, Eagle thought the wrestling tourney was bringing the three groups closer together, even if only for a day. He stayed out of the way and cheered, doing his best to praise the efforts of all the competitors. Falcon seemed pleased, too, until the partisan cheering and celebrating increasingly overwhelmed any larger community spirit. By the time the first rounds were completed, Hawk's children rooted for each other exclusively. Eagle's group and Falcon's group followed the trend, with Ram leading the shouts for Eagle's children until his ragged voice started to sound like old Coot. As the contests advanced toward the finals, Eagle strained to find one child cheering for someone in a different group—and that's exactly what he found, as Dove alone was bold enough to join in the rallying cries for just about everyone. Even Joy seemed reluctant to voice her support for anyone other than her comrades in Eagle's group. By the time Henna had disappeared with Mace, Falcon sat by his fire, alone, with his head in his hands.

The races three days later only made matters worse. Falcon and Justin met with Eagle early in the morning, asking him to help them foster and maintain some kind of camaraderie amongst the groups during the races. Falcon's face was pale; his eyes were sleepy slits. He mumbled something about wanting to cancel the races—he feared the whole idea would end up encouraging the very opposite of his original hopes. Eagle opposed the idea of cancellation, promising to do his best for everyone. He meant it, but both men read the lack of hope in each other's faces as they parted to round up their children.

As if intent to confirm Falcon's fears, the children abandoned all control during the second rounds of the races. Now they were cheering against their opponents even more than supporting their friends. The dispute of moons ago between Spider and Grouch seemed like nothing compared to the bitter heckling of this day's races. In the last heat before the finals of the youngest age group, Herb and Hoop jostled and shoved each other through the final turn. They never made it to the finish line. Herb took the other boy down in a move worthy of the previous wrestling matches. They screamed and clawed at each other while thrashing on the ground. Scorpion charged in and dragged Herb off by his single bushy braid and held back his arms while Hoop threw wild punches to his mid-section. Other children from each of the groups rushed in, led by Ram, Bison, and Clay, respectively. A frenzied brawl broke out. Fortunately, the men kept their heads, wading into the flailing children and separating them until the shouting, cursing, and punching turned to sniffling, whimpering, and crying.

Justin called out for everyone to disperse, ending the races. He stood like a tall pine amidst the squabbling men and children. He refused to hear any complaints. His steadfast certainty convinced the men to abide by his ruling. Hawk marshaled his children and led them off into the woods; Eagle and Sage took their charges to the archery range; Falcon, Coot, and Oak drove the children in the third group back toward the Stone and the center of the village. Eagle glanced back when he heard the despair in Falcon's voice. The man implored the children to return to their campfire at once; he sounded as if he might start to weep himself. Wolf lagged behind, nudging Clay and Tiller to follow the rest. The two boys seemed determined to straggle off—or maybe even defect to one of the other groups. Eagle stopped while Sage continued to herd the children. He caught Wolf's eye, holding him still for a heartbeat. The young man said nothing, as usual, but he shook his head several times before he turned to catch up with Moon and Sky at the back of Falcon's group. Justin followed none of the others —he remained at the site of the brawl until everyone else had departed.

That night, all three camps fell nearly silent. Only a few pairings occurred; most of the children stayed close to the campfires even though nothing was happening, not even the most casual of conversation. The men tended their fires with few words, even to their most trusted companions. Justin sat alone in Falcon's camp. Boys and girls stared at each other across the imaginary boundaries of each camp. Eagle wondered what they were thinking. Then he guessed they must be thinking the same kind of things churning now in his own mind.

How long would it be before fighting actually replaced the games they used to enjoy so much? In the morning, or even the next few days, would anyone be willing to talk to anyone from a different camp? And how long before the three camps transformed into two? Or four?

Indeed, the next morning proved all of Eagle's worst imaginings. The Ruck in each camp ignored the others, going about their business as if none of the others even existed. Eagle regretted this outcome, although his resolve to carry out his plans didn't change one bit. Falcon, however, seemed devastated. Even Oak couldn't convince him to get up and take some of the children out for a hunt. He simply lay on his back staring at the sky.

At the time, Eagle prayed for Falcon to regain himself. Nevertheless, he took advantage of the growing rift among the Ruck, working with Ram and Mace as often as possible over the passing days and nights while each of the three groups isolated themselves. Over and over, the trio measured the descent of the sun against the mountains in coordination with the changing of the Overseer. A whole moon came and went during their efforts while the division of the village began to settle in and feel normal. The groups kept to themselves, mostly, but the passing of time made it easier for the likes of Dove and Joy and Coot to cross the lines and interact, again.

When the men visited the women, Eagle went with enthusiasm. His confidence in his plan grew with each day of practice and fellowship with Mace and Ram. They had become good friends, Eagle realized, much more than simply a duo of young followers. When they weren't practicing, the three of them talked for hours about God and the story of the Ruck and Eagle's ideas about what existed outside of the *tekline*. The past moon had given Eagle much for which to be thankful; indeed, the luck of his three pairings lifted his spirits.

First, he visited Nightingale's yurt. As he passed through the gate with the other men, he heard the voices of a few women and children in the commons just beyond. For a heartbeat, Eagle wondered why they weren't in their yurts. Of course, he realized, these must be the women who had become pregnant and thus wouldn't participate in the visits. He heard laughter and squealing. When the men diverged, heading toward the yurts designated for each of their respective draws, Eagle paused and listened. No, more than that—he closed his eyes and listened intently, hearing their voices and feeling their exuberance, experiencing their togetherness, almost smelling their joy.

It struck him; it felt quite different from the pervading aura over the recent moons in the village. Here, even though Eagle knew there were divisions among the women, he felt a unified presence, rather than fragmented groups. They seemed to laugh and play with one voice. Their glee surrounded him, permeated him, penetrated right through him. He had witnessed it to some degree before. This time it suggested something he had failed to understand. The compound felt like ... like ... he struggled with the thought ... a distant, deep feeling overwhelmed him ... like something they had been missing ... like a *famlee* from the old stories.

Just then, someone spoke his name. He opened his eyes and saw Nightingale glaring at him near the flap of her yurt. Everyone else had disappeared, and the noises from the commons whisked away on the wind as if Nightingale had demanded they disperse. She stood tall and elegant as always, with her arms folded akimbo. She craned her neck at Eagle. He walked toward her, smiling. She huffed and went in before him.

She remained miffed for a while, but Eagle spoke gently, telling her how glad he was to visit her. He stroked her hair with one hand, sweeping slowly around her ear and cupping her strong cheekbones while massaging her long dark legs with his other hand. He described his reasoning for pausing outside her yurt as he kissed her neck and shoulders, telling her how wonderful it felt to hear the women and children playing and enjoying each other. Eagle tried to express his feelings while listening, smelling, feeling, everything in the compound. Nightingale relaxed little by little, with each of Eagle's thoughts revealed to her. Finally, she took his face in her hands and stared deep into his eyes, with the numerous candles illuminating both of them.

"I'm a little surprised, Eagle, that you would understand us so well." Nightingale drew in a deep breath, considering her next words. "Rarely do the men show any understanding of our ways here in the compound."

"I'm learning."

"Perhaps you are."

Their mouths met and they tasted each other, slowly at first. He had been with Nightingale before, but this somehow felt like the first time. He welcomed her advances; indeed she seemed to want to take the lead. Before long she had removed his leggings and straddled him, rubbing herself against his strong member. They continued to kiss and fondle each other for some time as she rubbed her pelvis against him. She moaned and stretched, gripping his biceps while she pulled him inside of her and rolled over until he could raise himself above her. Although they had stopped speaking some time ago, he sensed that she wanted him to lead now. He did, slowly pushing and pulling at first and then increasing his pace until he had spent himself inside of her.

The next night, Eagle went directly to Storm's yurt. Because he had insulted her those few moons ago, Eagle intended to make amends tonight. Even though he heard the voices again in the commons, and he wanted to stop and listen, he resisted. It became more difficult when he recognized Rose's melodious laughter. Eagle slowed his pace to let the laughter fill him before he passed through the yurt flap. Storm awaited within, having lit only a few candles. He found her already completely undressed, kneeling on the *ven* skins and blankets.

For a heartbeat, Eagle wasn't sure if that meant she was eager to be with him, or eager to get it over with. It wouldn't matter, he told himself, as long as he pleased her. Suddenly, he spoke without even thinking of his words.

"Storm, I know you favor Hawk. I respect your choice. But tonight, only you and I exist. I come here to please you, if you desire it."

Storm seemed only slightly surprised. Clearly, his words

weren't quite what she expected. Yet, she seemed willing to accept those words and their meaning. She extended her hand and Eagle took it, dropping to his knees. She rose from her haunches and they kissed, not with the same feeling he and Nightingale had, but passionately still. They embraced, leaning against each other while still on their knees. As they swayed and exchanged delicate kisses, Eagle let his hands roam across her pale back and buttocks, sometimes running his fingers through her short red hair. She pushed him away long enough to pull off his tunic and she ran her hands over his chest, back, and shoulders. He caressed her breasts, and she cooed. He squeezed a little harder, pinching her hardening nipples. She gasped and faltered, leaning backwards. Eagle gently laid her down and kissed her everywhere while she twisted and shuddered. He stopped between her legs and began to lick and suck with determination. She grabbed his head with both hands and rocked and swayed and thrashed. Her body convulsed and she let out a long moan, which reminded Eagle of the ominous wind sweeping through the valley ahead of a torrential rainstorm.

When she had recovered, she looked up at Eagle, who again knelt before her. She rose up and tugged at his leggings. He stood, removing them, and she lay back again, waiting for him. He entered her and thrust over and over until her gale-like moan returned and they climaxed together. They parted, but cuddled until Eagle drifted off, awakening later to find her hovering over him, half-dressed in her loose tunic.

"Nightingale told me to expect a different Eagle. I didn't know what to think, but I was willing to find out. You have become a real man." She put her fingers to his lips as he started to speak. "No, don't ruin this. I still support Hawk. I can't agree with your actions, as I have heard them. But, if you truly respect my choice, I can respect yours. Sleep and leave in the morning." She rose and disappeared behind the yurt's cloth divider, settling in with her young children.

Eagle awoke with the sun and left as Storm had asked.

When he returned for the third night, he entered the compound with a big smile and headed to Ruby's yurt. As in the previous moon, they enjoyed each other's company, physically, mentally, spiritually. They talked and loved throughout the night. When Eagle left the compound the next morning, something occurred to him. He felt more comfortable with Ruby than any other woman—even more than Rose. His heart burned for Rose; he thought about her all too often, he yearned for her, and yet he felt he would never have her as he wished. Those thoughts made him feel strange sometimes—even tormented. With Ruby, it always seemed like they had been together the day before. They always picked up where they had left off, enjoyed each other, and then moved on again.

After Eagle returned to the village, he engaged again in his plans without any delay. He traveled with Mace and Ram nearly every day; they continued to practice so often that they could now predict the changing of the Overseer within a few dozen heartbeats. A half-moon later, they sat together in the hills, Eagle telling them more about his God before they recounted the plan for Eagle's escape. Ram insisted that they try a real test—he volunteered to make the leap. He said he knew God was on their side.

"It's the only way we'll ever know for sure if it can be done," he said.

"And if you fail, our plans are ruined," Eagle countered.

"If we wait for you to try and it fails, what's the *fugging* difference?" Ram's emphasis carried in the woods. Eagle rolled his eyes and Mace's glance darted all around.

"Ram ... keep your voice down ..." Eagle said, "I know how you feel. You must trust me."

"Yeah, Ram," Mace added softly, "what's the *fugging* difference how we try to test it if everyone hears you calling out all of Eagle's plans?"

Ram balled up his fist, leaning forward. "Well, then, maybe you should stop telling your girl everything we do out here."

Now Mace leaned forward, snarling. Eagle held him back.

"This isn't helping," Eagle said. "You both swore to follow my plans. If you want to do it your way, go off and form your own camp. Otherwise, do it my way."

Ram huffed. "Well, what are we going to do?"

"We'll continue as we have, until I leave to visit the women. Each night, I will pretend to make the leap. We'll measure the sun, and you'll signal when you think it is time. We'll see how close we can get, without missing it. If we can get within one dozen heartbeats, we'll know we're sharp enough to do it for real. We won't have to guess, I'll just have to be close enough to the flash to see your signal, and to spring in time."

"That sounds hard," Mace said.

"*Fug.* Do you think?" Ram said. Mace just turned his head.

"We can do it. We're close already. Practicing the whole thing is best, now. It will be like shooting at the range—the more we do it, the better we'll get."

The brothers nodded.

They practiced for seven nights in a row. Finally, Mace counted nine heartbeats between the jump and the flash. Later that night around the fire, Eagle realized it was only one more night before the visit to the women. He slept fitfully, waking up after numerous dreams about Sprout and the burning *tekline*, or children tearing at each other's flesh and hair, or Hawk visiting with Lotus, Rose, and Honey, all at the same time. Finally, Eagle fell into a restful sleep until awakening to a blinding sun and the piercing sound of Chase screaming at him to get up.

7

"What? What is it?" Eagle's body seemed to respond before his mind could comprehend. He sprang to his feet, spun around, and looked for his bow.

"He's hurt bad, Eagle! Hurry! Come on!" Chase tugged at his leggings and took off running. Eagle followed, his body reacting, his mind wishing he knew why. She ran faster than the *ven*, it seemed. Eagle fixed his attention on her multiple dark braids whipping around her head as she ran. He barely kept pace; Chase sped into the foothills, picking her way around the rocks and ditches while he shook the remaining fog of sleep from his mind.

Chase turned and leapt onto a clear, short, jagged plateau. Eagle slowed when she stopped and then ducked out of his line of sight. He saw Fish on her knees, bawling. She looked like she had been rolling around in filth. Eagle had never seen her cry like that before—at worst she had sniffled and choked back a few tears, like when she dropped a toasty piece of *ven* in the dirt at the feast. A cloud of dust lingered all about; a few small rocks tumbled down a dusty slope to his left.

Fug, Eagle thought. A landslide.

He leapt as Chase had, landing just near Fish, who held her face in her hands, her tears mingling with grime and leaving smudges all over her head and in her hair. Eagle knelt by her and gave her a hug as he looked her over. She seemed unhurt —no blood, no breaks. Her heaving sobs now burst into wails.

She pointed a quivering finger. Eagle saw Chase hovering over a smaller child's twisted legs amidst a haze of dust and pile of rubble.

Eagle knew it was Badger. He wasn't sure whether he might have heard Chase say his name when she woke him, or if he recognized the boy's legs, or it was only natural, somehow, for Fish and Badger to be out digging on the hill this sunny morning. He hoped to God he was wrong, but when he moved up alongside Chase his hopes were crushed just like the boy's legs.

He motioned for Chase to back off. The body was half-buried under loose earth and rubble. Eagle could see Badger's chin and nose. He cleared away a few small rocks and debris. Badger was bleeding over one ear, although his head looked okay. Eagle craned his own ear to the boy's nose and mouth. Nothing. Carefully, Eagle swept away more of the rubble. Badger's trunk twisted too far. His feet pointed the wrong way.

Eagle hung his head. He heard Chase gasp over his shoulder. Fish lost what little control she had left, screaming wordlessly one moment and weeping the next. Eagle asked Chase to take the little girl back down to the village, to his yurt—and to stay there with her. He helped raise Fish to her feet and asked her to go with Chase—saying he would take care of Badger for her.

By the time Eagle had lifted the boy's broken body into his arms, others were scurrying up the mountain. He saw that some had turned back with Chase and Fish. But Willow and Thrush kept coming. Eagle didn't want his sister to see their youngest brother this way, but she gave him no opportunity to shield her from it. Like Fish, she fell to her knees and sobbed. Eagle asked her to rise and follow him down. Thrush helped her. They all descended silently.

They burned Badger later that day and before the draw for the women. Eagle cried with his brothers and sisters as they all huddled together near the pyre. Ox and Clay joined Archer, Willow and Eagle. Fish clung to Eagle, weeping with the others during the ceremony. She never left his side, not from the moment he joined her in his yurt to calm her down, until the men went off to determine the visitation draw. Others stayed close to Eagle and his siblings, especially Ash, Dreamer, and Fly. The whole village gathered; the boundaries seemed to melt for a little while. Justin spoke, comforting them with memories of the little boy.

Eagle's mind churned as he watched his tiny brother incinerated. He had—they all had—experienced the death of friends and siblings. The reality of The Hunt made it an expected event every three moons, or four moons during the long summer. He wondered how they had gotten so used to that, while an accident like Badger's seemed so unreal, so impossible and difficult to understand. He talked to God in his thoughts; he even asked aloud "why this would happen to my brother? What good would come out of it?" At least a death in The Hunt meant something. But this?

The men left Eagle alone with his thoughts during the draw. They carried on their business while he stood distracted nearby; he couldn't even think of it just then. When Sage came to tell the results, he welled-up once again. Eagle would visit neither his mother nor his sister; someone else would have to tell them the news. Instead, he would have to deal with Lotus, Mantis, and Nightingale.

His mood deepened when the men began to gather that night for the walk to the compound. Eagle's mind churned again, proposing impossible options as if he had a choice in the matter. He thought of charging through the gate when Honey opened it, wrapping her in his arms and telling her the horrible news. Actually, he had thought about jumping the compound wall several times during the day, defying all of the Overlords' rules about the separation of the men and women. Somehow, he mustered the strength to avoid such a mistake, even after the draw. Now, as they approached the gate, the urge re-surfaced and he realized that he hadn't even considered who would be with his mother that night. He couldn't think clearly; he couldn't figure it out now, and Sage had avoided communicating that fact. All he wanted was the comfort of his mother's arms and the chance to tell her what had happened. He whispered his feelings and confusion to Sage.

"No, my friend. You must not." Sage pulled him by the arm; they slowed behind the others. Although Falcon and Mountain took notice, they continued onward.

"Who's going to tell her?" Eagle winced, swallowing hard.

"We're all men here, Eagle." Sage pulled back again, letting a little distance pass between them and the other visitors. "We all grieve for the loss of a child. We all know the pain and uncertainty a mother must endure, waiting for news from the village."

Eagle stopped. He clenched his teeth, trying to count and sort the men and women. He couldn't manage it. "Who is it, Sage?"

"Hawk will do what is right, Eagle. You must let him."

"Hawk?" Eagle's heart leapt into his throat.

"He will do what is right. And you must do your duty. Lotus awaits."

Suddenly, Eagle found himself passing into the compound with Sage. The others were gone. Sage closed the gate and started off to Storm's yurt. He stopped after a few steps, realizing that Eagle hadn't moved at all. Grasping his friend's arm, Sage pulled Eagle across the commons. When they approached Lotus' yurt, they were hit by the fumes from a pungent brew wafting from a large stone bowl over a fire just outside her flap. Eagle shook his head, as if to shake off the odor. He inhaled deeply, nevertheless. It made him think of a trek through the woods just after a hard rain. Like a slap to the face, it made him remember the promises he had made to himself. To treat all the women with respect. To do his duty with enthusiasm.

"Go in, my friend," Sage said. He opened the flap for his friend and gave a little push. Eagle ducked through.

He found Lotus sitting with her legs tucked to one side, naked except for a thin piece of cloth tied around her hips. Two long candles on ceramic holders rested just behind her on each side. Her straight, dark hair fell about her face, keeping it in shadow. She beckoned him to sit to her left. He obeyed. He didn't know what else to do, and he couldn't speak just then. He was determined not to fail, especially with Lotus, no matter how painful his thoughts became.

She took his hand in hers. She held it for a number of heartbeats while he closed his eyes. He felt tears coming again. Still holding his hand, Lotus brushed the drops from his cheek with the back of her hand and pulled herself to her knees. She reached for a small wooden cup with her free hand and finally released his. He opened his eyes, and through the blur of slow, intermittent tears he saw Lotus squeeze through the flap. The brew's odor rushed into the yurt and once again Eagle breathed deeply, as if compelled by it. Soon, she returned with a filled cup. She offered it in both hands as she knelt again, this time facing him, and he accepted it in both hands.

"Drink, Eagle. Drink it all," she commanded.

He took a gulp. It tasted much like it smelled, sort of musty, earthy, and damp. He gulped again, turning the cup upside down and pouring the liquid into his mouth. His eyes were clearing. He took in the slender curves of Lotus's waist and torso when she took the cup back from him. She inspected it to make sure he had imbibed it all. She sniffed at it herself and craned her neck. She ran a finger around the rim and delicately licked the wet film from it. He watched, involuntarily licking his own lips. Her still-parted lips allowed a thin smile, not all like the mocking smirk she gave him the last moon from across the compound. Lotus slinked back out of the yurt and returned with another cup of the brew, kneeling in front of him again.

When she handed it back to him, she slid her hands down his chest, caressing his long muscles. One hand strayed to his thigh as he sipped, enjoying the flavor this time. She leaned over and gently kissed his neck and cheek.

Eagle welcomed her lead. It was much different than the last time he visited her yurt. She seemed interested in his presence, rather than simply obliged by it. She was no less headstrong, certainly, but everything else about her was different. He relaxed as her hands and lips continued to explore him. The day's tortuous thoughts and memories began to subside. He wondered how much it had to do with the brew. And he wondered why she gave it to him this time—she hadn't before. However unwillingly, his mind began to let go of his troubles, it seemed, until a sharp thought pierced through the growing sense of serenity.

She knew.

He started to voice that thought, but Lotus stopped him by engaging his mouth with hers, running her tongue around the soft underside of his lips. The thought he had wanted to voice melted away. His mind swirled. It felt like ... like ... happiness.

Lotus whispered to him, momentarily pulling her mouth away. "Later we talk. Now, we love." She continued to kiss and caress. He found no will to protest. Each touch felt more wondrous, more titillating, more incredible. He wasn't sure how, but she had stripped off all his garments and then straddled him. She rode him briefly, then rolled to her side and pulled him on top of her. Waves of strangeness rolled over him. He felt wonderful and weird at the same time. For a heartbeat, he thought he was with Rose, but when he opened his eyes to see his beloved, he was staring into Lotus' dark, narrow eyes. He didn't feel ashamed or disturbed by that revelation. The extraordinary waves continued as he thrust into her again and again, for long how he couldn't tell. Finally, he released, and it seemed like she had also, as she moaned, groaned, and squirmed underneath him. He collapsed on top of her, but soon found himself lying on his back alongside her, as if a dream had abruptly ended.

"Lotus," he said after many heartbeats, breaking the sounds of the valley's night, "thank you. I will never forget your kindness tonight."

She laughed. He heard a verge of the mocking tone he had come to expect, and yet it didn't materialize. It sounded more like sincere playfulness or maybe even self-reflection. "Eagle, I should be thanking you."

"I don't understand."

She laughed again, this time softer and contemplative. "It's not easy for the mothers, not even for me, wondering every moon about what is happening to their children in the village. I'm grateful for the way you have taken Dreamer and Fish under your wing these last two winters. Sometimes I pretend not to care, or the Ruck assume I am aloof, but those children are still my flesh and blood. I know you saved Dreamer's life at least once and I can sense he adores you. And Fish, well, our *gramma* has told me how you speak of her and I know she remained close to Badger, even after they left the compound."

Eagle opened his mouth to respond. He found no words. Everything about this visit continued to surprise him. His mind seemed to float away from him for a moment—the lingering effects of the brew, he guessed. Lotus propped herself on one elbow and stared into his eyes.

"I could see it in your eyes earlier—you guessed I knew about Badger. We mothers share much with each other. More than you can imagine. Honey wasted no time in telling me what happened. She came to me right after old Coot whispered the news to her when he came with the Black One to announce the draw."

"She asked you to help me ..."

"She didn't need to ask."

Eagle closed his eyes again. He felt her warm hand stroking his cheek. His mind was starting to clear. Not just from the effects of the brew, but from all the horrible events of the day. Another tear escaped and again Lotus swept it away.

"I thought ..." Eagle faltered.

"That I was against you, or at least not with you. No. It's important that I stay in between, just as Falcon and Coot have done. You see, Eagle, both of our ways are the old ways. I understand what you are doing, even if my methods differ."

Eagle opened his eyes and stared into hers. He couldn't help but believe her.

"I want the Ruck to go on," she continued. "But not as slaves to the Overlords."

"I almost ruined everything tonight," he confessed. "I thought to rush off to my mother—*fug* the rules of the visitation, that's what I was thinking."

"Fortunately, the Goddess was looking after us. Coot's message gave me enough time to prepare my potion for you, and your friend Sage delivered you here in time. It's helped, hasn't it?"

Eagle could only nod. He would have thanked God for it, and yet here was Lotus thanking her Goddess.

"You should sleep now, Eagle. Sleep and dream well."

He did both. When he awoke, Lotus offered him the wooden cup along with his skins. He hesitated, and she laughed, the mocking edge returning like it was connected to the rising of the morning sun.

"It's just water. Trust me."

He felt foolish again in her presence, although he now understood it wasn't because she thought him a fool. Rather, because she seemed to know so much more about everything than he did. He gulped the water, tugged on his clothing, and gave her a quick kiss before he left the yurt. She laughed again, smacking his backside on the way out.

Sage was waiting for him near the gate. Eagles paused, looking for Honey or Rose, seeing neither. He joined his friend. They spent the entire day together on the most remote hillside they could find. They didn't talk much at all, not once Eagle had assured Sage he would be okay.

As the sun set, he almost looked forward to his visit with

Mantis. After the encounter with Lotus, anything was possible, he thought.

That was until he entered her yurt, which felt cold and un-inviting, much different than the lambent feeling he had last night with Lotus. Mantis waited for him in the dark, with no candles, and apparently her children were fast asleep. Before Eagle could speak, she said she was sorry to hear about Badger; she said it was an awful way to die. Eagle agreed and they barely spoke another word the rest of the night. When Eagle sat down next to her, she immediately took off her leggings, leaving her top skins on and laying down on her back. They did their duty, and Eagle made sure to give it his best effort des-pite her staid preamble. No matter what he tried, she seemed to do her best to remain unmoved. After he had delivered his seed, he felt like he had just completed gathering firewood for another man's fire. He left as soon as he awoke in the morn-ing, a drizzling rain greeting him outside the yurt. No one was out here yet, it appeared, so he hastily left the compound and wandered around the valley for a while before settling in at his new spot on the bluff for the rest of the day. Ram and Mace found him there early in the afternoon. The sputtering rain had cleared by then, and they said they just felt like visiting the spot. They claimed they didn't expect him to be there. Eagle said it didn't matter. He told them all their plans would still take place after The Hunt. Both boys seemed relieved to hear it. They left him alone again before long.

He grieved for his brother the rest of the day. He cried again, stared out over the valley and mumbled to God. His pain was starting to subside, or at least it had dulled. He thought about The Hunt and realized that others would be losing their sib-lings, too. He needed to be strong in order to carry out his plans. The visit by Ram and Mace reminded him of that. He was glad they had come.

When he arrived at Nightingale's, she greeted him imme-diately, stooping at the flap, putting her finger to her lips and motioning to the yurt's divider. Eagle understood—the children were probably newly asleep. Several candles burned in her yurt and she was half-dressed, having already shed her top skins. She sat and beckoned him to join her. She blew out a few of the candles, leaving a soft glow.

She whispered. "I'm so sorry to hear about Badger ... are you okay?" Her melodious voice soothed him even in hushed tones.

"I will be," Eagle answered. "It's still too soon, you know. The Ruck must go on."

Nightingale smiled, her teeth gleaming compared to her brown skin and dark lips. "That's why we're here tonight, after all, isn't it?"

"Yes, and I have no intention of letting you down." Eagle reached out and cupped her cheek. Nightingale leaned in toward him and they kissed, nibbled, and fondled each other for a little while, trying to be quiet. She pulled away after a time, peering behind the divider and returning with a wink. They made love just once that night, but they didn't rush. Afterwards, they talked about the smallest of things until she began to drift off. Eagle relaxed and followed her to slumber before long. They slept until Nightingale's three children roused them with tugs and unapologetic whines. He gave her a goodbye kiss on the cheek before he left. He saw Mountain and Falcon leaving together and he caught up with them just outside the gate. None of them talked on the way back to the village. They had work to do that morning—preparing for the exchange of at least one girl who would become a woman and the children who would join the village—and none of them seemed inclined to talk about those things just yet. Of course, The Hunt itself loomed, just one day away.

◆ ◆ ◆

When the men gathered, Eagle realized nothing would be simple anymore. Their caucus made him wonder what would happen to the village after he escaped. Still, every moment made him more certain of what he must do.

First, the men had to determine which girl should go to the women. Eagle had assumed it would be Star, as they had already considered her seriously the last time when Shrew was chosen. But Hawk declared that Maize should go instead, or that neither girl should go at this time. That surprised everyone but Mountain, who, while towering quietly behind him, nodded his agreement with Hawk. Eagle threw up his arms and started to protest. Sage pulled him back. Justin and Coot calmly intervened, asking Hawk to explain his reasons.

His words were as transparent as worn out *ven* hide. Eagle stopped listening almost immediately. Everyone knew there was no good reason for Maize to go before Star, who was one winter older. When it was obvious that only Mountain supported the idea of sending Maize instead of Star, Hawk suggested that they should wait until the next Hunt to send another girl. Even Wolf voiced disagreement. With some of the women now pregnant, and others sure to follow, it made sense to send another girl right now. Eagle stewed as Hawk tried to garner support for sending both of the girls after none of the neutral men supported his push for Maize or neither. Eagle tried to pull away from Sage, but his friend kept a tight grip on him, whispering, "Eagle, he is only trying to provoke you."

"It's working. I'd like to rip out his tongue." He didn't intend to be heard, but he said it loud enough for Wolf and Falcon (and maybe everyone) to notice.

Justin let it go no farther. "Hawk, we have heard your reasons. It seems clear to me; most of the men agree that sending Star is our best choice right now. I see no reason to debate this further. Nor do I see any reason why Star should not be our next choice."

Hawk merely shrugged his acquiescence, as if he expected this result from the beginning. And it hit Eagle like a blow to the head—that must have been Hawk's goal anyway. Now Maize was almost assured to be next, even though Ash was also older. Surely, Hawk knew of the divisions in the compound; he strove to tip the balance of power both in the village and the compound—or at least to maintain the balance. He was looking farther ahead than Eagle in that regard, although his scope was limited to their imprisonment in the valley. Eagle's resolve had never been stronger; he must escape and prove his way. Everything else was just talk.

Next, the men began the task of the draw for The Hunt. Justin began per the custom, pouring the multi-colored stones from the ceremonial pouch, when Hawk interrupted again.

"I propose a change to the rules of the draw," he said. "I see no reason why Sage should be excluded." He held up his hand when Coot began to state what they all knew: it was the Ruck way to keep Sage, Justin, and Coot from all draws except the one that came just before winter. All the men exchanged glances while Hawk stood firm. They silently assented to let him state his proposal.

"Coot, I know the Ruck ways, but these times are different. Is there anyone who would debate that?"

No one spoke.

Hawk turned his attention from Coot, slowly looking around and addressing everyone. "Certainly, it is wise to keep Justin and Coot from the draw. We have lost a Justin too recently. And Coot's long memory is needed in the village. Sage, while wise himself, hasn't been chosen since he was named. And clearly, he has decided to support Eagle, while Justin and Coot have remained neutral."

The men stirred. Of course, they all knew exactly what Hawk meant. Until now, the men had rarely spoken so openly of the divisions between them when they had all assembled for any of the village business. Yes, the men had stared at each other from across the campfire; they had competed with each other to cultivate loyalty and allegiance—indeed wrestling with each other in many different ways without speaking their truths so bluntly. Perhaps the time for plain talk had arrived, Eagle thought.

"Protecting Sage means we are choosing Eagle's view of

leadership in the village. It's possible that both Mountain and I are chosen, and that we both die in The Hunt, while protecting the children. I would certainly trade my life for any of them. Everyone knows this. And so would Mountain, and so would every man here, I expect." Mountain nodded with a force that surprised Eagle, a near-outburst for the tall man. "If both of us perished," Hawk continued, "it would leave no men to lead the children who have chosen to follow us." He turned, reaching up to place a hand on Mountain's shoulder. "I believe it would be a terrible mistake for the Ruck. I've said it before, I believe Eagle's ideas will lead us to ruin. If the draw is fair, and that happens, so be it. As it stands, the odds are stacked against my way, which I believe is the only way, the necessary way, for the Ruck to go on."

Hawk paused, allowing the men to consider his words. Eagle scanned the men's faces; clearly, the three who had made the effort to remain neutral were considering Hawk's message. Eagle couldn't help but admire the man for a moment—perhaps Hawk did still have something to teach him.

Hawk continued. "I speak to you from my heart, with no hidden meaning. I ask you to discuss this like men."

For a few heartbeats, each man digested Hawk's words.

"Hawk is right," Eagle said. "It pains me to say it, but he is right ... in this case. Sooner or later, the rest of you will have to choose whether to support one of us, or to oppose both of us. Let's face it; keeping Sage from the draw complicates all of this. Truly, keeping any of us from the draw complicates all of this. Still, it is Justin's role to remain neutral and I trust him to do that no matter what. And Coot, well, I would propose he never enters the draw, but then, why have a draw? Perhaps, we could volunteer."

The men wouldn't hear of this: they all grumbled, shook their heads, and flatly said "no." Eagle raised his hand just like Hawk had.

"Of course not," Eagle said. "We would all volunteer, wouldn't we? Coot, isn't that why we have a draw in the first place?"

Coot smiled. "Yes, it is true, Eagle. Long ago the men realized that volunteering would lead to the death of the Ruck. Too many men would die, and no one would be left to lead the children. And certainly, we can't have the children volunteering. The draw was the only solution. The Black One tells us only to send twelve of the Ruck. Our fathers and their fathers and their fathers established the draw to ensure that the Ruck go on."

Sage broke in. "And they kept a few men from the draw as often as possible, knowing some of us would need to grow older for the Ruck to go on. They didn't think it wise to exclude anyone, always. And I agree." He laughed and shook his head. "I should think it pains me even more than Eagle, as my stone will go into the pouch today, but I also agree with Hawk."

The rest of the men nodded, chuckling or sighing despite themselves and the gravity of the situation. Only Falcon disagreed.

"It seems unwise to me," he said, "to change our custom at a time of strife. Still, I won't stand in the way of this change, if everyone else believes it is best. If Sage is chosen, the children will need an explanation. Or perhaps we will need to explain the change anyway, as his stone may be chosen next time, or sometime other than the winter's Hunt."

Justin spoke. "Falcon speaks well. My judgment is this: we will add Sage's name to the draw today. And I will take care of the explanation to the children ... whether today or another time."

It was settled. As the stones were chosen, Eagle asked God to keep Sage's stone in the pouch, pulling his own instead. Neither happened, and he wondered what message God was sending to him when Hawk and Mountain were chosen from the men—and Bison, Archer, Fox, Tanner, Dreamer, Red, Moon, Sky, Copperhead, and Rachel were chosen from the children's stones.

The draw bothered him until well after Moth and Star exchanged places in the compound and the village. A nagging feeling came over him when he sat by his fire, watching Mountain and Hawk retire to Hawk's yurt. Even later in the evening, while he sat with Sage and spoke with the children who came to him for comfort before turning in for the long night, he felt this draw was some kind of a sign. He couldn't decipher the message; his uneasy feeling grew stronger even while the meaning became more cryptic. As usual, he slept uneasily before The Hunt, and his dreams about escape all ended abruptly, with the memory of Lotus' brew snaking into his nose.

A full day passed after the chosen twelve walked into the woods the morning of The Hunt. A full day without their return. Many of the villagers still slept, or were doing their best to get some sleep, when the three horn blasts sounded the second evening.

Eagle had left his yurt at daybreak, bleary-eyed and still beleaguered by the unshakeable feeling of impending misfortune. He went to the fields and found Tiller there, weeding the growing rows of *veg*. He offered to help, and the boy accepte. It surprised Eagle, as Tiller agreed without his usual hesitancy. Eagle noticed much of the *veg* would be ready for harvest before long, and indeed that some of it had already been picked or uprooted by the boy—and probably other young helpers. Eagle found himself wishing he had spent a little more time in the fields.

After the horn blasts, which came as the sun began its descent, all of the Ruck came out and gathered in the three separate groups. Justin and Coot huddled together, preparing for the ceremonies to come—the first for Justin since being named after the last Hunt. The children stuck close to friends, awaiting and hoping for the return of their brothers and sisters. Suddenly, it struck Eagle: the brothers and sisters who had chosen to separate into different camps would soon be mourning together for a dead Ruck sibling. Or would they, he wondered? Had things changed so much that even this would be different? The time between Hunts, from the spring to the beginning of this temperate summer, had changed them all in ways he would never have guessed back when he was called Sparrow. He couldn't be sure of anything but his own plans.

The first shouts and exclamations answered that question. Axe proclaimed the return of Red and Copperhead. Children from Hawk's and Falcon's camps went rushing out to greet them together. There were hugs and tears in abundance, and the boundaries seemed be forgotten as the two worn-out, red-haired children were mobbed by the villagers. Snow and Fern clung to their sister, Copperhead, while Axe stood nearby grinning like he had just won a wrestling match but still trying to seem above it all as he stood next to Shadow. Dove and Nardo slapped each other on the back as they welcomed the return of their brother Red, laughing nervously about how his wild, uncut hair was even more matted and dirty than usual. They were soon joined by Wolf, their oldest brother, and Ash, their oldest sister, as well as some of Red's friends from Hawk's group, including Iris, Fisher, and Peacock.

The commotion was quickly rekindled when Tanner emerged from the woods. She looked completely beaten, Eagle thought, and his guess was confirmed when she collapsed in the arms of Potter, her brother, as he ran to greet her. It took some of the enthusiasm out of the crowd. Their elation would have waned soon anyway, Eagle knew, when the tension grew as more of the Ruck returned or failed to return.

Eagle's heart leapt despite all of that when Dreamer straggled from the woods not far behind Tanner. Fish squealed like she used to moons-ago during Eagle's stories. She ran ahead of Eagle as he went to greet the boy. Eagle quickly caught up to Fish, and they both hugged Dreamer with all their might. It was the first time since Badger's death that Eagle had seen Fish smile. Dreamer seemed confused by their greeting; incredibly, he appeared to have been daydreaming even at a time like this. Eagle remembered the last Hunt for which he himself was chosen, when he was still called Sparrow and had saved Dreamer. He decided this son of Lotus had some special charm that kept him from harm no matter how careless he was.

A short pause brought them all down—and for good, because the next to emerge from the woods was the Black One. It seemed like forever as it walked past them all without the slightest recognition of its dreadful effect, heading directly toward Coot and Justin. Eagle wasn't sure what happened when the two men huddled with the Overseer because it turned out Hawk followed closely behind him with the beautiful black-haired Rachel and the young girl Sky holding his hands. Eagle had thought to observe the meeting with the Black One, but his heart sank when he saw those three returning. All he could think of was Archer, who was still among those yet to return.

He wasn't alone in his calculation; the rest of the Ruck had also begun to agonize over the remaining odds. Mountain, Fox, Archer, Bison, and Moon still hadn't returned yet. Men and children from every camp wore worried faces, scuffling and murmuring while they waited and wondered. For uncounted anxious heartbeats, it seemed to Eagle like the village was whole again.

Coot and Justin moved to the circle while the Black One retreated into the woods. A few of the waiting Ruck took notice, and soon everyone had gathered around with backward glances towards the woods as inevitable as the still rising sun. Many of the children started to cry and the men now displayed pained and puzzled faces, as never had so many been taken at once. Eagle wondered if it were possible that five of the Ruck had died during The Hunt.

The answer was no, for Archer and Bison appeared at the edge of the woods. They slowly approached the others, joining the groups of brothers and sisters around the circle. Eagle tried to swallow the lump in his throat. His attempt only seemed to force out the tears welling up in his eyes. He held out his arm as Archer came near. He pulled her to his breast, her head falling on his shoulder as if she lacked the strength to hold it up herself. Bison moved directly toward Hawk's side; Shadow fell back a step and patted his leader on the shoulder while Fisher came to give him a hug.

Everyone looked around madly, still bewildered and unsure whether any of the remaining three would return. Soon, when Justin made his solemn walk to the Stone, the muted lament began among the brothers and sisters of Mountain, Fox, and Moon.

Justin stepped up. "We have lost three of our brothers and sisters today. They gave their lives so the Ruck would go on. We will thank them, grieve for them, and we will remember their names.

"Mountain was a man of few words, as strong and resolute as the name the Justin-before gave him. He cared deeply about all the children. During the draw, he told all of the men he would give his life to save every child he could, so the Ruck would go on. None of us doubted him. We all knew Mountain would watch over us for all his days, weathering any force that tried to wear him down." Justin paused, with a subtle nod to Hawk.

"Fox captivated all of us. She had a way of convincing us to try things we might not have tried on our own. She was quick, beautiful, and cunning. I remember a time not long after she joined the village, in one of the races: I saw her smiling as she came around the final turn at the edge of the pack, when she burst from the group and sprinted to victory. And Moon, he was dear to many of us. He often helped to care for the children who joined the village, teaching them about our ways and making them feel like they had always been here. His love made us glow like the moon that gives us light through the dark of night.

"We will miss all three of them. We will remember their names."

Justin turned slowly, casting his gaze over the assembly. Brothers, sisters and friends wept aloud now. Eagle watched the other children of Diamond mourning the loss of their third sibling in the last three Hunts, this time their eldest brother, Mountain. Eagle thought of Badger and tears came to his eyes again. Everyone in Hawk's group seemed devastated. Eagle realized the loss of Mountain and Fox meant that two of Hawk's strongest supporters were gone. Fox had become a leader among the young girls, and many of them had gone to Hawk because of her. While Eagle never welcomed the death of children or strong men, it occurred to him that these deaths would help his fight against Hawk. He felt ashamed for the thought. He also felt repentance because the thought gave him no pleasure. In fact, it pulled more tears from his eyes, and he found himself grieving for them as if they were his own siblings.

Eagle's eyes found Sky in the arms of Falcon, wailing like Eagle had never witnessed. Everyone knew that Moon adored Sky, but she had remained aloof—not mean or rude, in fact, they were seen together a lot—until now, when she allowed her feelings to show. Nearby, Oak and Herb huddled with Joy and Chase, all sons and daughters of the Lilly-before, trying to comfort each other for the loss of Moon. Rock and Brute left Hawk's group and joined Oak and the others. As brief as it might be, the ceremonies after The Hunt reminded them that, truly, it was one village, not three. Indeed, Mountain's brothers and sisters had stayed close together since the Black One's appearance. Earnest had left Eagle's group to commiserate with Bison and Fisher. And Joy had joined Oak, Herb, and Chase, exchanging hugs with Rock and Brute who left Hawk's group after comforting the friends of Fox.

Eagle looked back to Justin. The man swallowed back his own tears, trying to stay composed for the rest of their ceremony. He waited longer at this point than the Justin-before usually did. This Justin was still young, Eagle reminded himself, but in just three moons he had proven Coot's naming as a wise and meaningful decision for the Ruck. His words had weight, compassion and sincerity; his judgments so far had demonstrated great insight. Eagle glanced away; he didn't want to stare at the young man. He looked back to Falcon's group and saw the young girl Moth, daughter of Nightingale, cowering behind Spider. How strange it must be to join the village at such a time. He couldn't remember his own first experience.

Finally, Justin spoke again. "We will now honor the heroes of The Hunt. Who wishes to step forward?" The groups of grievers began to disperse, taking new positions at the edge of the circle. Two children stepped forward: Sky, quivering and wiping tears from her cheeks, and Red, whose wild look seemed to deny the loss of his older brother.

"Step up and speak your truth, Sky and Red." Justin stepped backward off the Stone, opening his arms and welcoming them.

Sky, older by one winter, approached first. She sobbed in between words and phrases. "I ... I ... there were ... two heroes, today. One who returned, one who ..." she broke down for a few heartbeats then gathered herself as Justin moved alongside her. She waved him off. "I'm okay ... Mountain helped us all ... during ... He, um, he moved around, checking on us. He told us to scream for him, if we were in trouble. Moon and I ... we ... they were after us. We screamed ..." Sky's sobbing increased; she gulped in lung-fulls of air, and her eyes were closed. She pushed on. "Mountain came out of nowhere ... he tried to save us. He attacked ... I mean, he jumped on it. He told us ... to run. I heard him scream when I ran ... I've never ... heard him ... I got away ... I looked for Moon, but ..." And that was all she could muster. Justin scooped her into his arms and carried her back to Falcon.

As Justin returned to his stance just behind the Stone, Red approached. The boy was crying now, too. It was hard to tell, because his red hair fell around his face, but Eagle could hear his sobs. Sky's speech had affected everyone.

"It was Tanner," he started, "who saved me." He paused again and took deep breaths. The boy's will proved incredibly strong, Eagle thought. He managed to stop crying before he continued. "She, um, she stayed near me all night. Um, she, she, she told me what to do. She said we would be okay. Early in the morning, they chased us. I was sleepy, I couldn't, uh, I was too sleepy. I couldn't run. A lightning bolt hit a tree ... she picked me up and carried me. I don't know how, but, um, she went faster ... the lightning bolts got far away. She dropped me ... and fell. I was ... scared, until Copperhead found us ... and we heard the horn. Tanner told us to come back, that she would, um, follow us." Red shrugged and stepped down. Justin patted him on the back before the boy ran back to Hawk.

Justin stepped up again. "It is the law. Some of the Ruck must die so the rest can live. We thank our heroes, and those who died for us. We honor them."

Everyone knelt and cupped both hands over their chests, fingers overlapped. They were silent for ten heartbeats, and then they rose.

"The Ruck go on," Justin announced. "Now, we remember our names. Heather, step up. Iris, step up. Shrub, step up."

The three children broke away from their friends. Iris and Shrub seemed proud to step inside the Circle. They stood side-by-side, emerging together from Hawk's group. Iris giggled, whispering to Shrub and taking his hand. Heather entered reluctantly, casting her gaze to the ground, her short-cropped and tangled brown hair looking like a *ven*-skin cap and her necklace of purple flowers shining against the dark hues of her vest. Eagle glanced at Archer, remembering when he had seen his sister teaching the girl how to craft arrow flights during the spring moons.

"Each of these children have lived in the village for a few winters, and each has been drawn for at least one Hunt—and returned to us.

"Shrub continues to grow and become faster, stronger, and more capable. I know he has been out hunting. He had helped bring in *ven* this spring. I have seen the fighter's look in his eye —just this moon I saw him coil up and shake his fist in warning when some of older boys cornered him. They were only playing, of course, but Shrub seemed prepared for any kind of threat. With that in mind, and my certainty that Shrub is no longer a suitable name for a boy with his skills, we will now call him Rattler."

The boy cast a sidelong glance back to Hawk, who smiled and pointed toward Justin. Rattler glided up onto the Stone while a few of the Ruck began to repeat his name in choppy succession. Others caught on and joined in while Justin kissed the boy on the forehead and spun him around to face everyone. Rattler recoiled, leaping backward off the Stone and raising his fists to Justin. The man laughed, and Rattler slinked back to Hawk, Shadow, and Bison.

"Iris, our young and beautiful flower is growing up, too. Sometimes, a name just fits, and the time is right. I don't need to say more, I shouldn't think, because she will talk enough for all of us, this girl, who is always buzzing around her friends with an enthusiasm worthy of the most productive Bee in the hive." Justin ended this with a wide smile and arms extended.

The girl started to run up to the Stone, then she turned and hovered, bobbing up and down as she waved to her friends. No one doubted that she was pleased by the name; how could they when she chattered about how perfect the name was right up until she finally zoomed up onto the Stone and gave Justin a big hug. "Thank you, thank you, thank you," she said, tittering and moving about when he tried to kiss her forehead several times before throwing up his hands. Her antics delayed the chant of her new name, but it seemed to work out just fine, as some of her girlfriends started to make a buzzing sound after each repetition of her name. It took many heartbeats for Onyx, Maize, and Copperhead to calm her down after she returned to the Circle.

Justin, who had waited patiently, now turned to Heather. The girl's plain, boyish face could now be seen; she smirked after the naming of Bee and seemed eager to learn her own fate.

"Heather has proven her value this spring, helping Archer make arrows for our hunting and bringing in a few *ven* herself, I'm told. While Archer has made a commendable effort to keep us supplied in our Fletcher's absence, we simply must have a full-time Fletcher for the rest of this long summer and for the winters to come."

The shy girl froze, her eyes wide and mouth agape. Justin beckoned to her, but she didn't budge. Falcon had to step into the Circle and shove her onward. She stumbled toward the Stone while the Ruck chanted her new name plainly. After Justin kissed the top of her head, she walked straight back to Falcon, her gaze fixed on him to avoid looking at anyone else. Clay moved over to congratulate her; she stood as still as the Stone itself, blinking and nearly tripping over her own feet when Falcon turned her around to face Justin again.

Justin raised his hands, palms upward. "We are the Ruck, we remember. We must go on. We will now eat and re-gain strength. We will thank the *ven* for keeping us fit and ready for The Hunt."

Eagle had to sneak away during the feast the next evening. With sudden clarity, while sitting with Sage, Ash, and Thrush —and watching the younger children play stones or chase—he had realized he might never see Rose again. He would either die at the *tekline* or make his escape the next morning. He didn't know what would happen after he left the valley, even if his escape succeeded.

Now, as he hid in the treetops near the lagoon while the sun sank behind the hills, he asked God to give him a glimpse of his love once more before he risked everything to prove the Ruck could be *free*. For a while, all he could see were the children playing in the commons, supervised by Ruby and Lilly. His vantage point didn't give him the best view of the compound;

some of the visitation yurts stood in his way. Still, when he had chosen this mighty pine, there didn't seem to be any better place from which to spy. It occurred to him that he might scale a few more in an attempt to get a better view, but he didn't want to miss any opportunity to see Rose.

He wondered whether he should risk calling out to her or somehow get her attention if she came into his purview. A flurry of such nonsense ran through his head, all to be rejected, of course. Any overt outburst this close to the compound could draw the attention of the Black One. He remembered the crisp fall day he saw her bathing in the lagoon and how they had defied the Overlords together by talking and kissing. It was pure chance—and they were lucky to get away with it. He wanted that again, one last time. He wanted to see her growing round belly, with a child he hoped might be his. Which must be his, he corrected himself. Alas, as night fell and Lilly and Ruby rounded up the children, there was no sign of Rose.

His eyes followed the two women as they herded the children back to the main sleeping area. His mother appeared—at least there was that!—and Lotus followed right behind. They were holding hands. Lotus leaned in and kissed Honey on the neck as they separated and took to the children. It was a parting kiss, the kind the men gave the women before leaving the visitation yurts in the morning, the kind Eagle had given to Lotus and Nightingale just a few mornings before.

Eagle almost slipped from his perch. Lotus' words from that recent night struck him with such force that he thought someone had tried to push him out of the tree. *"We mothers share much with each other. More than you can imagine."*

Once again, Lotus made him feel foolish, even when she was unaware of his presence. The sudden idea of it all didn't bother him; he had just never thought of it before. How obvious now, in hindsight, Eagle thought.

Now, his thoughts spun wildly, and he wondered about Rose. His cheeks burned. He felt just like the time when Hawk had chided him about being with Rose the next night. He remembered Rose's baby could be Hawk's, or another man's— perhaps the Justin-before. And he wondered whether she ... no, he told himself, it doesn't matter. All that mattered was that he loved Rose. He asked God, again, to show her to him before he left. He had been gone from the village for some time. He couldn't wait much longer—he needed to get back to the feast.

Rose didn't appear. Eagle knew he had waited far too long, and he climbed down the tree, as quietly as Spider sneaking up on an unsuspecting dupe. He plodded back to the village, knowing he would have to be content with the indelible images of Rose that burned in his memory. The last time he saw her, tending the soap vats. Her radiant face by the candlelight of the yurt when she told him she was pregnant. Her glistening, naked body at the lagoon. He knew then that he loved her more than anything, except for his desire for the Ruck to be *free*. The time for him to prove his belief had come.

Honey went to attend to Star while the other women worked together to arrange the children for a night's sleep. The young woman had sat off to the side, brooding, at all of their gatherings since she arrived. When they let her, she had wandered around the compound, alone, stopping to stare at the soap vats or standing silently at the gate. The only time she had shown any spark was when she was helping to watch over the young children. The other women were giving her a little time; they all remembered how strange the adjustment could be. Still, Star seemed to have more trouble than either Butterfly or Gazelle when they had recently joined, and so, that night, the *Gramma* knew she had to do more.

Star was weeping when Honey sat down next her. "It's hard to join the women, I know," said Honey. "Everything is different here, without the men and your friends."

Star turned her head and looked into Honey's gentle gaze.

Deep sadness drained the life from her face. Honey had seen the anxiety and stress of the young girls who came to the compound to become women. She sensed something different about this one.

Standing, Star wiped the tears on her forearm, sniffling. "Can we walk a little, Honey?"

"Of course, Star." Honey followed her toward the soap vats. When they came near to the now dormant vats, Star swallowed hard.

"It's not what you think. I ... I'm glad to be here," Star started, then paused, biting her upper lip gently, casting a side-long glance, and finally turning her head away as a few more tears escaped.

"Tell me," Honey said, now sensing something very different than she had first expected.

"It's Eagle," Star whispered. "He ..." she leaned in closer, hugging the *Gramma*, and whispering close to her ear ... "he's going to escape."

Honey thrust the girl away, holding her at arm's length by the shoulders. "What?"

"I wasn't supposed to tell, but I had to tell you."

"I don't ... how ... when?" Honey felt her heart in her throat, beating faster.

"Tomorrow night, I think. I can't say anymore ... you just had to know."

Honey's chest tightened. She gasped for air. She had heard the news of the deaths of Ruck children, even her own, but she was usually prepared for it by the time the men came to the tent or Coot managed to slip her the news when he came with the Black One to trade supplies. The recent news of Badger's death had pained her like never before. Now this. Honey stood there, dazed, her mind whirling. Like her son, crazy thoughts flashed like lightning. Run to the village and stop him. Call for the Black One. Tell Lotus.

When Star grasped her again, embracing her with all her might, Honey's senses returned. She would do none of those things. Her son was a man now, and he was a strong leader. She wouldn't question him. She wouldn't put any of the Ruck in danger. Gently pushing Star away, she nodded to the young girl —no, young woman—and started to walk. Star followed and Honey whispered once they had moved farther away from the commons.

"You must tell no one else, Star. I must compose myself. We will go back to the women and try to sleep, after we have walked a little longer."

Star nodded, taking Honey's hand.

"Thank you for telling me," Honey said, holding back a tear.

Eagle set out with Mace and Ram well after the sun had reached its apex and started to fall on the west side of the valley. As planned, they had convinced Clay to go hunting with them that day. Eagle was glad for that—he would have a chance to spend time with one of his brothers, even if he couldn't afford to tell him the plans. More importantly, Clay would be able to verify Eagle's escape if all went well.

The night before, Eagle had gathered with his closest friends. They enjoyed each other's company, watching the children and making the smallest of talk. Joy had conveniently lured Coot to Eagle's camp. Even though she seemed to have no idea of Eagle's plans, she ended up helping him to inform Coot, as Eagle had promised the other conspirators. Taking this as a sign of providence, Eagle caught up with the old man when he headed back to Falcon's camp.

Asking Coot to walk with him, Eagle blurted out his confession. He didn't know what else to do, so he simply told Coot the whole truth. He couldn't read any expression underneath the old man's tangled beard. Fortunately, Coot reassured him.

"I knew something like this was going on," he said, without a shred of alarm or concern. "I hadn't guessed exactly what, or when, but I suspected you were planning something that would change us all."

Eagle looked startled. Coot understood. "No, Eagle, don't worry. I doubt that Hawk has guessed any more than me. He has been busy plotting his own ends. Of course, I don't know for sure, but I wouldn't let the uncertainty stop you."

He paused and Eagle waited.

"You are the eldest son of the woman who gives me the will to go on. It has been hard these many winters, watching the children grow up and eventually die. I want the Ruck to go on, and yet with each season my faith in our future withers. I wish I had your resolve. The strength to do something about our plight. I admire you. And I think you were wise to hide this from an old man like me. Who knows what an emotional old fool like me would have done."

Eagle could only shake his head. "You're no fool, old man. Your love for my mother taught me the most valuable lesson I know. I feel the same for Rose."

"Thank you. Still, I know my behavior has been far too selfish. Yours, while risky, also promises something far greater if you succeed. Go with the Goddess, Eagle. Be *free*."

Coot turned away and walked off toward Falcon's camp. Eagle allowed a few tears to leak from his eyes, swallowed hard, and turned back to his own campfire.

Earlier this morning he had hung around with the children. He told an innocuous story, which was sparsely attended—he hadn't tried to round up any of the children; he just started telling one and a few gathered around. He realized it was the first one he had told since Badger's death—and might be the last one he ever told. Raven and Fly were there, with Fish, Fern, Hemp, Blossom, Dreamer, and Snow. By the time he finished, others had joined, including Ash, Thrush, Sage, Archer, and Willow. The first three conspirators had made sure Eagle's sisters were nearby that day because Eagle continued to insist that they not be told of his plans until it was too late for them to protest in any way.

Fortunately, Hawk had set off with a hunting party midmorning, easing Eagle's plans. Bison had stayed behind, with Grouch and some of Hawk's children. They were occupied with the routine of the day, and with the deft aid of Sage and Ash, it was easy for Eagle to slip away with his two sisters. They had come with bow and quiver per Sage's advice, and so Eagle took them to the foothills near the Archery range.

As Eagle told them his plans for escape, their reactions differed. Willow started to cry almost immediately. She mumbled and huffed, asking why he was doing it, before he could even explain himself completely. Archer's face went grim. She put her arm around her sister, telling her she had to stay quiet, or they might be discovered before Eagle could explain. Her even tone, same as her lessons at the archery range, calmed Willow enough for Eagle to continue. He admired both of his sisters, then more than ever.

Finally, when he had told them of the preparation with Mace and Ram, since the last moon, tears poured from Willow's eyes, and her shoulders wouldn't stop trembling. Under the comforting embrace of her sister, Willow managed to stifle any sound.

Archer whispered, speaking for both of them. "I think I understand why you didn't tell us, Eagle. I still wish you would have. We would have supported you." Willow nodded rapidly.

"I never questioned you. I hope you believe me. Like I just said, I knew that if you were involved, we would be more likely to arouse Hawk's, or Falcon's ... or anyone's suspicion. I made the others promise not to tell you anything, as much for your own safety as for the plans. I promised them I would tell you before I left."

"Thank you." Archer said. "I do understand, even if I don't like it. Everything has changed so much in the village. For all we know, they could have been spying on you all along. Our involvement might have hindered your plans. Or maybe it wouldn't have made any difference. Maybe Hawk even knows of your plan already. Maybe he wants you to leave. Maybe he thinks you will die trying."

Eagle smiled and Archer made a face. "No, don't misunderstand," he said, "I'm just so proud of you both. It makes me smile to sit here with you now. Whatever happens to me, I'll know you two will grow into wonderful women. The Ruck will go on."

Eagle leaned over to hug them. He breathed in and fixed their scent in his mind. He didn't want to forget how either of them smelled. They were clean and had the flowery whiff of the soap made by the women, having bathed the day of the feast. They held each other for many heartbeats before Eagle whispered that they should go to the range. Whether Hawk knew or not, Eagle said he would carry out his plans to the end. He told them that he would drift away during their practice session. They should say goodbye to him as they would on any other day, he added.

While they walked, Willow composed herself and she sidled up to Eagle, whispering. "Are you coming back?"

"I don't know, Willow," he lied, catching Archer's suspicious glance. He was almost sure he wouldn't, even though he held out a slim hope that he would come back to help them all escape. Proving the Ruck could escape was what mattered. Even if he did die beyond the *tekline*, Eagle would die believing the village would be changed forever if only he made it through.

Now, Eagle's mind returned to the present. The three boys walked ahead of him, Ram leading the roundabout way to the bluff where they had watched the Black One's ubiquitous sentry and practiced the timing of the leap so many times. The smallest doubts began to creep into Eagle's thoughts. Even after all their testing, so many things could go wrong. Sometimes, he felt it was too easy so far; he worried something would go amiss at the last heartbeat. Coot's and Archer's comments about Hawk began to gnaw him around the edges. Could Hawk know? If so, would he try to stop them? He found himself shooting glances all around, looking for signs of someone trailing them or shadowing their movements.

Mace had fallen back in step with Eagle, giving him a quizzical look. Eagle realized how obvious his current fretting must have looked. Regardless, Eagle smiled and nodded to Mace while increasing his gait. Mace raised a worried eyebrow as they caught up to the other two. Eagle patted the boy on the shoulder in reassurance. He told himself to cast aside all the lingering thoughts of turning back by the time they had reached the bluff.

The sun was starting to retreat from the valley, although it wasn't yet leaving the long shadow from the Black One at its post—the shadow Eagle and the boys had come to measure so well. They had a little time yet, plenty for Eagle to make his trek from here to the Point in time to make the leap. Clay's reaction to the view from the bluff allayed one of Eagle's doubts, relaxing him. Clay marveled at the view, saying he had never seen it quite like this. He compared it to the other spot, where Hawk had showed him the changing—just as Hawk had shown Eagle and Shadow and certainly others, Eagle realized. It didn't seem like there was any danger of Clay wanting to leave prematurely. He knew about the changing and wanted to see it.

It seemed so long ago, Eagle mused, since Hawk first revealed the changing. Eagle and his boys had come far since then. Clay's words help to soothe Eagle's mood; truly, the doubts dissolved now. Eagle was sure his brother's reaction was genuine, so it seemed Hawk had never shown him this new bluff. Eagle knew that Bison and his friends were trying to win Clay's allegiance, just like Eagle and Ram were doing. Perhaps Hawk hadn't discovered the bluff's significance. Everything was falling into place.

After a while, Eagle gave his brother a hug and asked him if he had enjoyed the day. Clay smiled.

"Yes, Eagle."

"Then I hope you enjoy the evening even more. I must go—I have a promise to keep. But Ram and Mace will be staying to watch the changing."

"Okay," Clay said. He paused. "Thanks, Eagle."

"You're welcome. Goodbye," he said to all of them, meeting their eyes, with an extra heartbeat locked on Ram.

Eagle couldn't help but run, albeit at a mild pace, to the ascent of the Point. He measured the shadows and knew he had time to catch his breath and make a sure-footed, unseen climb. During their practices, he had climbed close to the Point without drawing the Overseer's attention. At least, the Overseer never seemed to acknowledge Eagle's presence during the climb. Close enough to the *tekline* to make the leap, no matter what, he guessed.

He focused on a steady climb, just like his other attempts. He didn't want to change it, even though he did have an urge to proceed more carefully than usual. It had to be like he had practiced, whether anyone was watching or not. No one could stop him now unless they were already up there. He reached the pine that bore his markings, and he crouched down. Although the bluff was hard to see through the tangled low branches of the pines, Eagle saw the three boys. Ram was standing in the usual spot; Mace and Clay sat off to the side. Eagle glanced towards the Black One's shadow and saw that the time was near. He had a few dozen heartbeats, he thought. He looked out across the valley, and his eyes landed on Hawk's spot. He saw two forms there and smiled. He hoped one was Hawk, but the more witnesses the better, even if it were only two of Hawk's boys. Twice, when doing the tests, someone had been there. Perhaps Eagle was noticed on those occasions. Still, he hadn't done anything except guess the timing. They had practiced the run and leap only at the bluff.

In his thoughts he asked God for the strength to make the leap, waiting for a dozen heartbeats before he re-positioned himself, gently. Now facing the edge of the small plateau that served as the Black One's post, he turned his head to look at Ram. The boy had raised his hand. Eagle's heart hammered. He took three careful steps up to the plateau ledge, knowing he was in more clear view now and tensing for the final signal.

It came, and he lunged. Ram's hand hadn't even fallen all

the way to his side before Eagle rolled onto the plateau, jumped to his feet, and leaped toward the bright blue flash. Out of the corner of his eye he saw the changing of the Overseer. Then the jolt hit him, and he lost his sight for a heartbeat. He heard a sound like the one he heard the day Sprout had died. He fell forward to his knees, and when he felt his sight returning, he expected to see himself burning. He wasn't. His body tingled, nothing more. His pounding heart brought him back to the alert. He looked around wildly, seeing the Black One striding off.

He had done it! He wasn't noticed!

He ran.

8

And he didn't stop until darkness enveloped the woods and the hills. Eagle had been chasing the setting sun; it was the only thing even vaguely familiar to him. Out of breath, exhausted, Eagle slowed to a walk and surveyed his surroundings. Tall pines all around, like the Ruck valley but unfamiliar. None of them promised comfort to him. He picked one at random and settled in with his back against the trunk, tucked under the lowest branches. He closed his eyes and imagined he was back at the edge of the bluff, like the time he had taken shelter during the rain on his secret journey. But every sound alerted him, reminding him that he was hiding in a strange new land.

He slept in spurts. Everything called to him. The strange hills and trees pressed in around him; the noises kept him on edge. When he wasn't tossing for those reasons, Eagle stared at the sky through the clustered pine branches wondering what was happening in the village. Escaping scared him more than he had imagined. He shivered under the tree and thought of turning back in the morning. Only his hope sustained him. Hope that the proof of escape would help his followers to change things in the village. When the sun finally cast its rays over these new hills, Eagle chewed a small piece of *pem* and found his nerve. He told himself he would never think of turning back again, no matter how frightened he became. He would follow the sun. If he were ever to return, it would be to bring a boon to the village. Never in retreat from his goal.

Eagle chewed only two small bites. He had carried little out of the ordinary to avoid suspicion, but he figured the *pem* he had inside his vest could last a few days if eaten sparingly. He hoped to see *ven* and be able to hunt, but he wanted to get farther away first. The sobering possibility of Overseers on his trail pushed him onward; the few strips of *pem* would have to last. He sipped carefully at his water, too. He ran again, taking in the crisp morning air, feeling like he was pulling the sun's rise into the sky on a string behind him. Finally, the exertion overtook him as the sun was directly overhead. He stopped to rest, chewed a few more bites, and sipped water. The ground looked different, but it was starting to feel the same beneath his feet. Refreshed, Eagle chased the sun now, like it was dragging him on the string, until he found himself on a high, wide plateau. Daylight lingered for some time as it took a while for the sun to fall beyond the far away hills. There wasn't much cover here, but Eagle found a comfortable tree to settle under. This time he fell asleep after a few sips of water.

At dawn, he realized something. While he fasted for a few days in the valley, he had also conserved his energy whenever possible. Running for an entire day demanded nourishment. Eagle chewed the remainder of yesterday's *pem* and ate another full piece. Three remained, which he believed would last two more days. He figured his water wouldn't last that long. He took an extra sip before starting off on the run. He would have to find a good source of water; so far, he had seen only small muddy streams.

The day's travel went well. Eagle ran and rested a few times while traversing the plain and pushing into the new hills beyond. He had to make one difficult climb to avoid going well around these new hills. It slowed him down, but he felt like he was moving in the right direction. The climb also took him away from the stream he had been following while hoping to find a larger body of water—or at least a deeper, cleaner section. Eagle drank a little less that night, saving a few last swallows.

He slowly chewed the night's ration of *pem* and began thinking again. He had run for three days; he was exhausted, but the feeling that he had truly escaped became more real to him. *Freedom*! Finally, he began to understand what it meant. *Freedom* was exhilarating and frightening at the same time. To run and explore, not knowing what was on the other side of a hill, not having a *tekline*, or an Overseer, stop him from finding out but also having no assurance whether he would find pleasure or peril once he crested the next hill. Eagle realized he had been running so fast for so long that he hadn't taken the time to hunt for food or water. He resolved to slow down the next day. He would look more carefully for *ven* spoor; he would find water. He would survive if he kept his wits.

Still, Eagle wondered about his path. What else might be out here? Other Ruck? *Ven*? Wolves? Strange creatures? The Overlords? A shiver ran up Eagle's back. Thoughts churned while he stared into the night sky. Before long, fatigue overwhelmed his worried mind.

Morning brought a familiar breeze to his face, waking him. He blinked against the rising sun. Through sleepy eyes he spied the billowing smoky clouds that occasionally drifted high over the Ruck valley. It seemed like he was closer to them here, as if he had traveled toward their origin. In the village, those mysterious and smoky clouds were perceived as a sign of trouble. Now, the familiar sight emboldened Eagle. He set out slowly that morning, searching for *ven* spoor.

It didn't take long to find it. Actually, evidence was rather plentiful, showing a clear trail. But it was old and fading. At first, Eagle couldn't discern whether he was following the spoor to its source or its destination. He continued onward, still leading the sun in the morning and chasing it in the evening. Eagle stopped often, resting, chewing a little *pem*, and finding a place to hunker down for a bit to see what creatures might cross his path. He saw rabbits, rodents and birds, but no *ven*. He considered trying to shoot or snare a rabbit, but he knew it would be difficult. He didn't usually hunt such small creatures; the *ven* were always plentiful and there was little need to spend effort shooting something to feed a few, or only one, when a man could bring in a *ven* that fed many. Nevertheless, Eagle thought he would take one if he had to. Which might be soon, if the trail didn't lead to any *ven*.

Late in the day, he found more obvious tracks near another muddy stream. He thought a number of *ven* had passed by here, but again the spoor was old. Eagle decided to take this as an encouraging sign. He drained the last drops from his skin. He followed the tracks the rest of the day. They took him away from his pre-determined path, upwards on another slope with the sun falling to his left, but it proved worthwhile. As he climbed, it grew less muddy, expanding into a wider stream, which began to meander not far from the tracks. Eagle abandoned the tracks and walked along the edge of the stream, stopping now and then to cup his hand and check the water's depth and clarity. Before the sun had disappeared, he came upon a clean pool of water, as wide as a yurt and forming just outside a number of crevices on this ridge. Eagle knelt at the pool and thanked God. He had tried not to think about it, but his mouth and throat had grown thick with dryness. He splashed water onto his face with both hands, opening his mouth and gulping in mouthfuls and drenching his entire head.

He wanted to investigate the crevices to see if he could find the spring feeding this pool, but daylight was almost gone. He took a few moments to get his bearings and determine which way he would want to travel next. Then he sat down and rested. He enjoyed his last piece of *pem*. It was easier to eat with plentiful water. He drank more than his fill while he ate and then he drank more. He regretted it. As he tried to relax under the moonlight, he felt bloated. His stomach rumbled. Still, knowing he would have water for the morning—and enough for a few days after he filled the waterskin—renewed his spirit. When he finally did relax, he slept soundly through the night.

When Eagle awoke, it occurred to him that staying here for a full day might be wise. This pool would be the ideal spot if he could find a suitable stand nearby. Certainly, any nearby *ven* or other creatures would come by here to drink. First, he located the spring and filled his skin directly from the source. He drank with reason this time, before searching the slope for a place that he could hide and watch the pool. He settled on a decent spot, a little farther than he desired, although still a viable bow shot. He waited.

He stayed there most of the day, moving occasionally to stretch his legs or look for a better spot. No *ven* came, but he saw something he never dreamed he would see. A creature approached, smaller than the *ven*, on four wiry legs. It had a beautiful, menacing head, with piercing brown eyes, a long snout and pointed ears. It had claws on its feet instead of hooves like the *ven*. It had short, thick, grey-brown hair. It was lean, and it looked as hungry as Eagle felt. When it got near the pool, it paused and sniffed the air. Eagle saw the creature tense, with ears pointed and head tilted. It growled and showed the edges of yellow teeth. Eagle almost gasped. Seeing it now like this, he realized it fit the descriptions of the wolf or the *dawg* from the stories Garnet had taught him. Just then, another one came into view, quickly moving to the pool and lapping at the water with a long red tongue. The first one turned, its body still tense and now showing more teeth. Eagle thought it might see him, but it turned again to the pool after the other one stopped drinking. Finally, the pair turned and slinked off.

Eagle swallowed hard and regained himself. He had heard the distant howls in the night before and had told stories about the wild wolves in the hills, but none had ever appeared in the valley. Perhaps the *tekline* kept them out even though it allowed other creatures to pass. The wonder of it all reminded Eagle of his new *freedom*. It also reminded him of how lonely it was to be *free* and how new and strange this world beyond the village could be. He saw birds and other small creatures approach the pool that day. He just couldn't bring himself to take a shot at any of them. Despite his hunger, he held out hope for finding *ven*. They had to be around; nothing else made sense. He couldn't chance wasting his arrows while trying to bring in something as small as a rabbit, especially when he wasn't sure he could hit one from this range.

That night, Eagle built a small fire, his first since the escape. He felt safer here, despite the wolves, and he thought a fire might help to keep strange creatures away. It occurred to him that it might draw undue attention as well. So, he dug a hole, shielded near the ridge wall, and kept the fire small. He drank again and his stomach complained for lack of nourishment. He thought he smelled rain not far away, although none visited the area around the spring.

Would it be better, he wondered, to stay here and try to hunt another day, or should he press on? He talked to God, asking for insight. The answer didn't come to him, at least not yet. Like earlier in the morning when his mind seized on the idea to stay here, Eagle believed the choice would become clearer after rest had rejuvenated him, so he settled into sleep near the smoldering fire. He woke during the deep night—aroused from a dream that included both Hawk and Rose, his first such dream since he escaped—to the mysterious howling he had heard faintly in the valley over the winters. Much louder now, it startled him. He remained alert for some time. Eventually, he could tell the wolves weren't close to the spring, but their presence still gave him pause. They had definitely sensed him earlier in the day. He could probably shoot one if he had to; they didn't look any faster than the *ven*, although they certainly looked more dangerous. If he didn't kill one, or even both, they might threaten him. He decided to fill his skin after the sun rose, continuing his journey.

Eagle could only doze from time to time until the sun beckoned him. His mind stayed sharp, anticipating the approach of wolves or God knows what else. Now, haggard and a little weak from lack of food or sound sleep, he roused himself and drank until he felt full. He washed his face with the water remaining in the skin then re-filled it from the spring before starting off. He intended to resume his previous course if possible.

He had started to get used to the hunger, as he often did

by the second day of his fasts, and most of a day's rest and sleep helped him recover. Still, as the day wore on and he used his limited energy, the gnawing feeling in his belly returned. Even at a slower pace today than in his first three days after the *tekline*, his lack of nourishment began to take its toll. Eagle fought through it. He picked up *ven* spoor around mid-day and followed it again. For a while, it went generally in the same direction as the setting sun. The farther he followed it, the more it seemed to age and vanish. At one point the trail split; Eagle picked what appeared to be fresher sign, which took him up into the taller hills again.

As the sun descended inexorably to his left—like the other day when he climbed to find the spring—Eagle's vision blurred and his mind wavered. He felt his arms and legs tingle and decided he needed to take a decent rest before he pushed himself any higher up the hill. Plopping down on the hard slope, he slid up against a gnarled pine and sipped water. He scanned the way farther up the hill; it was easier to do so when not expending effort just to keep his balance and move upward. After a few sips and deep breaths, Eagle's vision cleared. He shook his head, trying to shake what he thought must be a hunger-induced dream. It changed nothing; a dark figure remained on the precipice of the hill. Fear overtook Eagle for an instant. His mind gained clarity and he grasped the truth. It was a Black One!

Again, ripples of fear swept over him and he couldn't move at all. His mind screamed to get up and run, but his muscles remained deaf to that plea. His paralysis helped, as it turned out, because he watched long enough to comprehend that the Overseer faced the other side of the hill. Probably, he didn't need to run. If he carefully backed down before it turned around, he might avoid an encounter. For a heartbeat, Eagle considered trying to creep up and shoot it. That was madness, he knew, but something compelled him to consider it. After many more heartbeats, he started back down the slope, with painstaking slowness, so he wouldn't attract the Black One's attention.

He returned almost to the split in the trail before darkness made traveling impossible. Eagle couldn't be sure he had evaded the Overseer, but he knew it was folly to travel at night. Besides, his body beckoned him to rest again. He pushed off the trail a ways, toward the setting sun, finding a thicket where he wedged himself among the brambles. It was damp in there, and he had scratched his arms and legs in his haste. Still, it seemed safe from view. He stayed alert for a while, in case the Black One came near. His stomach growled again. He still thought he could go without food for another day or two, but he doubted whether he could continue to exert himself traveling at the same time. He wished he had tried to shoot one of the rabbits, maybe even the wolf. If he saw a clear shot at another one, he wouldn't hesitate. He thought of Tiller and wished he had learned more about which of the wild flowers and roots one could eat. He looked around and was tempted to try any leaf, weed, or root he could find nearby. Tiller's words of caution echoed in his head. Some *veg* might be dangerous, and Eagle just didn't know how to tell the difference. He had spent all his efforts—while growing up and still as a man—on learning how to hunt *ven*. He had always considered the boys and girls like Tiller as oddities in the village. The *veg* was always secondary; a pleasant diversion and sometimes interesting taste but not important for the Ruck to go on. He had never even learned to fish, not very well at least. Understanding his ignorance now, he couldn't bring himself to try just anything he saw. He hadn't reached the desperation of starvation. Not yet.

Eagle rolled over to his side, into a particularly muddy patch. He grumbled and rolled back. Wait, his groggy mind told him, something important about this. Wet ground and a dark thicket. The smell of rain still reaching his nose from time to time. *Shrooms?*

"*Fug,*" he said aloud, then shushed himself. "I should be looking for *shrooms,*" he muttered. Maybe he could find some that looked familiar, like the ones Tiller said were okay to eat. At least he had some idea what he was looking for. Now, with the night taking over the sky and the Overseer possibly still nearby, Eagle knew he would have to wait.

All that night, Eagle's mind competed with itself over thoughts of food, of his encounter with the Overseer, and of events in the village. Would he find *shrooms* that were safe to eat? Was the Black One looking for him atop that ridge? Why were the *ven* so scarce in these hills when they had returned to the valley not long ago? What was happening in the village? Were there more Overseers combing the area? Did Rose think of him and wonder whether he lived after his escape?

Thus, another night passed with only spurts of sleep. There was no sign of any Black Ones. He hadn't been discovered. He decided to move steadily today, following his nose and searching for *shrooms* anytime he found a sheltered, damp area. By mid-morning he entered a likely patch of woods where the rain had apparently fallen as recently as the day before. Eagle slowed and searched in earnest now. His heart pounded when he found a small cap, then a second and third. On his hands and knees, he crawled through the wet undergrowth, finding and plucking handfuls of the delicate *shrooms*. He emptied his pouch of dried flowers and stuffed in as many caps as he could. He tucked others into his vest, where he had kept the *pem,* and carried yet another handful. Eagle left the woods and headed back toward his original destination. The sun was nearly overhead now, so he found a secluded place to sit and rest.

He sipped his water and stared at the *shrooms.* They looked a lot like the ones that he had collected in the valley. Tiller had given his approval of those—although it didn't mean anything here and now. Eagle wrestled with a decision. By the time the sun passed directly over him, his hunger beat down any other thoughts. He didn't know how much longer he could travel without eating. The urge to move on was powerful. After one more sip of water, Eagle stuffed a few of the caps into his mouth and chewed.

Immediately, the taste reminded him of Lotus' brew. It hadn't killed him; in fact, it had helped him. Eagle ate more, chewing them more thoroughly now and washing them down with measured gulps from his skin. Their texture grew stranger as he chewed, not anything like *ven*. Still, his appetite seemed to grow as he ate. He finished all the ones he had carried in his fists and dug into the ones inside his vest. He even ate one or two from his pouch before beginning to feel like he could eat no more. The hunger hadn't really abated, but he felt like could chew no more of the strange-tasting caps right now.

Staring into the sky and sipping from his skin, Eagle rested after his meal. The lingering odor of the *shrooms* prompted a memory of his last visit to Lotus' tent. He remembered how the brew had calmed him and how wonderful he felt lying with her. Eagle's breathing slowed and he relaxed in the midday sunshine. His thoughts wandered to Rose, to his friends and followers, his mother, back to Lotus, then again to Rose. He missed all of them. Tears welled in his eyes. He saw Rose standing naked, at the edge of the lagoon, her belly now full with child.

It made him smile, watching her in his thoughts. Soon, Lotus joined Rose and they bathed in the shallow water. They dried each other off. They were radiant, both of them. He thought he heard his mother's voice calling to them. Eagle got up; he wanted to walk to them and find his mother. As soon as he stood, his surroundings reappeared, and he found himself alone and feeling empty in the hills.

A sudden surge of energy coursed through Eagle. He had to do something. Sitting here wasn't the answer for him. The thought sobered him; it countered his sorrow without quite erasing the longing for Rose and his friends. The feelings of vital urgency and of great misfortune wrestled with him at once, like two young children tugging at his leggings and begging for a ride in a *cart*. Turning toward the early descending sun, Eagle set off in the direction he knew he had to go.

For a time, he was sure he was traveling again within the

Ruck valley, just a quick jaunt from the bluff back to the archery range to see his sister. He picked up the pace, a brisk run now, weaving through the trees and underbrush. Suddenly, everything changed again. He found himself on an unrecognizable path between two bare hills. The sun blazed ahead of him. He felt its rays penetrating his pores, filling him with energy. He could feel each ray drilling into him; he stopped and extended his open hands, palms to the sun, drinking in strength and replenishing spirit. He began to feel kind of dizzy; waves came and went until he sat down, closing his eyes, breathing, breathing, breathing. Breathing. Opening eyes again.

Sage was there, with Ash and Mace. They laughed at something. Eagle laughed, too. Embarrassed, he laughed again because he had no idea what they were laughing at. They turned and pointed at him, now suddenly rolling on the ground and almost choking on their mirth.

Eagle stood up. He had to run from them. He felt like young Sparrow again, when the older boys teased him during his first winter in the village. He didn't like that, so he ran. He ran like the day he had escaped the *tekline*, but now with an odd sense of purpose. Navigating this rolling plain, Eagle dodged in and out of trees, leapt over shrubs and rocks until he turned into the last leg of the championship foot race. He sprinted into the open field, seeing the finish line ahead ... he felt other racers lurking off his shoulder ... no, just one contender, Hawk, waiting to make his move and overtake Eagle in the straight-away. Eagle gave everything he had, running so fast he passed into a whiteness where his eyes didn't work but his feet remained sure. He stretched out and knew he had crossed the line before his rival.

Suddenly, the whiteness left his eyes. He opened them (or did he close them? it all seemed the same) and found himself again in the wilderness. The sun poured into him again ... he laughed out loud, standing tall, extending his open palms again to receive the myriad tiny rays ... he knew he had to keep chasing the sun, he was connected to it, it pulled him onward, by a string, forward, fast, urgent, life or death. He ran across familiar fields and places he had never seen … he turned to see Archer running alongside him, but she couldn't keep up, and she said she would meet him back at the campfire, and Eagle yelled to her saying he had to go on a secret journey, fasting as Sage had told him, but first he needed to rest, he told her, and so he sat in the shade of a clump of pine trees, closing his eyes and listening to the birds. He relaxed while the birds talked to him, telling him he was on the right path, that he should keep going. Slivers of light penetrated the pine limbs and tugged at him. Thoughts of rest meant nothing. He left the shade, dusted himself off, breathed, breathed, ran.

Reconnecting with the sun, Eagle felt more powerful strings of light grabbing him and leading him through dense woods onto an open field at the bottom of a slope. He slowed and surveyed the area. For one heartbeat, or a dozen, or three hundred, Eagle thought he was standing in one of Tiller's fields. No, it was different … much smaller, like Hawk's wrestling ring, but it was certainly a field of *veg*. Eagle fell to his knees and dug in the dirt, loosening a root that looked familiar to him. He called out to Tiller, delighted. He dug some more, extracting a few other roots. He felt hungry and thought to eat one right there, but the thought of eating dirt made him pause. Looking at his water skin, thinking to rinse them, he shook his head and laughed at himself. Just carry them, fool, he thought, it won't be long before we pass another spring or stream, and they can all be washed. He stuffed roots into his vest; they bulged and peeked out. Eagle didn't care. He grabbed a handful of dirt and heaved it in the air, dodging the clumps and grains as the dirt fell back at him.

The sun's strings pulled Eagle again. He took off into the hills. Soon, his yellow guide began dipping below the higher hills ahead. Eagle felt a rush of excitement. The end of this journey would be marked by the setting ball of fire. He knew it! He ran faster and yelled at it to wait for him to catch up; it seemed to stop and obey, then suddenly drop in front of him, mocking him.

Out of nowhere, Eagle saw two men, their long, stretched-out shadows preceding them. They were watching him ... he slowed down, and the world seemed to build itself around him, becoming more solid with each new breath. He studied the men now. They hadn't moved yet. One of them looked old, he had a thick, coarse beard; the other was lean and young. Eagle could hardly believe it when he realized it must be Falcon and Coot. His heart leapt and he ran to them, laughing again.

"My friends, I didn't expect to find you here!" he said, throwing his arms open as he approached to embrace them both in a life affirming hug. As Eagle came close, Falcon stepped aside, tripping him with one foot. Eagle sprawled into the under-brush, rolling forever down a hill until he landed with a final thud. He opened his eyes, saw a flock of birds in the sky, he wanted to rise with them, his wingless body held him back, his eyes grew heavy, he sucked in air, and then everything went black.

When the light returned, it was hot and smoky. The sun had never felt so near. No, it wasn't the sun now, it was a camp-fire. Not his campfire to be sure. Eagle bolted upright and felt another surge of energy. He looked for his companions, search-ing for Sage and Thrush and the others, but they weren't there. Wait, two men were here, the men he thought were Falcon and Coot. They weren't them at all. One of them held up a water skin, tossing it to him. Eagle stared at it; it looked exactly like his. He reached around for his to compare .... it was gone! His swollen tongue filled his mouth; he sipped at the new skin until he realized, of course, it was his water skin. He giggled even before he had swallowed, spitting out some of the water and feeling like a wasteful fool. The men just watched him.

So, Eagle studied them again, regaining himself and feeling completely awake, as if sleep was just something he had pre-tended to do in a story he told the children. They wore *ven*-hide with strange markings, much different than Tanner's, and they also had something on their faces, random smudges or careful patterns he couldn't be sure. He saw their bows and quivers. The one with the beard also wore something on his head.

Finally, the bearded one spoke. His words didn't make sense. Eagle thought he said something about finding a section of pine trees that looked like home. He wasn't sure if it was a question or a statement. Whatever it meant, he couldn't guess, so he shook his head gently and continued to gaze at them. So many people had come and gone today, well, no they hadn't really (but it seemed like they had, didn't it?), and Eagle expected these men to go away soon, too. They didn't, and now a shiver ran from Eagle's toes to his skull, where it lingered and turned into a trembling, crawling feeling all over his scalp. The young one asked him something important—this time it sounded like a question, anyway—something about home and the Overlords. He was sure he had heard those words correctly. The mere sound of the latter caused another crawling in his scalp, which sent ripples throughout his body, but then for some reason he remembered he was *free* of them, *FREE!*, and all he could do was laugh. Increasingly, he had to force himself to stop smiling.

They looked at him and then at each other. One of them reached into his clothing and pulled out a flat object. He waved it and then tossed it. Instinctively, Eagle snatched it out of the air and just as quickly dropped it by his side. Inspecting his hand for burns or something—he wasn't sure what—a marvelous smell reached his nostrils. It came from his hands ... it was ... what was it? ... it was, something ... it was *pem*! He grabbed the piece again and bit into it. Incredible! He had never tasted *pem* so well-prepared. He chewed it with enthusiasm, and they smiled at him now.

Between bites, Eagle thanked them for the *pem*. They seemed to understand what he said, so he tried to ask them where they had found the *ven*. Some of their words made sense, others were incomprehensible ... they sounded sort of like silly words the children made up for something they didn't like, or when a young child adds an extra sound to a word. For a long, long time (or maybe only a few dozen heartbeats), Eagle and the two men struggled to understand each other. Clearly, they all understood the *ven*, but the subtleties of question and answers about the *ven* went nowhere at first. The two men seemed puzzled, amused, interested, bewildered. Eagle refused to give up until he learned where to find the *ven*. He felt the energy surge again, this time drawing power from the large crescent moon. He paced back and forth, gesticulating and raising his voice, pleading for them to understand, sitting down, explaining, standing, ranting, pantomiming, laughing, sobbing. Breathing. Smiling. Breathing.

When they finally pointed a direction and counted on their fingers what he believed were days, Eagle collapsed. On his back, he stretched his hands out to the sky, he thanked God, he sat up. Why was he wasting time? He needed to get there as soon as he could. He could sleep later.

He leapt over the fire and slapped them on the arms and clasped hands with them. They smiled and looked even more bewildered, amused, entertained. They offered him another piece of *pem*; he took it and ran.

The moon gave him enough light to see, but he bounded off too fast. Soon, his limbs grew tired; his eyes betrayed him. He would have sworn a tree root reached out and grabbed him, but whatever happened, Eagle turned his ankle and went down hard. His head throbbed; he wasn't sure why, but now rest seemed like a good idea again. Breathing, breathing, breathing. He closed his eyes.

◆ ◆ ◆

The sun roused Eagle. His head still throbbed; his ankle screamed at him. He tried to put weight on it without standing up just yet. He could, he thought, but he would bear great pain if he tried to walk. Sipping at his skin, Eagle looked around. How did he get here? A pass between two hills, under the rising sun, was sort of familiar. Maybe he had come from that way. He felt strange: tired but serene, in pain and yet peaceful.

He remembered following the sun yesterday, running and running, visions of his friends ... visions of Rose ... visions of, yes, that's what they all were, visions. The *shrooms*! Of course. He had eaten them yesterday morning; they reminded him of Lotus' brew. They had given him a fever ... some sickness ... no, it was something else, something more, something he couldn't quite define.

Eagle breathed deeply. Whatever the *shrooms* did, they didn't kill him. He would have to be more careful. He needed food he could trust; he needed *ven*.

It all made him think even more about food, which made him remember more about his journey yesterday. He remembered the smell of soil, pulling roots, the patch of *veg*. Feeling around his vest, he found it was smudged with dirt and held a few large clods in the folds. None of the roots he suddenly remembered. Another vision? It seemed so real, but what happened to the roots?

The men. The other men. The campfire, the *pem*, talking ... no, more like trying to talk, everything flooded back to him. Yet another vision? They had given him *pem*; he looked for it, but he saw no more a sign of *pem* than the roots; no, wait, he remembered clutching the *pem* as he ran. He had never tucked it away after he raced away from the men.

Eagle scanned the area. Perhaps he had dropped it. He tried to stand; pain shot through his lower leg. He dropped to hands and knees and searched the ground. Soon he located his tumbling trail from the night before; he crawled along it until, with amazement, he found a thick, short piece of *pem* wedged in the dirt.

They must have been real! Eagle's heart pounded. Ruck from another village, or some other place! *Free* men, in the wilderness! Eagle thanked God for everything: for the courage to escape, for the guidance ... even for the *shrooms*. Eagle's escape now meant everything he had hoped for. The Ruck could be *free.*

The pain in his ankle rudely reminded him of his situation, tempering his excitement. He needed rest, at least for a while. On his hands and knees again, Eagle found a nice spot to recline while propping up his swollen ankle. He had enough water for another day, perhaps two. He wondered if the *free* Ruck had filled it for him. Resting here might be wise. He could drink, sleep, eat the *pem,* and start again the next morning. Biting the corner, he chewed. The flavor brought more memories of last night.

The men had told him where to find the *ven.* Two days to the northwest. That's what they had shown him, wasn't it? Eagle couldn't be sure. Real or not, the images in his mind from the day of *shrooms* were muddled. What was real and what had he imagined? He could only trust God to guide him in the right direction.

When he awoke the next morning, Eagle first checked the swelling in his ankle. It was no worse. He tested it again. The pain hadn't changed either, but he could hobble on it. In general, the day of rest helped enough for Eagle to continue his travel. He lacked food, again. He was running out of water, again. He needed to keep moving. Limping along, with many fleeting rests, Eagle covered precious little ground, but long after noon he stumbled across what appeared to be a large overgrown path. Eagle stopped and pulled at the brambles, uncovering what looked like many small rocks that had been arranged purposefully along the path, lining it in two long rows. It made him think of the field where they had the foot races —over time a path had worn in where the children ran close to the turn markers. This path was wide, a little more than an arm's length between the two strips. Studying the area, Eagle guessed the path extended for some distance in both directions. One direction generally went the way Eagle had been traveling, so he decided to follow it as long as it didn't turn far away from the setting sun.

Eagle plodded along the rock path, at times dragging his bad ankle and clenching his teeth. As the moon replaced the sun, he had to slow down. As his eyes adjusted, the path remained easy to follow. In some stretches, the brambles cleared, and trees were scarce, showing the path more clearly even in moonlight. One section posed problems. The path was broken, charred, almost lost. The small rocks had scattered. Eagle wanted to stop; his ankle complained more with every step and his other leg began to complain, too, tired of bearing most of his weight during the long day. He knew that it would be hard to start again once he had stopped for longer than his frequent, quick breathers. He suspected that a night's rest would probably stiffen the ankle now and make the next day's travel even slower. He could see the path well enough in the moonlight; he would continue until fatigue demanded sleep.

Ahead, it appeared the path was clearing again and turning into a more open plain. Eagle forced himself onward, reaching the opening and seeing something large and dark looming alongside the path. It looked sort of like a yurt, one of the bigger ones where they slept together during winter. His heart quickened, and he dragged himself closer and closer. It wasn't really a yurt, it seemed to be made of stone and wood … no wait, there were two of them, near each other, the stone one in the background rising high in the air and a shorter one, made of wood, close by. The path split just before it reached these yurts, one way leading up to the stone yurts, the other continuing into the plain. Eagle stopped, peering ahead. It looked like more of these yurts stood further along the path.

Sucking in air, steadying himself, Eagle pushed up to the wooden yurt. There were no markings; it looked old, creaky, and unstable. He came around a corner and found that it had only three sides, and a collapsed top. There was something large inside it. Something strange, dark, with the top of the yurt crumbled all over it. He couldn't see enough to discern what the thing was. He backed away, bumping his heel on something and almost doubling over as the pain shot through his ankle. With the last of his strength, Eagle dragged himself to the stone yurt. He saw several openings in the stone, not unlike the flaps on their yurts, which allowed air to pass through on a warm summer day. The path led up to the largest opening. Near the front of the opening, planks of wood were lined up and held together, sort of. No, they seemed to be falling apart together. He stepped up, and the pain shot through him again. Stumbling to the opening, he found something heavy blocked the way. Eagle had nothing left; he thought to push past the block, but as he leaned feebly against it, his will left him. He slouched to a squat against the stone yurt wall.

He tried to understand what he had found here, what it all meant. His body and mind had no intention of cooperating; they demanded he succumb to exhaustion, to collapse, to sleep. Eagle knew he had pushed harder than ever before. He didn't welcome the results that would surely come tomorrow. He fell asleep thinking about this stone yurt. No matter how strange, it was probably the home of some other Ruck, perhaps the men he had encountered.

He dreamed about his friends, about Rose and the other women, about how all of them would be living in new yurts made of stone, with all the *famlee* together in a large circular room, with wolves guarding the entryway on the wooden planks, and with *ven* roaming the hills all around.

The next morning was like no other in his life. As soon as he opened his eyes, he looked out over a new world. He propped his back more flatly against the stone yurt and gazed down the rock path. It actually went downwards, along a gradually sloping hillside. Last night, he couldn't see as well; the slope wasn't obvious, and he hadn't really tried to look past the yurts. Now, in the glorious morning sun, he could see the village of stone and wood yurts extending out before him. This one was just the first along the path.

For a heartbeat, he wondered if he were safe. Surely the villagers would come out to greet each other, to start the day's hunting or weaving or tanning. In the light of day, Eagle realized he had slept against the stone yurt's version of an entry flap. Now, just an arm's length away from it, he felt vulnerable. Who were the residents? Ruck? Overlords?

Eagle stood, grimacing. The ankle was impossibly swollen. He staggered around to the side of the yurt and slid to the ground. He could still see down the path, but no flaps gave entrance here, so he wouldn't be seen by anyone leaving. He watched, welcoming the warmth of day. The village remained still. The sun ascended. Stillness, except for the small animals and birds.

Eagle eyed the crumbling wooden yurt. It looked like no one had touched it for a long time. He felt odd, hobbling over to it while harboring a nagging feeling that he was being watched even though half the morning had burned away with no one passing by—no Ruck, no Black Ones, no Overlords, no wolves. He ducked around the corner, bumping into the large object he had seen last night.

Under broken wood, grime, and leaves, what must have been a *cart* sat before him. It smelled funny, had green stuff growing on it, and tilted, sort of, toward one of the four corners, which rested on square stones. One of the stones was half-crumbled. It had to be a *cart*; he could see that its only reason for existence was to move, by some miracle of God, and to carry Ruck or their belongings safely. It had a massive, hard shell, made of a strange material. Holes had worn through in many places. There was a space in the back of it that looked like it could carry several *ven*. It looked like one of the legendary *pickemups*. It didn't look capable of going anywhere now. Once, it must have been a wonder.

He thanked God again, considering this a sign. If only he could somehow show this to the other Ruck. No, they would have to follow him and find these wonders, too.

Hunger began to call again. The amazing village had distracted him for a time; as the sun lingered directly overhead, his stomach started to take over. It complained more than the ankle; the combination forced Eagle to look for shelter and sustenance. He dragged himself back to the stone yurt, stepped onto the wood planks, and leaned against the opening. The wooden barrier held when Eagle pressed on it with one hand. He tried two. It budged, so he pushed harder. Something seemed to be pushing back. Eagle let go, stumbling backwards. He froze. He waited many heartbeats. Nothing happened.

When he approached again, he took one hard step on his good leg, leaning his full weight against the barrier. It creaked. He lunged again. It pushed open a crack and something slid behind it. He pushed again, extending the crack and meeting the obstacle behind it. Light streamed in, like it was the first time in a lifetime. He pushed one last time. It opened enough to squeeze through.

Eagle staggered in and blinked against the dust he had stirred up. He saw a couple of sturdy partitions, dividing different areas of the yurt. A strange set of wooden steps blocked his immediate path, just behind the obstacle that had held the door. It turned out to be a large wooden box. The steps seemed to lead up to another yurt, up above this one. He passed the steps and entered an opening before the next partition.

This area was a mess. There were strange objects strewn about; they were all broken, twisted, splintered. Some appeared be wood, or fabric, others ceramic or strange material similar to the *cart*. He picked at the pile, removing an item or two to see what was beneath. Many strange objects. One caught his eye.

It was a *book*. A real *book*. He saw the cover—dirty, broken, but still holding together. Garnet had been the first to tell him about the *books* and the days when the Ruck knew how to *reed* and *rite*. As Hawk had pointed out in one of their last public arguments, the Overlords punished the Ruck severely when the men tried to teach the children anything about them. Garnet had told Eagle about *books*. In turn, Eagle sometimes told the children stories about them, never in large groups, only in private, like during his time with Mace and Ram. Certainly, he had never seen one. Picking it up with care, Eagle found that some pieces of it had fallen or been torn out. He picked up a couple of pieces and stuffed them into his vest. He carried the *book*, while looking for something like food or water.

Another opening led to another partitioned section of the yurt. Larger, it too was ruined, as if someone or something had picked through all its contents, discarding the undesirable in search of some valued item. Here, he found something of interest. A container, made again of material like the *cart's* shell, with a faded image on it, an image of one of tiller's root *veg*. It was old and completely empty. The edge was sharp, too; he nicked his knuckle reaching into it and sucked on it to stop the bleeding.

He saw that he could go back to the entry barrier from here, toward the steps. He could also try to pass another strong barrier, which appeared to lead outside. A third exit seemed the most interesting. A battered wood barrier leaned against an opening, failing to hide another set of steps, these going down. Eagle hesitated. Not much sunlight penetrated down the steps, and it didn't look like there were any flaps down there. He would need light before going down.

He chose the steps up. First, he pulled the wooden box out away from the front barrier so he could open it all the way and let the sunlight spill in. It took forever, as every tug caused his ankle to shout at him. Still, his efforts gave him plenty of light to use the steps. He found two entryways at the top and more steps continuing upward, behind him. Through one of the entryways, thin rays of light intruded. He stepped through.

Another ruined area. Most of the space was taken by something that looked like a bed. Softer and thicker than the Ruck beds of *ven*-hide or cloth, it certainly looked like it would be comfortable for sleeping. If he cleaned off some of the debris, he might get good rest here. Eagle had convinced himself by now; no one would find him here. This must have been one of the *sitties* of the *Yewessay*, old and unused since the Overlords came.

He peeked into the other area and saw much of the same, although it was darker in there. He decided not to go further up the steps. He would need to build a fire, and then carry a torch with him. Eagle wished he had one of the women's candles. He descended and paused near the front barrier, his ankle sore from going up and down the steps. There were scraps of wood in the ruins. He could save himself some effort. No, better to collect firewood as always and build something small outside, perhaps shielded by the wood yurt. After sliding down each step one at a time, and hobbling out of the stone yurt, he dropped the *book* behind the wood yurt and went hunting for wood.

Eagle's ankle complained more than ever as he collected the dry twigs. He found enough to start a small fire. He hastily snatched a few larger branches, hoping one of them would make a decent torch. Cloth or other tinder would help, too. He thumped his head and realized he should have taken some from the stone yurt ruins. He shambled back to the front barrier and retrieved some tattered old strips that looked like they would burn easily.

Slowing down now he had gathered supplies, Eagle patiently started his fire. He nursed it until it was burning hot, then he added the pieces of branches he had chopped up. He stretched the pieces of cloth around one end of another sturdy branch, tying them off. When the fire was hot enough to burn on its own for a while, Eagle held the branch over the flames and caught the cloth and wood on fire. He knew it wouldn't last long.

He lumbered as fast as he could up onto the planks and through the front barrier. He slid past the wood box and into the ruined area with the steps down. The light helped just enough. Eagle could see the steps below him. He descended, slowly, and found more ruins. Actually, this place had very dim light, coming from a small, dirty, crusted flap just under the roof on two sides. Various things were once kept down here, like tools and materials, he thought, similar to the things that Tanner and Archer kept in their work areas. He searched hard while his torch held. He stumbled across a filthy, crumbling box of small clothing; the pieces looked strange, but Eagle thought they might fit the likes of Moth, the little girl who had recently joined the village. He found a spilled box of small-pointed spikes, again made of a strange hard material like the *cart's* shell. Quickly, he tucked a couple into the fold of his vest with the pieces of the *book*. He found a large pile of clear, sharp fragments interspersed with circular pieces of *cart* shell. He knelt near the pile, carefully picking up a few larger fragments. Incredibly sharp, they surprised Eagle. You could see right through them, but they were as strong as one of Potter's bowls and sharper than a stone knife.

He pulled away more fragments and circles. Beneath, he glimpsed something darker. The torch waned; he thrust it down over the pile and saw what looked like a clear container with one of the circles affixed to the top, holding something dark within. Eagle tried to brush off more of fragments, cutting a finger on one. Finally, he uncovered the intact container. The smashed pieces were once containers like this one, he thought. Somehow, this one hadn't been crushed. Eagle held it up to the torch, but the flame had nearly flickered out. Eagle cradled the container under one arm and pulled himself up the steps again. He shuffled back to the front barrier and stumbled outside to his fire.

Eagle looked at the top circle. He had removed a few from the pile; they looked like they were made to hold tight on the container, yet still be removed somehow. He stared at it, turning it around in his hands and wondering how to make it work. He could break it open if he had to. First, he held the container in one hand and grasped the top in the other, trying and failing to pry it off. Grooves were shaped in the weird material. Eagle ran his fingers along then and wondered what the grooves were for. Extending his fingertips, he gripped the grooves and slid his fingers around in both directions. Instinctively, he grabbed tighter and tried to twist off the top. The container slipped from his grasp and he fumbled with it before tucking it under his arm. He set it on the ground between his knees and tried to twist it. He felt it give way; it worked! The top was turning and loosening. Finally, it spun off and fell to the ground.

The smell rushed up his nostrils. A sweet smell. Nothing he knew compared to it. His mouth watered, and his stomach screamed as he looked at the thick goo inside. He stuck a finger in it and licked. He stuck two fingers in and licked them clean. He could only fit three through the top, so that's what he did, scooping out the sweet goo and devouring it. It tasted marvelous, but he realized he was eating so fast he had barely noticed. With the container half empty, Eagle realized it was getting harder to reach the rest. He slowed down, carefully cleaning the edges with his forefinger and enjoying the taste as he licked off the sweetness.

He fumbled for the top on the ground. He twisted it back on and sat down by his fire, sipping water while leaning against the most solid pole of the wooden yurt. Before long, he dozed off. When he awoke, the moon was above him, and his fire had reduced to embers. He remembered the bed up the steps, but it seemed strange to sleep in the stone yurt, and he had tasked his ankle beyond its limit already. Stretching out, he lay on his back and gazed at the stars until sleep took him.

Dreaming again about Rose, Eagle awoke refreshed. The goo had nourished him, his ankle felt a little better, his spirits were lifted. Another day of rest would do, but he would need water. There must be a source near the *sittie*, he reasoned.

It didn't take long to find. A clear sturdy stream ran along a row of yurts to the outside of the village. Eagle limped down to it and sipped from his cupped hand. It smelled and tasted clean. He drank most of the remainder of his skin, filled it again. It occurred to him to investigate a few more yurts then fill the skin again for the evening. No sign of life appeared any-where in the village. He figured he could search for as long as he wanted. Along the stream he saw that some of the yurts had outside steps, as well as inside, leading down under ground. This helped him to see and explore quickly. None of the other yurts had anything of value, even down below. He found other containers, all empty or broken. He thanked God for the lucky find in the first yurt. Passing another ancient *cart*—and exhausted from using the steps—Eagle filled his skin and re-turned to his camp. Another meal of goo remained. He ate all that remained, resolving to get back on the trail the next morn-ing. He hoped to find the *ven* soon.

Leaving the village of the *Yewessay* in the morning, with all those yurts unexplored, Eagle considered staying a little longer. There might be more to eat underground. He felt the sun on his back; it pushed him into action. Must find the *ven*.

When the day began, Eagle could almost walk without limping. He covered a decent bit of ground, and as he chased the sun toward the horizon, the pain began to mount. He found more and more spoor, getting older and older. At dusk, he saw the drifting, smoky clouds ahead him, thicker here than usual. They seemed to rise from over a hill just north of Eagle's position. He stopped, watching and resting. He looked at the *book* again, which he kept tucked into the waist of his leggings while traveling. The respite helped, but now the sun dipped out of sight. Eagle found a place to sleep and settled in. The cloud intrigued him. Tomorrow, he would mount the hill.

◆ ◆ ◆

When he did, he saw more of the smoky clouds billowing from the other side. Eagle pushed harder, straining his ankle, ignoring it while pushing still harder. When he crested the hill, he looked down into a valley. Not just any valley.

This place had many *ven*. Beyond Eagle's ability to count.

Pressed together within barriers, some of them shifting nervously in small moving groups, others lying down and huddling together in sleep. Beyond them was a giant yurt, so big Eagle didn't think it made sense to call it a yurt, with long rounded pillars reaching to the sky, spewing the smoky clouds.

Eagle froze on the hillcrest, trying to comprehend the size of this ... whatever this was. He watched the *ven* mill about, strangely, unlike the bucks and does Eagle was used to hunting. The sheer number of them continued to astonish Eagle. Enough to feed the Ruck for many winters. Someone had trapped them here. The Overlords? Overseers? *Free* Ruck?

Finding out became the most important thing to Eagle now. The slope wasn't steep; he hobbled down quickly. As he neared, he saw some of the *ven* eating from a long shallow box. Coming closer to the barrier, Eagle slowed and picked a tree to lean against. If the Overlords had anything to do with this, there might be a *tekline*, too. Fortunately, he hadn't hit one yet.

Eagle hoisted himself up into the lower tree limbs, getting a better view. From this new perch, he could see something new in a large opening on this side of the massive yurt. A structure of steps, or something like steps, rose from the ground, up into the top of the yurt. No, not steps, more like ropes, which appeared to be moving, sliding up along poles. Now, things were being pulled up by the ropes, lifted from the ground and jerked up toward the roof of the yurt.

He couldn't tell what the ropes lifted, not at first. He studied the moving lines, watching them dip under the roof. Shapes became clear. *Ven* carcasses, hanging upside down, some with their blood draining out. Eagle stared. None of this made any sense. Suddenly, the ropes picked up something different, larger than the *ven*. Eagle focused. As the thing reached the middle of the line, Eagle shuddered.

It was a man. A large hairy man ... as large as ... Mountain.

Eagle nearly fell out of the tree. He caught himself and climbed down. He moved closer, to the edge of a clearing. He saw other Ruck being hoisted up the line, men and children interspersed with the *ven*. He counted almost a dozen. Mountain remained the only one that Eagle recognized. Unlike some of the *ven*, Mountain's body was long since lifeless—drained of blood, Eagle saw, as it ducked under the roof. All the Ruck bodies looked like that.

Trying to set himself gently on the ground, Eagle winced when he put pressure on the ankle. He knew he had to get away from here. Still, he wasn't leaving without taking one of the *ven* and understanding more about this strange place. He snuck in closer. It was the easiest hunt of his life. He wondered if the arrow would trigger a *tekline*. It didn't matter. He was going in. He shot the *ven* cleanly, apologizing to it, and perhaps to all of them, out loud. Moving up, Eagle climbed over the low rails of the wood barrier. Other *ven* scattered in front of him. It seemed silly now; he could have walked up and grabbed one. In any case, he found his kill and prepared it for travel.

While he did, he also watched the other *ven* calmly eating from the long rows of boxes. His eyes following the boxes back towards the large yurt, Eagle saw that the rows continued upwards into this side of the structure, forming a slide. With the *ven* slung over his back, Eagle hobbled along the length of the box until he neared the yurt. The stuff the *ven* ate came directly from the yurt, down the slide. For many heartbeats, Eagle's haggard mind wrestled with these strange findings. The dead *ven* and dead Ruck going in. The stuff coming out. Eagle tried to step over the box, to go directly around the side of the yurt with the rope pull, but the *ven* was too heavy. He almost fell over the long box, catching himself just in time to limit the damage to a bruise on the shin above his bad ankle. He stumbled down the length of the box row and turned around the end of it. Trembling, Eagle reached the rope pull. He could see into the yurt from here. He saw the *ven* bodies jerking up the rope and dropping into a giant bowl. He froze, staring, until his instincts took over. He stumbled backward toward the slope, breathing hard.

When Eagle reached the low barrier, the Black One on the

other side blocked his path up the hill. Eagle halted. Suddenly, he felt powerless. The fatigue of his journey, the sight of the lifeless Mountain going into yurt, the stuff coming out, his ankle, the sheer weight of the *ven*, it all overwhelmed him. He reeled.

The Black One ended Eagle's pain and confusion, releasing a lightning bolt from its staff and striking Eagle in his chest.

9

When Eagle awoke this time, he had no idea where he was. Darkness enveloped him, even while small streams of light forced their way into his vision. He had no recollection of how he got there, either. The sweet smell of wildflowers demanded his attention. He inhaled the scent, filling his lungs through his nose and exhaling through his mouth. The aroma awakened his senses.

He was on his back, in a yurt. The sunlight peeked in through the flap and it also penetrated the seams where the ven-hide was too loosely stitched. It seemed familiar, this yurt, but it definitely wasn't his. Rolling his eyes around, he decided it was smaller than his, more like one of the visitation yurts in the women's compound. This thought crystallized in his mind. Like the women's yurts. Exactly like ...

Bolting upright to look around, Eagle's entire body revolted. He gasped, then screamed. Or rather, he tried to scream. Instead, a horrible scratching sound issued from his throat. His limbs seemed to throb in time with his beating heart, and every beat brought waves of agony. He fell onto his back again, moaning. Despite the pain, he had glimpsed the divider in the yurt before he collapsed again. Also, he looked down a row of low wooden blocks supporting numerous candles just in front of the divider. The same candles the women made in the compound, arranged just as he remembered from his numerous visits. Although Eagle didn't know whose yurt this was, he knew he was back in the compound.

The flap opened. Sunlight poured in and Eagle lost his vision. Even the sun caused him pain. The flap closed.

"Eagle?"

Even though Eagle could see nothing but whiteness, he knew the voice. "Star?" The word, dry and rumbling in his throat, barely escaped.

"You're alive!" She dropped to her knees, hugging him. Eagle cried out again.

"I'm sorry," Star said again, "I should have known even after all these days—well, you still haven't recovered."

"What?" Eagle strained, but he couldn't put words together. It felt like a piece of bone was lodged in his throat.

"What?" Star stared at him.

Eagle focused on one concept. "Days?"

Star looked even more puzzled. "Days, um, what about days?"

Eagle strained again. Star waited, reaching for a water jug and cup.

"How ... many ..."

"How many days have you been here?" she ventured.

He wanted to nod. He managed a blink.

"I don't know exactly. I mean, almost a moon, I guess. We've had a visit from the men since the Black One brought you here."

"What ... when ..." Eagle grimaced with each throat-gouging word.

"Don't talk. I'll tell you what I know." Star had filled a cup and now she knelt beside him. "Here, I'll lift your head so you can drink. I'm tired of dribbling it in your mouth with a cloth."

Once he had taken a few sips, Star began to talk. Eagle let her words fill him. He stared at her face—beautiful, a woman's face now. She told him of some of the events since his escape. Her words reassured him and frightened him. As she talked, he remembered some of the escape and the journey afterwards, but seemingly only pieces of it all. She would remind him of something, which led his mind on a trail of disjointed memories—vague images—from outside of the valley. He had to ask her to repeat things frequently; he couldn't keep up with her narrative as his bursts of memory distracted him.

To learn that the Ruck had gone on, and that his escape had changed them, lightened Eagle's heart. Nevertheless, to learn all over again about his capture, to realize how close to death he must have been, to face the unavoidable truth of his re-imprisonment now ... it hurt Eagle as much as his physical ailments.

It took several days for Eagle to learn everything that had happened and to regain his memories—recent and long past. He slept often, for long periods of time, finally shaking the stillness but remaining weak. Star sat with him most of the time; he also saw his mother and Rose, individually, on a few occasions. Eagle had problems remembering much of anything at first. When he saw their faces, some fond memories flooded back to him. He was too weak for much more than a broad smile and a few words here and there, as each of them sat and spoke to him. They held his hand, made him drink strange smelling liquids (not the *shroom* brew!), and wiped his brow with a cool cloth.

Rose's presence lifted his spirit. Her belly had grown so much; she took his hand and placed it there. Eagle's heart pounded when he felt the child kicking and squirming inside her. Rose's now plump face glowed in the sunlight that streamed in through the open flap—or from the candlelight when she visited after dark. Each time, Rose seemed pleased to see him, although she seemed equally troubled. Eagle realized all three of the women acted the same way. He treasured the time he spent with each of them; he felt connected to each of them in a different way. This thought made him cry; it made him feel weaker. He had sobbed himself to sleep the night after Rose's first visit.

Star told him that the Overseer brought his almost lifeless body to the compound, about half a moon after her first visitation. The Black One commanded Honey to care for Eagle until he could stand on his own, and then he turned and spoke aloud for all the women to hear. A rarity, Star told him. The Overseer said any future attempts to leave the valley would result in the death of those attempting to escape, as well as an equal number of additional villagers in the next hunt. Later, the women learned that the Black One had given the same speech in the village.

Because Star was one of the few women without children (or at least without one on the way), her yurt was chosen for Eagle's recovery. Eagle remained in the stillness for more than a dozen days, long enough for Star's second visitation to take place. She giggled when she told Eagle how they had to move him into the common area for those three nights. No one knew what would happen if they moved him; he had lain there motionless, breathing but showing no other sign of life, getting thinner and thinner. They felt they had no choice; Star needed her yurt, and no others were available. They couldn't put him with Rose; her children prohibited that, the same as the other pregnant women. So, they hung a blanket in a corner of the commons and set him down there. It took the combined efforts of Honey, Star, Nightingale, and Butterfly to lift him and haul him across the compound. They feared he wouldn't make it through the night without Star's constant care, but Rose managed to sit with him for a time each of the nights.

Eagle learned that he had awoken from the stillness three days after they had moved him back to Star's yurt. He wasn't sure how many days had passed since then. In the last day or two, he had gained a little strength, stayed awake a little longer each day, and asked a brief question now and then instead of laying helpless and silent, listening to whatever the women chose to say when he first awoke.

Many of the names that Star mentioned had eluded him initially. Even though they sounded familiar, he couldn't remember why he knew them. Star had become Pearl, she told him; this became perhaps the most difficult thing to remember while he listened to her. His voice returned, slowly, painfully, as the piece of bone seemed to dissolve, slowly.

He discovered that the women now believed his sister Faith was pregnant for the first time. It seemed that Nightingale had also conceived again. Apparently, they would both participate in the next visitation, even though Lotus had predicted it wouldn't make any difference. For some reason, Star—no, Pearl, he reminded himself—mentioned that Faith had been with Coot, Bison, and Thrush during the previous moon. Pearl just knew that Thrush was the father of Faith's child. The last two names, Bison and Thrush, surprised Eagle, although he couldn't say exactly why in that moment. He thought about it more, later, understanding it meant those two boys had joined the ranks of the men in the village. Now, Pearl's insistence that Thrush must be the father of Faith's child consumed Eagle's mind. After he told her there was no telling, she continued to insist, more vehemently. Eagle couldn't stifle a chuckle. He regretted it; immediately, he felt like someone was squeezing his chest with a taut rope. He coughed and sputtered, struggling to breathe. Pearl did her best to comfort him and pass a cup to his lips while they sat awkwardly and silently for a while.

While everyone thought Faith and Nightingale would have their last visitation for some time, Mantis was among the women skipped for the visit during which Eagle spent unconscious in the commons. She had missed two circles; it was obvious to everyone that she would bear another child. And Lilly's child was expected any moment. Pearl said Lilly was a big as a yurt and getting bigger every day! While she talked of the other women, Pearl kept dropping hints about the arrangement of the men during her first visitation, noting that Mantis had lain with Justin, Oak, and Sage at that time. Eagle wondered if she wanted him to know with whom she had lain, even though she couldn't bring herself to say it aloud. He wouldn't ask. If she wanted him to know she would have to make up her mind to tell him. Besides, some of those names remained confusing to him.

Eagle learned that Jade had died in childbirth, shortly after

Eagle returned. At first, Eagle couldn't remember who Jade was. The baby, a boy, had survived. Pearl didn't elaborate on the complications of the birth. She told him about the burning of Jade's body and the ceremony led by Lotus. All the women gathered the following night in the commons with all the children (Pearl said Rose, Ruby, and she took turns checking on Eagle during the night). Faith held Jade's baby most of the night, but Pearl said she held him from time to time. Pearl said they sang and danced, which surprised her at the time. Not the same kind of singing as the night of the visitation. They stayed together longer; they each spoke about the goodness in Jade; they danced to a much slower drum; they sang to grieve, not to rejoice.

Suddenly, Eagle remembered the night he and his mother had talked about Jade. Somehow this particular memory opened the gate to many more. Faces and names danced in his head; he remembered Jade and Lotus, a man named Wolf, a boy named Tiller. The rush of memories shocked him, and he closed his eyes, hoping to slow the torrent. Seeing Eagle's pained expression, Pearl insisted that the singing and dancing was the best way to say goodbye and for the women to remember it could happen to any of them. She had mistaken Eagle's expression; the story and rush of memories had now rekindled his memory of Badger as well. Images of his little brother's funeral hurried back to him, as if he had awakened from a dream. His brother, just a small boy! He shed tears, while he explained his sudden recollections to Pearl. They sat quietly the rest of the evening.

Such recovered memories became a daily occurrence for Eagle. As the women continued to tell him about the events of the two moons, things burst into his mind without warning. At times, physical weakness overwhelmed him, or his emotions became more than he could bear. Often, he would fall asleep under the stress. As the days passed, he sometimes awoke refreshed, hoping to learn and remember more. Other days everything seemed pointless, or he would grow too tired to comprehend, asking the women if they could simply feed him and leave him alone.

And so, news and history of the village came slow to Eagle. He did learn that Falcon had joined with Sage and Thrush in leading the children who had chosen to follow Eagle before his escape. It hadn't happened right away, but soon after the news of Eagle's escape had spread throughout the village, Falcon announced that Eagle had proven escape was possible. He wanted freedom, too. According to Rose, the man encouraged the older children to join with him. Justin stayed, but he never questioned Falcon's decision. He simply told the younger children they could stay with him and Spider and Coyote for as long as they wanted. Some did stay—especially the youngest of them all. Oak and few of the older children went with Falcon. Oak's name rung as important in Eagle's mind, but he still had trouble recognizing many of these names. Aside from Sage and Thrush—oh yes, and Mace and Ram—Eagle couldn't remember the names of most of the children who had sided with him before the escape. His inability to remember names made him feel ashamed. Nevertheless, the importance of the escape itself was clear to him. All the details—how he had escaped, why he left, and what he did before the Black One brought him to the compound—stayed in fog, even while he remained sure his escape held great significance.

By and by, Pearl did tell him about the men who had visited her yurt. Eagle had begun to feel stronger for longer stretches of the day. He could sit up for short stretches. He had begun to chew on small pieces of *veg* and *pem*. Something about the *pem* seemed odd to him; it tasted the same as he remembered, although a thought nagged at him as he chewed. Something told him he shouldn't be eating it even though it made him feel better. He was able to stay awake longer, and he sometimes had conversations, rather than simply taking in whatever the women decided to share with him. One morning he listened to Pearl talk without any prompting, as he chewed the *pem* and sipped a steaming brew. She spoke quickly, like she needed to get something out before he spoke. That first moon, there was an extra woman, she explained, so three of them had one night each without a man. Pearl was the first one of the three to be skipped, and then she had been with Falcon ... and ... on the last night ... Hawk.

Eagle felt like a defeated fool the rest of the day. Rose had visited him later, after Pearl told him her story. He couldn't face her; he asked her to leave. Over the days of recovery, the three women had spent time holding his hand, helping him sit up for a bit, telling him about the events in the village and the compound. And throughout all the foggy, weakened days here in Pearl's yurt, Eagle hadn't thought of Hawk or their battle for supremacy, or what his own return would now mean for the village. He had listened to the women's stories, but they had rarely mentioned the man's name. How could Eagle have forgotten Hawk's name? How could he forget their rivalry? Perhaps that's why Pearl had hinted so much about the visitation. Eagle could forgive himself for the first days of recovery, when he could barely talk or think, but by now he should have focused on his return to the village. He shouldn't have needed Pearl's mention of the visitation to shock him from his sick bed. *Fug!* By now, he should have started figuring out what he would do when he could walk again. With the awakened memory of his rival, the events leading up to Eagle's escaped returned like a rockslide in his mind.

Eagle felt foolish and powerless. For the next three days, none of his caretakers could rouse him from his despair. He couldn't even stand; he reminded himself over and over, (as if he needed to be punished for his weakness). How was he going to go back to the village and lead again? How was he going to face Hawk, having proved that Hawk was right about an attempted escape costing the lives of other Ruck? How would he answer Hawk's inevitable arguments? How would he overcome the fact that everything Hawk predicted had come to pass? Yes, Eagle thought, he had escaped, but only to be captured and returned as a weak and helpless man who had endangered everyone. Would his followers (whoever they might be now) keep their belief in his words of freedom? Or would they conclude Hawk's way was better for the Ruck to go on? He tortured himself with these thoughts. He allowed the women to sit with him for those three days, but he told them to sit in silence. Honey refused to stay at all, and she told him what she thought of his orders. Rose and Pearl continued his feedings, although they stayed for shorter stretches and refrained from touching him or saying anything beyond requests for Eagle to sit up and eat or drink.

The despair gave him one benefit—it focused his mind on remembering everything he could dig from his cluttered mind. Eagle started to piece together what happened before the escape. Piece-by-piece, he remembered more about the journey on the other side of the *tekline*, even the horrible parts and memories some barrier in his mind had fought to keep secret.

The rift that divided the Ruck into three groups solidified in his memory. The many arguments with Hawk had grown more open and all save the youngest children began to choose a leader to follow. A boy named Fly had continued the story-telling, which, in Eagle's mind, was the most important ritual of the Ruck. Stories of *freedom* could help the Ruck to go on. Young men and older boys and girls had chosen one man or another—Eagle or Hawk—and pledged to follow his lead so the Ruck would go on. And Falcon, yes, of course ... the square-jawed, powerful man with the green eyes who had stayed neutral for so long. He had joined Justin—or was it the Justin-before?—when the rift began, insulating the smaller children from the unfathomable decision about whom to follow. Those who were too young to understand, those who simply couldn't choose because of their natural disposition, or those who had friends in both camps—they had all taken refuge in the neutral camp.

Eagle finally remembered his long-executed plan for escape. He tried to see the names and faces of the men and children who had chosen to follow him. Sage and Thrush, the brothers, of them he was certain. Fly and ... Fly and ... no, Raven and Fly. They weren't part of his inner circle; no, it was Mace and Ram, the eager young boys with whom he spent many days, speaking of his relationship with God while they practiced the jump across the *tekline*. The three of them had done it; they had figured out how to escape during the changing of the Black One. And Star! (No, Pearl now, he reminded himself again). How could he forget, even as she sat with him in her yurt, helping him gain strength? She, too, helped to make the escape possible. The realization only made him feel more isolated and more helpless during his bout with this spiritual malaise. Still, each recollection led to even more. Now, Eagle could visualize many of the children, from Fish and Dreamer to Ash and Chase.

Who had gone with Hawk? Eagle struggled to remember the individuals. For a whole day, all he could see in his mind was the image of the black-haired man lecturing the children around the fire after he objected to the storytelling. Gradually, other images returned, such as Hawk sitting at the spot—watching the Black One with the boy called Shadow—or Hawk and Bison rounding up a hunting party. Eagle tried to picture the children in Hawk's group. Some faces and names became clear: Nardo, Fox, Tanner, Ox. Yes, it was true, Ox, Eagle's own brother. And Tanner, the young woman whose long orange hair and round hips always made Eagle pause. Something didn't ring true about the girl named Fox; he couldn't figure out what. And Eagle remembered a tall man who rarely spoke. A man he respected even though he had chosen Hawk's side. The memory felt like it was hidden from him. No matter how hard he tried, he couldn't recall anything else about the tall man.

Still, Eagle knew the tall man was important. During the third day of his funk, Eagle fought to remember why. Strangely, new images returned while he struggled to reassemble his broken memories. He saw himself running and running, not in the valley, but beyond it. The leap across the *tekline* flashed in his mind often, then the running, but he couldn't remember where he ran to. He focused on those memories, seeing himself running, feeling the thirst in his throat and the ache in his limbs. Every time, his mind ended up back at the village, trying to recall the name of the tall man who lingered over Hawk's shoulder.

Eagle became more and more determined. He shunned the women one afternoon, declining their offers to feed and clean him. They left shaking their heads. He closed his eyes, concentrating, reaching deeper and deeper into his mind. Finally, other images crept in. He remembered a pool of clear water, a place where he quenched his thirst and filled his water skin. A place where he hoped to find *ven*, but none came near. He remembered searching for the *ven*, running and searching. Another village flashed before his eyes—yes, the empty village, with the large stone and wood yurts. The memory triggered a smell ... something special ... something he could almost taste now. The sweet, sticky goo. He remembered it now! A gift from God. This thought faded quickly, as he now remembered pain. Body-wracking pain. He had turned his ankle— he remembered it now—but that injury seemed like a nuisance compared to the memory of the agony in the darkness. No, this other memory of suffering endured; it never ceased. It pounded in his head and rippled through all his limbs, coursing up and down the length of his body like a blanket being pulled on and off during winter. Involuntarily, as he succumbed to the excruciating memory, Eagle's eyes rolled back into his head, and he began to choke.

Pearl ducked through the flap and fell to her knees beside him. She raised him up, with great effort, until he caught his breath, sputtering. Eagle's head pounded. He passed out.

When he awoke, Eagle found Pearl staring at him. Dim candlelight filled her yurt. Eagle's saw the tall man's face again in his mind. He saw the man and the *ven*, together, images alternating between blinks of the eye. He started to see more

—a giant yurt with ropes and long boxes of muddy liquid. As Eagle focused on the yurt, the pain returned. It began in his head, pressing against his skull, as if every thought of the huge yurt—and now, the thought of many *ven* around it—increased the anguish and bounced it back and forth in his mind. Eagle shook and frothed at the mouth; Pearl held his hand while she mopped his forehead and cleansed his lips. He pushed back against the pain, trying to see the giant yurt more clearly in his thoughts. He saw ropes pulling *ven*. Agony seized him, making the images in his mind white and formless. He fought it, pushing through the whiteness, shaking, and shivering through the pain while Pearl gripped his hand and stared, unable to help him. He saw the ropes, *ven* eating out of long, low boxes, a man, a child … pain … whiteness … a man, a child … blinding, piercing whiteness … agony … a man …

"Mountain!" he screamed, so loud that Eagle shocked Pearl out of her paralysis and knocked her from her knees to her rear.

"Mountain!" he cried. "No!"

Deep in the night, Eagle stirred. His body demanded sleep; his mind resisted. Remembering Mountain and the giant yurt opened another gate in his memory. Things came back to him through the darkness, in fits and starts and long stretches.

His whole journey seemed to play itself in reverse in his mind, starting from The Black One striking with its lightning bolt. As Eagle now recalled what he had seen at the giant yurt, with all the *ven*, the meaning also became clearer. When he had seen the rope pull and the *ven* slop with his own eyes, his mind had shut down. Now, in recollection, everything he found during the journey began to make sense. The tracks, the smoke, the behavior of the *ven* (whether in the valley or at the giant yurt). He noticed a few pieces of *pem* by his side, left by the women in case he awoke hungry. He had been eating it for days now, with the strange aftertaste nagging him as he chewed. Now, the taste seemed vile. Eagle felt a lump in his throat. He couldn't imagine himself eating another piece of *pem*. The vision of Mountain's dangling body, dropping into the huge bowl that fed the *ven*, made the thought unbearable.

He remembered the whole stone village. The *carts*, the beds, the mess, the underground. The stream. The *book*. What had happened to it?

Before the stone village, the fall in the dark and his wounded ankle. The men. For the first time since finding himself in Pearl's yurt, he thought of the *free* Ruck he encountered outside the *tekline*. The *pem* they gave him, his frantic attempt to communicate. Eagle wondered how many more of them were out there. And the *shrooms*! The strange visions. The power of the sun coursing through him. Running and digging and talking and laughing. And breathing. And running and running. Before that, the days and nights without food. The pool and the wolf—no, two of them. A man named Wolf. When Eagle returned to the village, he would have to find the man and tell him about the legendary creatures for which he was named. He remembered the rabbits and the birds. He remembered *freedom*. Running through the hills as if carried on the breath of God. Finally (or rather, initially) the *tekline*, his escape.

Eventually, Eagle would drift off to sleep in Pearl's yurt that night, only to awake with the sequence playing in his mind again. Even though he had recalled much, his memories seemed like a closed hoop, holding certain things in while refusing to let other things in or out. Eagle had convinced himself—something was missing. It nagged him because he couldn't point to any remaining gaps in his memory, despite his feelings. Not between the moons of planning and his actual escape. Not in the specific events leading up to his plan or any of the moons since well before the last winter. Those things all came together. All the arguments with Hawk, the races, wrestling, storytelling, the Hunts, everything had returned to him. Yet, his mind wouldn't rest. Something else.

Eagle searched his memory. He relived the last several moons at a rapid pace, enjoying some good memories and feeling foolish for some old mistakes. Mostly, he recounted good things, like the day he rounded up five children and took them for archery lessons and hunting, even though he knew there were no *ven* to be found. Again, the thought of hunting *ven* became bittersweet. So much of his life—all of the Ruck's lives—depended on it. He had proved his skill, from a boy to a man. It was one reason he had become a leader among the Ruck. It only confused him now, as every good memory of hunting reminded him of Mountain.

Each time he ran through the events of those many moons, he always ended up back at the *tekline*. Then he ran and met the men and found the pool and found the village and seen the giant yurt and the *ven* and then ...

The Black One. That's when it ended. Until he woke up here, in Pearl's tent. That was the gap. What had happened to him after the lightning bolt struck? He should have died, as had many other Ruck struck with the Overlord's weapons during the Hunt. From the descriptions of his condition given by the women, and his pain when he awoke, Eagle surmised he had been very near death. Maybe God had given him another chance. Or perhaps the Overseers or the Overlords kept him alive for some reason. Something was still hidden from him; he felt certain. Something about the time between the giant yurt and Pearl's yurt. He tried to count the days of *freedom*, comparing it to what Pearl had told him of the number of visits since his departure. He couldn't be sure of his count, but anyway he figured it, he was always left with a large difference.

Sleep threatened Eagle again, but now he fought it. The missing time, he must remember it, he told himself. Now. Before the sun rose again. He would have to return to the village soon. He would have to stand on his own. The memory of that time meant something. It felt like he was trying to control the direction of the smoke from his fire in the village, defying the wind and God's whim. And what was God's whim? Eagle spoke out loud, asking God to make things clear to him, to reveal the elusive memories. He asked whether his capture and return was part of a plan, a mysterious plan to help the Ruck. At first, the thought comforted Eagle. The more he thought about this possibility, the more it gave him strength to fight off the sleep, to keep searching for that last gate in his mind, the one barring his way to the truth. Still, his faith wobbled. Why would God hide these memories? Why had his attempt at *freedom* been denied? He had kept his faith, followed his heart, and trusted in God's guidance to escape the Overlords and find *freedom* beyond the *tekline*. And yet, everything he recalled seemed to mock any plans of the God that Eagle knew. Eagle couldn't help but wonder what it all meant.

Suddenly, he remembered Coot's parting words: *"Go with the Goddess."* Lying in the women's compound, unable to remember anything about the time after the Black One's strike, Eagle began to wonder why the old man had said that. Did he truly believe in the Goddess? Like the women? Could they be right? If so, what plans did she have for the Ruck? Why would she deny his memory? God or Goddess, none of it made any sense to him, anymore.

Eagle pushed himself up onto his elbow. He grew tired of lying there helpless. Perhaps this itself was the problem. He had lingered here too long, exhausting his mind while letting his body heal. Fresh air, if he could get it, would clear his head. Watching the sun itself rise above the valley, instead of welcoming only the tiniest of rays that managed to penetrate the yurt's seams ... yes, that would help. The night waned; before long, the sun would appear over the hills. He decided he would stand up, right now, and leave the yurt.

Pushing from his elbow to a sitting position, Eagle winced. His back ached, but he refused to stop, tucking one leg underneath him as he prepared to lift himself to one knee. That accomplished, he inhaled deeply, ignoring the aches rippling through his entire body. He planted one foot squarely next to the knee. Pausing, Eagle steadied himself with both hands on the ground, realizing the foot he intended to stand on belonged to the ankle he had injured during his journey. He had hobbled on it for days before reaching the giant yurt. Now, he pushed up with all his strength, and—for one heartbeat, before the tremendous pain shot up from his ankle, through his leg, into his torso, and right up behind his eyes—Eagle felt strong again.

He gasped, closing his eyes. The ankle buckled and he fell hard. He didn't scream. He dragged himself back to the layers of *ven*-hide and cloth, trying to settle in on his back. Waves of agony coursed through him, reminding him of a pain he had felt once before. When? His mind swirled. He had never been hurt like this. Even when it happened, even when he had first injured the ankle, it hadn't overwhelmed him so. Of course, the *shrooms* changed everything that night, but something didn't seem right. Eagle cried out now, like he had ... when? Again, the real pain of the now mingled with some memory of before. Excruciating, beginning in his ankle, no, his head—maybe both —and running up and down his arms and legs and pounding in his head and tearing at his groin. He cried out now as he cried out then, begging for them to stop, begging and pleading for them to let him *free*. Them. It came to him, like an arrow piercing a morning fog and striking its target. Them. Three of them. Three Overlords. And an Overseer. Gripping and twisting his ankle, attaching things to his head, his arms, his genitals. Feeding him pain as the Overseer commanded him to talk. About what? The escape? How? Who? When?

His reward for silence: agony and repeated questions.

Eagle drifted off, awoke in pain, and repeated this circle until the sun rose. The throbbing in his ankle continued to awake in him the memories of those days on end, helpless, abused, beaten. He wished he had never remembered. He thought he was healed enough to stand and go back to the village. Physically, perhaps he was close. The ankle truly hurt, but he did stand for a heartbeat. If he eased into it, with some support, perhaps his departure from the compound was only a few days away. He had the strength to stand, if he could bear the pain. Still, the wounds to his spirit, his mind, those would take much longer. He could almost see himself on the Overlords' massive slab (it reminded him of the Stone in the Circle) looking up at the beasts. They were hideous and huge. Their long faces hanging from stumpy necks atop massive bodies supported by four, tree-trunk legs. He had forced himself to keep his eyes open as long as possible while they tortured him, trying to see as much of them as possible. Of course, he had seen them during the hunts, but usually from afar or only for a glimpse up close. Now, the Overseer followed their instructions—orders that sounded like screeching baby birds to Eagle's ear. He remembered something else, when he first awoke on the slab of pain. The Black One took something from him, something he clutched in desperation, as if it might deliver him from captivity.

The *book*.

That was what happened to it. They took it from him. Instinctively, he patted his breast, touched the tunic where he had carried the *book* and the *pem* and the *shrooms* and the *veg*. Incredibly, the thing he searched for was still there! The piece of the *book*, the hanging piece he had torn from book that day in the stone village. And a single, hard, thin object deep in a fold of the *ven*-hide. He pulled both of them out, holding one in each hand. He remembered the hard object now—the small *cart*-shell stick with a pointy end and a flat end, the one he had found underground near the life-saving goo. He thought he had taken more of them. He tucked the *cart*-shell stick back into his tunic and dragged himself to the yurt entrance, still clutching the torn piece of the *book* while pushing open the flap and letting in the sun's earliest rays. He squinted, seeing the marks on the torn piece of the *book*. Yes. *Riting*. Carefully, Eagle tucked the piece back into his tunic. He stayed right there, on his back, with his head and shoulders peeking outside of the yurt. He thanked God for the scrap of the lost *book*.

He fell asleep.

The night of fitful memories helped to shake Eagle's despair. He apologized to the women the next morning after Pearl saw his head protruding through the flap. She had called out to the others, afraid her finding would mean the worst, and Eagle awoke before other women had answered Pearl's call. Eagle asked Pearl, Rose, and Honey to tell him more about the village since his escape. He asked that they bring him only *veg* and their brews, no *pem* or fresh *ven*. His mind and body healed together now. He had remembered everything about his journey. His resolve returned. He also remembered he had stuffed more *shrooms* into his pouch, although that was gone now. When he asked Pearl about it, she said they had found the pouch. Its contents were so rotten they had burned it. She also told him Lilly's child was born overnight, a baby girl. Eagle welcomed this news. He asked Pearl to give the mother and child a kiss for him.

For the next few days, the women often found Eagle sitting up when they came to him with food and water. He felt sure he would be able to stand soon. He wanted to, desperately. Returning to the village would be difficult, but he had to face it, and he truly wanted to go back. The sooner the better, since the next visit by the men drew near. He had no intention of being moved to the commons again, awake and aware this time, while the other men spent the three nights in the women's yurts. Eagle decided to learn as much as he could from Rose, Pearl, and Honey before he stood and walked through the gate.

Before long, he realized there was much he needed to know. Things had changed at a rapid pace. The three camps had shifted in composition. Hawk gained a few followers after he gave fearful speeches about Eagle's escape bringing retribution from the Black One and the Overlords themselves. Telling the children they would be safe if they sided with him because his camp had remained loyal to the Overlord's wishes, Hawk had quickly swayed Clay, the new Fletcher, and Tortoise. The news of Clay's choice hurt Eagle until he thought about how his brother must have felt about being a witness to the escape. Honey told Eagle others also seemed to be leaning toward Hawk, especially after the unusual warning from the Black One, although not everyone had been frightened enough to join Hawk's camp.

Before the Overseer's warning, Falcon had declared that Eagle's escape proved many of the arguments for *freedom*. He joined with Sage and Thrush and began to fill in for Eagle, at least according to Pearl. Falcon also encouraged the older children among the Rest—that's what the villagers were now calling the neutral group—to come with him, to stand up and fight for *freedom* rather than submit to the servitude of fear offered by Hawk. They had revived the stories, which had gone dormant during Eagle's early absence. Sage had coached Fly, convincing Raven to join him in the storytelling. The duo told at least one meaningful story of *freedom* every day. Honey said that Falcon (along with Oak, who had also joined their camp) stood up to face every challenge by Hawk until Eagle's rival dismissed such actions as futile and predicted everyone in Falcon's camp would eventually suffer. A few others had followed Falcon to Eagle's camp (now Falcon's camp, Eagle wondered?), including Sky, Herb, and even Wolf. News of the quiet man's choice warmed Eagle. He looked forward to clasping the man's hand and talking with him by the fire. Or, more likely, talking to Wolf while the man stayed silent.

It also pleased Eagle to hear about Justin, who had remained neutral and kept several the smaller children with him. Even Hawk understood the wisdom in allowing the smallest of the villagers to remain insulated from the unsavory truth of the Ruck's situation. Honey said Hawk made subtle attempts to bring the younger ones into his group while he had refrained from overt action. This seemed to be the only thing Falcon, Justin, and Hawk had agreed upon.

Piecing together the information imparted by the three women, Eagle admired how much they all knew about the village. He remembered his visits with his mother and how he would bring her the news. Obviously, other men did the same, and then the women shared their knowledge with each other. They possessed the ability to remain so close, so cooperative, even though some of them were rivals. A few times, Rose and Honey indicated their information came from Mantis or Storm, who continued to support Hawk. Eagle remembered how Storm had welcomed him to her yurt in the visit before his escape, perhaps reluctantly at first, despite her opposition to his actions in the village. He had probably misunderstood the divisions among the women when he learned of the men they supported. They had never separated into camps or stopped communicating and interacting; they had simply declared to each other their support for Hawk's or Eagle's (or neither's) ideas ... and then went about their daily life as they always had.

Finally, when Honey told Eagle she suspected the visit would begin in the next night or two, he told her he would be leaving. He stood up and hobbled, much as he had during his journey, convincing them he was able to leave the compound without help. He saw several of the women, including Rose, as he limped around a small patch of the compound the last day. He asked his mother to join him in Pearl's yurt, and he told her the whole story of his time outside the *tekline*. She seemed to absorb it all, asking questions now and then while listening attentively. She said she would tell all the women the story after he left.

On the final night, still in Pearl's yurt, reflecting on all he learned in those final days of recuperation, Eagle prepared himself for his return to the village. He thought about what he would say, and what he would do, and he wondered how the villagers would greet him. He hoped to enter his camp without encountering any of Hawk's followers, although he prepared himself for the possibility.

With sleep beginning to overcome his thoughts, Eagle focused his remaining energy to review the facts he had gathered about the current state of the village. He had surmised that all three camps were still intact, while he concluded that the makeup of Eagle's (Falcon's) group and Hawk's group indicated an inexorable shift toward two competing groups. Wanting to remember all the names as he used to, Eagle recited the names, almost singing to himself, until he succumbed to slumber.

◆ ◆ ◆

Coot, Justin, Coyote, Carver, Fern, Double, Happy, Huff, Shorty, Snow, Spider, Dove, Tiller, Peck, and Curly.

Falcon, Sage, Archer, Ash, Raven, Fly, Willow, Thrush, Dreamer, Oak, Sparrow, Chase, Henna, Hemp, Earnest, Fish, Blossom, Joy, Rachel, Ram, Parrot, Mace, Newt and Buck, Herb, and Sky ... and the quiet Wolf.

Hawk, Clay, Bison, Axe, Potter, Bear, Tanner, Rock, Rattler, Boar, Weaver, Bee, Nardo, Maize, Fisher, Grouch, Rabbit, Brute, Onyx, Peacock, Red, Shadow, Scar, Fletcher, Hoop, Tortoise, Ox, Copperhead, and Scorpion.

10

To Eagle, it seemed all the women and children had gathered in the morning, all watching him hobble from Pearl's yurt to the compound gate. He felt humbled. The women knew his situation—he had been there for more than a moon; nevertheless, it made Eagle uneasy to feel the eyes of the congregation watching him limp away.

The journey proved slow and painful. By the time the yurts at the edge of the village came into view, Eagle had little energy left. He paused, moving from the path and steadying himself between the lowest branches of a pine. While resting, he composed his thoughts, finalizing what he would say when greeted by the villagers from his camp. He could make an approach to Coot's yurt, as the path came quite close to it, possibly avoiding the happenstance of meeting any of Hawk's followers before finding the old man and asking for his help. After dozens of deep breaths, Eagle saw some movement in the village. He decided waiting would only complicate things. He winced as he moved back to the path, following it for more than a dozen heartbeats before diverting toward Coot's yurt.

He didn't make it. A few young children chased each other near the circle—under the watchful eye of their guardian for the morning, Dove. At once, the gaggle of youngsters spied Eagle. Curly and Peck squealed while Double pointed furiously.

"It's Eagle," the twins shouted, nearly in unison.

"Did you come to play with us?" Double asked, racing toward Eagle with the others just a few steps behind.

Eagle braced himself, remembering the times he had tussled in fun with the children, especially Fish, whose charge would knock him off his feet in his current condition. She wasn't among these children, but Eagle feared that someone else might rush him just as she used to do, latching on to his injured leg and taking him down like a lame *ven*. Fortunately, Dove perceived the imminent danger, loping past the smaller children and interposing himself between them and Eagle.

"Children," he said. "I'm sure Eagle is happy to see you, but he must be tired from his journey."

"We just want to give him a hug," Snow said.

"*Yeeee!*" The others tried get around the older boy but Dove held them off.

"It's so nice to see you all having so much fun," Eagle said. "I will play with you later, I promise."

The cheers began to stir the other Ruck. Dove tilted his head and shrugged. "So much for a quiet return," the boy whispered. "I might as well call the old man." Dove hollered loud enough for everyone in the village to hear.

So much for a quiet return, indeed, Eagle thought. He accepted Dove's arm, leaning against him as they tottered toward Coot's yurt while the commotion spread throughout the village like ripples from a rock skimmed across the lagoon. Eagle had time for only a few words with the old man before much of the village had assembled around the circle.

"Much has changed," Coot said.

"I know."

"They will expect you to speak."

"I'm ready."

Justin sidled his way through the Ruck and stepped inside the circle. He stopped just short of the Stone and addressed the gathering.

"Eagle has returned to us. I'm sure many of us have questions, perhaps even rebukes, but I can see he is weary, and we must not rush things. His escape and return mark a new time for the Ruck. I ask that all of us to be patient, and to respect for each other, in the coming moon. I will ask Eagle to speak, although I expect his words, now, are only the beginning of his story—and ours—since he left us."

Justin stepped back toward Coyote, Spider, Tiller, and the smaller children among the group they now called the Rest. Eagle noticed that Dove had moved to join them. Coot started towards Justin as soon as Eagle starting limping into the circle. Clenching his jaw so he wouldn't grimace from the pain, Eagle weighed Justin's words while searching among the Ruck to smile and wave at his sisters. Justin spoke with more authority than Eagle remembered. His words were wise. Eagle determined to do his best to heed the man's message, keeping brief his first words to the Ruck while still saying what he had say. He paused near the Stone, as Justin had, then stepped up.

"I escaped. I was captured. I was *free* for a time. You can't imagine how it felt. Now, here I am, a prisoner again, a prisoner of the Overlords, as are all the Ruck—at least for now. It seems Hawk and I were both correct." Eagle paused for three heartbeats, deliberately turning his eyes toward Hawk, Shadow, and Bison (and glimpsing Clay and Ox among them). Eagle continued to scan the villagers and continued. "Yes, escape is possible, and yes, the Overlords intend to punish us for it. In the days ahead, all of us must decide whether we will let them punish us, or if we will fight back."

Eagle paused again, briefly locking eyes with a few men, including Justin, Wolf, and finally Hawk. Sensing that his rival wanted to interrupt; Eagle continued. "Yes, I'm weak now, but I will recover. I say 'yes, we fight back,' and I ask each of you to fight with me. I will talk to anyone who wants to hear my story, and I'll listen to anyone who wants to tell me I am wrong. Together, we will decide how the Ruck will go on. I ask you for one day of rest here in the village, and then we can begin. That is how I see it: this is a new beginning in our struggle for the Ruck to go on."

Eagle stepped down. Before anyone else could speak or even step into the circle, Justin had stepped up again with his palm raised. "Please. I know we will exchange many words. Hawk, I know you wish to respond. We have heard your thoughts over the last moon. You do not need to respond. Not yet. I think it is best to give Eagle his day of rest before we debate."

Hawk merely turned away, and his flock followed on his wing. Falcon's camp lingered until he asked them to go about their chores. Willow wanted to approach, but Archer whispered to her. Instead they waved to Eagle as they left. Eagle glimpsed Ash, who was standing near his sisters before they moved on. He smiled at her and she returned the greeting before turning away. Eagle admired her shapely figure; no doubt she would be joining the women before long. He noticed a few of the older children lingering among the Rest, particularly Carver and Tiller. Soon, Thrush, Sage, and Falcon surrounded Eagle, urging him to make his way to his yurt.

Eagle accepted their aid; no need for any pretense of strength. Thrush slid under his left arm while his older brother Sage supported Eagle on the right. Falcon strode in front, chasing off any persistent boys and girls.

"We weren't sure if we would ever see you again, Eagle," whispered Thrush, "until the Black One brought the news."

"And when he did," said Sage, "we weren't sure whether to rejoice or lament."

Eagle glanced at each of the brothers. The elder looked just as Eagle remembered, but Thrush had the air of a man—and not because his wispy patch of reddish chin hair had spread and thickened to the point where he had begun to chop it off. Eagle recalled Pearl's insistence about the father of Faith's child. Visions of his sister and Thrush in the woman's yurt flitted through his mind, to the point of distraction, he realized, as Sage was demanding his attention.

"Eagle, I wonder if you will need more than a day to rest."

They had reached Eagle's yurt and the three men stared at him with doubtful expressions. "No ... I'm sorry, I was just thinking about how much Thrush has grown since ... well, you are truly a man, now."

"Right!" Thrush gesticulated toward his brother and Falcon. "So, tell these two that I should join in their counsel. They want me to stay out here and chase away the children."

"Brother, it's not the children that concern us," said Sage. "We must speak in private with Eagle. You understand well enough."

Thrush scowled at Sage's remark. Eagle raised his hand before the younger man could spit out a retort. "Thrush, perhaps your brother is right. I welcome the chance to hear your counsel. First, I ask you to make sure the three of us are undisturbed, just for a short time. I will tell you everything we discuss. Your brother can take your place when you and I talk."

Sage and Thrush exchanged glances. "Whatever you say, Eagle," Thrush said. He pulled open the yurt flap and swept his arm wide as he bowed his head, beckoning the three men to enter. Eagle and Falcon chuckled; Sage rolled his eyes as he passed by, and Thrush let loose the flap.

Eagle drank in the familiar yet distant odor of his yurt. So different than Pearl's, where he had spent more than a moon. Almost strange to him now, after his time beyond the *tekline*, living under boughs and the stars. Sage and Falcon encouraged him to sit—helping him to a relatively comfortable position, with his ankle propped up on a rolled-up *ven*-hide. As they began to tell Eagle of the time after his departure, Falcon and Sage discovered that Eagle already knew many of the changes going on in the village. So the three men decided instead to delve deeper into the thoughts and spirits of the men and children, rather than re-hashing the shifting allegiances or the mundane events in the village. First, Falcon asked Eagle how he had learned so much.

Eagle explained. He had learned much from Pearl, his mother, and Rose—despite himself, he chuckled—in the days and nights of recovery in Pearl's tent. Not simply about the events in both the compound and the village, but in the ways the women shared their lives. Quite different from the village, he had come to understand, and important for all the men to learn. While the men had wrestled to achieve superiority in deciding how the Ruck would go on—keeping secrets and recruiting followers and trying to influence the paths of the younger men—the women shared every piece of information they gathered about the village while they helped to raise and prepare each other's children for joining the village and for ensuring that the Ruck did go on. They lived under the same common shelter, using the individual yurts only for the visits. Yes, Eagle answered, after Sage pointed out that the women had their divisions, disagreements, and allegiances, too. Even so, they didn't feel the need to hide their motivations from each other, nor did they compete for power. Regardless of what Mantis might think of Rose and Lotus, she accepted their positions as leaders. At least, they didn't seem to play games with such important matters, while the men had made a habit of it —even manipulating games such as the races and the wrestling matches.

And Eagle told them he was tired of those games. He regretted the way his rivalry with Hawk had played itself out. He didn't regret his decision to escape. He didn't regret telling the stories or passing on his thoughts about God to Ram and Mace. He wished only that he hadn't kept the secrets, even from his own brothers and sisters. Sage protested, reminding Eagle of the danger they faced and why they had decided to proceed in such a way. Falcon agreed; in fact, he ventured to say that he might have tried to stop Eagle back then, had he known of the escape plan. Granted, Eagle answered. Maybe, at the time, it was necessary. Now, he asserted, was the time to have open discussions, to listen to each other. To let the children hear the truth so they could make up their own minds. He laughed out loud.

"Even now, with Thrush protecting us from the treacherous ears of other Ruck, we find ourselves trapped by our old habits. Do you see? Sage, please let the young man in."

Shrugging his understanding and looking a little like one of the children who had been scolded for a known discretion,

Sage stood and threw open the flap. "Come in, brother. Our wise—and apparently now *free* even beyond our understanding—Eagle welcomes your counsel."

Thrush stepped in, half-pleased, half-suspicious. He started to secure the flap. Eagle laughed again, so loud and boisterous it made his chest ache. He coughed.

"No, Thrush," he sputtered as Falcon tried to calm him, "let the air freshen our discussion. We have nothing to hide from our brothers and sisters."

The men gathered around again, sitting cross-legged while Eagle shifted his rump and re-positioned his elevated ankle. Falcon offered him a draught from his skin, which Eagle accepted. They awaited his words, like the young children when the patting had ended, and the story was about to begin.

"Thank you, Falcon. Obviously, I do need to rest. So, I ask each of you to help me in a few tasks to begin our new ways. Falcon, please seek out Hawk. Tell him I would like to have a storytelling at the circle, tomorrow morning. Each of us—and anyone who wants to bare his or her heart—will have our say, for all the Ruck to hear. If Hawk objects, tell him I will be there to speak from my heart in any case. Tell him I am resting now, and even so, I welcome a meeting anytime, here at my yurt, between now and tomorrow morning. I expect he will refuse; perhaps he will surprise us."

"I begin to grasp your intentions, Eagle," Sage said. "Still, this may come as a shock to some of the Ruck. Do you want all of the children to hear such a debate? Even the youngest?" He raised an eyebrow as he asked.

"My heart says yes, although perhaps some are too young. While I recovered in Pearl's yurt, this occurred to me: even Hawk had the sense not to push the youngest children from the shelter of Justin and Coot. What do you think, Thrush? You are the youngest among us here, and even though you are now a man, perhaps your mind is not too far tainted by the ways of men to help us understand the feelings of ... of children such as Curly and Peck."

"I think I would want to hear the ideas of the men. Yet, I think I might also be frightened. I would ask Justin and Coot for their counsel, as they have been looking after the youngest children for a few moons now."

They all nodded. Now, Falcon spoke. "I, too, was with Curly and Peck and the others for some time. I think if they are told what to expect, they won't be so frightened. I would like to hear what Justin has to say. His wisdom has increased by leaps and bounds since your escape, Eagle."

"Indeed. Thrush, I ask you to seek out Coot and Justin and explain my ideas. Tell them they I would be grateful if they paid me a visit tonight. Make no secrets; find them and talk to them no matter who might be listening."

"And what may I do for thee, *free man*?" Sage bowed at the waist from his seated position, making them all laugh.

"Spread the word: Eagle has much to say, and he will say it at the circle in the morning. Again, tell them openly and without hesitation."

"As you command, *free man*, although expressing myself has always been one of my weaknesses, I shall do my best."

The men chatted briefly, reaffirming Eagle's plans. Before they left to carry out their tasks, the faces of Mace and Ram appeared through the open flap.

"Eagle!" Ram exclaimed. "We couldn't wait to visit, but we knew you were resting."

"We have word for you," added Mace. "The Black One has just come. Justin says that the visits to the women begin tomorrow evening."

The men looked to Eagle, who nodded. "Thank you, boys. Seeing you and talking to all my friends—I can't think of a better way to rest. And thank you for bringing word of the visits. It sounds like perfect timing."

Eagle caught each man's eye. "These men were just leaving," he said, speaking to Ram and Mace, while gesturing towards Sage. "Come in, my young friends, and tell me what you have been up to since you helped me escape."

The visits continued throughout the day, making it some-what difficult for Eagle to get the rest he really needed. As soon as he would begin to drift off to sleep, new visitors would peek into the tent and ask if he would mind some brief company. He knew he needed more sleep, but seeing his old friends, followers, and siblings—even opponents—lifted his spirits. He concluded it just as valuable as undisturbed sleep.

Among the well-wishers were Willow, Archer, and Fish. The youngest girl nearly threw herself on top of Eagle, wanting to give him a smothering hug. Archer restrained her, allowing Fish to give him a gentler embrace and then keeping the young girl by her side as Willow knelt to kiss Eagle's cheek. They brought him *pem* and dried *veg*—Eagle declined the former, telling them he would explain later, but he hungrily chewed and swallowed the *veg* while he talked. Eagle couldn't stop smiling the entire time, even as his emotions tugged at him, bringing tears while he laughed with them. He took note of how they had all grown even in a mere few moons. Archer was nearing the age of womanhood. She wouldn't be ready to leave before the coming winter, but certainly before the next win-ter. Willow's long legs had gotten even longer, and she seemed to be entering an in-between stage of awkwardness. Her sin-cere joy in being here with him put a lump in Eagle's throat. And Fish, well, she was as wound-up as ever, nearly escaping Archer's grip several times and launching herself onto Eagle like the days when a man's only cares were to tussle with the children and hunt *ven*.

Hawk never came. Falcon brought word from the man, who said he would bring his followers to the circle in the morning, while he had nothing to say to Eagle this day. However, Eagle's brother Clay did come, along with Onyx. No visitors surprised Eagle more than these two children from Hawk's camp. It began clumsily, with no one quite knowing what to say and the two young people hovering near the yurt flap. Eagle propped himself up and tried to put them at ease.

"My brother, I missed you. Please, sit. And Onyx, you too are most welcome." They hesitated. "Please, I know this must feel strange, but you have already arrived, so why not sit and speak with me?"

Onyx took Clay's hand and they sat on their haunches a few feet from Eagle. The man waited for his younger brother, or his new friend, to speak.

"Why ... why didn't ..." Clay stammered.

"Why didn't I tell you I was going to escape?" Eagle drew a deep breath. "Because I was blinded by pride and my rivalry with Hawk. I couldn't see then what I see now. I'm sorry I deceived you. Things are about to change, I hope."

Clay stared at the ground. "I hated you for that, and I felt like ...." When he stopped, Onyx squeezed his hand.

"Tell him, Clay," she said.

"I felt like you used me."

Eagle swallowed hard, keeping his gaze on the top of his brother's head as it was the boy kept his eyes downcast. "I'm sorry."

Clay looked up. Both children stared into Eagle's eyes. His glanced moved between them, waiting.

"I think he means it, Clay," Onyx offered. They nodded to each other, and she continued while the boy shifted to sit cross-legged. His stare returned to the dirt in front of his feet. Onyx continued. "Some of us wonder about what you found ... out there." She seemed to expect an answer, and Clay's eyes darted up for a heartbeat after she said it.

"I found *freedom*. A beautiful and frightening thing. Feeling *freedom*, even briefly, and then being captured has taught me so much. I plan to tell everyone tomorrow. Can you wait to hear the rest, along with everyone else?"

Onyx and Clay looked to each other again, saying they could. Clay wasn't finished, though.

"Eagle, I did hate you. But when the Black One came and told us ... I ... I wondered. And I wanted to see you and ... talk to you."

"Brother, never have I been as proud of you as right now. It took great courage to come here. I can see you are already becoming a man. And Onyx, thank you for supporting my brother."

They smiled at each other, briefly. "We should go," Onyx said. They got to their feet and started toward the flap.

"I love you, Clay." Eagle said. "I'm sorry I hurt you. I will do my best to make amends."

Clay stopped, a hint of a smile reappearing for a moment. He shrugged and they left.

Finally, Eagle did have short nap before nightfall and before the arrival of Coot and Justin. He hardly slept soundly, especially after Clay's visit, but it was enough to refresh him. The two men had waited until their children settled in for the night, under the care of Tiller, Dove, and Spider. Now, they huddled close to Eagle and spoke with him in the dim candlelight within Eagle's yurt.

The meeting didn't take long. Eagle explained the same things he had shared with Sage, Falcon, and Thrush. He expressed his regrets about the secrecy before the escape. Interestingly, both men still believed it was the right thing to do. Justin said it disturbed him at first, especially when he later learned that Eagle had told Coot the night before the escape. After reflection, Justin said he realized the rivalry between the two men had created such terrible divisions among the Ruck, and he was glad for Eagle's escape. It didn't make things easier or answer questions about how the Ruck would go on, but it broke the impasse. It forced everyone to ask questions of themselves and each other. So far, no one had put it quite this way to

Eagle, not the women, not his friends. It helped Eagle to hear such a perspective. Eagle said the Ruck were lucky that Coot had recognized the insight possessed by this new Justin, once called Earnest.

As if to prove he deserved such praise, Justin then wondered aloud if the Overseers would allow them to have such a day of open debate, as Eagle had proposed. It seemed quite possible they would forbid such a gathering at this time. Still, no matter how the men looked at it, this possibility made no difference. They all believed they had to try. They would face such an outcome if it arose.

And with that, they discussed the main issue at hand—how to proceed with the children during the next day's events. Both Justin and Coot decided all the Ruck should hear the truth as the men saw it, even the youngest ones. It was better to exclude no one from such an open debate, whether they simply listened or wanted to speak. Of course, they knew Eagle would speak, and they expected Hawk to respond. If others wanted to have their say, Justin said he would encourage it, limiting their stand on the Stone only to ensure there was time enough for all that needed to be said before the men went to the compound. Coot said he wanted to speak, too. On this measure, they all agreed—this was a time for complete openness if the Ruck were to go on.

Coot then returned to the question of how the children might react to such open debate. Certainly, they should hear the truth as each speaker believed it. Still, the youngest would just as certainly become confused and torn and even hurt as the men and older children debated. Coot said he believed each of the Ruck children must decide whom to follow for the Ruck to go on. Children need guidance—they want guidance, he stressed—and the men would have to balance the children's need to hear with their need to be protected, even directed. Coot suggested that Justin make a proclamation before anyone spoke: any child who wasn't ready to choose would be able to stay with Justin. And that no matter what anybody chose, every child would still be loved by all the Ruck. And if they didn't want to listen now, they could go to the clearing near Tiller's fields and play until the gathering was over.

All three agreed, with Justin pointing out this should apply even to those who had already seemingly chosen, from Fish and Herb to Nardo and Red. Shaking his head, Eagle had to admit that he hadn't thought about the reactions of children who had already become part of either Hawk's or Falcon's camp. (Both of the other men made a face when Eagle referred to latter camp as Falcon's). He ignored them, telling them about Clay's visit. He wondered aloud how many children might switch their allegiance and whether the debates might throw the village into chaos. Justin put up his hand, and Eagle stopped short.

"Eagle, the Ruck must go on. Until we bring this to light, we can't go on; we merely go round and round. Chaos or not, the time has come. We have one day before the visits and then three days before The Hunt. My only concern is whether Hawk will agree with to these ideas. I must go to him now and persuade him."

The men stood and embraced before Coot and Justin departed. Eagle felt the pain return when he put weight on his leg. It had diminished over the course of the day; it returned when he stood. He eased down into his blankets and *ven*-hide, but sleep eluded him for a time. Having left the yurt flap open, the dim starlight seemed to call to him. He crawled on hands and knees to the opening, dragging his blankets behind him and taking care not to put any more pressure on his lower leg. With his head protruding through the flap, he settled on his back and stared at the sky. It didn't take long for him to fall asleep, although he woke from time to time with both horrifying and beautiful images fresh from his dreams—images of Ruck children at each other's throats among the yurts, running *free* beyond the *tekline*, crying and alone, or building new stone houses amidst fields of freshly sprouting *veg*.

◆ ◆ ◆

Eagle heard the Ruck gathering. He watched many of the young children in Falcon's group passing by his yurt. It seemed most of them had wandered by with a purpose, as they all waved to him and then whispered to each other as they moved past. Eagle stopped Chase, asking her to find Ram and Mace and to tell them to come by after their breakfast. Her face brightened, and she started to run. She stopped suddenly and returned, asking Eagle if he had eaten. Chase offered him a piece of *pem* she had tucked in the fold of her tunic. Eagle thanked her, but declined, asking her instead to bring him some fresh or dried *veg* after she found the boys. A quizzical look passed over her face, but Chase told him she would be back soon. She took off like a startled *ven*.

By the time the boys arrived, Chase had delivered a bowl full of *veg* and a fresh skin of water. Eagle chuckled. Apparently, without the *pem*, Chase assumed Eagle would need to eat a mound of *veg* to even things up. Eagle doubted she would have brought him so much *pem*, had he asked for that. As he was chewing a sweet root and sifting through the bowl's contents, Mace and Ram eyed him with bewildered looks on their faces. Of all the things he had to say, he had begun to realize his new ideas about *ven* and *veg* might be the hardest for the children to understand.

After he finished his meal, the boys helped him to his feet. Eagle noticed that Mace had used only one arm and seemed to be hiding something behind his back. Before Eagle could say anything, Mace presented his secret: a freshly carved cane. Though crude—hardly worthy of Carver's fine craftsmanship —it looked sturdy enough. The boys beamed as Eagle accepted it and smiled. He tested it, moving in a small circle. It seemed perfectly sized.

"We made it last night, taking turns," Ram said.

"Outstanding. I feel better already." He patted each of them on the shoulder, and they all made their way to the circle. Eagle felt awkward using the cane, but there was no doubt it helped relieve the pressure on his still-healing leg once he found a rhythm.

Much of the village had already assembled. Eagle and the boys mixed in with the Ruck from Falcon's group, grasping hands and nodding and smiling. He saw the three groups had taken positions around the circle, with clear spaces between the thirds. Finally, Justin entered the circle and stood at the edge of the Stone. Immediately, the Ruck stopped their individual conversations and waited for Justin to speak. It reminded Eagle of a gathering after The Hunt.

"This is an important day for the Ruck. I believe with the passing of many winters to come, we will remember this day before the summer Hunt as a day of reckoning for the Ruck.

"My hope is this: we will remember this day for its promise of a better way for the Ruck. I don't know what that is, yet. That's why we have gathered today. To listen to the men here in the village—to listen to anyone who wishes to speak. And then to choose how we will go on. Our choices will come with the rising and setting of each day's sun, as we consider each other's words and actions, not with the end of today's speeches."

Justin had begun to trace a path around the Stone. While he paused in speaking, he continued to walk, smiling gently at the younger children in every group. "Some of you younger children may find this frightening. Please, do not worry. All of the men," Justin gestured to each camp, "have agreed that no child will be forced to choose before you are ready. You don't even have to listen. Our friend, Dove, has agreed to take any children ... any children ..." Justin repeated, making eye contact with the smaller ones around Hawk and Falcon "... over near Tiller's fields to play and enjoy the summer day. And any child who is confused or frightened by the idea of choosing will be welcome to stay with me in the days to come. No matter what you want to do, all of the men and all of your friends will still love you.

"In this, all of the men are in agreement. Are we not?"

Coot lifted his voice, saying "Yes, Justin," prompting other men to follow. Eagle added his voice, as did virtually all the men, including Hawk and Bison (it seemed that perhaps Wolf was the only man remaining silent). Eagle had wondered whether Justin had been able to resolve this with Hawk. It lightened his heart to know the all the men felt this way—or at least were willing to say they did to ease the children's anxiousness. The change was palpable; the children seemed to breathe a collective sigh, many of their dismayed faces perking up.

"Good." Justin beckoned to Dove, who moved toward Coot's yurt. "Dove will remain here, collecting any of you children who wish to go and play. He will come and go as needed, taking you to the fields." Some of Falcon's group, who were close to Coot's, pushed together to allow a space near the circle. No children went there, yet. Dove sat on the ground.

"I have decided that our first speaker will be Eagle. I promise he won't be the last."

Justin returned to stand near Coot, Spider, Coyote, and the others in his camp. Eagle limped into the circle, leaning on his cane and stopping near the edge of the Stone, just as Justin had done.

"As you know, I escaped the *tekline* and was captured by the Overlords and the Overseers. I would like to tell you a story today."

Instinctively, Fly and some of the children began the patting. Eagle smiled and gently gestured to them to stop, raising and then lowering his arms, palms downward.

"I'm glad to know you have continued the stories while I was gone. Glad to know that you remember our ways. The stories are important to the Ruck, I believe, as they remind us of the Ruck-before. Today, I want to tell you a true story—one that I know is true because it happened to me. A story about what I found beyond the valley."

Eagle proceeded to tell them everything he had painfully

remembered while recovering in Pearl's yurt. He left out only a few select details, although he blurred some of the particulars in the descriptions of his agony on the Overlord's stone slab. A few of the children became frightened at that stage, and even before this part of the story, several the Ruck called out exclamations when Eagle told of seeing Mountain's body in the giant yurt. Still, no one interrupted; in fact, the Ruck hushed each other from time to time so Eagle could be heard. None of the children went to Dove. It seemed everyone, even Hawk and his staunchest followers, wanted to hear Eagle's tale. As he neared the end of his story, Eagle said there was more he wanted to say, especially about the incredible yet terrifying feelings of *freedom*, but he knew there would be questions for him, and he supposed others might wish to debate his story. Before he could say anything else, Hawk stepped into the circle. The Ruck deferred to the two men.

"Well-told, Eagle. Your skill at telling stories hasn't diminished. Yet, much of what you say ... well, you must allow me to ..."

"Of course, Hawk. That is why we are all here." Eagle braced himself, with his ankle starting to throb after standing for so long, not to mention in anticipation of the expected onslaught from Hawk.

"Yes. How should I begin? I suppose there is only one way. How are we to know this is all true?" Some of Eagle's friends objected and Hawk raised his hand. "Please, let me finish. After all, Eagle admitted that he was delirious with hunger and thirst and the effects of the *shrooms* and the pain from his injury. I don't mean to suggest that Eagle is making this up. I am asking how can we know whether these events were real, or imagined?"

Eagle chuckled, inwardly. Hawk remained a formidable opponent. His question was sure to introduce, or reinforce, some doubts among the Ruck.

"You are right, Hawk," Eagle said. "I have wondered about some of what I experienced, especially during the night of the *shrooms*. I have two answers. I hope they will convince all of the Ruck." Eagle waited to see whether his rival wished to say more. Hawk indicated, with a nod, for Eagle to give his answers.

"The first is answer is this: much of my story took place before the *shrooms*. The days of running, seeing the legendary wolves—yes, Wolf, your name comes from a real creature, I am now sure—and seeing the Black One on a hill far from the valley." Eagle limped a few steps toward Wolf as he spoke, catching the man's eye. "All of these things happened when my mind was still sharp. Yes, I was hungry and thirsty, but I have fasted before, while here in the valley, and I was prepared for such hardships."

Again, Eagle turned to those in Falcon's camp and met the gaze of others, including Clay, Tanner, and Tiller. "Many of you know about these fasts, I spoke to you during them ... or perhaps you are aware they were Sage's idea, some time ago. He said I should fast in order to clear my head and gain perspective. So, up until I ate the *shrooms*, I believe the memory of my experiences are clear and true. And I believe everyone knows that none of the men here in the village would knowingly lie to the children about such important matters, so I put my trust in you, even if there is doubt about what I tell you—before or after the *shrooms*—that what I say is what I truly believe happened to me."

"Of course, no one would suggest that you are lying, Eagle." Hawk answered. "But what about your experiences after the *shrooms*? Or after your resistance to hunger began to wane? How can we be sure you met *free* Ruck when you thought you were seeing your friends, even me, running alongside you? Obviously, we weren't there. How can we know your visions of a stone village, and a field full of *ven*, weren't visions caused by the *shrooms*, or hunger, or both?"

Hawk now turned away from Eagle and was addressing the other Ruck. "As Justin has wisely said, this is a day of reckoning for the Ruck. I find it difficult to change my mind when presented only with the memories of a man who has admitted he experienced impossible visions."

Murmurs rumbled throughout the Ruck. Brothers and sisters and friends traded questions and answers and assertions and more questions. Eagle waited.

"Let us hear what Eagle has to say," Bison hollered. "What more do you give us, besides your memories?"

"Proof," said Eagle. He hobbled over to Bison and Shadow. Others closed in as Eagle reached the edge of the circle. Most notably, Clay, Onyx, and Rock. "I took some things that I found —some were lost, but these remain. I kept these hidden from the Overlords, deep within my tunic."

Eagle dropped his cane, wobbling, as he pulled forth the torn piece of the *book* and unfolded it. Mace rushed up to help steady him.

"I tore this from the *book*. You can see: it has *riting* on it, just as the stories tell us. I found this in the stone village, which I have already told you. You can see how old it looks, from the time-before, I think, from where I believe the Ruck of the *Yew-essay* lived, with their *freedom*, before the Overlords came."

This time, the ebb and flow of the Ruck voices almost thundered through the gathering. Eagle wondered if this would be the thing that brought the Black One down to stop the proceedings. He almost hoped for it; as it would only lend credence to his assertions, he wagered. So far, nothing. He handed the piece of the *book* to Bison.

"Take care with this Bison, no matter what your beliefs about my story. Everyone here should see it."

Bison took it, carefully. Those around him crowded into to get a glimpse. Others clamored for their chance, moving across the edge of the circle and pressing in around Bison and the others.

Justin entered the circle, bellowing. "Please, let us remember our customs for the circle. Only those who are speaking should enter. We will all have a chance to see this ... this proof ... as Eagle calls it."

The Ruck obeyed, resuming their places at the edge of the circle. Now members of the three groups had co-mingled as a result of their movements. Mace knelt and retrieved Eagle's cane, handing it back to him and standing near Clay and Chase (who had beaten most of the others to the spot), waiting for a turn with the *book*-piece.

"There's more." Eagle said. "This strange stick, made out of something like the *cart*-shell." He had extracted it from his tunic during the commotion and now held it aloft in one hand while leaning on his cane with the other. He hobbled over to Coyote, on the other side of Bison's group. As he went, he became aware that Hawk had moved in closer, deliberately.

"I found more of these, but only this one eluded the Overlords. I say this is further proof of my story about the stone village. A piece of the *tek* from the days of *freedom*." Eagle handed it to Coyote, carefully reaching through the numerous outstretched hands of the children.

Conversations and smaller groups of debate among the Ruck rose and fell as the items circulated. Hawk and Eagle both remained silent, observing. Eagle stepped back, nearer to his rival. Hawk remained stoic, unfazed. Eagle guessed the man had expected something like this. It also seemed like no child would depart the gathering now. Finally, as the fuss died down, Hawk spoke again.

"Truly, Eagle's items are amazing. Even at a distance, I can see they have meaning. Let us think about what that meaning is. Let us assume these things do prove that Eagle's story is true —or rather, that at least some of his story is as true as he remembers it."

Hawk began a sweeping circle around the Stone as he spoke, catching the eyes of followers and opponents alike.

"I suspect Eagle would now tell us these things mean we can have *freedom*, just like we did before the Overlords came. I say it means exactly the opposite."

Eagle was tempted to interrupt, as Hawk was stealing some of his fire, but he held back, just as Hawk had when the items had caused such a stir.

"Think about it, everyone. These things are wonders." Hawk had stopped near Oak, who now held the *cart*-shell stick, putting out his hand. Oak handed it to Hawk and now the man raised it over his head.

"None of us has ever seen the likes of this. Of course, we have all heard the stories of the *tek* and the amazing things the Ruck-before could do. Still, these pieces of *tek* were no match for the Overlords. They captured the Ruck-before as easily as Chase might outrun Curly and Peck—or as easily as Bison could pin Nardo in a wrestling match. They took the Ruck-before, maybe from the very stone village Eagle found, and they put them here in the valley. They have kept us here ever since. We live and die at their command. Why should we believe that any of these things mean we can be *free*? There's no reason to believe so. I say to you, the only thing these things prove is that the Overlords are our masters. The best way for the Ruck to go on is to do as they say. For now, and forever, to reject the idea that *freedom* can be real."

Hawk dropped the stick, and it fell into the grass, disappearing.

Some of the younger children had begun to whimper and clutch at the older children around them. Curly and Peck ran to Dove; he hugged them deeply. The mood of the whole gathering had changed—at least it seemed so to Eagle. Slowly, other young ones joined Dove—even Fish, Nardo, and Dreamer. The debate took a natural pause as everyone waited for the children to decide whether they would stay or go. Among the older Ruck, only Eagle moved, slowly limping up to Hawk. He stooped down, steadied by the cane, and picked up the *tek* stick. Finally, Dove took the gathered children away, somewhat reluctantly it appeared, as he wanted to hear more himself.

When they had moved out of earshot, Eagle spoke again.

"Hawk's view saddens me. Partly, because he might be correct … partly, because such ideas hurt us worse than the Overlords could ever hurt us. Perhaps we can't be *free*. I believe we can, and I think it's better to keep this hope in our hearts. Better to strive to achieve *freedom*, than to admit the meaninglessness of the Ruck going on, as ... as prisoners of the Overlords."

"That is precisely where we differ, Eagle. I don't think it helps the Ruck to believe in something if it can't be true. I think the only way we can go on is to admit that we are prisoners. I have one regret: I should have said this bluntly before. I thought it better to shield the children from such a truth, to maintain our ways without questioning what our fathers taught us. I have learned from our disagreements. I'm as surprised as anyone to admit that your escape has been a good thing for the village. It has brought us to this point, where we can honestly debate what is best for the Ruck to go on."

As Eagle was about to respond, Hawk held up his hand. "Please, I must finish. You had your chance to present your story. Now it is my turn to present my ideas."

Eagle nodded.

"I ask everyone to consider these ideas and questions: Why did the Overlords and Overseers bring Eagle back to us, alive? It seems clear to me. To prove that escape isn't possible—to allow the Ruck to hear Eagle's own words about how he was captured and punished. If we try, they will stop us. They will bring us back here, or they will hurt us and our brothers and sisters and perhaps even kill us—as they have told us quite directly. They could have killed Eagle and brought his lifeless body back as a warning. Yet, they control us completely and they have no reason to fear his talk of *freedom*. Bringing him back alive shows us just how powerful they are. They can kill us if they choose; they can let us live if they choose.

"So, why do they keep us here? Because we have value to them. Eagle would tell us now ... he would say they use us as we use the *ven*. Perhaps that is true. I say, that is the way of things. The bugs eat other bugs, the birds eat the bugs, some birds will eat other birds, or their eggs. We eat the *ven*. And if Eagle's story is true, then perhaps the *ven* eat the Ruck. It is disturbing, but it changes nothing. We need the *ven* to survive.

The Overlords need us, we need the *ven*. It is the way of life. It is the way the Ruck go on. I believe, someday, the Ruck will prove that we can live among the Overlords. I believe they are testing us. The Hunt is one of the tests. They wish to see if we are strong enough. I say, we must continue to go on as we have, proving our strength, proving our ability to go on, until some-day, the Overlords reward us."

Again, murmurs rippled through the gathering. Eagle raised an eyebrow to Hawk, His rival turned up both palms, de-ferring to Eagle.

"I am also glad we have reached this point," Eagle started. "It seems that both Hawk and I have put our foolish rivalry be-hind us. We still disagree, but now, rather than bickering and plotting, now we are speaking from our hearts and asking you to help us decide how the Ruck will go on.

"My thoughts are different. To answer Hawk's questions, I say these things: The Overlords brought me back to frighten us into believing we can't escape. If they hadn't brought me back, you would never know what happened to me. Some of you might have believed I was living *free* beyond the *tekline*. The belief could have grown and given hope … hope that you could follow me. If they had brought me back dead, there would still be doubts about what happened. The only truth would have been that I was dead. Bringing me back alive casts doubt on the belief of *freedom*—it has convinced Hawk, and maybe others of you. Obviously, the Overlords know what they are doing. My return makes escape seem impossible, no matter what we believe.

"Even so, I say it shouldn't stop us from trying. No one thought it was possible to escape the *tekline*. Now we know it is possible. My capture shouldn't shatter our hope for the *freedom* we deserve. I felt it, even for a short time. It was frightening and wonderful, uncertain and exciting, painful and exhilarat-ing. I would trade anything to feel it again. While I love the Ruck and I want us to go on, I know this: going on without striving for *freedom* has no meaning. I would rather die than live as a prisoner, waiting for the Overlords to grant me what I believe only God, or maybe the Goddess as the women believe, can give me. Or maybe *freedom* is something we possess even if there is no God."

This comment caused another rumble through the Ruck, surprising some of Eagle's closest friends and allies. He pressed on, as Hawk seemed content to listen.

"Yes, this is something else I would like to talk about, but first, I believe what Hawk says is 'the way of things' doesn't have to be so. We don't have to eat *ven*. We can live without it. I recovered, among the women, without it. I ate nothing but *veg* and the women's brews—which I understand are made from nothing but water and *veg*—for almost two moons. I was near death, but I regained strength, without *pem*, without fresh *ven*. In fact, I feel better in some ways than ever before. I'm thinking more clearly. It's as if eating the *ven* had poisoned my mind, and now I'm *free* of the poison. I say there are reasons not to eat *ven*. What I saw at the giant yurt, it sickens me even now. The *ven* were eating the Ruck, and themselves. And those *ven* must have been driven here. Why else do the *ven* come in abundance for the hunting seasons, and then disappear across the *tekline*? Because the Overlords wish it. We end up eating the *ven*, and we end up eating our brothers and sisters. And who knows what else was in the *ven* meal. I beg you, if you believe nothing else that I say, think on this. We have Tiller—he can lead us to growing more *veg*, enough to survive without the *ven*. If only we choose to do it."

Eagle paused, as he knew this would cause another stir. He was correct. "Give up *ven*?" he heard. "I don't think I could" and so forth.

"Listen, please. I know it's hard to understand. If you had seen what I saw, with your own eyes, I think your doubts would disappear. To me, this has great meaning. My eyes are open, like never before. We have been living falsely; we are just as the *ven*, barely more than unthinking animals, penned in like I saw at the giant yurt. We can be more, if we choose to be.

That's what this debate is about. Our choices. Please, hear me. Choose to be more. We can try to escape, to be *free* again. Even if we die, we will become more than we are now."

Hawk interrupted. "Eagle, I have listened, and I have heard enough. I still say your beliefs are madness. The only thing you have said that makes sense to me is this: there might be no God, no Goddess. The way I see it, the Overlords are the closest things to gods. It makes no difference really. Here are my last words. Fighting and dying for nothing won't make the Ruck *free*. It won't 'make us more' and it won't help the Ruck go on. *Freedom* is a story from the Ruck-before—perhaps it was true then, but it is meaningless now."

Hawk began to walk away. Several of his followers started to join him. Coot stepped into the circle.

"Hawk, please wait for another moment." Hawk paused, bowing his head to the old man, who continued.

"It seems this debate has come about much differently than I expected. Only you and Eagle have voiced your ideas. It is okay; much has been said, and we all have things to consider. Still, as the oldest of the Ruck, I would like to add one thing before we disperse, or at least before some of us do, because I hope there are still those among us who want to talk about these things."

"We're listening, old man," Hawk stated.

"You are right, Hawk. I am an old man. Old and tired. I have seen many winters—thirty by my feeble count. I grow weary of living this way. Even before Eagle's escape and capture, I had begun to question things. I was too weak to do anything. Eagle's courage has given me new hope. I don't want to go on this way. I will tell you all something now. Something that is forbidden by the Overseers. I am completely in love with one of the women. My greatest wish is to be with her, always—to have what the Ruck-before called a *famlee*. For years, I have yearned for this, but my fear of the Overlords has been stronger. I love Honey, and if I could be *free*, I would take her away from here. I would spend the rest of my days with her, even if those days numbered only one. I will choose Eagle's way. The rest of you must consider and choose for yourselves."

Hawk simply shook his head. "I truly pity you, old man. You will certainly die, and we will certainly miss you. Strangely, I do agree on one thing; we all must choose. I have heard enough. Those of you who feel the same, I welcome your decision to follow me now, or later. Stay if you like and listen to more of this meaningless talk. You will still be welcome in my camp, whenever you decide to join us." Once again, Hawk turned to leave.

Justin spoke. "Hawk, we men must still convene later today to determine the draw for the visits. We must continue to the visit the women—if we don't, we know the Ruck won't go on." Eagle realized that Justin said this for the benefit of everyone. They all needed such a reminder, it seemed.

Hawk spoke loudly, without turning around. "Indeed, Justin. I will return at your command."

Bison, Shadow, Tanner, and others followed Hawk immediately, while some others lingered. Friends spoke to each other hurriedly, some staying and some running to catch up to Hawk. Justin gathered those remaining from his camp (although Eagle noticed that Spider had gone with Hawk, after a quick word with Coyote), and he sent Carver to relieve Dove. Among those remaining included all of Falcon's group (except the younger ones who had left with Dove) along with Clay, Rock, Onyx, Copperhead, Scar, Oak, and Maize. The last two were talking to Tiller, who seemed incredibly uncomfortable, while Ash, Archer, and Ram listened in. Eagle left the circle and walked up to them. Others quickly gathered around, including Justin and Coot. Everyone stopped talking, looking to Eagle.

"Please, don't stop because of me. I want to hear what you have to say as well. I see that all of Falcon's camp has remained. All of you must follow your heart. If you believe Hawk is right, I want you to join him."

Sage spoke. "Eagle, I think I speak for all of us: we want to hear everything before we choose. Some of us might change our minds; I can't say. For now, we all have questions for you and each other, I suspect, and I doubt anyone plans to join Hawk's camp before we satisfy our questions." Words and nods of agreement rippled through the gathering.

"That is good to hear," Eagle said. "I hope you don't mind if I sit down." Mace rushed to help him again. Eagle's sister Willow sat next to him and clasped her brother's hand.

Oak spoke up. "I believe Sage speaks for most of us, too. Eagle, your words about the *ven* have shaken many of us. Even those of us who disagree with, or just wonder about, your ideas of *freedom*. I was asking Tiller if he thought we could actually grow enough *veg* to feed the whole village."

Everyone turned their eyes to Tiller. The young boy was shaking, terrified. Eagle remembered how shy Tiller had been on the other occasions when they had spoken. He wondered if the boy might just run away. Archer patted Tiller on the shoulder, and Dove (who had just run up, nearly out of breath, in time to hear Oak's question) told him it was okay—they all trusted him.

"I ... I ... I don't know," Tiller cast eyes back and forth, then to the ground. He knelt down and dug his fingers into the dirt. It seemed to steady him. "I mean, if we had enough seeds, enough ... well, it's just a matter of ... of ... working the soil."

Tiller looked up, brown eyes wide. "I couldn't do it myself! I mean ..."

"We would help." Archer said. "I believe what my brother tells us. If we're not hunting the *ven*, we won't need as many archers. You can teach me." Others agreed, saying they would learn, too.

"Wait," Sage said. "It's not so simple. I doubt we have enough *veg* right now to feed everyone who might want to stop eating *ven*. We haven't prepared for this. Your harvest is nearing, isn't it Tiller? There won't be time to plant much more."

The boy nodded.

"I hadn't thought of that," Eagle admitted. "I suppose it will take some time to wean ourselves from the *ven* altogether."

"Perhaps as we learn and plan," Oak said, "a few of us can stop, as a sort of test to see what happens to us without the *ven*. I would be willing." Several voices echoed Oak's.

"A wise suggestion," Justin stated. "A few of us to start. Some from each camp would be best. Obviously, Eagle would continue, as he has already shunned the *ven*. How many others are willing?"

Nearly twenty of the Ruck raised their hands and volunteered. Their immediate enthusiasm surprised Eagle. While many of those listening hadn't volunteered, it seemed the idea of eating *ven* had suddenly become sour enough for a change among the Ruck. Sage suggested that Justin simply choose twelve of the Ruck to stop eating *ven*. Meanwhile, anyone who was willing could begin to learn from Tiller. Everyone agreed. Sage added another thought. While some of them might feel strange eating the *ven* after Eagle's story, they would need to do so until there was enough *veg*. "No matter what our choices," he stated, "the Ruck must go on, and that means we must eat." Clearly, there was no alternative, for now.

After more discussion, during which the Ruck began to break up into smaller groups, with some going about their own business, Justin chose from among the remaining volunteers. He selected:

Eagle, Oak, Archer, Thrush, Copperhead, Coyote, Tiller, Chase, Onyx, Henna, Raven, and Happy.

The smaller groups of Ruck continued to converse and question each other well into the afternoon. At first, Eagle enjoyed watching and listening as the men and children talked about his story, debated whether they thought they could live without *ven*, or discussed the possibility of *freedom* and their beliefs about God or the Goddess or neither. (Coot talked much about his views in this regard, sharing what he learned during his childhood and from the women he had visited over many winters). As the sun moved overhead, Eagle became weary. They had asked him questions from time-to-time, and he had participated enthusiastically, but the events of the last two days began to sap his strength. He asked them to allow him to return to his yurt. With the openness now established, Justin reminded everyone that they could continue these conversations anytime they chose.

Ram and Mace volunteered to help Eagle back to his yurt after he returned a succession of hugs from his brothers, sisters, and friends. Along the way, the boys asked him what he meant about the possibility of God not existing. Eagle had noticed their silence when the topic arose among the small groups. After his many talks with them about a personal relationship with God, he expected them to have questions.

"I'm not really sure," Eagle answered, truthfully. "Come sit with me for a while. I need to lie down, and have a short nap, but I do want you to hear my thoughts—and I want to hear yours."

It turned out to be a confusing conversation. By the time the boys departed, and Eagle reclined in sleep, none of them felt certain anymore.

Eagle had explained the doubts that had crept into his mind after he escaped the *tekline*. Or more accurately, he voiced his own questions and doubts (some of which he realized had come from Hawk's statements), and then he and the boys explored their feelings. Why would God allow the Overlords to imprison the Ruck and hunt them like *ven*? If God was all-powerful, what purpose would he have in the *ven* eating the Ruck and the Ruck eating *ven* who had eaten other Ruck? Of what purpose was it to give *freedom* to the Ruck and then allow the Overlords to take it away? What was the purpose of the death of a boy like Badger?

Eagle also reminded himself and the boys about some of the recent events, as well as some elements of faith that reaffirmed his own belief in God. When he was half-starved, Eagle had found the live-saving goo, and he still felt compelled to thank God for it. It seemed impossible that he had stumbled upon the container on that day, when subsequent searches turned up nothing, without guidance from God. When he needed strength and courage in the foreign woods, he found comfort deep in his faith, comfort that helped him see clearly and conquer his fears. Eagle reminded the boys of the time when they worried Hawk and his followers had discovered their plans to escape. Eagle had felt the presence of God watching over him and making sure they had the time they needed to complete their work. Above all, Garnet had taught him that God had given him the *freedom* to make his own choices—a gift no one could take away—and Eagle didn't want to abandon this part of Garnet's teachings.

Finally, they all talked about Coot's lecture on the women's belief in the Goddess. Eagle admitted their view made more sense as he thought about it. All the things which reaffirmed his God could also apply to a Goddess. When you had turned over all the leaves and stones of such a debate, in the end, the women are the ones who give birth to the Ruck children. Didn't it make sense that the Goddess had created the Ruck and the land, just as the women gave birth to the Ruck children? Or as Coot put it, "the land is the Goddess and the Ruck its children." Wasn't the women's circle like that of the moon? Weren't the seasons an endless circle of death and re-birth? Doesn't the women's Goddess embody all the notions of these circles? Doesn't creation belong to the women?

As they left, with Eagle fading from fatigue, Ram said he was beginning to think it was easier to believe in neither a God nor a Goddess with the mastery of the Overlords hanging over them. It was, Ram said, the only thing he for which could agree with Hawk.

◆ ◆ ◆

Sage woke Eagle and helped him to the meeting for the draw of the visits. While the sun was still visible above the mountains, the meeting was taking place far later in the day than usual. Sage mentioned that Coot was pained by the late start—he almost always brought word to the women by mid-day, so they could prepare themselves for the first night's visit. Honey and the others must be wondering about the delay. They would manage, Sage insisted.

As they walked to the meeting, Eagle watched the sun. For many winters, his view of its setting had been the same. Now, after seeing the sun fall beneath different hills beyond the *tek-line*, the sight took on a new wonder. He imagined the shadows it cast over other hills and valleys, thinking about other Ruck who must be looking up and wondering, too.

The draw took little time. Justin had gathered only the number of men needed for the visit after Coot had confirmed the number of available women with the Black One. The order would be: Falcon, Sage, Oak, Justin, Wolf, Thrush, Coot, Hawk, Eagle (the return of Eagle meant that Bison wouldn't return to the women, at least not this moon). After the draw, Coot told them which women would be receiving the men. Eagle had already guessed, based on what Pearl had told him. Eagle would visit Pearl the first night, then his mother, and then Lotus. Eagle couldn't help but think: if there were a God or Goddess (or perhaps both, it struck him suddenly), then Eagle himself had somehow earned a favor.

Eagle went back to his yurt and made a meal from the remaining *veg* Chase had brought him earlier this morning. While Eagle was eating, Tiller stopped by with Archer. Eagle realized he must have made an awful face because the boy shrunk away, quickly, and Archer apologized for bothering him.

"No wait. I'm sorry," Eagle said. "You aren't bothering me. It's just that it has been a long day ... and well, it might be a long night, and I haven't rested nearly enough. Please come in. Just understand it would be best if this meeting went quickly."

Tiller still hesitated, but Archer dragged him. "Tiller is afraid," she blurted.

"I'm not ... afraid ... it's just ... uh ... I don't know."

"He's afraid that we can't grow enough *veg*, at least not for a long while," Archer said. "So are others. We've been talking all afternoon."

Eagle sighed. "It won't be easy. We must try. I didn't dwell on this during my story, but it became so clear when I was out there. The Overlords want us to eat *ven*. For that reason alone, we must find a way to stop. I was starving out there and I knew nothing else. I felt like a small child, incapable of feeding myself. All around me, there might have been *veg* that I could eat, and yet I knew nothing about it. I was lucky; Tiller had explained to me that some things could harm us. If not for this, I might have eaten something deadly. I picked the *shrooms* because they were the only thing I knew—again, thanks to Tiller. I ate the goo because I believed it was a gift from God and it smelled like … like life. Otherwise, I would have starved. If we are going to be *free* of the bonds of the Overlords, whether by escape or by defying their wishes, we must stop eating the *ven*. We must learn how to survive by eating *veg*.

"What about other animals? And more fish?" Archer asked. "That came up in our discussions."

Eagle paused and smiled. "I'm not sure. It is the kind of new thinking we need. Indeed, while I was out there, I saw squirrels and birds and other small creatures. I thought about trying to take them with my arrows, but I had no experience with such hunting. I didn't know how to capture one either. Again, I felt helpless. If we could learn to take other animals, even the birds, then we might not need as much *ven*. And we will still need to hunt *ven*, for clothing and tools."

"That's what we thought," Archer said, smiling. "What do you think now, Tiller?"

The boy had relaxed a little. "I still don't know. Uh, maybe."

"That's good enough for now," Archer said. She grabbed Tiller's hand. "Let's go. Eagle needs his rest." She winked at her brother as she left. Eagle blushed, felt silly for it, and then he finished eating before getting some sleep. He was sure Sage and Thrush would come get him before the men gathered, just before nightfall, for the walk to the compound.

11

Fortunately, Eagle had guessed correctly because he might have slept through the night without Thrush jostling him numerous times and pleading with him to wake up.

Eagle wiped the slumber from his eyes, found his cane, and followed Thrush to join up with the other men. It was a quiet march, with the each of the men lost in his own thoughts of the day's events or of the night's impending activities. That was fine with Eagle. He kept thinking about Pearl. It would be strange to visit her yurt tonight after spending so many days there recovering.

Eagle hesitated for a moment outside of the young woman's yurt, closing his eyes and listening to the entire compound as he leaned heavily on his cane. He heard a few of the men and women greeting each other; he heard the cry of a baby and the sound of a mother still trying to get her children to sleep. He drew several deep breaths, taking in the now familiar odors of the compound. Mostly, he smelled the soap vats, cooling down not far from Pearl's yurt. The flap opened, startling him.

"Are you okay, Eagle?" Pearl asked. She stepped out of the yurt, wearing only her leggings. She had her light brown hair braided close to her scalp, making her green eyes dazzle in the darkness. Eagle couldn't remember ever seeing her this way before. They had spent so much time together, in the village, when she was called Star. He remembered the times when Star and Ash flirted with him. He had wanted to reciprocate, but they were some three winters younger ... now, here was Pearl, standing with her nubile breasts bared to him, ready to welcome him into her yurt. He thought of Ash, who he had seen only briefly in the village since his return, and how she too would be here soon, perhaps in three days.

"Eagle?" Pearl shrugged when all he could do was blink to break his stare.

"I'm sorry, Star, uh, Pearl. It's just that you are so beautiful. I have waited so long to kiss you. I was just thinking back to the night after the Justin-before gave me my new name ..."

Pearl laughed. "You always were a tease. Hobble in before I take you right here." She disappeared behind the flap. Eagle followed.

She had changed her yurt. Everything was sideways—from the low row of candles (only two were lit, with the warmth of summer making any more impractical) to the arrangements of the blankets and *ven*-hide. Pearl helped him down to the bedding, ensuring that his leg was comfortable and setting his cane near the flap. She began to kiss his hands and bare arms, working her way to his neck. Eagle reached up with his left hand, guiding her mouth to his, while gently cupping each of her small breasts with his right hand. She moaned and fell on top of him. After more kissing, he gently slid her off and slowly removed his tunic, *mocs,* and leggings. She watched him and then stood, allowing him to remove her leggings as he knelt before her. Eagle winced as his ankle complained from the stress. Pearl insisted he lay on his back, and then she continued to kiss him slowly, all over his body. They continued leisurely for some time, touching and teasing each other like they never could back in the village. Finally, she mounted him. They rocked back and forth until she shuddered, and then Eagle rolled her over and thrust until he spent himself inside her. He rolled off, dropped alongside her. They held hands for some time, staring at the shadows on the yurt top and regaining their breath until they drifted off long enough for a few of the candles to turn to nubs.

Pearl woke him with kisses and whispers to his ears. She wanted to know what had happened in the village since his return. Eagle told her everything about the meeting at the circle and with the Ruck who came to his yurt. She asked about her friends, especially Ash, and he told her what he had seen in the short time since his return. He told her about their plans to grow more *veg*. To his surprise, she asked him if he planned to escape again, and if he did, would he want to take any of the women with him.

He leaned up on his elbow, grinning. "Are you saying you're tired of the compound already?"

She slapped him, playfully. "Not me. Well, I would go, but I meant Rose. She will give birth soon, and I know she cares for you and it might be your child and ..."

"Slow down!" Eagle shifted himself onto his rump and balled-up a *ven*-hide to prop up his leg. Pearl helped him settle into a comfortable position.

"I haven't given it much thought, yet," Eagle said. "Yes, I suppose I do plan to escape again, and this time not alone, but you're way ahead of me. I don't know how to bring the women. Do you think Rose would want to go—would she be able to travel? It won't be easy."

"Not the day after she gives birth, but if you wait a while, yes, I think she would be willing. And maybe your mother, or Lotus or Ruby ... or me."

"It will take much planning. I will talk to my mother tomorrow night. It's nice to know you still think of these things, even after leaving the village. I never would have escaped without your help. Still, it doesn't sound like you really want to go."

"We know each other too well, Eagle." Pearl paused, lighting another candle from one of the nubs before it extinguished itself. "No, this is a new life for me already. Living with the women is wonderful. *Freedom* sounds wonderful, too, but ..."

"I understand," Eagle said. "I was just telling some of my friends how much I had learned about your ways, while recovering here. And Coot has been telling the children about your Goddess."

Pearl looked alarmed. "Really?" She made another less-surprised, more-thoughtful face. "I guess he might know more about her than I do. After all his visits with Honey and the other women, I mean. It is still a new idea to me. But I like it."

"I can understand why. Anyway, trying to take any of the women will prove risky. Best to consider the idea of taking one or two, at most." Eagle beckoned for Pearl to come closer, and she obliged. "Pearl, you have always been special, both in the village and now here with the women. You have given me even more to think about." He leaned over to kiss her.

"Think later," she answered, reaching for Eagle's member and returning to the kissing of his earlobe and neck.

After Eagle and most of the men had gone that morning, Pearl sought out Honey and Lotus. She told them about her conversation with Eagle. The elder women exchanged glances. Honey told Pearl that she and Lotus would be looking after the children today. Honey instructed her to tell any of the mothers who wanted to bring their children to the play area to do so, thus having some time to themselves or with their friends until the men returned. As Pearl started to leave, Lotus asked her not to speak of the escape until after she and Honey and shared their thoughts.

"Don't worry, young beauty," Lotus added. "It won't be a secret; it's not our way, as you have already learned. We old crones simply like to be prepared before the others start talking about such an idea."

Honey and Lotus herded their children through the commons into the penned-in dirt area. Marvel, who was apparently wandering around on her own, had caught up to them and asked what Pearl was doing and if could she go with her instead of staying here like her mother Rose had instructed.

Lotus said no, because all the other children would be coming here anyway. So, the little Marvel began to boss around the rest of the children while the two women took advantage of the precocious girl's initiative, moving closer together and talking about what Pearl had shared with them.

Pearl wandered around the yurts, finding Storm first. The poor woman looked completely frazzled, squatting just outside her yurt, with her young girl held cradled in one arm up to her breast. Meanwhile, her oldest child, Trey, ran around and around the yurt, shrieking each time he whizzed by and startling the baby girl (and making Storm wince). The baby was of walking age, but still young enough to suckle. While Trey disturbed her breakfast with each shriek, she didn't cry out, preferring to resume her suckling.

Putting her finger to her lips, Pearl ducked around the side of the yurt after Trey raced by again. Storm cocked an eyebrow and shrugged. When Trey turned the corner, Pearl stepped out and scooped him up. It scared the daylights out of him, and he started to cry.

"It's okay, Trey," Pearl cooed. "You were going to make yourself dizzy before long."

"Or cause his mother to throw his sister at him," Storm grumbled.

"Was Justin so terrible last night, Storm? What happened?"

"No. It's just that he wanted to talk about the Goddess all night ... well ... you know, afterwards. We barely slept. What does he care whether I get to sleep?"

"This is your lucky day. Honey and Lotus told me to round up the children and take them all to the common area. They said today all the mothers could do as they please." Trey had stopped crying but was now fidgeting under Pearl's grip.

"Perhaps the Goddess doesn't hate me after all." Storm let a smile escape. "Hold on, she's almost done."

Pearl told Trey that he would be going to play with the other children.

"Now?" he asked, brightening.

"Soon. If you can wait just a bit, I'll take you and your sister, and we'll go get Rose and Ruby's children."

Just then, Butterfly floated over, humming to herself. Her skin shone in the morning sun and her cheeks were slightly flushed, like she had been running or jumping. Pearl still couldn't believe she was the same person who had left the village several moons ago. Butterfly had changed so much. Pearl knew that she herself was changing, too, and she wondered if Ash would recognize her when she joined the women.

"Good morning," Butterfly said, smiling.

"Not another bright-faced young thing," Storm said, standing. "Oh, that's right, you had Coot. He already knows about the Goddess, I imagine. Here, she's all yours." Storm handed the baby girl to Butterfly, while the young woman looked bewildered.

Pearl laughed as Storm disappeared into her yurt, saying "Goodnight."

"She didn't get much sleep, and these two terrors haven't helped," Pearl explained. "You're just in time to help, Butterfly. Honey and Lotus asked me to tell the mothers to bring their children to the play area."

"Okay."

Pearl expected to find Rose still in her yurt. The woman could barely move. Sure enough, she was there, and so was Ruby with all her children. Pearl and Butterfly greeted Ruby, who was standing outside the open tent flap. They told her about the "old crone" instructions. Ruby laughed and told them she had come to to see if there was anything Rose needed that morning.

"'To have this baby', is what she said," Ruby stated, chuckling again.

"And I meant it," Rose added. "You say you've come to take the children? Wonderful. I'll just scream when it's time to take this one. Don't go too far away."

They all laughed while the children began to play right there. Pearl knelt down and said a more personal hello to Rose.

She remembered telling Eagle how Rose was as big as a yurt. Now, seeing her trying to get comfortable inside the yurt, Pearl couldn't resist a giggle. Even in her discomfort, Rose looked radiant.

"Let's get these children off to the play area," Ruby said. "Then I'm going to obey the old crones and get some rest. Don't forget, I was with Wolf last night."

"It's always the quiet ones," Rose yelled from within her yurt, as the women herded the children back to the play area.

Pearl and Butterfly continued their duty, seeking out the two remaining mothers. It was easy. By now, most of the women had left their yurts and were congregating in the commons or setting forth to their daily tasks. The two young women escorted the children of Mantis and Nightingale and then decided to spend the rest of the morning together. Butterfly suggested that they leave the compound and take a swim in the lagoon. Pearl was surprised—she said she thought it wasn't allowed. Butterfly laughed and said of "of course it isn't allowed," but they all did it sometime or other, and Mantis had told her the men hardly ever stayed close by. As long as they didn't stay too long or make too much noise, the Black One would never know. They snuck out and enjoyed the refreshing coolness of the lagoon, and then spent the rest of the day together.

Meanwhile, Honey and Lotus talked well past mid-day, allowing the children to do as they pleased (stopping them only at the inevitable moments when they hurt each other or started bickering and crying).

They shared what they had learned overnight while Falcon lay with Honey and Sage visited Lotus. The news from the village didn't surprise them entirely, as they knew Eagle had already returned to tell his story after his recovery. Still, the openness of the debate and the men's decision to allow the all the villagers to choose their leaders couldn't have been predicted. More than anything else, the questions about eating *ven* troubled them. While the women grew some small roots and knew the secrets of the *shrooms*, they depended on the *ven* brought by the men during the hunting moons. Eagle had already made his feelings known during his restoration in the compound. A few of the women had found the idea of eating *ven* repulsive after hearing Eagle's story. Lotus and Honey had made it clear that they would have to eat *ven* to survive, at least for now, but the reaction in the village would become known here quickly. Some of the women might want to stop eating *ven*, like the volunteers in the village.

They also discussed Pearl's information about another escape with some of the women. They thanked the Goddess for bringing Eagle to Honey's yurt this coming night. Honey could speak to Eagle before any of the women could learn of this idea, assuming Pearl respected their request to keep it to herself, for now. Of course, they would all discover soon enough—in fact, Lotus proposed they meet the next day to tell all the women what they had learned. Regardless, they agreed that Honey would need to point her son in the right direction, helping him to understand the dangers involved in such an idea. It couldn't be avoided, this plan, they concluded. While it could lead to the wrath of the Black One for the remaining women and villagers, their intuition told them more attempts to escape were inevitable now. Eagle's desire for *freedom* would spread. And maybe, just maybe, the Ruck could truly be *free*.

At that point, Lotus confided to her lover—she wanted to escape as well. It would be hard to leave the women, but *freedom*, which seemed so remote before, now seemed possible to her. The signs were clear, she said; the Goddess wanted the Ruck to be *free* of the Overlords' rule. She couldn't be certain if now was the right time, but the Ruck couldn't wait forever. Eagle had started something. It had to continue through its complete circle. Some of the women would have to go with the

men who escaped—to start anew if the Overseers didn't capture them. Women would be needed to bear *free* children, to
help teach the girls how to become women, and to guide the
formation of new villages. Obviously, she added, the men can't
be trusted to start over by themselves, even if they had the
power to bear children.

Honey laughed. Lotus never seemed to miss an opportunity to exaggerate the men's flaws, but a seed of truth always
remained at the center of her barbs. Honey had to agree; she
wouldn't even trust her own son to start a new village. Although Eagle had grown and matured—and she was proud of
him—he had also shown a tendency to be rash and unpredict-
able. Honey told Lotus that she was right. Some of the women
must go whenever Eagle and other villagers decided to escape.

So, they discussed and debated. Which of the women? How
would they convince Eagle as to how to proceed? They agreed
on this: only a few women should go, perhaps only two.
Women who had shown the ability to bear healthy children.
Lotus reiterated her desire to be one of those women. Reluctantly, Honey agreed. They would miss her in the compound,
but her insight and wisdom would help Eagle beyond the *tekline*. Honey then suggested that Rose might be able to go after
she gave birth.

Lotus objected at first. Not because she found Rose unsuit-
able, in fact, she could think of no better woman. Rather, Lotus
knew of Eagle's feelings for Rose and wondered whether that
would interfere with the realities of bearing multiple children
by multiple men—that is, could Eagle continue the ways that
had always ensured the Ruck would go on? They would both
need to mate with him and any other men who escaped in
order to bear strong children who could then mate with each
other and with the *free* Ruck (if Eagle's story could be believed).
And Rose wouldn't be capable of traveling soon. What if Eagle
planned to leave before the next moon?

This question, Honey answered, may become an advantage
to suggesting Rose. Eagle would have to wait in order to take

her—and Honey was sure he would want to take her. It would give the women time to prepare. Not only for the escape, but for the repercussions of the escape for those remaining in the valley. Assuming the Overseer kept his word, escapes would mean death among the remaining Ruck. They would need time to plan for such events, time to prepare the women and children, and time to help the remaining men to prepare the village. Perhaps they could even fight back. Or while the Overseer might take random Ruck as punishment for the escapes, he might allow the leaders of the village and compound to choose, much as the twelve villagers were chosen for each Hunt.

Yes, Honey said, as Lotus questioned each possible outcome, this was all speculation. She repeated her point: The more time they had to plan and seek the Goddess' wisdom, the better the chances for escape to succeed. Even if Rose couldn't or wouldn't go, convincing Eagle to wait for her to be ready gave them more time to auger the Goddess and assess the situation.

Of course, they weren't even sure that Rose would want to go. Clearly, no woman could be forced to join an escape. Now wasn't the time to ask her—they laughed as they reminded each other of every woman's state of mind near the birth of a child (and Lotus was sure Rose would deliver the baby soon). So, it would have to wait.

In the end, the best course of action became clear. Honey would speak with Eagle tonight (they thanked the Goddess again for the fortuitous sequence of the visits). She would tell him they hoped he would escape again but not too soon. She would stress the need for careful planning. She would say they believed two women should go with him. Honey would further suggest Rose and Lotus as the best choices, asking Eagle to wait for Rose to recover before trying any further escapes. He could use the time to plan and build support for his ideas in the village. Honey would begin to lead Eagle toward the idea of taking only a couple of men and a few children. Finally, Honey and Lotus agreed to meet again tomorrow to see how things went with Eagle before talking to all of the women. Lotus had argued they shouldn't wait another night, but Honey said this should be considered a mother's prerogative. All of the women would understand that.

◆ ◆ ◆

When Eagle stopped in front of his mother's yurt, he thought he heard Rose cursing. He had been thinking about her during the day after some of the things he and Pearl had talked about. During his recovery, Eagle hadn't felt the same longing for Rose as he had before the escape, and he began to wonder whether his feelings had changed. After spending the morning with Thrush, Sage, and Wolf, he had sat in the woods alone, trying to rest his ankle and pondering whether his love for Rose had diminished. No, he concluded. He still loved her, although so much had happened. Alone with his thoughts today, his mind had returned to Rose, remembering the day at the lagoon. He wanted to see her again. He glanced around, seeing the other men had entered each of their respective visitation yurts, so he stepped lightly toward Rose's instead of entering Honey's. Indeed, she cursed again, and then Eagle heard the voice of Mantis trying to comfort Rose. Eagle stopped, only a few paces from the yurt. Of course, with Mantis omitted from the visitations (now with child herself), she was keeping an eye on Rose, who could give birth at any time. Looking again to see if anyone had witnessed his approach, Eagle quickly retraced his steps to his mother's yurt. He entered.

"What were you doing, Eagle?" Honey asked. "I heard the other men, but you lingered."

"Seems I can't hide anything from you, mother." Eagle smiled and sat, taking her hand after she carefully propped his leg on a bundled-up blanket. "I heard Rose and thought to see her, but then I heard Mantis and realized my mistake."

"It seems you are taking more and more chances, Eagle. Perhaps you should take more care during the next moon and save your luck for something more important."

"Honey, are you scolding me?"

"Someone has to do it, before you start believing you can break all of the rules, whether made by the Overlords, the Overseer, or the Ruck. You'll have us all eating *shrooms* and running for the *tekline* with bone knives brandished ... at least that's what I hear."

Eagle was taken aback. He started to protest, caught himself. He laughed. "Mother, your wit still gets the best of me."

They laughed and made small talk. Unlike other visits, Eagle knew he wouldn't need to provide his mother with all the news of the village. After all, he had only been there a few days since his recovery—and he knew that Sage had told her of the events since his return (according to Sage, Honey had "pelted him with questions like Fish during a story about the *tek*"). Yet, Eagle expected she would want to share some things with him alone. Indeed, Honey immediately asked him about his brothers and sisters. Eagle enjoyed telling her how Archer was growing into a woman now and how she had ideas about working with Tiller to grow more *veg*. Willow, too, had grown. Eagle said he saw some of her older sister beginning to show in Willow as well—especially when she came with Archer to his yurt, and he had a chance to speak to them together for some time. Mostly, Eagle spoke of Clay, telling Honey about his brother's surprise appearance with Onyx. Eagle held back a few tears as he told the story. He hadn't realized how much it had affected him until he tried to put it in words to his mother. Honey helped when she remarked that Clay might finally mold his own opinions instead of letting everyone else shape his views. She asked about Ox. Eagle had to admit he knew little, except that the young man seemed steadfast in his support of Hawk.

Throughout, even though Honey paid attention to his news of her children, it seemed she was waiting to get to some other news. Or perhaps she had news for him.

"So," he said, "just what have you been hearing? I know Sage likes the sound of his own voice ..."

"No. Not Sage. Pearl."

"Ah, I see," said Eagle. "The women keep no secrets. It's one of the things I have been telling my friends ... and rivals. So, what did she say?"

Honey paused for a heartbeat, sensing how her son was a much more profound man than even just a few moons ago. She decided to take up her suggestions head on. "She asked you about future escapes—including whether you planned to take women with you."

"That's about all of it. I was planning to ask for your thoughts, mother. It seems Pearl has simply given us a head-start."

"What are your plans, Eagle?"

"I believe the Ruck must try to escape again. We must not allow the Overlords to rule us. Or the Overseers—and we know there are more than one of them. Have I ever told you that Hawk believes they are actually Ruck who have earned the favor of the Overlords?"

"Yes ... well, I don't recall who told me ... I'm aware of his ideas. Do you agree?"

"I don't know. I hated the thought of it when he first presented it to me—in truth, I still hate it—but now I suspect he might be correct. Anyway, I've told the Ruck we must fight for our *freedom*. For me, escape is part of the fight. It's dangerous, and I don't intend to try again too soon, but it must happen."

Honey sighed. "I was hoping you would say that. It makes the rest easier."

Honey explained what she and Lotus had discussed during the day. She and Eagle talked about which women might go with him—when the time was right. She was relieved that she didn't need to coerce Eagle to agree with the delay. He had arrived at that conclusion on his own. While he didn't say how long he might wait, he certainly would wait for a moon. That might not be long enough for Rose, Honey said.

Eagle eyed her for several heartbeats. "Mother, we have talked about a few of the women. Tell me who you and Lotus think should go."

"Lotus has told me she wants to go. You couldn't ask for a stronger woman. And both Lotus and I know Rose is also a good choice, provided she has recovered from the birth. Lotus has predicted it will be very soon. Still, we haven't asked Rose, yet; it's no use in her condition."

"Yes, I heard her cursing about the child's delay. Her voice was unmistakable; I heard in it the spirit of the Rose who I came to love … .and at the same time … well, the raging of a mad-woman."

"You'll never understand all of it, Eagle." Honey laughed. "Although it seems you are now wise enough to acknowledge what you don't understand about us."

"Do you think Rose would go?"

"You still love her, don't you, Eagle?"

"Yes. I want her to come, but …"

"You're afraid she might refuse."

"I wouldn't say afraid," Eagle answered, thinking for a few heartbeats. "It would be painful if she refused."

"Lotus and I will ask her, soon after the child arrives. I believe she cares for you. When she has begun to recover, we shall see how see feels."

"And what about you, mother, would you come with me?"

Honey drew in a deep breath, and Eagle knew the answer.

"It's okay, mother. I would prefer you stay. I don't want you to suffer if things go wrong. I believe you have a better chance here. And with Lotus gone, you will be needed here."

Honey smiled. Indeed, her first son had become a powerful man, in many ways.

Eagle continued. "For the same reason, I'm not sure I should take any of my brothers and sisters."

They discussed that idea, going round and round about whether it made sense for Archer, Willow, Ox, or Clay to escape with Eagle (or perhaps separately if an eventual plan included more than one group of the Ruck) whenever the time came. In the end, they agreed any such decision could wait. Eagle would have to determine what was best as he and his followers made plans.

They hugged and held hands for a little while, again making small talk. It seemed they both understood, this time more than ever, that it could be their last night together. Finally, Eagle said he needed a good night's rest, so they settled in to sleep.

Eagle slept well past sunrise. He awoke to the sounds of men leaving the compound and the faint smell of one of the women's brews. He groaned as he shifted his ankle from its perch and pulled himself to one knee. Each day brought him closer to a complete recovery, but the ankle remained sore and stiff, especially in the mornings. Honey pushed open the flap and the smell of the brew flooded in. His mother handed Eagle a cup.

"Drink this, Eagle."

When he made a suspicious face, Honey laughed at him.

"It's more of the healing herbs we gave you while you were here. You've had a few days without them; a few new doses will help now. And eat these roots as well."

Eagle obeyed, sitting in front of the yurt and sipping from the cup. He watched as Oak departed through the gate after kissing Storm goodbye; she had escorted him all the way there, and she seemed happier than Eagle had ever remembered seeing her before. Storm glided back to her yurt waving to Honey, who returned the wave and whispered that Eagle was now the only man left in the compound. It made him slightly uncomfortable, but not nearly as much as it would have five or six moons ago. While recovering in Pearl's yurt, he had learned to recognize the sounds of the women starting their daily routines and toward the end he had occasionally watched them moving about the compound. Today, he watched with a clearer head, munching the roots and finishing off the brew (which his mother insisted on refilling once already, in addition to filling his water skin with the yellow-brown liquid).

He saw Butterfly and Pearl speaking with Lotus at the edge of the commons. The younger women started to play with Marvel and Trey. Soon, other children gathered at the urging of Lotus. The older, black-haired Lotus made some sort of sign toward Eagle and his mother—it was a signal certainly intended for Honey. Eagle didn't catch the meaning, even as he glimpsed his mother returning the sign and laughing. Glancing back and forth between the two women, Eagle felt he might be the object of their exchange. Even with Lotus staring at him now and winking as she approached, Eagle didn't feel the wave of embarrassment her penetrating gaze usually gave him. He sighed and ate more of the *veg* as Lotus sat next to Honey.

"Planning to stay all day, Eagle?" Lotus asked, grinning.

Eagle swallowed, turning his head to consider the woman's jibe. "No, Lotus, I'm sorry. You'll just have to wait until tonight."

Lotus chuckled, stroking Honey's hair. "Your son has developed a sense of humor. Perhaps he will please me yet."

Honey rolled her eyes and leaned away, pulling her hair from Lotus' fingers and making a face.

Eagle got to his feet, leaning on the cane. "Perhaps tonight I will make an effort."

"Now you've raised my expectations," Lotus said. "You had better rest if you plan to rise to the task."

"Okay," Honey interjected. "Time for you to leave, Eagle."

Eagle was already limping away. "Goodbye mother. Until tonight, Lotus."

As he neared the gate, Eagle saw Rose and Mantis strolling into the commons. Rose was enormous; she leaned against Mantis for extra support as each small stride seemed an effort. Eagle stopped and watched them—thinking Rose was never more beautiful—until they noticed him. He waved at them and grinned, but both of the women scowled in return. At first, Eagle thought to take offense. He remembered Rose's cursing last night and his mother's words about her present condition. Plus, it wasn't his place to linger in the compound like this. He smiled, waving again and bowing his head before departing.

Lotus and Honey saw the exchange, giggling and waving to each other, imitating how Eagle had waved to Rose. Then they laughed out loud, and Lotus said they shouldn't be acting like those fresh young beauties over with the children.

Honey disagreed. "Any chance to feel young again is welcome."

"I make it a point to feel young every day. Now, we must shoulder our responsibilities. Assuming all went well with your 'mother's prerogative,' I think we should gather everyone and tell them about the talk of an escape involving the women."

Honey sighed. She took Lotus' hand, and they sat silent for a few heartbeats. Finally, she spoke.

"Yes, Lotus, it went well. And, of course, you are right. We must tell them. I just wish we could wait longer." Honey shook her head as Lotus began to speak. "I know. You don't have to say it. Please gather the women at our meeting place. I will join you soon."

Honey entered the meeting area, and the women hushed themselves and their children. They had gathered around much as they did two days before to hear the news of the pending visits. This time, still well before the sun ascended directly overhead, the mood felt different. The children had more energy, the babies required more attention, and the women sensed that this meeting held an unfamiliar significance. Honey saw Rose had taken a position in the rear, leaning against the picket wall while her caretaker Mantis reigned in their children with Butterfly's help.

"I'm sure each of you has been trying to guess the purpose of his meeting," Honey began in a low voice. "It's unusual for such a gathering during the visits. This is a time of reckoning for the Ruck. You all know things are changing in the village. The men tell us, and we share with each other. That is why we are here now.

"I speak softly to avoid the ears of the Black One. While we don't keep secrets from each other, we all know of the risks of speaking too openly. During the passing of moons before some of you women ever arrived in the compound, what I'm about to say might have been considered impossibly dangerous. We would have passed it from mouth to ear among the women. Now, things are different. I will speak openly, but not rashly. Even though I doubt the Overseer will notice, I see no reason to cast discretion aside, completely."

Honey paused, casting her gaze over the women and children. Her measured, mysterious tone had captured the attention of the children as well as the women, as she had hoped. Marvel and the others watched intently; in fact, the young girl had quieted some of her friends when Honey started to speak.

"My son Eagle has told me he intends to escape again. I doubt this comes as a surprise to any of you. He … and Lotus and me … believe that a few of the women should go with him."

Collectively, the women drew in their breath and gasped. Honey saw that Pearl remained impassive for a heartbeat before joining with the other women, exchanging glances and chattering quickly. Honey caught the penetrating gaze of Mantis.

"I believe there is no turning back," Honey continued, speaking directly to Mantis before sweeping her gaze over all of the women again. "It might mean punishment for those who remain. It may also mean escape from the valley and another way for the Ruck to go on. If men leave the valley, and avoid capture, they will need women to start a new village and bear the next generations of the Ruck.

"I know all of you won't agree. We need to discuss this as we always discuss important things: in small groups during the course of our daily routine. Of course, you may wish to share this with the men tonight. We all must make our choices in this matter. We have time to consider all of this. Eagle has no plans to attempt escape again soon. But he will attempt."

Lotus stood. "And I, for one, support Eagle's ideas. I want to go with him, when the time comes."

Honey didn't expect this from Lotus, although it didn't surprise or alarm her. Lotus' words carried great weight with the women, and she often spoke bluntly. She had proven her wisdom and foresight many times, predicting the birth of babies, discovering remedies from brewed herbs, or anticipating the thoughts of the other women. Her statement brought a natural close to the meeting. The women began to speak to each other or leave in twos with their children, whispering their thoughts about Honey's news and Lotus' proclamation. Mantis asked Butterfly and Pearl to take all their children. The young women obeyed, although convincing Marvel to leave took some doing. Finally, only Rose, Mantis, Honey, and Lotus remained.

Lotus walked over to Rose, who had climbed to her feet with the aid of Mantis. "Your baby will be born before the next sunrise," Lotus said.

Rose's eyes grew as wide as Marvel's during the meeting. "Thank you, Lotus. That's the nicest thing I've heard in moons."

Mantis stood still, calmly acknowledging Lotus' prediction and staring into her eyes. "You know I disagree with these ideas of escape. It will only bring more death among the Ruck. And yet, I won't interfere. I ask only that you teach me whatever you can before you leave. The women will need your talents, even if you are gone."

Lotus smiled, reaching out to take Mantis' hand. "You will be splendid. We can begin tomorrow."

The four women exchanged glances and clasped hands before leaving the meeting area.

◆ ◆ ◆

Eagle spent this day much as the previous. First, he found Thrush, Wolf, and Falcon not far from the compound, along the path. They had waited for him. Wolf and Falcon were chewing *pem*. They didn't offer any to Eagle. Thrush ate dried *veg*, but he didn't seem to enjoy it much.

They talked about the next day's events—especially the draw for the Hunt and the decision about which woman should leave the village. They all agreed: Ash, being the oldest and most mature, was the natural choice (Wolf's nod spoke for him). Eagle reminded Falcon and Wolf about Hawk's support for Maize the last time. Hawk would probably push for her to go. This surprised Thrush, who hadn't been among the men at the time. He said he was still new to all of this, but he didn't see how or why they should let Hawk get away with such a stand. Eagle suggested they think about sending both women. Hawk would get what he wanted, and Ash would still go, as she should. Eagle further suggested Falcon was the best man to suggest such an idea if Hawk insisted on Maize.

When the sun had risen overhead, Eagle told the others he wished to rest again, alone. They all decided to split up for the afternoon. Eagle returned to his preferred spot, propped up his leg and dozed off a few times, waking only to sip the now lukewarm brew in his skin. He watched the sun dip beyond the hills, thinking of the land beyond the *tekline*. When he returned to the compound gate, he found Justin and Coot waiting there for the other men. They smiled but said little to each other as they waited.

When Eagle entered Lotus' yurt, he found her sitting right next to a single lit candle, which melted onto an overturned bowl. She wore only a small tunic and sat so close to the flame it seemed as if it might burn the curve of her bare hip.

While he no longer felt foolish standing in front of her, the image Lotus presented this moment almost unnerved Eagle. She had a way of taking people off-guard. She beckoned to him. He sat across from her, gingerly arranging himself to keep weight off his leg.

"It is getting better," Lotus said. "By the full moon, you won't need the cane."

"I'm just beginning to like the cane." Eagle patted it.

"Which is why you must stop using it when the moon is full." Lotus grinned and raised her eyebrows.

"Ah. I see. Is there anything you don't know, Lotus?"

"Plenty enough to keep life interesting. Eagle, I look forward to chatting with you about the all the mysteries of life. I hope we will have much time for such, later. I'm sure your mother told you that I want to go with you when you escape again."

"You make it sound as if we're leaving tonight. Do you know something imminent?" Eagle asked.

"No." Lotus laughed. "Well, yes, just not that. In truth, for all my sight, it is hard to see what lies ahead for me. I can see for others, although it is harder to see for myself. For that, I thank the Goddess. Still, I believe you will pay only one more visit to the women before you go. And I expect that Rose will want to go with you, which is why you will wait even that long. I can't say why any of us do what we do, but I have strong feelings about what may happen."

"Have you ... or my mother ... spoken to Rose?"

"Again, no." Lotus leaned closer. "Still, I know her well."

Eagle didn't know what to say. He stared at the candle. Lotus leaned back again.

"We told the other women of your plans."

"Already?" Eagle snapped his head, staring into Lotus' dark eyes. He felt silly, immediately. He thought the ways of the women couldn't surprise him anymore. He thought he was beyond worrying about secrets. He regained himself after a heartbeat, realizing he still had far to go.

She chuckled. "Yes. Your mother told them about the idea for some of the women to escape with you. And I told them I would go with you. Of course, I assume you would want me."

"I'd be a fool not to. But ..."

"Don't worry, Eagle. I know you are beginning to understand our ways. I have heard that you even spoke to the men about not keeping secrets. There is nothing in the valley that can stop your plans. It doesn't matter who knows. You will escape again. Beyond this truth, I cannot see. It is one of the reasons I want to go with you. If I cannot see it, I must believe it is because I will be there. Even if I could see nothing, I would want to go with you."

"Thank you."

"And I must repeat: I hope we have much time to discuss the mysteries of life, given to us by the Goddess. Tonight, there is no time for it."

Again, Eagle didn't know what to say. He leaned in and waited, hoping Lotus would continue. He didn't realize he was holding his breath until she spoke, and he exhaled.

"Rose will give birth before the sun rises." She put both her hands on Eagle's chest, sculpting his torso with her fingers. When he started to speak, she moved her fingers to his lips. She knelt in front of Eagle, pulling off her tunic and then slowing undressing him.

Eagle awoke, hearing the cries. He had been dreaming again —of running beyond the *tekline*, this time, with Rose and Lotus. Rose had fallen, and she was calling to him. He tried to run to her, but the distance between them never shrank. Awake, he realized the cries were real. Rose's voice pierced him like an arrow.

He felt around in the dark for his cane, finding it as his eyes adjusted. Lotus was already gone. He dragged himself out of yurt and pushed himself to his feet, leaning on the cane. Lotus was standing nearby in the darkness. Eagle stopped next to her and tried to see. Soon, Mantis emerged from the yurt, holding the crying newborn.

"And the circle continues," Lotus said, taking Eagle's hand.

Eagle couldn't sleep after the baby's birth. He and Lotus sat together under the light of the single candle. They talked a little, now and then. Eagle asked if Lotus knew whether the child was his. She shook her head. He asked again—did she mean that it wasn't his or that she didn't know? She would only say it didn't matter and refused to say more. Eagle wondered if the other men could sleep. When the sun rose, he left the compound, stealing a glance at Rose's tent while Sage caught up to him.

The men returned to the village and went their separate ways. Justin had told them to convene at the circle before sundown for the draw. Eagle was met by Mace and Ram, who walked with him to his yurt. He thanked them for their company, even as he asked them to allow him to rest. He answered their inquisitive looks with the truth—Rose had given birth, and he hadn't been able to sleep afterwards. They didn't seem to understand, but they did as he asked, telling the other Ruck of the news and letting him sleep.

He awoke from Sage's repeated jostling. "Come now, Eagle, even Curly and Peck don't sleep this long into the afternoon."

Eagle pushed himself up on his elbows, blinking at the sunlight pouring into his yurt. The angle of the light told him it was well past mid-day. He rubbed his eyes. "Is it time already? It feels like I just fell asleep."

"Justin wants us to gather for the draw. We have a little time. You've been sleeping most of the day."

The two friends talked for a time, mostly about Rose's new child. Sage said he had heard the noise, but quickly fell back to sleep in Storm's yurt, knowing the women would take care of things. Eagle confided; he hadn't been able to sleep at all after he heard Rose's cries and witnessed Mantis announcing the baby's birth to the Goddess. He wondered again whether the child might be his. Sage put a stop to such talk, reminding him why Garnet had told them never to follow that path—such speculation leads to jealousy and spite; nothing good comes from it.

When they joined the other men at the circle, everyone was present except for Justin. Bison had accompanied Hawk; even though he didn't participate in the visit this time, he had still become a man and deserved to attend the draw, having his name entered with the other men instead of the children. They all greeted each other as usual, although little was said as they waited. Eagle noticed Bison staring at him from time to time. Eagle made no issue about it. Finally, Justin arrived—looking more than a little concerned, Eagle thought—and escorted them into the woods.

When they reached the traditional spot, the sun was just beginning to dip down to the tops of the hills. Justin greeted everyone. He recommended they begin with the choosing of the woman. Hawk immediately proposed the name of Maize, surprising no one.

Sage and Thrush began to respond in less than a heartbeat. The brothers stopped and looked at each other before Thrush deferred to his older sibling. Sage said Maize wasn't the oldest and thus wasn't the most likely girl to choose. They had discussed this before the last Hunt, he reminded everyone, when it was obvious that Star, now Pearl, should go to the women. Sage agreed on one point: Maize continued to mature quickly. Even so, she was still not the oldest, or the readiest, even if she had been considered last time. Nothing else mattered.

Bison took up the argument for Maize, speaking of her physical growth and her leadership with the younger children in

Hawk's camp. He said Maize was ready to bear children, which was what really mattered.

So was Ash, Thrush countered, and she was also the oldest girl. The other men allowed the two youngest to trade barbs and make their cases. The argument for Ash was simple; she was the oldest and ready to bear children. Bison argued something that had never been an issue, at least in anyone's memory, including Coot's. Star had gone last, and she was from Eagle's camp, Bison stated. This time, the girl who would become a woman should come from Hawk's camp, he declared.

Coot spoke, after having stood silent while pulling at his beard since they had arrived. "I see Bison's point. Things have changed. We should consider this."

He paused as everyone looked to him in surprise. "Perhaps we should make sure to balance things among the camps. Now then, since Pearl was from Eagle's camp ... and before that Gazelle was from Hawk's camp ... it would seem to be time for a girl from Justin's camp to go to the compound. So, Spider it is."

The men reacted with verbal disbelief, laughter, or both. The idea was ridiculous. Spider was much too young, even though she was the oldest girl in Justin's camp. Coot had made his point. The question of which camp meant nothing.

Justin stepped in while the men chortled and scoffed. "The men have always chosen one of the oldest girls, one of the most mature, one ready to bear children. That is what we must discuss. There have been times when no girl was sent, because none were ready. And there have been times when the oldest girl wasn't chosen, because she wasn't ready. Isn't that true, Coot?"

Coot nodded.

"Now we have two women who both seem to be ready," Justin continued. "I suggest we agree to make the decision based on chance, like the draw."

When the men exchanged glances and began to weigh the idea, Falcon spoke.

"Why not send both of them?"

"Yes, why not?" Eagle offered, almost too quickly, he guessed.

Again, the men exchanged glances and murmurs.

"Has this ever been done, Coot?" Justin asked. "I know we rejected this idea last time because we agreed such a decision would be reserved for extreme cases, like unexpected deaths among the women."

The old man pulled at his ruddy beard. "I don't recall for certain. If it has, it was likely for the very reason you mention, Justin, and rare indeed."

Oak spoke up for the first time. "We know the women will die, too young, just as most of us will. Jade died in childbirth. She was the first in many moons, but she won't be the last. Mantis and Lilly are pregnant now. Maybe Falcon is right."

"The women also believe Faith is pregnant," Eagle said.

"And Lotus told me that Nightingale will also conceive," Sage said.

The men fell silent, each one thinking about what had been said. None of them wanted to think of such things, but it was possible one of those women wouldn't survive childbirth. Eagle reflected on what Oak said—Jade was the first in a few seasons. They had been lucky. And with so many women becoming pregnant, sending two women might be a good idea. Of course, Eagle had another reason he hadn't yet shared. If he took women out of the compound—out of the valley—they would need replacements. He wondered what the others were thinking and considered revealing his true thoughts. The men conversed in small groups now, speculating on the outcome of the pregnancies in the moons to come. No secrets, Eagle reminded himself. It didn't mean recklessness. So far these were only ideas, not a plan he had shared or formulated with anyone else. Waiting to hear the others seemed best.

Indeed, after listening quietly since his opening bid for Maize, Hawk spoke again.

"I don't think we should send two women. Maize can wait another season. Ash cannot."

Everyone turned to face Hawk. Of all the men, Bison and Oak seemed more surprised than anyone. "Maize can wait," Hawk repeated, addressing them directly.

No more was said, except for Justin asking if the men were unanimous in choosing Ash to join the women. No one dissented.

"Then it is time for the draw." Justin poured the colored stones onto the ground. "First, we will choose the two men. Eagle, I believe it is best to keep your stone out of the pouch."

"What? Why?" Eagle struggled to form an intelligent response, failing.

"It's obvious, Eagle," Bison said. "You can barely stand without that cane. How will you defend yourself? How will you defend the children?"

Eagle looked around at the other men. He glanced at Sage and Thrush, then Falcon and Wolf. Thrush stared at the ground; Sage just stared. Wolf shook his head slowly.

Falcon spoke. "Justin is right, Eagle. There are plenty of men for the draw."

Eagle locked eyes with Hawk. The man glared back. "And you, Hawk?"

"As Bison said, it's obvious. I doubt the Overseers brought you back just so you could die in a Hunt, without even a chase."

Suddenly, Eagle felt terribly tired and weak. He nodded and watched, somewhat distracted, as Justin placed all the stones, except for Eagle's, in the pouch. Justin drew out two. Sage had stepped closer and patted Eagle on the shoulder while Thrush continued to stare at the ground.

Bison erupted after the stones for Hawk and Wolf were selected. "Hawk, not you, not again! That's four Hunts in a row. We must choose again!"

"No, Bison. The draw is the draw," Hawk said. He stepped over to Wolf and put out his hand. The quiet man accepted it. "Wolf, I know you will do your best to protect the children."

Wolf nodded and spoke at length. "And you," he said.

Justin drew the children's stones. Eagle shook off his temporary malaise and hobbled over to watch Justin extract and line up the stones:

Ram, Carver, Red, Spider, Clay, Dreamer, Grouch, Henna, Bee, Archer.

◆ ◆ ◆

As they returned to the circle, Thrush volunteered to give Ash the news. She left with Coot, who returned with Marvel. The small, clever girl's rapid-fire questions left everyone blinking, chuckling, and trying to keep up with appropriate answers. At first, a few of the men and older children wondered why the women had sent such a young child—and some fretted that for the second consecutive Hunt only one child had joined the village. Because some of the men had witnessed Marvel's precociousness in the compound, it didn't take long for everyone to accept her as a new villager. They all reminded themselves that their numbers fluctuated with each passing winter. Marvel's presence lightened Eagle's mood. Directly, she told him "the mother and the baby are well." When Sage asked Eagle to help comfort the children who needed kind words and reassurance, he readily agreed. It helped him to feel less powerless.

Being kept from the draw affected him profoundly. There were times when he had thanked God for not being drawn, and there were other times when he had wished he were chosen instead of another friend. But never had he been excluded from the draw itself. It made him feel like he was a burden on the village, not a leader. He thanked the Goddess for sending Marvel—the little girl provided just the slap in the face he needed. When a group of children came to him—including Fish, Newt, Snow, Happy, and Fern—Eagle told them a light-hearted story about the *tek*. They all felt better, especially Eagle. Strangely, he had the feeling Marvel was memorizing everything he said during the story.

Eagle slept uneasily, although far better than the night before. He awoke early and gathered with the other Ruck to watch the twelve enter the Hunting grounds. Marvel stuck close to Eagle. He expected her to ask what was happening. Instead, she summed it all up.

"I wonder who will come back," she said.

As it turned out, the Ruck didn't have to wait long to find out. The Hunt ended before the sun had risen completely over the valley. When the first survivors returned—Bee and Carver —the villagers learned there were two Overlord parties in this Hunt. Eagle thanked God, and then the Goddess, for that. A quick Hunt meant less suffering for everyone. It didn't diminish the painful wait to see if brothers and sisters would return. Everyone had someone close among the twelve, as always. For Eagle, it was his sister Archer and his brother Clay, as well as the trusted Ram.

Eagle's heart pounded when he saw his sister emerge with Henna. Archer came straight to him. They embraced for a long time. For so long, Eagle missed the return of Spider and nearly missed the unusual sight of Wolf walking hand-in-hand with Grouch and Dreamer. The silent man, who almost always walked alone, seemed awkward holding the young people's hands. Judging from their faces, the children seemed grateful to walk with Wolf.

In the mix of celebration and anxiety, it became clear that only four of the chosen were left. The members of Hawk's camp were clearly distressed; they demanded aloud if anyone had seen Hawk fall. None of the survivors had seen anyone taken by the lightning bolts, although Archer said she had seen Hawk with Red and Clay not long before the horn sounded thrice. No one had seen Ram. Relentlessly, Bison, Tanner, and Boar pressed Archer about what she saw, while Eagle worried about Clay and Ram. The thought of losing his brother, after they had just begun reconciliation, struck deep in Eagle's heart. Ram had become a loyal follower and more: a true friend. Eagle couldn't stifle tears as he wondered and waited, leaning against his cane and holding Marvel's tiny hand.

Finally, as some of Hawk's followers began to fall to the ground weeping and wailing, while others held each other and did their best to reassure themselves, Clay emerged alone from the woods, staggering, followed by the Black One.

12

Archer ran to Clay. Eagle faltered, losing the grip on his cane. He nearly collapsed, knocking down Marvel as he fell to one knee. Thrush helped Eagle rise, handing him the cane, while Sage tended to Marvel (who shook it off quickly). Fish hugged Dreamer, and both closed in near Eagle, along with others.

The Overseer had already begun to confer with Justin. The Ruck all around the circle fell into complete disarray. Always, the brothers and sisters of the dead lamented. Today their grief went far beyond. With a few exceptions, Hawk's supporters lost all control. They cried and cursed; they fell upon each other and tumbled down to the ground; they pulled at their hair and threw down their belongings. Only Scar and Shadow seemed unmoved; the latter stood alone, as if still obediently positioned a step behind Hawk's shoulder. Others joined the distraught children, including more of Diamond's brood, who had lost yet another sibling in the Hunt. Chance, Fletcher, Mountain, and now Red. Eagle noticed something: Dove, Happy, and Wolf sought out their youngest brother, Nardo, amidst the weeping followers of Hawk. Many of Eagle's camp mixed in with the others. The divisions that had separated them for moons seemed to dissolve with the magnitude of the loss of the man named Hawk.

Eagle thanked Thrush for his help, briefly turning his attention to Mace, who was standing apart from most of the other Ruck. Eagle saw Joy moving to hug Mace and Tiller—yes, Tiller was the middle brother, between Mace and Ram.

Coot had made his way to them as well to help Joy console the two remaining brothers, the sons of the Jade-before. Just then, something occurred to Eagle: Hawk had no remaining siblings. He was the last of the surviving brothers and sisters borne to a mother whose name Eagle had never sought to add to his memory.

Archer and Clay approached Eagle, banishing this line of thought. The brothers embraced, but no one rejoiced. Too much sorrow surrounded them. Instead, they stood side-by-side and watched as the Black One departed. Justin moved painstakingly into the circle, stopping at the Stone. He waited much longer than usual, letting the younger children subdue themselves while the older children eventually took notice of his presence in the circle.

"We have lost three of our brothers today. They gave their lives so the Ruck would go on. We will thank them, grieve for them, and we will remember their names.

"Hawk was a father to many of the Ruck. He was a leader among us for a few winters, unsurpassed with bow and arrow, and a hero in too many Hunts to count. His name was drawn ..." Justin's pause was odd and belabored "... each of the last four Hunts. He never questioned it; he went among the twelve and did his best to protect the children. This time he gave his own life; willingly, I am certain. Hawk's deeds went well beyond the Hunt. He taught the children the ways of the woods, of the *ven,* and the river. He stood by his ideas for how the Ruck would go on, setting an example for all of us to remember in the days ahead."

Justin paused again. While the children tried to compose themselves, to uphold the ritual of the remembering, the loss of Hawk seemed too much to bear. The wailing began anew. Justin allowed them dozens of heartbeats—letting Scar, Rock, Tanner, Bison, and Maize calm the others—before he continued.

"Ram, nearly a man, was also taken from us. We will all remember his strong will and desire to make his voice heard among the growing children. He had the courage and the resolve to do what he thought was right, no matter what others might believe. His role in Eagle's escape will surely become a legend in the stories told to the Ruck children."

"Red was known to many of us as a friend and good spirit. Still a young boy, he had proved his skill as a hunter. He also had a wit as striking as his red hair and he made many of us laugh without offending any."

"We will miss all three of them. We will remember their names."

Justin waited while Hawk's followers, along with Diamond's children, exclaimed and lamented yet again. Eagle let his gaze flow from them over to Mace and Tiller, who had moved closer to Eagle. The two boys were now wiping tears from their eyes and trying to remain stoic. The lamentations continued for some time, and still Justin waited.

Eagle began to study Justin. Something was amiss. After the last Hunt, Justin had also let the children have their time, for much longer than the Justin-before. The man had even had trouble holding back his own tears, still young and not fully accustomed to the demands of his station. Today, he seemed different; he had the appearance of sorrow, as did everyone, but he also seemed to be struggling with other thoughts. For a few heartbeats, Eagle observed Justin muttering to himself while the Ruck expressed their grief. Eagle then looked to his friends and siblings who hadn't gone to cry with the others. They stood solemn. Archer held Clay's hand, who held Onyx's. Finally, Hawk's followers began to regain themselves, with some of them breaking off into smaller groups around the circle. Clay kissed his sister's hand and limped away, supported by Onyx. Those two walked to join up with Rock—away from Bison and others.

Seeing this, Justin shook his head, as if clearing his mind. He continued with the ceremony as the Ruck had for as long as Eagle could remember. "We will now honor the heroes of The Hunt. Who wishes to step forward?" From the newly forming clusters of the Ruck around the circle, Clay stepped in, as did Dreamer.

"Step up and speak your truth, Clay and Dreamer." Justin stepped backward off the Stone, taking a stance just behind it and beckoning for them to take his place.

Clay struggled to reach the Stone. Eagle had seen him stagger from the woods and limp along with Onyx; still, he hadn't realized until now that his brother had been injured rather than simply fatigued. Clay stepped up, pulling his left leg over the lip of the Stone and facing the Ruck.

"I ... I wish I didn't see it, but I did ... I saw Hawk hit by the lightning bolt while trying to save Red. Hawk had told us to stay close and to run across each other's paths. See, the Overlords tried to trap us between the two, uh, groups. Hawk said to move apart and come together, running in different directions, to confuse their scent. We ran back and forth a lot. I tripped ... I, uh, twisted my leg and I fell." Clay paused, swallowing hard and wiping his eyes. "Then they were chasing Red. I saw Hawk run out ... well, across, like he said, trying to distract the Overlords. The other group came up fast. One group shot Red, the other shot Hawk. He wanted to save us both. I believe ... well, even though I'm not sure I understand his ideas anymore ... I still believe Hawk was a hero." Shaking his head, Clay stopped. He wiped his eyes and swallowed hard again. Before moving to back to Onyx, he gazed at the followers of Hawk who had assembled near Bison, and then he locked eyes with Eagle.

Dreamer swayed, still one step in from the circle. Archer had to reach in and nudge him. He walked to the Stone and stepped up easily.

"Wolf saved me. He, um, well, he found me asleep, or, well, you know ... He told me to follow him, and we just started to run, when ... when ... when the things, the Overthings, um ... the monsters ... pounded out from behind us. He told me to run one way, and, um, he went the other way. I don't know how he got away ... they were, they, they were right behind him." He shrugged and stepped down.

Despite themselves, some of the Ruck giggled nervously, for a heartbeat or two. Even a few who stood near Bison. Dreamer's name might never change, Eagle thought.

Justin stepped up again, still troubled. At least it seemed so to Eagle. Justin continued, regardless. "It is the law. Some of the Ruck must die so the rest can live. We thank our heroes, and those who died for us. We honor them."

Everyone knelt and cupped both hands over their chests, fingers overlapped. After ten heartbeats, they rose.

"The Ruck go on," Justin announced. "Now, we remember our names. Scar, step up. Grouch, step up. Shorty, step up."

Scar seemed the most surprised. He stood mostly by himself, though very near Bison and the others. He hesitated, but Maize moved over and kissed him on the cheek, before gently pushing him into the circle. Eagle remembered when a Justin-before had named him Sparrow, at a similar age as Scar. He had felt awkward and unsure at the time. When nearly a man, the naming took on much more importance.

Meanwhile, Grouch was hugging and kissing Ox while the other young girls exclaimed for a moment, excited for their friend. Grouch stepped in proudly, ready to shed her old name. Eagle heard Archer whisper "It's about time, what an awful name she had." Shorty also stepped in quickly, from among Fern and Snow and the young children gathered near Falcon and Coot.

"These children have been in the village for different numbers of winters," Justin said, "but each has grown and changed much this season. They all need new names, names which attest to their character rather than their appearance."

"Shorty has marked only one winter in the village. When he arrived, he was named for his stature. Since then, he has learned fast and sprouted up like some of the *veg* in Tiller's field. I have watched him take wonder in everything around us —from the crafts he learns to the ways of the woods. More than anything else, I have seen him awake at night, when the other young ones have drifted off, staring at the moon, and thinking of what I cannot guess. We shall call him Moon."

The boy paused, unsure, but smiling. Justin smiled and beckoned to him and he took measured steps up to the Stone. Eagle noticed that several of the children around him had turned to Sky, to see her reaction. Tears came, but she also bore a slim smile as she remembered her friend, lost in one of the Hunts-before. Eagle smiled, too. He turned to observe Justin, admiring the man's ability to begin shifting the mood of the Ruck. The naming meant so much, and Justin had already mastered it by all accounts. He had helped soften the blow by naming two children in Hawk's camp while still managing to touch the members of his own group and Eagle's. As Justin kissed the boy on the head, the Ruck chanted slowly, repeating the new name in low stretched-out tones, while raising their heads toward the hills over which the moon would re-appear in a few days. Moon left the Stone and received hugs from his young friends. Coot reached over and patted the boy on his head.

"For a time," Justin bellowed, recapturing everyone's attention, "our friend Grouch seemed as if she had just a moment ago bitten into a bad piece of *ven*. A smile came no more often than a winter snow, a happy word even less often. Still, this young girl has begun to find her way here in the village, and her name is more than simply wrong, it is offensive to the friends who know her well." Justin paused as murmurs went through those around Bison. "Yes, I see these things—and you wouldn't want to know what else I've seen when you thought no one was looking! Worry not, those matters are of no concern today. Like a young bird that has found its wings, we shall now call you Robin."

Robin sped to the Stone, with arms spread wide. She swooped once around the Stone and leapt up to hug Justin. Her quick leap took him off guard, and they staggered together before the man caught his balance and held onto the young girl. He bent to kiss her on the head, but she gave him a quick peck on the cheek and slipped from his grasp, circling once again before flying back into her friends' arms. The Ruck picked up the quick choppy chant of "Robin-Robin-Robin" started by Bee and Copperhead.

"Finally, this boy stands before us, wondering. He isn't yet a man, but he has shown signs of becoming a strong, wise man. He has learned well from Hawk and others, never closing his mind to anyone's ideas even while making his choices about who to follow. I know this, because he came to hear my thoughts during the difficult times we have all faced in recent moons. I have seen him talking to many of the Ruck, from all three of our camps, since Eagle's escape. And I have known him as a friend, even before my naming and first visit to the women. Like Robin and Moon, his present name represents only the exterior. In this Owl's heart, I see, hear, and feel an abundance of wisdom, patience, and strength."

The Ruck had fallen completely silent as Justin spoke. Now, a few people began to hoot like the bird whose name was given. The harmony spread, until the newly named Owl calmly strode up to the Stone. After he stepped up, he knelt before Justin, who kissed him on the head and then pulled him up for an embrace. Eagle reminded himself: while Justin had become an important man in the village, he was only two winters older than his friend Owl. When the boy left the Stone and glided back to receive greetings from Rock, Clay, and Onyx, Eagle saw Justin's face turn sour once again. The man looked somber, perplexed, if only for a few heartbeats.

Justin raised his hands, palms upward. "We are the Ruck, we remember. We must go on. We will now eat and re-gain strength." He paused, apparently considering something while Eagle mused about his odd behavior. "We will thank the *ven* and the *veg* for keeping us fit and ready for The Hunt."

Eagle had rested, at the insistence of Archer and Sage, while the Ruck prepared for the feast. He didn't return to his yurt; instead, he lounged near Coot's, chatting with the old man while watching the children. It had been some time since Eagle had done so. He noticed that Hawk's children began to mingle more with the others than he remembered from before his escape. Coot noticed too, telling Eagle this had happened before, when a leader died. The old man reminded Eagle of the changes after Garnet's death.

By the time the feast had begun, the Ruck had congregated into several small groups, nothing like the three distinct camps that formed after the last two hunts. In many ways, Eagle felt a sense of uncertainty and strangeness during this feast. Most obvious were the twelve who ate no *ven*. Their decision became awkward. The freshly skinned animals were roasted over great fires; the charred flesh passed around among the men and children as they had always done. Eagle himself felt odd at refusing the *ven*; for so long he had joined his brothers, sisters, and friends in filling his belly and thanking the *ven* for another season of life after the Hunt.

Justin's words echoed in Eagle's ears. *"We will thank the* ven *and the* veg ... ." Eagle knew that the stories and the ceremonies changed slowly as the children grew, as the men died, and as the Ruck went on. Many times, he wondered how different the stories he told were from those told by the men many winters before. He had observed the subtle changes in Fly's re-telling. This change—not eating the *ven* during a feast, and Justin adding the *veg* to be thanked—seemed quite poignant to Eagle this night. He turned his attention to Justin, who played with some of the young children near his fire, along with Spider.

Willow was talking to him, Eagle realized, as both his sisters and other children gathered nearby enjoying the pleasant late summer evening.

"Eagle?"

"Yes, Willow." He turned to look at his younger sister and saw that Mace was sitting very close to her.

"We cooked this for you. For all of the *veg*-eaters." She

proffered a steaming bowl with water and *veg* and fish.

Eagle took the bowl and inhaled the rich aroma. "It smells wonderful." Eagle noticed that Archer and Thrush also held bowls. They smiled at each other.

"We thought, for this feast, we should do something kind of new," Archer said. "Marvel and Tiller helped with the seasoning—not quite the same as for *ven* or how we usually eat the *veg*."

Eagle looked around and found Marvel playing with Fish and others. That young girl is well-named, he thought, thinking of Rose and the times he had watched Marvel in the compound. He noticed that others of the twelve *veg*-eaters, scattered among the various groups, were also holding bowls of the liquid. They all seemed to be waiting for him.

"Thank you, everyone. Let's eat." Eagle held up his bowl and then put it to his lips, drinking, plucking out a piece of fish and popping it into his mouth. It all tasted good. He smiled, watching Archer and the others follow his example.

The feast continued through the night. Eagle politely refused offers to play stones or join some of the children for a walk as many of the Ruck began to pair off or gather in their small groups of friends. He had a feeling the night's activity would signal the intentions of many of the children now that Hawk had gone. Coot had stated it; things were changing fast. Already thinking of what would happen in the next moon, and how he would plan the next escape, Eagle preferred to observe the Ruck and measure their allegiances. Sage had joined him, and they talked of what they saw while watching the followers of Hawk.

As the children began to disperse, Bison tried to keep all of Hawk's followers together. He made an impassioned plea for them to follow him now, saying he wanted to preserve Hawk's ideas exactly as they were, even in his absence. Eagle and Sage watched while the latter whispered his doubts about whether Bison's attempt would garner any followers. The cohesion was gone, he surmised. Eagle questioned what Sage meant, and his friend clarified: while Sage thought many of Hawk's children would cling to the beliefs Hawk had taught them, he suspected they wouldn't trust Bison as the new leader. The loyalty of Hawk's group had much to do with the man's presence, his leadership, rather than the ideas themselves.

The unfolding events proved Sage correct. Only a few stayed with Bison—including Shadow, Bear, Nardo, Axe, Tanner, and Brute—after a debate about what they should all do. Almost all the children spoke well of Bison. They said they wanted to remember Hawk and his ideas, too, and yet no one seemed willing to follow a single leader in place of Hawk. Owl stated clearly: no one could replace Hawk, not yet. In fact, he said it would be a mistake for anyone to try to replace him. Some expressed support for the idea of *freedom*, including Clay and Onyx. This caused Bison to erupt, probably damaging his chances with some of the children, Sage wagered. Bison declared that Hawk would be ashamed of them now. In response, Owl and Rock said Hawk would never berate his children that way. He always gave them the choice to follow him or choose another way. That was one of the reasons everyone loved and respected Hawk, Owl said.

Eagle watched as the caucus ended peacefully, even though Bison and Boar seemed ready to fight with Owl and Rock. Owl reminded everyone that Hawk had talked about the wrongness of fighting amongst the Ruck, even when they disagreed strongly. Eagle and Sage exchanged amazed glances when they heard Rock follow Owl's words with a story about Hawk. Eagle strained to hear it all, eyes widening. It seemed that Hawk had confided to Mountain, Bison, and Rock, revealing his strong desire to beat some sense into Eagle but telling them he knew such actions would never help the Ruck to go on. Hawk wanted the Ruck to be unified. All his efforts, until very near the end, were to convince Eagle and his followers that their ideas would bring the wrath of the Black Ones, leading to the end of the Ruck. It would be no better, Hawk had said, to destroy the Ruck from within, by fighting, wounding, or killing each other.

"Do you remember his words, Bison?" Rock asked. "What would Hawk say if he saw you were about to fight with those who share your beliefs, but choose not to follow you?"

"I remember," was all Bison would say.

And so, Hawk's children began to split up, with some remaining close to Bison and others choosing to depart in groups forming around Rock or Owl. Eagle noticed that Clay and Onyx went with Rock. When he mentioned that to Sage, his friend cautioned against premature conclusions. They shouldn't overstate what was happening this night, he added. Sage didn't perceive the children choosing new leaders, not so soon anyway. He knew that Owl and others had begun to question Hawk's ideas after the escape. Sage guessed the children were just choosing friends to spend this night with, after rejecting Bison's attempt to assume Hawk's place. The children would need time to figure out what they wanted and who they might follow if anyone.

Eagle nodding, accepting his friend's insight. The next moon would hold many changes among the Ruck, he thought. His own plans would involve anyone who wanted to join him. He promised himself to talk about his plans in the open. Not in speeches for the Black Ones to hear, although not in secret as the last escape had taken root. He would gather with his friends to discuss his ideas and listen to theirs. He would also approach Justin, Rock, Owl, and even Bison.

Sage and Eagle passed the rest of the night together, watching the boys and girls settle into groups of friends, start-up impromptu games of chase and stones, or wander off in pairs. The sight of young boys and girls leaving to enjoy an evening of private play reminded both men of their adolescence. Sage remembered some of the girls they had followed into the woods. Some of them were now women wile others had perished in the Hunt. Eagle felt a pang of protectiveness when Mace took Willow into the woods, sitting up abruptly and drawing an amused chuckle from his friend. Eagle raised an eyebrow toward Sage when Tiller and Archer went off together—both men agreed they were an unlikely pair, but Sage reminded Eagle that the feasts often had such an effect on the Ruck. Indeed, the children's ability to carry on, and their willingness to observe the rituals of the feast, came as a relief. It reminded Eagle: the Ruck would go on, as long as they continued to care about each other, even when leaders such as Hawk, and Eagle himself, threatened to divide them.

◆ ◆ ◆

Over the next several days, while the moon grew larger each night it passed through the night sky, the Ruck adjusted to the death of Hawk. Eagle acted cautiously at first, playing stones and organizing races with the children, learning from Tiller along with many of the other Ruck, and participating in Fly's storytelling each night. Eagle was pleased to see Copperhead and Onyx encouraging other children to attend the storytelling. Those girls reminded everyone that Hawk had always believed the stories were valuable, even while he objected to some of Eagle's tales. They brought the likes of Bee, Rattler, and Rabbit, intermingling with Fish, Snow, Herb, and Double around the evening fires.

Heeding the reminders himself, Eagle chose his stories carefully. He found himself beginning to understand Hawk's viewpoint, now carried forth by the children who loved the man. With Hawk gone, his ideas became more understandable. The rivalry, now finished, began to seem silly. After telling his stories, of the *tek* and the *dawgs* and the *sitties*, Eagle would sit with Coot, Sage, Mace, Thrush, Falcon, and others, talking about his ideas of *freedom* and escape. He kept these discussions separate from his stories of the time-before. A time and place for everything, he reminded himself each morning, learning to choose his words more wisely without hiding secrets. Before long, their discussions became an every-evening meeting. The men and some of the older children gathered with Eagle to discuss the events of the summer, the impending time of the fall harvest, and what they would do in the moons to come.

They laid plans for better development of the *veg* and talked about how the Ruck might adapt. Each night, new members of the village joined in, and more of the Ruck spoke up. Archer told everyone about how she and others (including Dove, Spider, Parrot, Blossom, Hoop, and Peacock) had been learning more from Tiller. In hope of expanding their store of *veg* for the winter, they had planted some quick growing *veg* after helping him harvest some of the roots already planted. At Archer's urging, Scorpion told the Ruck how he and Fisher had begun to set traps for some of the smaller creatures. Fisher was also teaching a few of the younger children how to snare fish in the river. Copperhead and Happy thanked both boys for that— they had enjoyed the small strips of roasted flesh and asked to be included in the next day's lessons. Archer suggested Scorpion and Fisher should become teachers of these crafts—just like Carver, Weaver, and herself. A number of the Ruck children volunteered to participate in such lessons. The two boys divided up the children with Archer's guidance.

Eagle admired his sister then; she was becoming a leader among the Ruck in the village. It was unusual for a young girl to do so, he thought. For so long, the boys had followed the men in this regard, while the maturing young women took care of the youngest children, preparing for their time to leave for the compound. When he mentioned this to Sage, Eagle's friend scoffed, saying the young girls had always done their share to lead. Only the men who struggled for dominance— and who thought primarily with their members—could fail to see that. Eagle hung his head and laughed, acknowledging Sage's biting wisdom, keen humor, and uncanny ability to provide a verbal slap of perspective just when Eagle needed it.

Eagle smiled when Owl and Maize joined them one evening, near the time when the moon rose to a new fullness. He also noticed that Justin had joined Owl and Maize over the past few past nights, although the man usually said little. He just seemed to listen, no matter whose company he sought. Eagle could sense that Justin remained troubled. The man played with the children, but otherwise he seemed withdrawn and introspective. He sometimes attended, but didn't participate in, the evening meetings.

Looking around, Eagle also counted how many of Hawk's former followers had joined them that night, including Boar, Ox, and Copperhead. Predictably, Bison, Shadow, Tanner, and Bear stayed away. Still, Eagle perceived the opportunity to foster openness, to reach out to some of Hawk's followers as well as the Ruck who had remained neutral. He told them all he believed more of the Ruck could escape. He said he had plans to make it work. No one seemed surprised, but Eagle saw doubt in many faces.

"I have been out there." Eagle said. "I know that if we work together, some of us will be able to evade the Overseers."

"How can we possibly evade the Black Ones?" Owl asked. "While our fathers believed there was only one Overseer, we know better now."

Eagle smiled. "Yes, Owl, we do know better. It was Hawk who first opened my eyes, as I assume he did for many of you. He showed me the changing of the Black Ones. Until then, I thought, like many of us ... I believed there was only one Overseer. One all-knowing, all-seeing, all-powerful Overseer. In truth, they aren't any of those things."

"Hawk said they are from the Ruck!" Clay shrunk after blurting this out, staring at the ground when everyone turned to him. Eagle paused, noticing Justin's face darkening.

"Yes, my brother," Eagle replied. "Hawk told me, too. I didn't want to believe him. I'm not sure I do now, but perhaps he was right about that, too. In any case, he opened my eyes and while I could never accept his ideas about how the Ruck should go on, he did influence my thinking. Hawk's revelation eventually convinced me escape was possible. Ram, Mace, and I watched the exchange many times, counting the *tekline* flash and practicing the leap to *freedom*. It worked. And it can work again."

"Okay, but it only answers how we might escape the *tekline*," Owl said. "They still hunted you and brought you back here."

"True. They hunted one man. I was like the *ven*. Afraid, tired, outmatched. Without a plan for survival. Think of the Hunt; it takes at least three of the Overlords to track us down when we work together. Yes, eventually, they win. Still, we know there have been times when the Ruck evaded them for days. Even in the hunting grounds. The land beyond the *tekline* is vast. And the Overseers, whether of the Ruck or something else, are not as powerful as the Overlords. In numbers, with a plan and working together, some of us can evade them. They can't catch us all. That's why I found the *free* Ruck out there. Of this, I'm certain."

Justin stood to leave. He wore the same perplexed visage that Eagle observed during the naming, and several times since. Eagle decided to seek out the man later in the evening. For now, this gathering was more important.

"If we escape and manage to evade the Black Ones and the Overlords, what then?" Maize asked.

"We find a place where we can grow *veg*, fish, and trap." Eagle spoke directly to Maize and then bowed his head to Fisher and Tiller, who sat near each other. "We make babies and the Ruck go on. Yes, we might have to live on the move, without a permanent village, to evade capture. Please believe me; one day of *freedom* is worth a lifetime enslaved in the valley. I was there, I saw the stone village of the *Yewessay*, I saw the wolf, I smelled the air at the top of the hills. It is worth it."

The assembled Ruck fell into murmurs and small conversations. Eagle waited.

"Wait, wait," Thrush said, almost shouting over the others. "Make babies? Are you saying the women will go?"

"Perhaps. Or perhaps the oldest of the girls will be ready." Eagle purposefully turned to face Maize and another round of conversations erupted.

Owl stood up and put his arms up. It reminded Eagle of Garnet's way, winters ago when Eagle was still Sparrow. Soon, the Ruck had calmed down.

"Eagle, you have changed the village almost beyond recognition for many of us. Now, you are talking about the end of the village—and with it the end of what we have all been taught for the Ruck to go on. I'm not sure I'm ready for that, but you have given us much to consider." Owl turned and spoke to the other Ruck. "Eagle's words hold hope and danger. I will need time to think about these ideas. I hope everyone will think long and hard over the next few days, talking to each other." He bowed to Eagle and walked away, followed by Maize and Rattler, then joined, surprisingly (at least to Eagle) by Ox and Boar.

Others departed in their small groups, while some stayed to talk some more, including Thrush, Tiller, Mace, Copperhead, and Willow. It pleased Eagle to see them discussing his ideas without looking to him for guidance. When he was gone, when any of them decided to make their escape, they would need to work together to survive. He remembered Garnet saying something similar to him—how Sparrow would need to learn to evade the Overlords without his help—and it occurred to Eagle that he had built upon many of Garnet's teachings, sometimes without realizing and quite probably well beyond anything that Garnet had hoped for or even imagined. If the new leaders such as Owl and Archer could do the same, the Ruck would survive.

Eagle stood, leaning on his cane and looking to the moon as the darkness started to envelope the valley. He remembered what Lotus had said. He promised himself to start the next day without the cane. His leg ached only after long walks or attempts to run. It was time to let it gain strength without the crutch. He slowly backed away while the other Ruck carried on with their ideas. He set off to Justin's camp, determined to find the man and learn what was troubling him.

Eagle smiled as he approached, watching Curly, Fern, and Peck chase Coyote around the camp fire while Dove and the other young children cheered them on. Eagle sat next to Dove, asking the boy if Justin were around. Dove said he hadn't returned from the gathering.

"Is something wrong?" Dove asked, observing Eagle's pensiveness.

"No." Eagle stared into the fire. "Actually, I'm not sure. Do you think Justin has been himself lately?"

Dove stood, rousing the children near him. "Go get Coyote. Help your friends catch him!" When Snow, Double, and Huff had taken off, leaving Dove alone with Eagle, the boy sat again.

"Owl asked me the same question last night."

"What did you say?"

"Sometimes yes, sometimes no. He smiles when he plays with us. When he talks to the men or goes to your gatherings, he seems different."

"Where might he go, if not here, and not in the village?"

Dove hesitated, turning to face Eagle.

"I mean, does he have a place where he goes to think, to watch the stars, to ..."

Dove brightened. "Yes. He does. Owl would know."

"Thank you. And don't worry. I just want to talk with him."

"I know, Eagle."

It took a while to find Owl and his friends. They had retreated to a place they favored, near the foothills beyond the archery range. Eagle knew of the place; it wasn't a secret by any means. Before he found them there, he first went to their regular camp, where he stopped to speak with Clay and Onyx. He invited them to go on a trapping excursion the next day. They told him they had seen Owl and Maize with a few others, heading toward the archery range.

While he walked under the light of the moon, Eagle thought about Justin's behavior since Eagle's return to the village. Even before the draw, the man had seemed different. His words were always wise, and his handling of the gathering showed how much he had grown in the last few moons. At the time, Eagle thought of these changes only in positive terms. Now, in reflection, he could see beyond that, reading trouble into Justin's face when remembering the night in his tent before the draw.

Images from the painful time during the draw, when Eagle's stone was removed and Hawk's was chosen, also replayed themselves in Eagle's mind. He remembered Bison's words: "*Four in a row.*" Even as he spotted Owl's small fire, those words continued to echo in his head.

Owl stood and greeted him, wary. "Eagle, is something wrong?"

"No, not exactly." Eagle continued to approach. "I'm looking for Justin. Dove told me you might know where he is. He hadn't returned to his camp after our gathering. I don't think anything is wrong, but I would like to speak to him and, well, as I said, Dove said you might know."

Owl asked his friends to wait for a moment. He came closer to Eagle.

"Yes, Justin and I have a place where we sometimes talk. I go there by myself now and then, and so does he. It is our place."

"I understand." Eagle laid his hand on Owl's shoulder. He could feel the muscle and sinew of the older boy's arm. He was growing strong in many ways. "I won't ask you to tell me." Eagle took his hand away and looked to the moon again.

Owl looked up, too, then turned his gaze back to Eagle. "We were just discussing your ideas about escaping with the women and living outside of the *tekline*."

"I'm sorry to have interrupted. Perhaps I can find Justin tomorrow." Eagle began to move away, reminded of his promise about the cane as he leaned heavily against it.

"When we're done," Owl said to Eagle's back, "I will see if Justin is still there and tell him that you seek him." He paused as Eagle ambled away, then called out. "Eagle, I'm worried about him, too."

Stopping, turning, Eagle nodded. He didn't know whether Owl could see him clearly in the moonlight. Eagle returned to his yurt and settled in to sleep with his head poking out the flap as he had become accustomed to doing since he returned to the village. He dreamed of a new village, much like their home in the valley, but near a vast body of water. He saw Owl and Archer, grown old like Coot and Honey—or maybe even older—and surrounded by children chasing each other around a campfire.

Eagle enjoyed his diminutive breakfast, becoming more and more accustomed to his ration of *veg* and the root brew Marvel had taught them to make after she arrived (having memorized the instructions given to her by Lotus). Eagle and the other *veg*-eaters had learned to eat a little less than everyone else until they could bolster their supply of *veg* and fish. Already, they had begun to adapt, supplementing with more fish and *scurries* (as the small animals they now hunted had been named by Newt). Eagle looked forward to Scorpion's trapping lesson this morning.

It came as a surprise to many of the Ruck, but the *veg*-eaters all claimed to feel better in the last several days despite their rationed meals. Onyx was the most vocal about it. She would tell anyone willing to listen: she now understood what Eagle meant about thinking more clearly than ever. She said it was like peering beyond a lifting fog in the valley, suddenly seeing the hills for the first time. Interestingly, most of the twelve *veg*-eaters had assembled together this morning—and Eagle realized the children chosen from Hawk's and Justin's camps increasingly spent their time among new friends in Eagle's camp. All of them were active under the tutelage of Tiller, Fisher, and Scorpion. The latter two teachers had broken completely from Bison, associating primarily with Clay and Rock, who seemed willing to do whatever Onyx suggested. Meanwhile, Tiller had become noticeably self-assured and decisive, giving work orders to younger and elder children alike.

And so, that morning, three large groups of Ruck set out

on their chosen ways—some to the fields with Tiller, others to the river with Fisher or into the woods with Scorpion. Eagle wanted to count and recite the names, even though he understood these groups weren't like those of the rival camps before his escape. While many of the Ruck now engaged in the newer activities, others continued the traditional ways. The other crafters—such as Weaver and Carver and Tanner—still practiced their skills and taught children as they always had. Everyone agreed: the Ruck had to learn the new ways, but the old ways were still needed, too.

Indeed, Eagle saw two separate hunting parties had formed for the third day in a row. These hunters continued to bring in *ven* for the fall and coming winter while the others learned lessons for the future. No one had lost sight of the need for the *ven*—not just for sustenance in the moons to come but also for the hides and bones they used for so many purposes. Eagle watched as Bison, Shadow, Bear, and Axe headed off into the woods, hardly talking to anyone else, while Falcon, Oak, Wolf, and Chase strapped on their quivers and bid a good day to Eagle and the others. Eagle noticed that Owl and Sage weren't hunting today, although he had seen each of them join one of the hunting groups in recent days.

As Eagle tagged along at the rear of Scorpion's group, moving more than a little slowly without his trusty cane, he saw Justin heading off to the river behind Fisher, Mace, Willow, Huff, and others. He waved. Justin quickly turned away. Eagle felt certain the man had seen him. It became all too obvious. Justin was avoiding him.

It bothered Eagle throughout Scorpion's morning lesson. He was fascinated by the boy's ideas about how to trap *scurries* without damaging them, but he couldn't focus on the task while thinking about Justin. Eagle made a promise to himself —to learn more from Scorpion after he had spoken with Justin and resolved whatever was going on. More than once, Eagle had an urge to go to straight to the river and take Justin aside right then. Each time he fought it off and told himself that forcing the issue would do no good.

As the sun alighted high overhead and the children were busy practicing what Scorpion had shown them, Eagle patted the boy on the back and congratulated him, saying all the Ruck would benefit from his talents. Then, he took his leave and went to the fields, where he hoped to find Owl. The older boy had been spending time there when he wasn't hunting *ven*. Indeed, he found Owl among the others as they took a long break during the hottest part of the day, drinking water and talking under the tree shade.

Owl saw Eagle coming. "Hello, Eagle. Ready to get dirty? Tiller says we'll be back to work soon."

"Happily," Eagle said. While the man meant it—he had been spending time in the fields since the Hunt—Owl appeared unconvinced at the moment.

"Did Justin speak to you yet?" Owl asked.

"No." Eagle said. "Did you expect him to?"

"Yes, well, sometime today, anyway. I found him last night, lying on his back and staring at the stars in his favorite place. He seemed okay. I told him you were looking for him. I didn't stay long, once he promised to find you."

"I waved to him earlier, and he turned away. I suppose he might not have noticed, or he just wasn't ready ... I don't know. It seemed like he wanted nothing more than to avoid me."

"Please give him time, Eagle. I've never seen him like this. I don't want to push him."

"Agreed. Still, I need to speak with him sometime soon."

Owl didn't answer immediately. They sat and watched as some of the children chased each other, now that the break was ending and Tiller was rounding up his workers. As he rose, Owl turned to Eagle.

"If he doesn't come to you by the time the youngest children go to sleep and he disappears again, I will take you to his place."

"Thank you, Owl. Let's get to work."

◆ ◆ ◆

Eagle remained distracted during the evening gathering. Justin hadn't made any effort to fulfill his promise to Owl, despite their proximity at the evening meal, when Fisher and his friends passed around lightly charred chunks of fish from their day's catch. Justin had helped with the catch, and he now celebrated with the others until Eagle, Oak, and other men arrived. Justin's mood changed in a heartbeat; his smile disappeared, and his face grew more somber than the day of the Hunt.

Determined to give the man the full day, as promised, Eagle could only sigh and watch Justin drift away from the group, turning toward his yurt. Now, as the gathering was ending without an appearance by the man, Eagle sought out Owl, who lingered in a light-hearted discussion with Falcon.

"Friends," Eagle said, "Sorry to interrupt. Owl, it seems I must ask for your help, as Justin has disappeared again."

Falcon nodded. "So, I'm not the only one who has noticed."

"Not at all," Owl said.

"What can we do?"

Owl faced Falcon. "I'm taking Eagle to speak with Justin. I know where he goes. Please, Falcon, it will be hard enough ... for ... for me to take Eagle. Justin has been my friend for so long. I know something is wrong. Whatever troubles him, it seems to concern only the men ... and he won't speak of it to me. I'm hoping that Eagle ..."

Falcon clapped Owl's arm. "I understand." Falcon's smile reappeared immediately. He moved over to Buck's side as the older boy was telling a story to Blossom and Chase while the young girls listened intently.

Owl led Eagle to the foothills, not far from the landslide where Badger had died. Eagle paused, remembering his little brother. Memories from that day rushed his thoughts. It seemed so long ago, although only several moons had passed.

Owl and Eagle moved cautiously in the dark, with only moonlight to guide them, because Owl insisted on approaching quietly, and without light. He seemed reluctant to give away the spot he and Justin had discovered when his friend was still called Earnest.

They startled Justin. He jumped to his feet and reached for his knife. Owl held up his hands.

"Justin, please forgive me. We are worried about you."

Justin growled, clenching his fist. "Go back to your yurts."

Eagle and Owl gave each other sidelong glances, but neither moved.

For several heartbeats, all three of the Ruck waited. Finally, Justin flicked his knife to the ground, sticking it in the earth. "I'm a fool. My friends come to help me, and I threaten them. I don't deserve to be called Justin."

He slumped to the ground, dropping his head into his hands. Again, Owl and Eagle exchanged glances, pity filling both of their eyes this time.

"Justin, I brought Eagle here to speak with you, because we care about you. Others have noticed, too. I'm not yet a man, but I am your friend. I will leave, so you two men can talk."

Eagle put out his hand to Owl. "You might not be a man by custom, Owl, but your actions say otherwise. Thank you."

Justin looked up, watching his younger friend leave. Eagle watched them both, remembering how difficult it is for young people to cast aside childhood after only twelve or fourteen winters, as Owl and Justin had. Eagle himself would be seeing seventeen winters. He wondered if the Ruck-before faced such responsibilities at this age.

Eagle sat across from Justin, cross-legged, watching the man who once again buried his face in his hands. Eagle knew he must not demand anything of Justin. The man bore wounds deeper than those of flesh and blood. Eagle waited.

"I'm sorry, Eagle, I have failed as Justin."

"Not in my view." Eagle paused. "Please tell me what troubles you."

Justin folded his hands in his lap, continuing to stare at the earth in front of him. "I don't know where to start."

"Garnet once told me that the only place to start was the beginning."

Justin laughed, despite himself. "I was a young boy, fresh from the compound when Garnet died in the hunt. It seems so long ago ... and yet ..."

"Like yesterday," Eagle ventured a guess to finish Justin's sentence.

"Yes. And yesterday, I was a boy named Earnest, who couldn't tell a lie. Today, I'm a man, named Justin, who lied because he thought it would help the Ruck go on."

"The beginning ..."

Justin looked up. He hesitated, and Eagle waited.

"For the past two Hunts, I have cheated the draw. I chose Hawk's stone on purpose. I cut grooves into it and made sure it was drawn." Justin bowed his head again.

Eagle breathed deeply. Somehow, this seemed like something he already knew. Of course, he hadn't known. Now, he remembered Justin making a face during the gathering when he and the younger Ruck had discussed Hawk's ideas about the Black Ones. He also recalled Justin's uneasy face during the last draw.

"Why?" Eagle asked.

"I made a pact with Hawk," Justin said, still staring at the ground. "He wouldn't oppose the gatherings; he wouldn't question my rulings. He wouldn't try to stop your plans. He would encourage his children to listen to your stories and to welcome the debates ... I, in return, I ... would ensure his stone was drawn."

Eagle felt like he had been hit with an Overseer's lightning bolt.

"Hawk is alive," he said.

Justin's head snapped up. "What?"

"Think about it, my friend. Why else would he make such a bargain? You heard our conversation the other night. Hawk made no secret of his beliefs. The Ruck were being tested, he said. He believed the Ruck could go on, but only by proving our worth to the Overlords. He believed the Black Ones were from the Ruck. He wanted to be chosen, to prove himself, and be taken during the Hunt. Not to die. To join them. I don't know how I can be so sure, but it must be the truth."

Justin stared at Eagle, eyes wide. The two men sat in silence for dozens of heartbeats. Eagle reflected. The image of Lotus in her tent filled his thoughts. He tried to focus on Justin, but Lotus pushed him aside. Her image nodded. Eagle shuddered. He remembered seeing Hawk emerge from the hunting grounds, alongside the Black One, as if they had been seeking each other's counsel. Again, Lotus nodded.

"I lied, Eagle." Justin brought Eagle back to the now. "To you, to all the men, to all the Ruck. To the children I love. How can I bear the name of Justin any longer?"

"Because Coot gave it to you. And because you deserve it. Yes, you deceived the men. Still, you may have given the Ruck a gift beyond the hopes of any man. We can be *free*. Your decisions have pushed us to this day—where the Ruck are changing their ways and considering *freedom*."

Eagle's face softened, even while Justin's tortured face made him want to cry.

"Justin, you made a choice for the Ruck. You chose to lie to the men. Your heart was pure, and you have done us a great favor. I am sure of these things now: Hawk is alive. The Overseers are nothing but men, of the Ruck, and they are vulnerable. Forgive yourself and come with me."

Eagle stood, feeling power coursing through his palms, like the night of the *shrooms* beyond the *tekline*. He shuddered again as he extended his hand to Justin.

"Our time is coming," Eagle said. "Return to the village with me and we will share this with the men—and those who are about to become men."

◆ ◆ ◆

Eagle had assembled all the men around his own campfire. Maize and Raven and Dove and Spider and Archer and Coyote had made sure the children went to their yurts. Justin, sitting next to Owl and Oak, still looked troubled but he had agreed to tell the men everything when Eagle asked.

Bison and Boar joined them. Owl and Shadow came, too, even though Bison objected. Eagle told Bison he could leave if wanted. The young man sighed, sitting and staring into the fire. No one else questioned Eagle's leadership on this night.

Eagle thanked them all for joining him. He stood without his cane, awkwardly. He wasted no time. He told them he believed Hawk was still alive. He waited for the exclamations, objections, and bewildered looks to die down. He told them why he had come to such a conclusion. They all listened, exchanging glances and intermittent whispers. Then they heard Justin's guilt-ridden story. Eagle watched all the men carefully. Those who had once followed Hawk remained impassive, as did the old man Coot, as if this came as no surprise.

Eagle asked Bison to stand. The young man obeyed, reluctantly.

"Bison, you know what Hawk taught you. Do you believe what we say?"

Bison closed his eyes. Before opening them, he steadied himself. He now stared at Eagle. "As much as I hate to admit it, yes, Eagle. Well ... at least ... I believe it is possible. Hawk taught us our only hope for *freedom* would be to join the Overseers. He said they were from the Ruck. He said he had spoken to them. He said we could never escape and live as you believed, Eagle, but that we could move from the valley and live in greater service to the Overlords. Faced with the choice of believing he is dead or alive, I must believe what he told me was true. And then, that you also speak the truth."

Others, including Owl, Shadow, and Boar, nodded. Owl spoke. "Hawk shared his beliefs with many of us. He took us to the same place he took Eagle and told us what he thought about the Overseers. Now, it seems many of us accept his ideas. It is nothing more than a child's small step to believe Hawk may be among them now."

Sage spoke. "It may be a small step, but the smallest misstep can lead to death. We don't know Hawk went with the Overseers. We can only guess. The point is: what do we do now? Do we accept Hawk's truth, and hope to follow him to a new life as Overseers while leaving the village behind? Or do we accept Eagle's truth and follow him beyond the *tekline*, to escape and to make a new life for the Ruck?"

The men looked to each other. Many eyes turned to Justin and Coot, but no one spoke for several heartbeats until Falcon stood to have his say.

"It's all too clear to me." He moved to stand beside Eagle. "I choose *freedom*. I wouldn't fault anyone for choosing Hawk's way. It may ensure the Ruck go on, but it is a meaningless path."

As others began to rise and join Falcon or shake their heads in disagreement, Eagle called to them. "Wait, please. I don't want to divide the village so soon after we have begun to come together again. We all want the Ruck to go on. We simply don't agree on how. I welcome all who choose to follow me—and I will share my ideas for escape and *freedom*. Still, those who wish to follow Hawk must be respected."

Eagle turned his attention to Bison, Shadow, and Boar. "I don't expect you to follow me. I do ask you to consider your actions and how you may affect my plans. The Overlords must need us—even if they capture all of us who try to escape, they won't destroy all the Ruck. You and those who choose to stay must carry on in case we fail. Let us agree to respect each other's ways, and hope at least one group of the Ruck succeeds. If we can agree on this, the chances improve for the Ruck to go on."

Bison listened carefully, then whispered to Boar and Shadow. "Eagle, we don't agree on much, but we all want the Ruck to go on. The Overlords are powerful enough to stop you without our interference. I believe they will want the rest of us go on when you have been captured and killed."

The three steadfast followers of Hawk walked off. All the others remained. Owl spoke.

"Eagle, it seems you have many allies, now."

"Although, I must not remain among them," Justin said, surprising everyone. "Eagle, while I believe you are right, I must stay in the village with the Ruck who remain. It is the only way to redeem myself. They might need me." He walked off alone.

The others looked to Eagle. "My friends," he said, "I have many ideas. From now until the visit to the women, we must talk and plan and choose. Some of us must stay, while some of us must escape, taking women and children with us."

The men nodded and took seats around the fire once again, listening to Eagle's plans and talking deep into the night.

Eagle and the other seven men waited outside the compound gate. It was odd to stand here without Hawk among them. Eagle remembered the awkward moments here when his rivalry with the man had reached its peak. He felt the blood rushing to his face as he thought of the time when Hawk had pressed the reality of his night with Rose. Then, it had brought fire to Eagle's thoughts; now, it was nothing more than an embarrassing recollection—a foolish moment kindled by jealousy.

All the men gathered here had agreed to the plans for escape, as discussed and debated for a dozen days now. Bison, who had so far kept his word of non-interference, remained behind in the village. A few the women were with child now or had recently borne a child; even with Hawk gone, the number of men needed for this visit had dwindled. Thrush would be the youngest man to visit with the women.

All the men had agreed—except Justin. He had kept to himself and the children, working in the fields or going on hunts for *ven* or *scurries* during the day and playing stones in the evenings around the fire. He would occasionally share a meal with Coot or Owl, but mostly he stayed with the children, where he seemed content. Now he stood apart from the other men, refusing to meet even Coot's glance.

So, while the seven others would soon whisper the plans of escape to the women, Justin would carry on his duty as the Ruck men always had, as if the impending new moon would bring only more races and games and hunts (and Hunts) and babies.

Eagle turned as he heard the gate opening. He saw his mother and smiled. He would visit her tonight, incredibly, as the draw paired them once again. Eagle couldn't help but think that God or the Goddess had granted him this one last chance to be with his mother. He expected her to stay behind, although none of them knew for sure, just yet, which of the women would join them in three days' time. For a heartbeat, it occurred to Eagle that his fortune in these pairings was as unlikely as Hawk's four draws in succession for the Hunt. He glanced at Justin as the men filed in, wondering, before taking his mother's hand and walking with her to the yurt.

They talked until Honey's candles had burned to puddles. First, Eagle summarized the events of the dozen or so days beginning with his talk with Justin and the meeting with the men. Coot, Falcon, and the other men would be doing the same with the women they visited, although Eagle doubted they would delve into the same level of detail demanded by Honey. He wouldn't even hazard a guess as to how the conversation between Falcon and Lotus would transpire.

Eagle told Honey how the chosen men (and a few select children) had tested the leap beyond the *tekline* from various locations around the hills enclosing this valley—the only place that the Ruck had ever really known, Eagle mused—when the changing of the Overseers occurred. It seemed so obvious now, he said, as he explained how they studied and measured the flash for several evenings. They could cross the *tekline* from any point in the hills, if the timing was right, allowing each of the chosen groups to escape.

Honey stopped him, abruptly.

"Eagle, how many groups of the Ruck are you talking about?"

"I'm sorry, mother. Things have changed since we last spoke and I'm getting ahead of myself. When we realized escape from different locations was possible, Sage and Coot suggested we send more than one party beyond the *tekline*."

"I see." Honey paused and Eagle let her think. "I suppose it's sensible, assuming your tests prove true. How do you know?"

"We don't. Not for certain. We do know the flash in the *tekline* happens at various points around the valley. It looks the same everywhere—the same as it did near the Overseer when I escaped. We all believe it will work."

"And so, I ask you again: how many groups? We have planned for only three women to leave with you."

Eagle smiled. "Three? Mother, you have already anticipated the need for more women than we talked about last moon. Is this the work of Lotus? In any case, we hope for four of the women."

"Yes, Lotus foresaw the need, but she counted only three. She suggested we plan for herself, Butterfly, and Rose—who agreed only if she can take her new baby—to leave the valley with you. Is three enough?"

Eagle's heart leapt. He had hoped Rose would agree. Yet, to save himself the pain of learning otherwise, he hadn't allowed himself to count her name among the escaping Ruck. He forced himself to focus on the issue at hand.

"No, not as we have planned," he said.

Eagle then told his mother their entire plan, as determined over the last few nights of meetings, while she listened intently without interruption. The men had gone back and forth trying to name pairings of men and women; they wanted to ensure that each group had at least two women for each man or two men for each woman. Sage suggested that they should also take a few children, not the youngest, but not all of the oldest. Coot added that some of the older girls should go, too, as it could be too risky for too many women to leave the compound. That made them consider just how many of the Ruck should be in any one group. They devised some games to help determine how many of the Ruck could make the leap at the same time. Eagle digressed, telling Honey about the fun they had one warm morning, leaping in unison and laughing and falling in a heap with one another.

Before tonight's visit, Eagle said, they had debated round and round until they came to agreement on how many of the Ruck could go together.

"No more than six of the men, and no more than six Ruck in a group, we agreed," Eagle answered. "That turned out to be the easy part. Naming the six was another matter. And we realized we couldn't choose them all without your counsel. Of course, I mean the counsel of the women. In all, we hoped four of the women could join us—while planning for four groups of escaping Ruck."

Eagle acknowledged Honey's quizzical look, at what seemed to be only part of the story. "By including two of the older girls," he added, "we thought that six possible child-bearers would give us the combinations we sought. You have planned for three women, so it seems we are close. Could there be another?

"Perhaps." Honey pondered again, while Eagle began to recite, in his thoughts, the names the men had identified. "Tomorrow, I will speak with Lotus. I expect she will have an answer ready for me, after her night with Falcon."

Eagle nodded.

"Now," Honey said, "tell me who you think will go. Any of my children, other than you, Eagle?"

Eagle recited the litany:

Rock, Falcon, Wolf, Thrush and Owl. Archer, Maize, Henna,

Buck, Onyx, Clay, Spider, Mace, Dove, and Chase.

"Two of my children." Honey stated. "Not counting you of course, Eagle. Leaving Willow and Ox in the village." She nodded. "And my old Coot, he will stay, too?"

"He wouldn't leave you, mother. He said he was too old to escape. We didn't agree. Some of us thought he should go. Some of the men had to stay, and he insisted."

"I'm not surprised. I am relieved. Selfish, but relieved."

Eagle took his mother's hand as he told her about the possible groupings. Honey said she would discuss all of this with Lotus, including the possibility of another woman and who she might be. They sat in silence for a little while.

"One last time, Eagle," Honey said. "Tell me about my children."

Eagle drew a deep breath, hearing the finality of this visit in his mother's words. He had felt it before—the night before his first escape—and he remembered how he had climbed the tree outside the compound, searching for a glimpse of Rose and forcing himself to bid goodbye to all of women, including Rose and Honey. At that time, he wasn't even sure if he would live through his attempted escape, let alone return to see his mother again. This time it felt certain. Somehow, he knew he would never see her again.

He choked back his feelings and put on a smile, telling his mother about Archer's leadership and her developing friendship with Tiller. In addition to the fact that Archer was near child-bearing age, her rapidly increasing knowledge about growing the *veg* would be needed beyond the *tekline*. Eagle told his mother how many of the children were learning more about producing *veg*, saying the decision for some of the Ruck to stop eating *ven* had proven successful so far. This also prompted Eagle to tell her more about their efforts to trap *scurries* as they adjusted to life with less *ven*. Eagle also told his mother of Willow's increasing independence, and how much more she grew to look like her sister and her mother with each passing moon. And he told her of Ox's shifting allegiances—

the boy had started hanging around with the children in Owl's group. Finally, Eagle mentioned how quickly Clay was becoming his own person, just as his mother had suggested during the last visit. They talked again about Clay's visit to Eagle's yurt with his friend Onyx. Eagle shed a few tears as he confessed his guilt for deceiving his brother during the escape. Honey hugged him and said Clay couldn't wish for a better older brother. She told him to stop punishing himself because she was sure it was all for the best. After all, wasn't Clay now being chosen to escape, too?

And with that, they lay down side-by-side and talked about the winters gone by. Honey told him stories he never would have remembered, even back to the days when he lived in the compound. Eagle thanked God and the Goddess once more for the gift of knowing his mother, even as a man, and being able to share this night with her. Suddenly, it seemed silly to him to thank anyone for the privilege. He told his mother so, noting that he meant no offense to her Goddess. She laughed at him, saying the Goddess didn't care what Eagle thought. For a moment, he took offense. As she laughed at him again, a silly feeling overtook him, and he began to chuckle along with her. She told him another story, this time about Archer's time in the compound, when she had strutted around bragging about the number of times she had pooped all by herself—keeping careful count and challenging the other young ones to match her prowess. Eagle and Honey giggled and hushed each other, but they ended up laughing and crying until they drifted off to sleep shortly before daybreak.

◆ ◆ ◆

The next morning, the men met in small groups as planned. They informed each other of the discussion with the women, and then went their separate ways as the traditions demanded. This was Coot's idea—he convinced them that so many of their customs were being challenged during this moon, and so it was best to keep a few intact to avoid alerting the Black Ones at this stage of their plan.

When they returned to the compound gate, the men exchanged greetings and waited patiently for the women to let them in for their second night's visit. Before long, Eagle found himself in Lotus' yurt, staring at her shapely body, half-shrouded by the sparse candlelit shadows. The yurt seemed entirely different than he remembered from the last moon. He wondered, but couldn't remember, if he had thought the same thing the last time.

Lotus sidled up to him and they kissed. He started to talk but she put a finger to his lips and said, "Everything is in place, Eagle. We'll talk later."

She then slowly dragged her finger from his lips to his chest and kissed him on the spot her fingers had vacated. Eagle relaxed, returning the kiss and letting her direct their encounter. Her familiar touch put him at ease, as she stroked his chest and tweaked his nipples; the embarrassment he had previously felt in her presence now vanished. Tonight, he welcomed her mysterious ways and let himself be taken in by her advances. In fact, he found a strong desire welling inside of him, a strong feeling of connection with Lotus. A feeling he thought she shared. Not the same as with Rose, but strong, and vital, nevertheless. They teased and pleasured each other for some time before he mounted her and drove his seed deep within her.

Afterwards, they lay side-by-side and talked, staring at the wavering shadow patterns on the yurt's top. Truly, Lotus talked, and Eagle listened, for the most part. She said Falcon had given her the whole story, and that she and Honey had discussed all the women and children named so far in Eagle's plan.

She surprised him with two things. First, the fourth woman to join the escape had come down to a choice of Pearl or Diamond (who was called Ash in the village). The inclusion of Pearl was the surprising part—just a moon ago, Eagle remembered, Pearl had said she would rather not go, having only recently begun to enjoy life among the women. Still, Pearl had volunteered—while Diamond was proposed by Mantis—because she had only recently joined the women. In the end, after some debate, which Lotus alluded was less than civil, the women decided Diamond should be the fourth woman to go with one of the escaping groups.

The other surprise caught Eagle completely unprepared. Lotus demanded for Dreamer go with them. In fact, that Dreamer be part of the group composed of Eagle, Lotus, Rose (and the baby), Henna, and herself.

He asked her why such a specific group was so important. She avoided answering the question, saying only that she had seen things.

He balked. Instinctively he realized, as he had no reason to disagree. While he believed Mace would be a good companion, there was no practical reason why it couldn't be Dreamer.

She insisted while also refusing to say more. She would say only this: she saw this group together beyond the *tekline,* and she wanted to be part of it. Eagle could only nod his head, trusting her vision. They went on to discuss the rest of the groups and their plans for meeting at the appointed spots the next night. It turned out that Honey and Lotus had filled in all the names:

Eagle, Lotus, Rose, Rose's baby, Henna, and Dreamer.
Falcon, Diamond, Rock, Archer, Chase, and Dove.
Wolf, Butterfly, Rachel, Spider, and Buck.
Thrush, Owl, Maize, Clay, and Onyx.

On the third night, Eagle's mind remained pre-occupied with the impending escape. He and the other men had met briefly again in the morning, confirming with each other what all the women had presented the night before regarding the four escaping groups. Some of the men were mystified by the certainty the women brought to this decision-making, but Coot put a halt to any debate.

"I have learned many things over my thirty winters," he said, "but none more important than this: when a woman has made up her mind, there is no sense in arguing. The groups have been determined. Why waste our energy discussing it?"

All the men had shrugged. They drifted off to their own musings. Eagle had clasped the old man's shoulder and said, "I will miss you, old-timer."

Now, inside Storm's tent, Eagle forced those thoughts from his mind and focused on the half-clad woman facing him. Storm's face was dark and serious. No, more like distant than anything else. He stroked her hand and arms, cupping her face and giving her a quick kiss, but she only frowned.

Eagle remembered Coot's words and decided the only course of action was a direct one. "What is it, Storm?" he asked.

"What do you care? You're gone."

Eagle stared at the yurt flap for several heartbeats. "No, now I am here. Tomorrow, I will be gone. Tell me what bothers you."

For some time, she refused, and they repeated this exchange. Eagle was determined to hear what Storm had to say, even more so when she continued to refuse. Finally, she relented, telling him she wanted to escape with one of the groups. The women had to choose four, she reminded him, making sure he understood her displeasure with the choices. Storm asked him why he wanted those four, and he reminded her that he didn't make those choices. He told her, honestly, that he wanted Rose to come, and he shared his deepest feelings about her. He surprised himself—he hadn't really talked to anyone before about how much he cared for her—of course his mother knew and Lotus knew, and while Sage, Coot and some of the other villagers understood Eagle's feelings, he had never articulated them as he did this night in Storm's yurt.

Eagle assured Storm that, other than Rose, he had asked for no woman in particular. He admitted having Lotus was beneficial, but he didn't see any reason why Storm couldn't have been one of the others.

Before he could finish his last thought, Storm grabbed him and thrust her mouth against his, parting his lips and probing with her tongue. She almost knocked him over; before long she was pulling at his leggings with a force and strength of will that Eagle realized could only be yielded to. She took him with an amazing vigor and passion, riding him and then demanding he lick her until she shuddered and thrashed wildly. In the end, she pulled him on top of her, urging him to finish. Afterwards, she fell asleep quickly, like one of the winter rains passing fiercely through the valley, leaving no trace of its fury.

When Eagle awoke in the morning, Storm was gone, along with her children. He dressed and left her yurt, dawdling in the compound until he saw Sage exit from Butterfly's yurt. He caught up with his friend and they headed toward the gate. Eagle stopped there, turning around and scanning the compound for what he thought would be the final time before Sage closed the gate.

13

After they returned to the village, Eagle said goodbye to Sage. They made little show of the moment, pretending it was just another morning after a visit to the women, but as they clasped each other's arms Eagle stared into his friend's eyes for a few extra heartbeats. They both knew what lay ahead of them this day, and how important it was to maintain a regular demeanor. Still, it struck Eagle heavily. This was no way to say goodbye to a dear friend who he would probably never see again.

The plan required patience and diligence throughout the day. Each man knew his tasks, knew things must proceed as they had agreed. Each man also knew how delicate the entire situation was. To appear at ease, to maintain the Ruck routine —even while many of them undertook extraordinary actions —would test them all.

Eagle walked among the children who assembled in their morning groups, seeking out Mace. Fish and Double spied him. Eagle smiled as they rushed toward him, shrieking. He shifted his weight and prepared to snatch them up before they could latch on. Eagle managed to ensnare Double in his right arm, but Fish was too quick. She darted away and back, sliding through Eagle's legs and hooking her limbs around his left ankle. Soon, Happy and Fern joined in the fun, giggling, screaming Eagle's name, and asking for rides.

Eagle succumbed. He dropped to his knees, letting the children swarm around him, even as he saw Mace and Dreamer standing near a group of the other children, including Copper-head, Buck, and Robin. Eagle let the smallest children pile on —they were now more than a half-dozen strong. Playfully and gently tossing them off and then letting them latch on again, Eagle laughed until his chest ached. The children begged him for more, but they relented when he told them he needed to speak to some of the older children, who were standing nearby and laughing along with the young ones.

Brushing himself off to appear aloof, Eagle surprised Fish —swooping her up with one arm and then turning her up-side down as she strode over to Mace. The boy beamed when Eagle approached; his grinning face struck Eagle like an arrow through his heart. Eagle turned Fish upright, lower her feet to the ground and hugging her around the mid-section.

"Go play with your friends, Fish."

She obeyed.

"Mace, Dreamer, I'm glad I found you here. Would you like to go on a *scurry* hunt with me?"

Dreamer shrugged, staring out past the other children. Mace's eyes and face darkened briefly, then he regained him-self. Eagle understood the boy's reaction. Mace knew the schedule for the day. This wasn't part of their plan.

"Sure ... Eagle," Mace said.

"Let's go, then," Eagle said.

Surprisingly, Mace seemed relieved when Eagle told him of the change. Dreamer looked as confused and detached as ever, stopping to pick up some sticks and holding them up in front of his face, in some sort of pattern understandable only to himself.

"I was worried you had called off the escape," Mace whis-pered. "I'm glad to know it's okay." He seemed about to speak again but paused as they walked.

"I expected you to be disappointed, Mace." Eagle took two deep breaths. "You seem to understand."

"No, I don't understand. I have learned we must work to-gether for the Ruck to go on. If Dreamer takes my place, what can I say?"

Now Eagle could see that the boy clearly was disappointed. Also, sincere.

"There is nothing to say. Except that I'm proud of you." They stopped and Eagle put out his hand, as he would to one of the other men. Mace grasped his arm and smiled.

"Is there something else I can do?"

"Perhaps," Eagle answered. "Someone should keep an eye on Bison."

Mace nodded. "I see. You can count on me, Eagle."

"I know." Eagle smiled. "In one way, I'm glad you'll be staying. The village will need you, Mace."

They walked and talked about how to make sure Bison and his friends didn't break their word. And they talked about how the village would go on after the escape and how the Ruck might face retribution from the Overseers. Mace swore to protect the other children; Eagle hugged him and told him to take care of himself, too. Finally, they met up with the other Ruck who had been hunting *scurries*. The rest of the day went as planned.

◆ ◆ ◆

As Raven and Fly began to tell an elaborate story, Eagle lingered at the back of the gathering. Many of the Ruck were there, including Bison, Tanner, Shadow, Mace, and nearly all the younger children. A select few were missing and a few more would drift away, soon. Eagle glanced toward the sun as it dipped near the top of the hills—and beckoned him to follow it beyond those hills. He savored the sight; one he had seen over many moons and winters. He remembered watching the sunset as a younger boy, enthralled by the orange sky at the end of a day's hunt with Garnet. Between then and now, most of the sunsets had grown plain and uneventful. Today, the reddish-orange sky brought back many memories, especially of the last dozen moons.

Eagle thought of the evenings with Hawk, watching the Black Ones; he remembered races and hunts and feasts around a blazing fire. The smell of *ven* roasting over the fire filled his nostrils; for a moment, he wasn't sure if it was a memory or something happening now. The smell made him think again of the feasts—of young children playing chase or stones while the older ones paired up and went into the woods. He saw himself making the one and only trek into the woods with Jade, and then he remembered his first fast, and then he saw himself during his awkward visit with Tanner on the third day of the fast. Eagle couldn't suppress a chuckle when he thought of how she could still distract him.

As if she knew Eagle was thinking of her, Tanner got to her feet and rounded up a few stray children who hadn't yet been captured by the story. He found himself staring at her until he realized she had noticed. She shook her head and went back to Bison's side. Eagle felt his face flush. With a shrug he reminded himself that some things never change. His mind went back to the plan of escape.

Falcon and Wolf had disappeared shortly after the afternoon's work in Tiller's fields and not long before this gathering started. They had taken their chosen travelers with them, except for Archer, who lingered at her yurt as long as possible before joining them in the hills.

Thrush and Owl met with the rest of their group near the archery range, where Eagle had found Owl the night he was searching for Justin. From there, they would move to their appointed spot, waiting—as did all four groups—for Oak's signal. With no women from the compound joining Thrush's group, Eagle thought they had the best chance of escaping. He remembered saying goodbye to his brother and making light of it all. After all, they would see each other later this night, or the next morning—that is, they pretended they would. Eagle had watched, trying to appear disinterested, as Clay and Onyx walked away hand-in-hand, like so many of the older Ruck children going off into the woods.

Eagle found it difficult to wait any longer. He had insisted on staying at the storytelling as long as possible, asking Coot to make sure that Henna and Dreamer made it to the meeting place for Eagle's group. The old man had indeed taken the two children aside just as the storytelling began. Dreamer had balked, wanting to hear the story and apparently forgetting everything about the plan.

It made Eagle chuckle again, despite himself. Dreamer's reaction was so natural it would probably help the plan—assuming the boy did as Coot instructed. Fortunately, Henna kept her wits, helping Coot to convince Dreamer about more fun waiting for them where Coot was taking them. She had proved as sharp as she was fast in these last few days. Eagle thanked the Goddess for Henna's presence in his group.

Now, Eagle realized, it was time for him to join Henna, Dreamer, and the women. He hoped all four of the women would be able to slip out of the compound as planned. He had no doubt that Honey and Lotus had a well-coordinated plan, but it meant each of the women would have to make their own way to join with each of their groups. Butterfly and Diamond surely knew their way, as both had joined the women no more than one winter ago. Eagle couldn't help but worry about Lotus and Rose, especially with Rose carrying the baby. For many winters they had been secluded in the compound. He had voiced this concern to Lotus. As usual, she had simply laughed at him. No matter how much they had assured him, Eagle imagined the baby crying as Lotus and Rose made their way into the hills, alerting the Black One and endangering the entire plan.

As Eagle turned away, he heard Fly telling the children about the *birds* and the *carts* and the *Yewessay*. The children laughed and made the traditional sounds and movements. Eagle's heart grew stronger with the telling, even while his mind continued to worry about the women. He passed by his yurt and then purposefully took a turn toward Tiller's fields before heading into the hills, with the setting sun ahead of him.

◆ ◆ ◆

When Eagle reached the meeting place, he found all his worries were completely without merit. The women had already arrived, and Coot had gone. Lotus held her son's hand while Henna kept watch and Rose rested against a tree, with the baby neatly swaddled in a pouch secured around her chest and belly. The child slept soundly. Eagle closed his eyes for a moment and breathed deeply. They all greeted him silently with bright eyes and smiles, even Lotus.

They had little time for much else as Eagle sensed the time grew near. He oriented himself and found Oak in the distance, standing tall at the secret spot. Their current position was chosen because it provided a view to that spot, as did each group's location. Oak's solid frame cast a long shadow under the waning light, reminding Eagle, for just a heartbeat, of Mountain. Eagle assembled everyone as they had practiced. Henna helped, making sure Dreamer paid attention while Eagle prepared Lotus and Rose. This was the weak strand in their plan's web—the women had never practiced the leap. Eagle and the other men had done their best to describe the process during the visits, but, in the end, they would have only one chance to make it work.

They stood together in a row, holding hands—Lotus, then Eagle, Rose, Dreamer, and Henna—with Eagle looking over his shoulder toward Oak.

Eagle's heart beat faster than ever before. It seemed to pound harder and harder as he waited for Oak's signal. Of course, he didn't count the beats, but they seemed to mount beyond his expectations.

He glanced at Rose and the baby. They appeared completely calm. So did Lotus. Eagle scolded himself for taking his eye away from Oak, but the pause helped him to breathe and regain his composure. When he did look back to Oak, he saw the man raise his hand—the preliminary signal—and Eagle whispered the countdown to the rest of his group. Although he heard Lotus whispering something, he focused all his attention on the lone man at the point.

When Oak's hand fell, Eagle and the others saw the flash of blue light in front of them. He squeezed the women's hands and they all leapt.

◆ ◆ ◆

Eagle felt the energy rush through his limbs, just like the last time he had leapt beyond the *tekline*. He landed on his feet and immediately checked to see if the others had passed without harm.

Lotus still clutched Eagle's hand. She wavered, but remained on her feet, blinking. Rose's hand had slipped away, and she knelt one step in front of Eagle, cradling the child inside the pouch. A quick glance showed Henna and Dreamer shaking their limbs as if trying to shed water after a swim; they finally let go of each other's hands and stared wide-eyed into the alien wilderness. Everyone seemed to have made it through unharmed. Eagle knelt beside Rose and cupped the back of her head with his hand, peering around her shoulder to see her face. Before he could say anything, Dreamer startled them all back to their wits.

"*Fug*! Can we do that again?!" The son of Lotus turned back toward the *tekline*, his mouth agape and eyes as wide as one of Potter's bowls.

Eagle couldn't stifle a belly-laugh as he stood and grabbed the boy's arm. "We must move quickly. This way ... Henna, please help Rose."

Pulling the boy behind him, Eagle beckoned to Lotus, who caught up in a few steps, and they began to push their way into pristine woods. Eagle remembered how shocking it was for him to see new trees and shrubs for the first time. He wondered if the others felt as frightened as he did back then, but he didn't take the time to ask anyone, urging them on and glancing back a few times only to make sure that Henna and Rose weren't falling too far behind—and halting for several heartbeats now and then until they closed in again. While this wasn't the same path he had followed before, he knew the direction he needed to go, leading the group at a brisk and steady pace until the sun had disappeared completely over the hills. As it grew dark, he looked for a place to stop and rest, finding a suitable niche on a ridge under a bunch of pine trees. Eagle slowed as Lotus took the children ahead. He took Rose's hand and helped her crest the ridge. They joined the others and the baby stirred; its mother cooed and began to unwrap the swaddling while Eagle watched. Lotus and the children sat down in a triangle and pulled out some of their provisions. Eagle heard Lotus telling her son to eat only one piece of *pem*—to but to make sure he ate all of it—and to drink three measured sips of water. She also handed each of the children some kind of small leaf-wrapped food from her pouch.

Now, Eagle noticed that Rose had a similar pouch, from which she extracted a few of the leaf rolls and passed a larger one to Eagle while she held her infant in one arm. She asked Eagle to sit behind her and support her, and then lifted the child to her breast, cradling it upside down underneath her armpit, with its little legs stretched out toward her elbow and its feet touching Eagle's ribs. She fed the child, seemingly drifting off to sleep while the boy suckled. Eagle breathed deeply, enjoying the feeling of Rose's back pressed against him and welcoming her body's warmth. He chewed the roll with vigor —it was somewhat bitter and had hints of *shrooms* and spice. The taste made Eagle think it held exactly what his body needed. He ate it all and then drank a few sips from his skin.

Eagle had planned to eat some of the dried *veg* that he had brought along, but the roll satisfied him for now. This time, he had surreptitiously packed more to eat during the journey. All of the escaping Ruck had hidden *pem* and *veg* in their layered fall and winter clothing, and they had grabbed an extra water skin before going to their meeting places. Sage and Falcon had debated the risk in appearing overburdened. Owl had reminded them that it wasn't unusual for hunting parties to take extra water. And the men had asked the women to pack whatever they could as their risk was already obvious—carrying a full *ven*-hide bag or traveling unburdened while straying so far from the compound would make no difference. Either they would be noticed or not. Eagle guessed his group had enough supplies for several days of travel.

They had all eaten without speaking, allowing themselves to recover from the travel and adjust to the new surroundings. Shortly after finishing her roll, Henna broke the silence.

"Eagle? I'm ... I'm scared."

"I know, Henna. We all are. I was frightened and alone when I escaped before. Living in the valley, we're unaware of all that surrounds us. The land is vast; unending it seems. And while these trees and hills look different to us, they feel the same. After another day or two of traveling, the ground beneath your feet will feel just like back in the valley."

Henna stared at her hands. "But where are we going?"

"We will look for the free Ruck I met before. They are out here, I'm certain. We will need to travel a few more days, following the path of the sun. We'll hunt *scurries* and look for more *veg*. It won't be easy, but we'll be together, and we will survive.

"I believe you, Eagle. But I'm still scared. What if the Black Ones ...?"

Dreamer interrupted. "I'm not scared. This is fun."

Everyone stared at the boy, even his mother. Eagle wondered if he understood what escape meant. Did Dreamer think this was a game, and when it ended, they would return to their yurts? And yet, perhaps the boy's attitude was the best fit for their journey.

"You are brave, Dreamer," Eagle said. "Our escape should be fun, even if it frightens us. There is nothing like the nourishment of *freedom*. Every moment is unknown and new. Scary in one way, fun and exciting in another way. Henna, when we travel tomorrow, under the warmth of the sun, you will begin to feel the power of *freedom*. I promise."

Rose stirred, shifting the infant to her other arm and breast. Henna got up and paced a little, peering into the dim new moonlit night as if trying to find something elusive. Lotus cuddled with Dreamer, whispering to him. Eagle heard Henna sniffling, perhaps sobbing.

"Henna, come sit with me," Eagle said. He put his arm around her shoulders when she pressed in close to him and wiped her eyes. He just held her for a while until he felt her breathing evening out and she began to yawn.

"Henna, the Black Ones may come looking for us. As I said, the land is vast and I doubt they have even learned of our escape yet. They found me the last time, but only because I was weak and foolish. No one knew what lay beyond the *tekline*. And I wasn't prepared for the journey. Now we know much more."

Henna yawned again. "Okay, Eagle." She wiped her eyes again. "I'm tired."

"Go lie with Lotus and Dreamer. Get some sleep."

Yawning a third time, Henna did as Eagle asked. Lotus helped the two children find a place to huddle together in relative comfort, and then she approached Eagle and Rose. The baby had finished its meal, and Rose had re-swaddled it. Lotus knelt beside Rose, taking the child from her.

"Rest, Eagle, we will need your strength in the morning. I will stay awake for a while."

"As you say, Lotus," Eagle answered. "You will need rest, too. Wake me later and we will trade places." Eagle shifted his weight and he and Rose reclined together, face-to-face on their sides, staying close to share their warmth. Lotus gave the infant back to Rose when the man and woman had settled themselves. The baby rested between their torsos. Eagle could feel its faint breathing.

He thought to himself: this was all he could ever hope for. The woman he loved at his side, their young child in their arms (he had begun to convince himself it was his, even if another man had planted the seed), and the *freedom* to choose where they slept. If he died tonight, he considered for several heartbeats, he would die happy and fulfilled. Then he realized how selfish this thought must be, as the Ruck children laying near him had never felt such *freedom*. For the Ruck to go on, Eagle would have to survive many more nights—he must lead them to the other Ruck he had found before in the wilderness. The thought sobered him, and he lay awake for some time before falling asleep.

He awoke to the baby's soft crying as Rose nudged him repeatedly. Lotus hovered over them, taking the infant while they re-arranged themselves. Rose sat upright again with Eagle's support, feeding the child, while Lotus sat nearby.

"We should name the child," Lotus said, abruptly.

"Now?" Eagle said. He immediately felt silly for his response. Even now, Lotus still had that effect on him.

"We are starting new ways, Eagle," Lotus replied. "We are a small group of Ruck. This child is important. It should be named."

"I ... agree," said Rose, yawning between the words. "He will be re-named someday, of course. For now, he needs his first name."

"Who am I to argue with two wise women?" Eagle stretched his neck, chuckling.

"A wise man," Lotus said.

"What should we ..." Rose yawned "... call him?"

"I don't know ... yet. I will consider it. Perhaps the Goddess will send me his name while I sleep."

"If you are to sleep," Eagle said, "I will need to wake up."

"Let's change places, Eagle." Lotus stood and came over to the couple. She braced Rose's back as Eagle stood up, sliding in behind the nursing mother and supporting her as Eagle had been. Eagle stood and watched them. They seemed as content together as he had felt while lying down to sleep alongside Rose. For a heartbeat, he felt a pang of jealousy. Surprising himself, Eagle let it pass quickly. He had grown fond of Lotus, and, while his feelings for her weren't the same as for Rose, he knew he loved her, too. They would all need to love each other to survive. He glanced over at Dreamer and Henna. They fidgeted as they slept, apparently dreaming. Eagle wished he could build a fire, but it wasn't wise. They weren't yet far enough away from the valley, he believed. So, he paced along the ridge edge, checking on the women and helping them to settle in for sleep, before sitting on the edge of the ridge to take his vigil for the rest of the night.

Eagle realized he had drifted off not long before the sun peeked over the hills, the hills from which they had departed the day before. He couldn't have slept for long, he assured himself. And a quick looksee confirmed everyone was okay.

He took a sip of water and chewed on a piece of dried *veg* while looking out over the landscape. He judged the sun's ascent and re-oriented himself, determining the direction they would travel today. He heard the others stirring behind him, and then the baby began to whimper. Soon they had all roused themselves, eaten a little, and talked about the beautiful morning sun. Eagle smiled when he saw the hope in Henna's face; he had expected the light of day would improve her mood, since it displayed the wonder of the foreign land around them. Rose asked Lotus if she had any ideas for the baby. The woman only shook her head in replay, saying, "Tonight." Eagle wanted to hear more, but Rose nodded in agreement and the women wouldn't speak of it any further.

When they had prepared to travel, Eagle and Henna produced their pouches of dried flowers and began to crumble them around the campsite. He told Henna to save some of hers, as did he. Eagle then led them down the slope to a pass that he intended to follow through the morning. He told them they wouldn't hurry for now, preferring to travel more slowly, single file, while attempting to cover their tracks whenever possible. When they reached the pass, he positioned Rose and Henna just behind himself, with Dreamer next, and Lotus last.

He asked Lotus if she had any special tricks for covering their tracks. She rolled her eyes. "Perhaps you should take up the rear and I will lead. We are simply following this pass, yes?"

"For a while." Eagle considered her idea. "Okay, Lotus. We'll do it your way." He laughed, and they exchanged places. Eagle paused for a moment as the others began the trek, crumbling the remainder of his dried flowers and spreading them to the wind or scuffing them into the dirt. He doubted it would mask their trail completely, although it might confuse any pursuers. He also picked up some fallen pine branches and strapped them together in a sort of broom like he had seen Shrew, now Gazelle, make back in the village. Eagle dragged it behind him as he followed the women and children. While he had little confidence in the idea, he figured it was worth trying.

Lotus led them in the projected path of the sun, stopping to rest occasionally, allowing Rose to feed the baby and tell- ing the children to eat a few bites of a leaf roll or *pem* or *veg*. Eagle kept a close eye on Henna and Dreamer, watching for any further signs of anxiety, but it seemed he was right about the sunlight improving their spirits. As they continued onward, Eagle would catch up to Lotus from time to time and discuss a course alteration. He would say a word to the children or walk alongside them briefly—and he increasingly saw the wonder in their faces and the bounce in their steps. At times, he paused and drank in the air of *freedom*, savoring it more than he had during his first escape. Other times, he lingered behind and scanned the woods behind them, searching for any indication of Black Ones closing in. So far, it seemed they had put a good distance between themselves any possible pursuers. They had kept in the valleys as much as possible, avoiding moving higher into the hills. While Eagle didn't say this to the others, he remembered seeing a Black One high on a ridge during his first escape, like the Overseer back at the Ruck village. He wagered it would be best to stay low and push through the lowland passes whenever possible.

They stopped for a longer stretch after the sun had passed overhead and began its descent. After they ate, Eagle watched as Henna held Rose's baby for a while, giving the women a chance to refresh themselves. Rose dozed, her head in Lotus' lap, and Eagle remembered the discussion about the infant's name.

"Lotus, did the Goddess send you a name for the child?"

She grinned. "Perhaps, Eagle. The signs are all around us. I think we may have our ceremony tonight. Your question makes me wonder, though: has your conversion to the ways of the Goddess become complete?"

Eagle stared into her dark eyes, tilting his head. In seasons past, he realized, such a comment would have made him uneasy and defensive. Now, he returned the grin.

"No, Lotus." Eagle glanced at Henna and Dreamer, considering his next words. It appeared Henna listened closely, while Dreamer may have been listening—or may have been visiting a far-away world that only he could see and hear.

"My beliefs have changed," Eagle continued, "although I don't think such a conversion is possible for me. Garnet taught me so much about my personal relationship with God. Shedding that would be like walking in these alien woods with my eyes closed or with my feet bound. And yet, I have learned about your Goddess and her ways, too. It seems to me they must both exist, in our hearts and minds if not in the world. The Ruck need them both, and they have been apart for too long. Just as that baby needs a mother and a father—something denied from the Ruck for too long."

Lotus' grin widened. "Your mother was right, Eagle. A few

winters ago, she told me you would grow into a great leader for the Ruck, if we let you. The Goddess gave me troubling visions ... of the conflict between you and Hawk. Honey said those visions gave us a glimpse of the events to come but showed us none of the meaning for how the Ruck might go on. She asked me to be patient with you and with the Goddess. At first, her advice made no sense to me. I listened because she is the strongest woman I have ever known."

"And what do you believe now, Lotus?"

"I believe in the Goddess. At the same time, I see that your God is important to you. And to the Ruck. Indeed, we will need our faith in both, and in ourselves, to become *free*."

Henna giggled. She quickly looked up to the sky when the man and woman turned to look at her.

"We are *free* now, aren't we?" she said, looking all around her and then shifting her glance from Eagle to Lotus. When Eagle nodded, words bubbled out of her mouth. "I mean, we're going where we want to go, no matter what the Black Ones want us to do. I'm still scared, but I guess it's a good kind of scared. It's so different. Men and women and a baby, together. It's like a dream. Weird and scary. Exciting."

A breeze swirled around them, hinting of the winter to come. They all breathed it in.

"Yes," Lotus said, "we can even smell the *freedom*. It isn't like the compound. Or the village, I imagine. It smells different."

Eagle felt a surge within him when the wind swirled again. A combination of exhilaration and urgency. He saw Dreamer shiver. "We should go now," Eagle announced. "We need to use the sun while it lasts. I fear we have moved too slowly this morning."

Lotus darkened, a shadow passing over her face, apparently transforming her mood. Eagle wondered if she felt the same thing he felt. "I will pick up the pace, Eagle."

Lotus did just so, pushing so hard that Rose became quite fatigued. Henna called to Lotus, and the group stopped briefly, while the women moved the baby's pouch to Lotus in the waning daylight. Eagle took the lead; he kept a slower pace as the sun dipped beyond the horizon. Still, they had covered more ground today. Eagle felt relieved when they made camp in the evening.

Dreamer asked if they could build a fire. Eagle glanced around and realized this camp wasn't as secure as the previous night's location. They were exposed. Not vulnerable or obvious but unprotected from approach. Eagle said it was still too soon for a fire. Eventually, they would need one, Eagle told the boy, just not yet. Dreamer made a face, plopping down by himself while the others sat together.

When they had finished their meal, Lotus gave the baby to Eagle while the two women whispered to each other—and Henna tried to listen in. Eagle immediately felt awkward. He realized he had never held a baby before. During all his visits to the women, it had never happened. Like their travels, the newness was both frightening and inspiring. He looked at the infant's tiny hands and feet, then at its eyes, nose, and mouth. He saw hints of Rose in the boy's face, but he couldn't discern his own or any of the other men either. Now, the baby seemed to be staring back at him, as if searching for his father's features in Eagle's face. A silly thought, Eagle told himself. Still, he couldn't shake the feeling. He thought of Hawk and the Justin-before, either of whom could well be the father. Thinking of Hawk turned Eagle's thoughts to the Black Ones. As he cradled the child, and the women continued their counsel, he scanned the area around them.

Just as he was starting to feel more accustomed to holding the baby, Rose knelt by Eagle and held out her hands. He gave the infant to her as she smiled. She kissed his lips and then stood and held the baby aloft, gripping the boy's back and neck with one hand and cupping her other hand under his bottom. Henna moved closer to Eagle, and he put his arm around her. Dreamer also stood nearby, apparently watching the proceeding.

Lotus approached Rose, rubbing something between her

palms. She invoked the Goddess, turning once around and announcing that another Ruck child had come to the age deserving of a name. She dragged two fingers through the palm of her other hand and then rubbed the infant's forehead with those fingers, leaving a dark smudge.

"This child shall be named Future, for he holds the future of the *free* Ruck, united under the Goddess and the God." Lotus' voice penetrated Eagle's soul and seemed to echo around them. "He will be raised under the sight of a mother and a father and his survival will be a sign to the Overlords, a sign that the Ruck will go on, and without their meddling."

Eagle almost staggered back. He hadn't expected such a heavy naming and Lotus hadn't held her voice in check at all. In fact, her words seemed to carry in the hills, almost in defiance of the Black Ones and the Overlords. It seemed to Eagle she might be heard back in the village, carried on the wind's breath of *freedom.*

Despite the danger in her strongly spoken words, the power in Lotus' announcement filled his heart with hope. As he watched both women kiss the child's forehead, smearing their lips with the mark Lotus had put there, he wondered if Lotus had seen something in the child's future. He felt a shiver run down his spine and back up to the base of his neck.

Rose approached Henna and softly told her to kiss the mark. She obeyed, breathing heavily, Eagle saw. He guessed she was as moved as he was. When it came his turn to kiss the child, he paused.

"It's all right, Eagle," Rose said. "This will be the way of the *free* Ruck."

Eagle wondered how she knew what had made him hesitate. He felt like he was intruding upon the women's ceremony—one he had never even seen before. Rose's gentle smile persuaded him. He kissed the child, faintly tasting the earthy smudge on his lips. He watched as Rose turned to Dreamer, who evidently had been paying attention, or at least was now. The boy also kissed the child.

The rest of the evening passed almost solemnly. The effects of the ceremony on their mood seemed to linger. Rose fell asleep first, with Future in her arms and her head in Eagle's lap. He had propped himself against a tree trunk and stared at the stars. Henna and Dreamer cuddled together at the edge of some bushes while Lotus took the first watch. Like the night before, the women woke Eagle as they shifted themselves to allow Rose to feed the baby. Eventually, Lotus took Eagle's position against the tree, and he wandered around the camp, shaking the sleep from his head and keeping a constant vigil until the light of day returned.

He had already eaten before the others awoke—so when Henna greeted Eagle, he asked her to keep watch while he napped briefly. He wanted to be fresh for the day's travel, he explained, and she nodded. Eagle saw a glimpse of fear in her eyes—fear of bearing such a duty out here in the wilderness. He leaned against a tree, saying "I trust you, Henna. If you see anything—anything—come and kick me awake."

Eagle dozed and dreamed. He saw himself and his companions hurrying through the woods and hills. Nothing seemed to chase them; in fact, they weren't running, they simply made haste. They were trying to catch up to something, someone. Ruck-sized figures in the distance. The Black Ones? No, that would be foolish. But who?

Henna yelled at him, trying to get his attention. He couldn't hear her. Her voice grew more urgent, although she seemed to move farther away, ahead of him in the woods. Finally, he heard her.

"Eagle, wake up. Lotus says we should go now. Eagle! Come on."

He opened his eyes and grabbed Henna's wrist. She gasped. Finally, Eagle recognized her actual voice, which his dream had joined in his mind. He stood quickly.

"I'm sorry, Henna. I was dreaming." Eagle released her wrist and put his hand on her shoulder. "I'm sorry I startled you. Are you okay?"

Henna's stunted breathing said otherwise, but she replied, "Yes, Eagle. Lotus says we should leave now."

"Yes. Yes." Seeing Lotus, Rose, and Dreamer heading down to the pass, Eagle gathered himself and his belongings, telling Henna to catch up. It seemed Lotus knew the way, so Eagle took his place at the rearguard. This third day, the travel seemed easier to all of them. They moved quickly and quietly toward a looming slope they would eventually have to climb over or go far around. Eagle recognized it—at least he thought so. It appeared to be part of the same giant hill he had climbed during his first escape, although they were approaching it from a different direction. He caught up to Lotus and they discussed their path, deciding to veer around the hill, staying in the low-lying area. This would take them farther north of Eagle's previous path, toward the stone village and the valley of the *ven,* although it would enable them to make a different approach than he had before. He thought their chances to avoid the Black Ones and find the *free* Ruck would improve if they took such a path. He didn't voice these thoughts just then; he only told Lotus he thought this would be the best way.

As the Ruck became accustomed to the travel, they began to take better stock of their surroundings. They saw a flock of birds traveling south overhead, and everyone took that as a good sign. Both Henna and Dreamer spotted various *scurries.* They fell back to tell Eagle—he nodded, telling them that once they had covered more ground, they would take the time to set snares. He asked them to count the number of *scurries* while he would try to spy wild *veg* that they might pull from the ground. This task seemed to occupy their minds until Lotus led them into a sparsely wooded plateau where they stopped to eat.

Eagle scouted the area while the others rested. Finding a running stream, he took a deep draught from his nearly empty skin and refilled it. When he returned, he sent Henna and Dreamer with other skins to fill, sitting down next Rose (who nursed Future) while Lotus napped. The children returned quickly, bearing the filled skins, but obviously out of breath.

Eagle realized they were afraid while on their own, even knowing he and the women were nearby. They must have run the whole way back. They didn't complain, sitting down to rest and sip from their newly filled skins, but Eagle and Rose understood what had happened, casting wide-eyed glances at each other.

And then, as they were nearly ready to resume their travel, deciding to stay on the plateau for a while even though it provided less cover than the pass below, Dreamer spoke up.

"I'm getting bored. All we do is walk around. When are we going back to the village?"

Rose and Eagle gawked, turning to each other and blinking. Struck dumb, thoughts raced through Eagle's mind. Had the boy completely misunderstood their escape? Did he really think they were going back to the village? How could he? They had planned everything, told him everything. All the talk of *freedom*, did it mean nothing to Dreamer, alone in his exclusive world?

Numerous heartbeats passed. Eagle felt himself staring at Dreamer while the boy fiddled with his waterskin. Eagle knew he should say something; he couldn't muster any words—at least any that seemed appropriate.

Rose had leaned over to Lotus, nudging her. "I heard, sister," Lotus said, eyes still closed.

Stretching and sitting up, Lotus crossed her legs, opened her eyes and spoke clearly. "Dreamer, of course you know we aren't going back to the village. We are *free* now, and we are looking for the *free* Ruck. This isn't a game. It's our new life."

The boy looked up, screwed up his face and then sighed. "Oh yeah. I remember." He shrugged. "It's still boring." Dreamer got up and looked around, wandering off a little and pretending to notch an arrow and let it fly.

Eagle had a strange urge to laugh, but he stopped himself. Instead, he exchanged puzzled looks with the women and Henna. Like Dreamer, they all shrugged and began to pack up for the remainder of this day's travel. While Dreamer appeared to be okay, his question lingered in Eagle's mind the rest of the day—and it appeared to affect everyone's mood. No matter how much they adjusted to their new surroundings, the tremendous change in their lives couldn't be denied. It would take much time, Eagle thought.

They pushed along the edge of the plateau as the sun fell slowly in front of them. Although winding around the large hill took time, Eagle reassured himself. He kept looking at its height, reasoning it would be a difficult climb for Rose. Her energy seemed to diminish with each day, and they had taken more frequent rests to accommodate her. Eagle began to feel great enjoyment traveling with the women. Spending time with them, without feeling the need—or the duty—for sex, made him feel even more *free* than ever. Still, he worried about Rose. They would have to stop earlier than expected today. As if the God and Goddess had heard his thoughts, Eagle detected what appeared to be a well-protected bluff just behind them as he checked for any signs of followers. He had completely missed it as they approached. He stopped and then moved off, telling Dreamer to ask Lotus to stop (and then wondering whether the message would be relayed). He pressed up the hill and reached the bluff. It seemed ideal for a rest and perhaps even a fire. He leapt and hopped his way back down to the others, who had indeed stopped to wait for him. They followed Eagle up the hill. He saw the relief on their faces when they reached the spot. They all rested briefly, eating and drinking. Eagle then took the children back down to set snares for *scurries* and search for root *veg* while the women stayed behind. They succeeded and also gathered wood for a fire, returning to show what they had found.

Eagle arranged a spot to build a small fire, getting it ready but telling the children he wouldn't start it just yet. He told them to rest a little longer, after which they could check their snares, and he would start the fire. Dreamer pulled a pouch from inside his tunic, looking surprised.

"Henna, do you want to play stones?"

"You brought stones and you didn't say anything?" Henna asked, shaking her head.

"I forgot."

Everyone laughed. Dreamer just shrugged. The children amused themselves until the sun had nearly disappeared, while Rose slept and Lotus arranged a manger for the baby. When Rose awoke, Lotus took Dreamer and Henna to check the traps.

Eagle approached Rose and took her hand. She stood with his help, and they walked to the edge of the bluff, looking at the last reddish rays of the day's sun. He glimpsed Rose's face out of the corner of his eye. She beamed, like the day she told him of her pregnancy. He thought she was more beautiful than ever. Her round face seemed serene, framed by her long, tied-back hair. Eagle took her face in his hands, and she turned to him. They embraced and kissed, pulling away from each other for a heartbeat to look into each other's eyes, then kissing again, like lovers would in a woman's yurt but without lying down together. To Eagle it seemed that Lotus and the children returned quickly, but he realized the sun had disappeared completely as they stood there, leaving the light of the slivered moon to guide them.

"I'm sorry, Lotus," he said as she crested the ridge. "I should have had my fire started to help guide your return."

She laughed at him. It reminded Eagle of the times in the compound, and, although the laugh had its usual mocking edge, it sounded funny to him.

"I'll forgive you this once, Eagle," she said, brushing past him with the children close behind.

Henna carried two *scurries* while Dreamer had firewood stacked up to his chin. Lotus had also collected a sack of something, tied to her waist by a strap of *ven*-hide (fresh *veg*, he learned soon thereafter). Eagle reluctantly let go of Rose's hand and went to start his fire. The women and children prepared the *scurries* and *veg* for roasting. Before long, Eagle had a small, manageable fire, over which they cooked a meal fit for *free*

Ruck—all of them huddled around it to help obscure the light and enjoy its warmth.

The night at the bluff seemed to rekindle everyone's energy. They laughed in hushed tones and talked about the journey ahead. It was something they hadn't done as a group. Lotus started the conversation, talking about how far they had come and asking Eagle how many more days he thought it would be before they could find the *free* Ruck. He recounted his previous journey. While they followed a different route now, he believed they would be able to find the rocky path that led him to the stone village of the *Yewessay*. He said he wanted them to see it, to understand more of what he had seen his first time beyond the *tekline*. And he told them, honestly, he didn't know where the *free* Ruck might be, but if they continued to travel and look for signs, he believed they would eventually encounter some.

When the conversation reached a natural lull, Rose said she was terribly tired, and even so, she had begun to feel her new *freedom* tonight, for the first time. She looked Henna in the eye and paused.

"I was just as scared as you were, Henna. I didn't want you to know it. I didn't want anyone to know it. My feet moved, but my heart was frozen. Now, *freedom* feels real. I understand why Eagle had said he would gladly trade many winters in the village for one day of *freedom* beyond the *tekline*. Whatever happens tomorrow, I will have lived as a *free* woman today. I want to celebrate every day this way. We had always made our choices in the village and in the compound, but we never chose to break our bonds until now. I look around and everything is a wonder. The smallest of *freedoms* has moved me more than anything I had imagined."

She took Eagle's hand as she continued. "I share a meal and a fire with a man who I have grown to love, with a woman I have loved through the passing of winters, and children who are brave and strong. It feels like a *famlee*. I was never sure whether to believe those stories. Now, I believe they must be true."

"I have always believed the stories, Rose," Eagle said, squeezing her hand. "What I can't believe is you just said you loved me."

The children giggled, and Lotus made kissing noises. They all laughed. Eagle felt a twinge of embarrassment, but Rose seemed to speak for them all this night. It did feel like a *famlee* as told in the stories—at least as much as anyone of them could guess. He could tell from the others' faces: this night would give them the strength they would need in the days ahead. And lest they lose sight of things, Lotus made sure they didn't forget what lay ahead of them and behind them.

"A *famlee*, of sorts, we are. I don't think I could ever go back to the valley. Still, many of our brothers and sisters are there. We haven't spoken of them either. I understand why. It's painful. But we must remember their names. We must tell their stories to our children. And to the *free* Ruck that we meet out here. We must promise each other never to forget where we came from. This is the promise the Ruck-before must have made when the Overlords forced them to live in the valley. They told the stories, and so must we."

"Lotus, you must have heard my thoughts," Eagle said. "While building the fire, I was thinking this would be the time and place for a story. Now you have given me an idea about how to tell it."

Eagle began his story. He reminded them of the Ruck-before and their wonders. He wove in the stone village of the *Yewes-say*, and the goo, and the *cart*. He told of how the Ruck had lived for many winters in the valley, raising children and participating in the Hunt and making sure the Ruck would go on. Then, he spoke of the friends they had left behind, as well as those who had attempted the escape as this group had. He said they must remember their names, as many as possible. He recited all the names, surprising himself with the long list. While he had spent time memorizing the mothers and brothers and sisters of the Ruck—everyone he had watched grow up in the village—he had never said the names out loud in such a way.

With every name, he felt strength. With every name, he could see that the others were moved. Henna and Dreamer shed tears while Rose and Lotus comforted them and each other. They took turns holding the baby after it awoke, and Rose nursed it.

The fire began to die down. Eagle let it dwindle as he finished his story. Rose put Future back in his makeshift bed, lying down to next to him and falling asleep quickly. Henna and Dreamer cuddled together at the edge of the embers, and they also fell asleep. When Eagle yawned, Lotus told him to sleep first, again—she would wake him later. He nodded and drifted off while the litany of names ran through his head again. He remembered the faces of his closest friends and brothers and sisters. He hoped they had fared well, wherever they were.

Eagle awoke abruptly, as someone or something poked and prodded him. He sat up quickly, alert. He relaxed when he realized it was Lotus. Then, he shook his head again, realizing something else: she wasn't simply waking him for his watch. No, she was massaging his now erect member and kissing the skin around his hips, between his tunic and leggings. She had already undone the ties at the top of his leggings.

"Lotus, what are you doing?" he whispered.

In between kisses, she whispered in return. "I should think you would know by now."

"Of course ... I mean ... now?" Eagle looked around and saw the others still seemed to be asleep. He felt silly—how did she manage to make him feel like a fool even in the most pleasurable of circumstances?

"Trust me." She loosened the ties further and tugged the *ven*-hide down past his hips. She took him in her mouth, delicately running her tongue around and around.

"What if ..." Eagle faltered.

"Just trust me," Lotus said, holding his member in her hand and then running her tongue around the head.

He gave in to her as she convinced him with her mouth but with no further words. She stopped momentarily and straddled him, her leggings already off. She rocked back and forth on top for a while, then rolled the both of them over until he was on top. Eagle thrust deep within her, enjoying the feeling, until out of nowhere, he remembered where they were. He didn't stop; rather, he paused only for a moment as the reality of their surrounding and situation seemed to excite him even more. He kissed her, and she bit his lips and neck as he continued to thrust, until finally, he filled her, and they moaned softly in unison. They lay still for several heartbeats. Lotus whispered into his ear.

"And this will be the way of the *free* Ruck, Eagle. We will make love when we choose, with whom we choose—not at the Overlord's bidding, but because we want to."

He understood, and yet he also felt quite conscious of the others. He pulled back and rested on his knees in front of her. Rose and the children were still asleep. He leaned forward again and kissed Lotus. Feelings swirled within him—both love and shame. He had never felt this way after sex before. He remembered his embarrassment after Rose swallowed his seed during the night when she told him of her pregnancy. Still, that felt much different. As they dressed, he began to understand why Lotus had come to him. He also knew that being a *free* man would take a lot more getting used to then he had ever imagined.

Lotus kissed him on the cheek and went to cuddle next to Rose. Eagle watched and saw the two women fit together like they had spent many nights just so. He sighed, sat down near the faint embers, staring at, and listening to, the alien world around him.

◆ ◆ ◆

The next two days of travel passed without incident. They had circumvented the giant hill, and Eagle turned them farther north. They had developed patterns of rest and travel, moving steadily while allowing time to refresh themselves—mostly to make sure Rose kept up her strength. All of them now took turns carrying Future. Eagle enjoyed the feeling of the baby against his chest. Each of them became rejuvenated during their shift, except perhaps for Rose.

As the sun's descent signaled the end of the fifth day of travel (Lotus had begun to keep a tally), Eagle thought he recognized the area they traveled through. Without saying anything, he began to search the trail for any signs of the rocky path that led to the stone village. By the time the waxing moon replaced the setting sun, he had taken the lead, pushing onward even though he noticed the others falling behind while helping Rose or struggling themselves.

He refused to listen as Lotus told him they needed to find a place to sleep that night. He pressed on, leading them along a meandering path, which frustrated the others even more, while stretching the distance between himself and the others and stopping occasionally only to ensure they didn't lose sight of him. Finally, he found the path for which he searched. He stopped, picking up one of the stones and hurling it into the woods in exultation.

Darkness began to envelope them. The moon gave just enough light for them to avoid losing him completely. Eagle waited for the others to catch up, calling their names softly to help guide them. When they approached he grew more excited.

"Do you see?" he asked. "This is it!"

Lotus spoke for everyone, between gasps. "We can't see anything except your silly smile, Eagle. What are you talking about and why have you pushed us to the edge of exhaustion?"

"This is the path to the stone village!" He made a face, realizing how loud he must have been just then. Softer, he said, "It can't be much further."

Rose spoke up. "Then we will be happy to see it in the morning." The others agreed.

Eagle frowned. "I thought we could push on, and ..."

"You heard the woman, Eagle," Lotus interrupted. "You have pushed us long enough. We must rest."

Eagle glanced around. "The village has shelter and water and ..."

"And a *cart*." Dreamer said. "Maybe you could go get it and carry us there inside of it." The boy seemed completely serious. His mother laughed, almost as loud as Eagle had exclaimed his find, and Henna giggled.

"Shush," Rose said, between breaths. "*Fug*, if the Black Ones are following us, we might as well burn down all of these trees as loud as we are being."

Dreamer's and Rose's comments brought Eagle back to his senses. Obviously, none of his companions could travel further, and he didn't actually know how far away they were.

"I'm sorry," he said. "We will rest and follow the path tomorrow. Still, we need to move away. The woods are thick here —I suppose if we move off a little ways, we'll be okay."

"Done," said Lotus, who led the way without asking anyone to follow. Soon they had found a small patch of brambles with a clear space, and they all settled in. They ate dried *veg*, *pem*, and leaf rolls in silence.

"You can have the first watch tonight, Eagle," Lotus announced.

Eagle merely shrugged his agreement. He struggled to stay awake himself, thinking of the stone village and how impressed the women and children would be when they found it in the morning. Without those thoughts to keep his mind working, he would have fallen asleep, he was sure. While he wished they had pressed on, Eagle knew the women had made the right choice.

He slept uneasily after Lotus took the next watch. He dreamed of the stone village, the free Ruck, and the village back in the valley—waking often and then resuming the dream each time he drifted off again. Every time he awoke, he felt like the dream had ended just a heartbeat too soon— another few beats and he would have learned an important secret. When the sun rose, he felt groggy and frustrated by the unfulfilling dreams. He reminded himself that the stone village awaited.

Indeed, it proved more than half a day's travel. Eagle saw the scorn in the women's eyes, as they trudged along the path while the sun rose directly overhead. They would have been foolish to have pushed on into the night. Nonetheless, his heart pounded, and his own fatigue melted away when he saw the first stone yurt and the wooden yurt where the *cart* sat. Leading the way, he stopped and turned to see if the others had seen the structures. They had all stopped and gathered in a bunch, staring past him.

"It's true," Henna said.

"I never doubted it," Lotus said, "but it's still a wonder."

Eagle took a few steps back toward them. "Come on. This is nothing."

They walked with him up the sloping hill until they reached the ruined wooden yurt. They all gaped as they walked around the *cart* and pointed at the stone yurt. Dreamer walked further up the path and held his head when he looked down into rest of the village. "Look at all the yurts. They're … they're … huge."

Eagle approached the boy, with the others straggling behind. "It's just as amazing this time. Follow me."

Eagle led them to one of the yurts he had inspected before, one near the stream. They passed other stone yurts and each time his companions slowed to look at them. The one Eagle had chosen seemed stronger than the others, and he had easily pushed open the wooden flap before. The others seemed timid as he entered through the gap, which appeared exactly as he had left it. Realizing they hadn't followed him in, Eagle poked his head back through the entrance, beckoning them to follow. The place was layered with grime, but the strange items inside were mostly intact. Eagle plopped himself in some kind of seat, raising a cloud of dust and soot, and enjoying the experience thoroughly. He propped up his feet on a wooden structure, like the women's candle shelves but larger, in front of the seat. He smiled.

Everyone else just stood there, barely inside the yurt. They looked around, glanced over at Eagle, and looked around some more. Eagle beamed now, throwing his arms wide, eager to show his companions the wonders of this place where the *Yew-essay* had lived. While they seemed genuinely in awe, they also seemed unsure.

"This is so weird," Henna said. "What are we supposed to do?"

"Why not make camp here?" Eagle said.

"I don't know," Rose answered.

Lotus and Rose exchanged glances. "Well, I could use the rest," Lotus said. "We all could. Listen, Eagle, it's just quite strange, all of this. How about if we walk around some more, fill our skins from that stream, and take this a little at a time?"

Everyone nodded. They backed out of the entrance.

Eagle slumped, disappointed. But he understood. He had seen the village before, searched through several of the yurts and stayed long enough for his ankle to regain strength. And while he had staggered through the first stone yurt those moons ago, in awe as his companions now were, he had slept outside that first night, hadn't he? Lotus was right, as usual.

He met them outside and apologized. As they moved behind the yurt to the stream, he told them about his first visit here and how it had affected him. They paused, resting briefly near the stream, until Eagle suggested that they move to another place he remembered, behind a few yurts in a more secluded area. When they arrived, they settled into camp, eating some of their supplies and talking about the enormity of the stone village.

After they had eaten and rested, Henna and Dreamer ran around a few of the yurts and began to investigate inside some of them. Eagle and the women stayed at their temporary camp, discussing their immediate plans and taking shifts with Future. They decided to stay here another night, perhaps two, but not for any longer. Rose suggested this could be a place where the Black Ones would look for them—it would be better to stay on the move. They each wondered aloud whether it might also be a place where the *free* Ruck would come. Eagle said he hadn't seen any when he visited before. In the end, they all agreed it was too soon to settle in, here or anywhere.

They used the rest of the day wisely, setting snares for *scurries* in the woods around the stone village and resting their tired limbs. Eagle and Henna even tried to fish in the wide section of the stream. That proved fruitless, but they both enjoyed it. Late in the day, they all took shelter in one of the secluded yurts. They went down to the lowest level of the yurt, down steps to an area below ground with ample ventilation from openings near the ground level. Eagle built a small fire, roasting some of the day's catch. When they had gathered in the yurt, they found more strange items—perhaps remnants of the *tek*. Eagle found a container like the one with the lifesaving goo. Broken and empty, it still served to augment his story of the first escape. He told them a story of that time, finishing with his trek to the valley of the *ven*.

They all slept well that night, with Eagle and Lotus taking watches at the edge of the steps. Eagle crept up the steps in the still of the night, sitting with his back to the yurt's entrance and staring at the stars. He heard noises, briefly, which sharpened his awareness. It didn't sound like any creature noises that he knew. Later, he heard what must have been the sounds of the wolves talking to each other in the night. Listening, he convinced himself it was nothing more, and he went back down to the bottom of the steps to resume his vigil.

In the morning, Rose and Lotus told Eagle they wanted to rest here one more day. He looked into Rose's eyes, saw the fatigue in her face and nodded his head. He remembered the noises in the night; he decided not to say anything. Better to rest now and travel well the next day than to push on too early and risk lacking the strength to flee or fight if need be.

Lotus and Rose stayed around the yurts during the day, searching for anything that might add to their supplies. Meanwhile, Eagle and the children roamed the area, checking their snares and searching for more *veg*. They gathered a good bit of the latter, replenishing their supplies as the leaf rolls and *pem* began to dwindle. And they caught more *scurries*, roasting a few for the night's meal and even saving some for the next day's travel.

The day proved far from ordinary. As they traipsed around, Eagle spied the billowing white smoke from the huge yurt in the valley of the *ven*. He thanked God and the Goddess for showing him—he judged it as a sign for their continued travel. Eagle had begun to think about whether they should go to *ven* valley. He thought he remembered the way, but he wasn't sure if they should go. After all, it was where he was re-captured by the Black One.

Seeing the puffy clouds of smoke made him resolute. He looked around at the stone village and then at the children. Seeing it with their own eyes certainly had an impact, a positive effect on them. Eagle sensed this helped them adjust to their trek of *freedom*. It gave them renewed hope, he believed. While it could be dangerous seeing the valley of the *ven* and understanding why Eagle had decided to stop eating *ven* ... well, regardless of its effect, Eagle believed it was necessary. This was the real world, he now understood, and the valley of the *ven* was part of this reality.

When they returned to the women and took their evening meal, Eagle shared his thoughts.

"I saw the white smoke, from the valley of the *ven*," he began. "I think we should go there."

"We saw it, too, Eagle." Rose said. "It reminded us of our valley, but it looked different from here."

"Much closer, larger." Lotus added.

Eagle glanced at the children to see if they appeared frightened. Predictably, Dreamer seemed far away. He had opened his bag of stones and was holding one between each thumb and forefinger—at eye level, as if he were talking to them or he was listening to them talk to each other. Unlike Dreamer, Henna seemed to hang on their every word.

"It will be dangerous," Eagle said. "Still, I think we should go there. I believe I can lead us by a more cautious route than I took before. I don't want to go down into the valley. I think we can find a place from which to observe it, safely. I suspect Overseers will be nearby, but I think we can avoid them, if we don't stay long."

Rose and Lotus turned to catch each other's eye. They nodded.

"We already discussed this, Eagle," Lotus said. "We agree."

"We want to see the *ven*, as you described them," Rose added.

"Are you sure?" Eagle asked. Suddenly, he felt he unsettled by the idea. He had thought he might need to convince the women, now he couldn't help but have doubts himself.

"Of course not." Rose rolled her eyes. "Sometimes, a woman just has a feeling."

Eagle glanced at Henna again, then turned back to the women. The girl seemed frozen, listening but unable to move.

"Okay. Let's get to sleep early," he said. "We'll start out at daybreak."

Eagle took the first watch. Henna came to him, unable to sleep. They talked for a while, with Eagle reassuring her about the valley and telling her the story of his first visit. She shook her head.

"So many *ven*. It's hard to believe."

"Yes, Henna. It is why you must see it for yourself."

Eventually, she dozed off, leaning against Eagle near the bottom of the steps. He was surprised she didn't wake up when he heard the wolves again, or when Lotus stirred and came to take the watch.

"It sounds like they are closer than last night," she said.

"You heard them?"

"Yes. And I felt something else. I think someone ... or something ... is watching us."

Eagle looked up the steps. "Do you think we should change our plans?"

"No. I think the Goddess is also watching over us. We should do as we decided."

Eagle turned back to Lotus and glimpsed something more in her face. "What else, Lotus?"

She hesitated, and they both heard the wolves again. Two of them, seeming to talk to each other from across the world —a world that was much wider than the Ruck had ever experienced.

"I have seen a confrontation with the Black Ones. It is coming." Lotus paused. "I don't know exactly what will happen. I can see few details, but it will be the telling point in our journey. The smoke is a sign. We must follow it."

"Then I should get some sleep, so I can lead us to it." Eagle gently laid Henna on her side as he readjusted himself and reclined. "Good night, Lotus."

"Sleep well, Eagle."

He didn't. The dreams returned to him, waking him often, repeating after he fell asleep again and still proving just as elusive as the previous nights. Still, the days of rest in the stone village seemed to be enough. When the sun greeted them and they had eaten, Eagle took the lead, with Lotus at the rear. They headed toward the white smoke.

For two more days, Eagle lead them in a circuitous route into the hills, finally ascending a steep slope to a bluff above the valley of the *ven*. The sun had more than half-completed its descent as they stared silently down the slope. They now perched on a ridge, looking down to the giant stone yurt and the wide expanse of *ven* huddled together within the wooden barriers. Eagle heard his companions draw in their breath at the sight beneath them. Even Dreamer seemed transfixed by it, his attention on the here and now rather than some far-away-dream-world.

The scene below struck Eagle as forcefully as the first time. Maybe more so. Before, he was fatigued, hungry, in pain. Now, with his senses sharper and the view from high above so all-encompassing—and knowing what he had seen in the giant stone yurt—it challenged Eagle to consider just how much he really understood about the world.

Glancing around, he guessed all his companions had similar thoughts and feelings. He wanted to give them time to take it all in, but he feared they had lingered too long already. As they had ascended, pushing higher and higher through the pines, Eagle thought he heard other movement in the woods below. He closed his eyes and listened intently for many heartbeats. While he reasoned that nothing more than *scurries* moved near them, he couldn't shake the feeling, put in his mind by Lotus, that they were being followed.

When he opened his eyes, he saw that Lotus was staring at him.

"Perhaps we should go, now, Eagle."

"Yes, the sun is already leaving us. We should move away and find a place to rest for the night."

Quietly, the small band of Ruck followed Eagle as he moved down the slope, away from the valley. Rose took up the rear while Lotus carried Future.

They had reached a plateau—heavily wooded—with the orange sun directly ahead of them, when Eagle again heard the movement around them. He stopped, turning to meet the eyes of Lotus. He motioned for Henna to come to him, and he whispered to her.

"Henna, I think we are being followed. Ready your bow."

The girl clenched her jaw and notched an arrow. Eagle turned, putting his back to Henna's and preparing his own bow. He motioned for Lotus and Dreamer to move on, with Rose behind them. Rose slowed down, glancing over her shoulder at Eagle. He waited for several heartbeats and then told Henna to catch up with Lotus but to keep her bow ready. She ran ahead, past Rose, while Eagle caught up to the woman, and the two of them followed side-by-side, farther back.

Eagle noticed that Rose seemed calm, as if she had been expecting this. He guessed Lotus had told Rose about her visions of a confrontation. Her calm helped him. He decided to trust their faith in their Goddess, waiting for whatever was to come.

He heard the noises again. This time, it sounded like someone approaching from behind—and from their flank—rapidly, simultaneously. He stopped, scanning the woods while Rose drifted off toward a thick patch of pines. Lotus and the children continued moving ahead.

Eagle studied the woods, listening. He saw the movement clearly now. Three figures approaching from the way they had come. Then he saw the black garments.

He took aim and fired his bow at the one most visible. It struck its mark, in the Black One's mid-section, but it bounced off. They began to move more quickly, not quite running, increasing their gait, and closing in on him.

"Rose, Lotus, RUN," he yelled while notching another arrow and moving backwards, half-facing the black-clad pursuers as he tried to see if Rose had obeyed. She had, weaving her way through the pines. The Black Ones split, two pursuing Eagle and the other changing course to chase Rose. That one began to run. Eagle judged quickly. It wasn't as fast as Rose—in fact, the heavy black boots and garments appeared to hamper its chase—but Eagle stopped and fired his bow at it, hoping to distract it if even for a few heartbeats. This time he missed; nevertheless, the shot seemed to have the effect he hoped for, as the Black One seemed startled by the arrow passing so near in front of it, pausing before resuming its chase. For a heartbeat, this emboldened Eagle. Perhaps the Overseers were just Ruck after all.

Eagle glanced again at his pursuers, before turning to run. One of them had stopped and readied its lightning weapon. The other had begun to move wider, past him and in pursuit of Lotus and the children. Eagle turned and ran, trying to intercept its path.

He felt and then saw the lightning bolt buzz over his head. The Black One had missed. Eagle ran faster, expending everything he had; he began to close in on the Overseer chasing Lotus. He caught a glimpse of the woman and children running further ahead into an even denser patch of pines. Another bolt passed near Eagle, between himself and the Black One he was chasing.

As he ran, Eagle saw Lotus stop. He couldn't understand why, but he had no time to ponder it. Now within a knife throw of the Black One, Eagle strained, willing his legs to drive him onward. As he felt his breath waning, Eagle decided to leap upon the Overseer ... only a few more strides ....

Two men appeared from nowhere, blocking the Black One's path. The Overseer halted, its large black boots thudding and digging into the earth. The men rushed it. Their presence caused Eagle to slow down, but his momentum carried him into the Black One's back, nearly at the same time as the other men struck him from the front. They all tumbled in a heap. Eagle found himself under the Black One, his legs pinned. It struggled above him, wrestling with the two men. Eagle saw their faces—they were Ruck! None that he recognized. Not from the village. The *free* Ruck he had seen before?

One of them grappled the Black One's arms while digging his knee into its back. The other one was trying to pull the mask from its face. Eagle thrashed and pushed at the bodies above him, grunting as he attempted to get out from underneath. The brief sight of Rose running toward Lotus made him pause.

Everything slowed down before Eagle's eyes, even his heart seemed to beat five times too slow. The Overseer stopped, aiming its weapon. The bolt struck Rose from behind, and she fell forward, lifeless.

Eagle screamed. He felt energy coursing through his body. Time resumed, and he kicked up his legs, rolling the Overseer off. As he scrambled to his feet, he saw many things all at once.

Other Ruck were pushing Lotus and the children into the woods. He couldn't count them. They seemed to number more than a dozen. The Overseer who shot Rose sent another bolt toward the group. It struck one of the free Ruck, but the others disappeared among the trees. One of the two men who now wrestled with the fallen Black One succeeded in ripping off its mask. He pulled a stone knife from his *mocs* and stabbed at the Black One's neck. Eagle saw blood spurting from the wound and glimpsed the face of a man where the mask had been.

A lightning bolt buzzed past Eagle, striking the man with the knife. He fell. Eagle turned, seeing the third Black One approaching from behind. Instinctively, Eagle dove to the ground near the fallen Ruck and the dying Black One. He saw the Overseer who had shot Rose closing in on them now. Another bolt buzzed overhead. The man near Eagle had raised himself to one knee. He held the Overseer's weapon, aiming it at the one who had shot Rose. Eagle shuddered as a bolt leaped from the weapon, striking the Overseer, and knocking him backwards. Eagle had looked directly at the bolt, and his vision left him for a few heartbeats, replaced by flashing white spots.

He heard another bolt before he could see clearly again. He scrambled to his knees. As his sight returned, he saw the Ruck man with the lightning weapon crumpled on ground. Eagle turned his head quickly from side to side, finding the last Black One aiming its weapon at him. Eagle wondered why the Overseer hadn't fired.

The Overseer took several steps sideways, beginning to circle Eagle. It seemed to be considering something, its head tilted sideways. Eagle decided running wouldn't help him. Nor would rushing. At this range, the Black One wouldn't miss. Eagle knew he couldn't get near it before it shot the bolt.

As the Overseer continued to move around him, a thought

struck Eagle—a thought as sudden and powerful as the bolts. The Black One circled just as Hawk had done during their stand-offs back in the valley.

Eagle spied the lightning weapon in the fallen Ruck's arms. It was no more than an arm's length away. He glanced up to the Black One, who continued to circle, seeming to dare Eagle to reach for the weapon. Eagle lunged for it, grabbing it and rolling away. Desperately, he fumbled with it, not knowing how to shoot the bolt. He looked up and saw the Overseer's weapon releasing the bolt. It struck Eagle just below the neck.

◆ ◆ ◆

Eagle awoke, his head and chest pounding. His arms and legs were bound; his body was strapped to some kind of table. He remembered his painful recollections while in the care of the women at the compound. For a heartbeat he thought he was back at that nightmarish place again. But something felt different. He sensed movement. As he lifted his head, he glimpsed Rose on a table beside him. Next to them both was a Black One, its mask resting on top of its head. Eagle tried to see its face, but it reached out and pressed something into his side. The object sent waves of pain through Eagle's body. He passed out again.

◆ ◆ ◆

Later when Eagle's senses returned, he barely had the strength to lift his head. Every muscle in his body ached. He felt bruises on his face, his hands, everywhere. He had strange memories of waking up from time to time and being kicked and punched and poked in the side with the pain-giving object. Vaguely, he remembered hearing Rose's pleading, desperate voice.

Now, he realized he was still strapped to the table. His feet were inclined. His head dragged near the ground. Dragged, yes. The table was being pulled by a Black One along rough ground. With all of his energy, Eagle craned his neck and glimpsed the shadowy back of the Black One. Everything seemed dark—he couldn't tell if it was night or if his vision failed him. He heard the Overseer say something, apparently to someone in front of it. Something like "Keep moving, woman."

Soon, Eagle heard the voices of other Ruck, calling out to each other. He couldn't understand anything they said, although it seemed urgent. Finally, the dragging stopped, and the table fell to the ground. Pain wracked him; he moaned.

Someone loosened the straps. He wanted to run, to fight, but he could barely move at all. It seemed to grow darker, even as he felt bodies around him. He realized his eyes weren't open. With great effort, he opened them and saw fuzzy forms around him. A few of them lifted him from the table and set him on the ground. They propped him up and offered words of comfort— or asked each other questions. They sounded familiar, but far away.

"Is he going to live?"

"Relax, Eagle."

"What happened?"

"Don't try to move, just rest."

"Where are the others?"

"I'm here, my love."

Eagle recognized Rose's voice, at last. He squinted and saw her face near his. She held him while others gathered around. He saw another face he recognized: Sage. Suddenly memories flooded back to him, and the haze lifted from his mind for a few heartbeats.

"The ... village?" Eagle asked. It proved a great effort to speak, but he felt compelled.

"Yes," Sage answered.

Eagle strained to see. He thought he saw several men, children, and even women there.

"Mother ..."

"She's dead, Eagle. The Overseers killed her, and others, after you escaped."

"Falcon ..."

"Falcon and the others are still out there, we think."

"Mace?"

"Dead, defending the children from the Black Ones. Eagle, what happened to Lotus?"

Eagle blinked. He felt his vision and mind fading in and out. Never had he felt such agony. His energy seemed to blink in and out with his sight. He knew life was escaping him.

"Lotus ... the children ..." Eagle faltered.

"What, Eagle?" It was Rose. Eagle summoned his strength, hoping to see her face. His vision cleared for a few heart-beats. He saw Rose, her face also bruised, although she seemed stronger than he was. He glimpsed others around her, including the small girl, what was her name ... Marvel. He saw the woman, Mmm ...Man ... Mantis. He saw the Black One, standing apart, watching. Eagle coughed out words, feeling a salty taste in his mouth.

"They ... they ... escaped ... with the *free* Ruck."

"They did?" Rose exclaimed. Eagle's vision went dark again, but he heard Rose continue. "I saw them, the *free* Ruck, they were helping Lotus and Henna and Dreamer and Future, but then I fell. The *free* Ruck helped us. They attacked the Black Ones. I was shot by lightning, but maybe the others ..."

"Nonsense. We captured and killed them all." It was the Black One's muffled voice.

Eagle felt life leaving him. He focused all he had, lifting his arm, and pointing his finger.

"A lie," Eagle said. "That is ..." he trailed off.

"Tell us, Eagle," said Rose.

He groaned, staving off death. "He is ..."

Marvel, who leaned close to Rose, listening carefully, spoke. "He is saying the Black One is Hawk. And he is correct. I would recognize my father anywhere."

Eagle heard gasps and exclamations, feeling movement

around him, even as the blackness slowly began to turn grey and then melt into white all around him. "The ... mask," he uttered.

"Take off his mask," Marvel commanded.

In the growing white glow, still in Rose's arms, Eagle saw many of the Ruck close around the Black One. Strangely, Eagle could suddenly see everything around him in a mist of yellow-white light. A lightning bolt shot from the Overseer's weapon, and Eagle heard screaming among the Ruck. And yet, they continued to press in on the Black One. They fell upon it, overwhelming it with their fury, taking it down and wrestling with it until they had it pinned.

The whiteness now exploded before his eyes, just as the Ruck ripped the mask from the Overseer. Eagle felt his energy leaving him, completely. He whispered to Rose.

"The Ruck will be *free*."

Hunted Like Animals — The Ruck (Surviving Mothers)

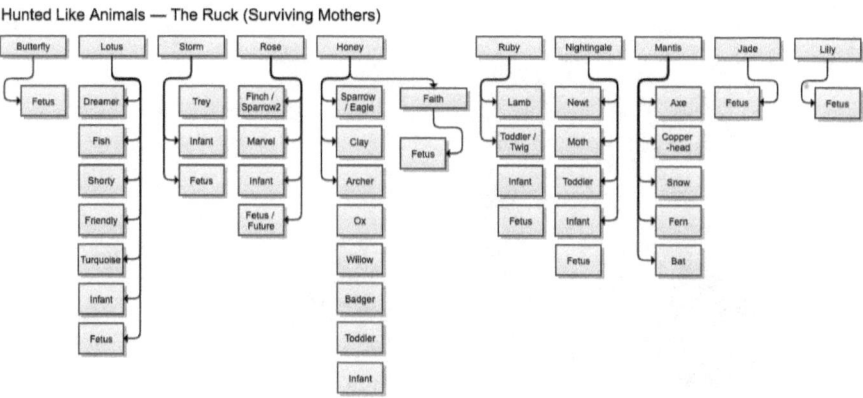

Hunted Like Animals — The Ruck (Dead Mothers)

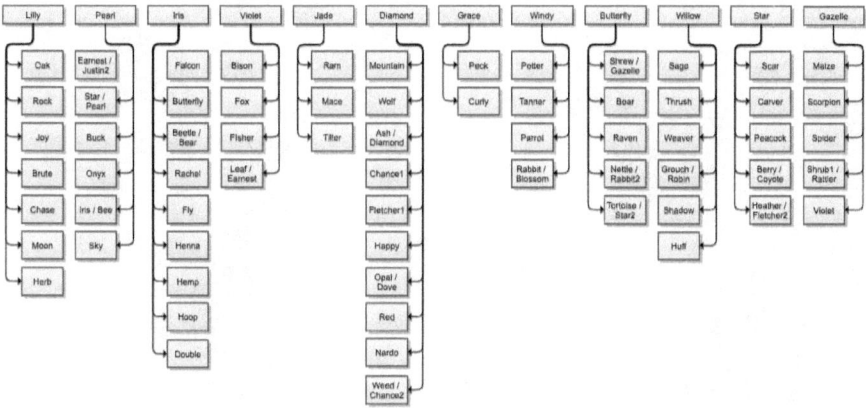

Hunted Like Animals — The Ruck (Dead Mothers Men with No Surviving Siblings)

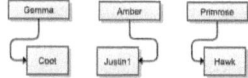

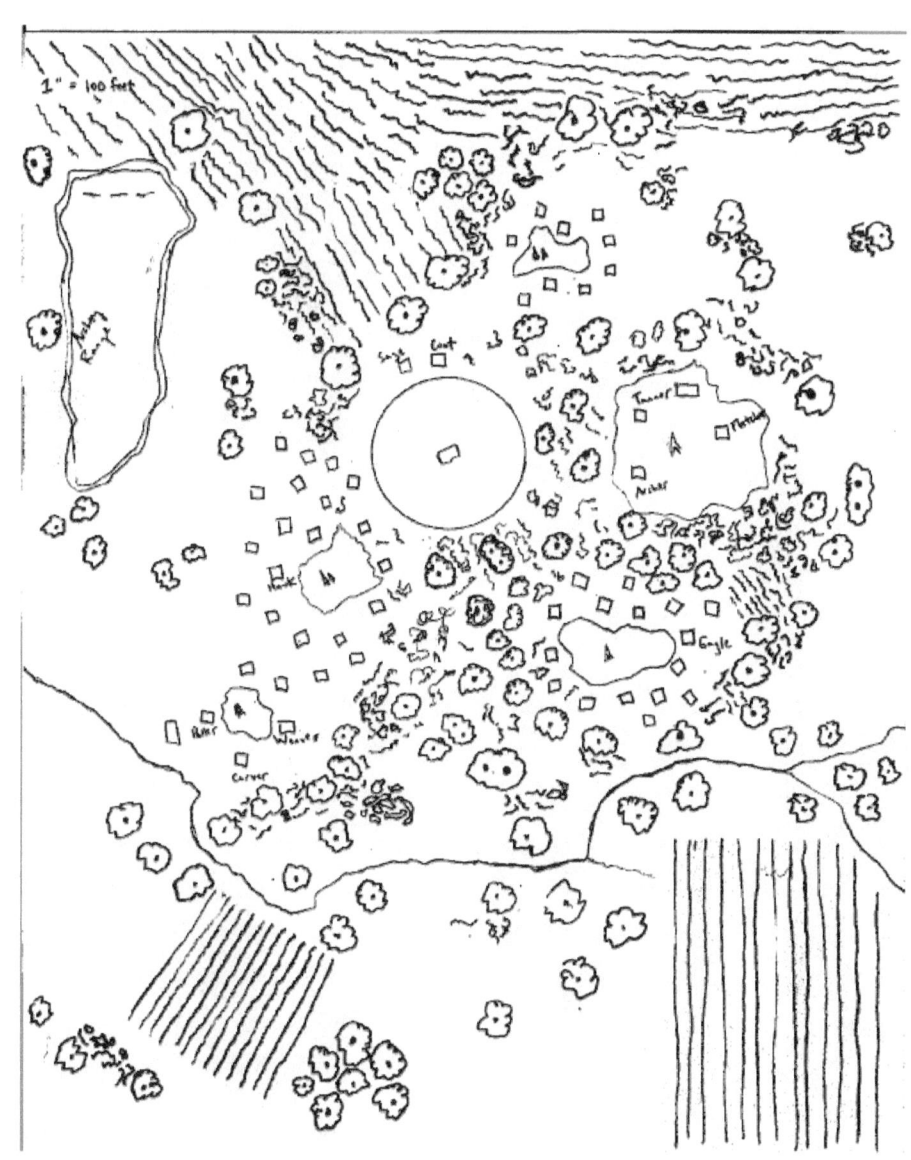

1" = 100 feet

ACKNOWLEDGEMENTS

Thanks to:

Dana Warner, my soulmate and inspiration.

Dirk Warner, my son, for editing, being a sounding board, and giving constructive criticism.

Kwame Workman, my old friend, for giving input on an early version, in chapter installments over time.

Karl Keesler, my friend, for a beautiful cover design.

Joseph Campbell, whose writings about *The Hero's Journey* remain indispensible.

Some influential authors, whose books inspired me to tell a story by building a new world, from John Brunner, to Samuel R. Delaney, Pearl S. Buck, Arthur C. Clarke, J.R.R. Tolkien, Shirley Jackson, Gabriel Garcia Marquez, Fritz Leiber, Frank Herbert, Ursula K. LeGuin, China Mieville, and Philip K. Dick.

All my friends and family who give support, even if they didn't like any given story. Perhaps more importantly, to all my friends and family who told me what was wrong with my stories, even if it was hard to hear.